EVERY PART OF H...

Terror exploded...

He could feel them coming for him. They knew who he was. They knew who he fucking was.

He had to get away… crawl away, if he had to…

Hands abruptly grabbed him.

Immediately, his terror exploded outward, making him cry out.

*They had him. They fucking had him.*

He tried to fight them off—

"Brother," a familiar voice said through gritted teeth. "Brother, stop fighting us! Let us get you out of here! They're closer than we thought. They're coming!"

Even as he said it, another sound ricocheted through Revik's mind.

He didn't know how he heard it, given the blindingly loud siren, the screaming behind his eyes, the voices of the uniformed soldiers who were trying to drag him to his feet.

That sound somehow lived in a near-silence behind all the rest.

Perhaps the sheer physicality of it simply overrode the Barrier noise he couldn't think past.

That, or the familiarity.

Something about that pure familiarity, of muscle memory, of years and decades of ingrained habit, lurched Revik back into motion, even when nothing else could.

He moved in spite of the paralysis, in spite of the silver strands, in spite of the pain that wanted to shatter his skull, in spite of the mercury light shaking of every muscle in his body.

It wasn't even that loud, that sound.

Not at first.

Revik knew exactly what it was though, and what it meant.

It was gunfire.

# THE EX-ROOK

## A BRIDGE AND SWORD NOVEL

JC ANDRIJESKI

The Ex-Rook (A Bridge and Sword Novel)

*Copyright 2023 by JC Andrijeski*

*Published by White Sun Press*

First Edition

ISBN: 9798393906696

Cover Art & Design by Damonza http://damonza.com (2023)

This book is licensed for your personal enjoyment only. All rights reserved. This is a work of fiction. All characters and events portrayed in this book are fictional, and any resemblance to real people, organizations or events is purely coincidental. This book, or parts thereof, may not be reproduced in any form without permission.

**No Generative AI Training Use.**

The Author expressly prohibits using the Work in any manner for purposes of training artificial intelligence technologies to generate text, including without limitation, technologies that are capable of generating works in the same style or genre as the Work. The Author reserves all rights to license uses of the Work for generative AI training and development of machine learning language models.

*Author's Note: No artificial intelligence (A.I.) or predictive language software was used in any part of the creation of this book, nor will it ever be for any of my works.*

Link with me at: https://www.jcandrijeski.com

Or at: https://www.patreon.com/jcandrijeski

Mailing List: https://www.jcandrijeski.com/sign-up

*White Sun Press* 2023

*For A.*

# CHAPTER 1
# DECONSTRUCTION

"That's not something we hear in here often, brother..."

Revik looked up, sharp.

His body had already tensed halfway into a fighting stance.

He hadn't heard the other male walk in. He hadn't heard the door. Something about the silent, ninja-like steps and movements of the monks still made him jump like a cat whenever they snuck up on him.

They would give most seer assassins a run for their money.

"...The music," the monk clarified.

The aged seer smiled at him where he held up a hand in a peace gesture. He waited until Revik stepped back. He waited until Revik eliminated or at least decreased the more aggressive aspects of his posture. Once he had, the monk changed the direction of his hand.

He did all of it without a single hint of accusation.

Revik followed the other seer's eyes back over his own shoulder, towards the small music player and its faintly crackly speakers.

It crouched on a stone bookshelf and blared a poor recording of one of Revik's old albums. The tinny strains of music echoed strangely against the walls of his small, cell-like room, which was really more of a cave than a normal monk's cell.

Somewhere in those few ticks of silence, Revik understood the monk's remark.

His eyes shifted back to the older seer.

Remembering himself finally, he bowed.

Like most of the permanent residents here, the male monk wore a loose-fitting, sand-colored robe. With his guileless smile and open expression, he came across as more friendly and cheerful than many of the older monks, especially those who spent most of their time meditating.

He was also more curious, particularly about Revik.

"What is it, brother?" the monk asked. His light blue eyes held a flicker of interest. "The music you are playing. It is human, is it not?"

Revik fought to stifle a snort.

Gods. He'd been lost in his own kind of bubble over the past few years, but never in his life had he encountered beings so out of touch with the wider world as the traditional seers who lived here, in the caves of the Pamir.

He'd been warned to curb his sarcasm, though.

Especially with senior monks.

He'd been warned to show respect, to remember himself when he responded to sincere questions from his betters, no matter how they might sound to his more jaded ears.

Revik's current teachers viewed his tendency to twist a lot of his off-the-cuff responses into sarcasm as a means of avoidance.

They were probably right.

Still, negativity, sarcasm, cynicism... they all proved difficult habits to break.

"It is, brother," he said. "It is human. This music."

"And what is it called?" the seer asked, his eyes and voice still curious. "It has a name, does it not? This type of music? Would I know it?"

Fighting the pounding in his head, and that denser feeling of claustrophobia that tugged at his chest whenever he spent too much time in the hollowed-out stone room, Revik kept his blank infiltrator's mask in place.

He made an inviting gesture with one hand for the seer to enter the room.

He fought to control his light, even then.

"They call it rock and roll," he said, deadpan.

The old monk grinned like a kid. He clasped his hands in front of his robe.

"Rock and roll? That is a curious name, is it not?" He looked back at the music player, as if examining the nature of the beings making the sounds through the speakers. "That is the *type* of music though, yes?" the Chinese-looking monk persisted. His blue eyes held more curiosity. "What is this *exact* group called?"

"Band," Revik corrected thoughtlessly.

"Band, brother?"

"They call them bands. Not really groups. Not anymore."

A flush of impatience hit Revik's light as the monk nodded with interest.

Revik struggled with a denser annoyance at being disturbed, and seemingly for no reason at all, other than for a curious monk to stare at a cheap cassette player. He rubbed his forehead and tried to shove his irritation back. He avoided the eyes of the other male.

His resentment didn't dissipate.

It's not like he got a lot of time alone here.

They were on him pretty much all day, every day, when he wasn't asleep.

Why the fuck wouldn't they just leave him be, the few minutes he had to himself? He couldn't possibly pose any kind of danger to them, not anymore.

The mind wipes Vash and his infiltrators performed when Revik left the Rooks made certain he'd be as harmless as a neutered kitten. Hell, he could barely function on his own at all these days, after so many years lived inside the Org's Pyramid.

He felt toothless.

More than that, he felt he had nothing to offer to anyone—whether in terms of a threat, or... *gods forbid*... some kind of benefit.

Even as he thought them, Revik struggled with his own thoughts.

He knew why the seer had come.

Revik had been indulging in more than a little "negativity" for the last hour or so, including around one of the worst bouts of separation pain he'd suffered in quite some time. He'd already been warned against trying to seduce any of the monks living in the enclave, male or female, so he'd taken to hiding in his room when he got like this.

They should have taken the fucking hint and left him alone.

Even knowing that compassion likely led the other male to come find him, Revik couldn't seem to make his anger less.

When the old monk stepped deeper into the room, Revik saw a flash of image behind his eyes. Dark, swift. It was gone as soon as it was there, but disconcerting enough to make him flinch, and leave a harsh taste in his mouth.

It also caused him to step back, to increase the physical distance between himself and the other male.

Somewhere in that image, he'd jabbed a flip knife in the male seer's eye.

Something about the light there, maybe.

Something about the monk staring at him—*seeing* him.

Something about the fucking innocence there, the...

(*sheep-like,* his mind muttered)

...openness of the monk's light, the compassion devoid of cynicism, of any guile whatsoever.

Something about the fact that they wouldn't leave him the *fuck* alone.

"Brother?" the monk prodded.

The older seer's voice held patience, along with a denser light. The warmth of his light wove into Revik's as he stood there...

(*Insidious,* Revik's mind accused. *Unwanted, unasked*)

...holding him, providing him with a measure of stability, grounding his light in a less angry, less aggressive space.

Reluctantly, Revik let the other male coax him out of the worst edges of his anger.

A few seconds later, he exhaled sharply.

Then he shook his head. He clicked under his breath, rubbed his temples with a hand.

He didn't look at the monk at all now.

"The Stones," he muttered tonelessly. "They're called The Rolling Stones, brother."

The other seer sent a warm pulse of light to Revik's chest.

Humor lived there, but also a denser understanding, one so complete, Revik had to fight not to yell at him. The compassion there threatened to pull more words out of him, even as his own reactions sickened him. They brought up a dense surge of self-hate strong enough that he had to fight not to yell at the other male again.

*Patience, brother Revik,* the male sent softly. *You are too hard on yourself.*

*And if I stab one of you in the throat, my good brother?* Revik sent back bitterly. *Will you think the same charitable thoughts of me then?*

*You will not.*

*You cannot know that. I've done it before. Many times.*

*Not here.*

*What difference does it make, where I am?* Revik's mind growled. *Who I am with? Do you think me so religious I would not kill a man of the cloth? Because believe me, I would. I've done that before, too.*

Truthfully though, Revik hadn't.

Not that he could remember, anyway.

Moreover, unlike some things he could not remember but suspected he had done anyway, or somehow *knew* he had done, he didn't feel that way about this. He didn't think he'd killed a lot of monks in his life, whatever other horrible things he may have done while living inside the Pyramid of the Rooks.

Something in hearing the lie in his own words caused him to relax, if only a little.

The old monk's blue eyes sharpened.

A faint smile touched his lips.

*In point of fact, brother, you are doing far better now, to express these thoughts where we can see them. It is progress, although you may not feel it as such.*

Revik let out a short laugh.

He nearly choked on it.

The monk, Tulani, only smiled.

*Thoughts are powerful with seers, it is true,* Tulani sent, humor still in his light, even as he looked at Revik thoughtfully. *But thoughts are still not* actions, *dear brother. Not even in a seer of your stature.*

He ignored the openly disbelieving look Revik gave him at the "stature" comment.

*Thoughts carry karmic repercussions of their own,* the monk added. *But do not make these things equivalent in your mind. Just because you think something, you should not treat that impulse as something you have already done, beloved brother.*

*And if I want to do it?* Revik sent, his jaw hard. *What then?*

The old monk clicked softly in rebuke.

*Do not waste time worrying what you may or may not do based on passing impulses alone.* He made a calming gesture, using his light. *We fear you far less now than we did before, brother Revik. When you would not express any feeling in front of us, when you refused to talk to us about anything at all going on inside your light… that is when we feared you.*

Revik shook his head.

He did not attempt to argue, though.

The monk's smile teased higher on his lips.

*Anyway, brother, I somehow doubt it is violence that truly motivates you at the moment. At least not violence of the sort you seem to imagine. I think if I was more your type in other respects, the impulse would have struck you somewhat differently.*

At that, Revik snorted a short laugh.

That one was almost real.

He still didn't look directly at the other male.

When the silence stretched, he conceded the monk's point with a gesture of his own, then backed deeper into the room when the monk walked towards him.

Rather than maintaining the distance between them, Revik doubled it, one of his arms folded tightly over his chest. He felt the gesture as protective, but couldn't quite decide if he was protecting himself from the other seer, or the reverse.

*You are too hard on yourself, brother,* the monk repeated. *Do not beat yourself up for feeling. The karmic repercussions of our thoughts are quite heavy enough.*

Revik nodded.

Truthfully, though, he wasn't really listening.

He only listened to about half of their words, even now.

He fought to push away the part of him that was tired of this, that wanted to sink into a different kind of depression, one based in a heavier futility.

The silence between them stretched.

"Are you ready, brother?" the seer asked aloud.

Revik nodded, but made no effort to move.

Tulani didn't wait. He turned smoothly on his bare heel. He exited through the only door in or out of the cell-like room, and moved as silently out as he had when he'd walked in.

After another sharp exhale, Revik resigned himself to follow.

He walked over to the bookshelf first. He leaned down to switch off the small cassette player, right as "Paint it Black" started to play.

He couldn't help but find that fitting, too.

---

The wooden door opened out to a rough-hewn corridor, which itself grew into the larger maze of passageways that crossed and splinted up and down countless floors inside the rock fortress that made up this part of the Old City.

The monastery was the oldest in the Pamir.

Therefore, it was also the oldest known to exist—at least that still existed.

It lived in the segment of the underground city directly opposite of where the famed Adhipan trained. They had maintained that same residence for training young seers since the infiltration group's inception.

Revik found it sort of ironic that, as a boy, he'd fantasized about living here.

Of course, he'd imagined himself on the opposite side of that dyad protecting the city's light. He'd imagined himself as one of the Adhipan, not as a broken man living in penance with a bunch of old monks—monks who, initially at least, viewed him as a somewhat frightening and murderous curiosity.

He knew it was a privilege to be here.

It was a privilege to even be allowed inside these rock walls.

It still felt like a prison.

Watching Tulani pad barefoot through the rock-hewn corridors in front of him, Revik felt a whisper of defeat go through his light.

He couldn't stop it, even knowing the old male probably felt it.

He never would have believed a bunch of kneeler monks could wear him down to such a nub. Not by hammering him with their ideology, although they lectured him at times, just as Tulani had done just now. Not even by molding his light, or trying to force him to see the world the way they saw it themselves.

No, most of what the holy seers of the Pamir had done since Revik arrived was simply to reflect Revik back at himself.

They showed Revik, Revik—without the masks.

Without the posturing, without the filters, without the stories and quasi-mythologies.

Without any of the rationalizations he'd designed for himself over the years.

They showed him his own mind.

Then they simply sat back and watched.

And they waited.

They waited and watched as Revik reacted to what he saw.

Now and then, they would approach him, usually with kindness, often with words of encouragement, sometimes with gentle advice.

It was fucking maddening.

It was fucking excruciating.

Yet, as it turned out, the patience of the Ancestors could outlast even his own.

Really, there was no contest.

In the battle of wills over Revik's soul, over his way of looking at the world, over his way of seeing himself... he was definitely losing.

He honestly couldn't decide if that was a good thing or a bad one.

# CHAPTER 2
# WATER ON STONE

Revik came out of the training session, if anything, angrier than before.

He'd expected to be alone, at least, once he got back to his monk's cell.

He craved aloneness, needed it by then, even if it meant returning to that fucking lightless, airless cave for the remainder of the afternoon and evening.

He more and more wondered if they'd saddled him with such a tiny monk's cell on purpose, knowing he was claustrophobic.

Rooms with real windows existed inside these caves.

Some even had real ventilation to outside.

Revik had seen many empty rooms of this sort on his wanders through the tunnels.

He knew the monks suffered from an excess of space, given how much the monastery had shrunk in the years since First Contact, when monks were slaughtered wholesale, along with the rest of their brethren.

That didn't even include the rest of the underground city, which now stood mostly abandoned, including caves adjacent to the formal spaces belonging to the monks.

Revik wasn't a monk

He could have lived in any of those caves.

They'd had an abundance of options when assigning him a room.

They also likely knew he wouldn't particularly want to admit to his own discomfort, if only because he wouldn't want to discuss the reasons why, or the precise incidents in his past that led to Revik being claustrophobic in the first place.

His claustrophobia was his own damned business.

Tulani, the old monk who had been in Revik's room, asking about his music, would probably have agreed with him on that point... right before he suggested Revik talk about it anyway, for his own benefit, not theirs.

Revik wondered if Tulani had been assigned to him, too.

The old monk might be hanging around to keep Revik from being alone too often with his thoughts... or to keep him from committing suicide, for that matter, or contemplating escape. He might be there simply to monitor Revik's reactions more closely.

Revik also wondered sometimes if Tulani overstayed his welcome on purpose.

Maybe they were waiting for Revik to snap... to have some kind of nervous breakdown they could all observe and use to pull him apart from the inside.

Revik knew by now, as "innocent" as the monks seemed, they were no strangers to penetrating difficult psychology. Nor were they fools, as much as Revik was tempted to treat them as such. The truth was, they were wearing him down.

Patiently, slowly, kindly... strategically.

They were wearing him the fuck down.

Revik's training sessions were a part of that, as well.

Right now, those consisted of opening structures in the light around his *aleimic* heart, which had been an exercise in fear, frustration, embarrassment, pain, and grief.

Mostly fear.

He hated feeling that goddamned vulnerable.

He hated feeling that goddamned naked.

Even breathing hurt by the end.

After over four hours trying to meditate with a bunch of happy, contented monks, who found the entire process effortless and illuminating, Revik more or less wanted to put his hand, and possibly his head, through a wall.

At the very least, he very much wanted to be alone.

He knew it was childish.

He knew he was hiding from them.

He knew on some level he even feared them, and what they saw in him.

He knew it was counterproductive to avoid getting to know any of the monks. He knew it likely wasn't helping him spiritually to hold onto his own music, his own books, his previous connections with the world... the fact that he'd read a fucking *newspaper* in the last fifty years.

But he couldn't seem to shake his stubborn desire to hold onto those things.

He couldn't shake his reluctance to truly understand their world.

He knew they'd call it attachment, avoidance, a kind of addiction, and he even agreed with them up to a point. He could see and understand how it kept his light and mind in a certain space, one that wasn't wholly healthy for him, especially right now.

He just didn't care.

Or maybe he *did* care, but not enough to change.

They'd told him, over and over, that they would not keep him here, that there was no danger they would trap him inside, or try to force him to be a monk forever.

Revik *knew* this.

He knew they meant him no harm, that they weren't trying to brainwash him, or force anything upon him, or convert him to anything... but he feared these things anyway.

After years spent inside the construct of the Rooks, who molded his mind, his light, his very sense of who he was, he was terrified of doing that all over again, just with different masters. No matter how "benign" those masters might seem on the outside, the thought was unbearable to him. It was fucking unbearable.

He didn't trust himself.

For the same reason, he didn't let himself get too close.

He isolated himself from them even as he hated the feeling of disconnection. He held onto things he knew didn't define him even as he hated how erased he felt.

He hated not knowing who he was anymore.

He hated knowing he'd disappeared to the rest of the world.

He hated how *irrelevant* he felt.

It was as if the last thirty years of his life had pretty much been a wash.

Worse, really—those years now felt like steps backwards. He looked back at who he'd been under the Org, and saw nothing but delusion.

Of course, the monks saw all of this somewhat differently.

The monks told Revik that his depression was as much organic as it was psychological. They likened it to a drug addiction. They told him that he missed the symbiotic nature of the Org themselves, and the way in which they fed upon one another's light. They told Revik he'd grown completely dependent on the Org, while living inside their seer network.

They called that network, "The Pyramid."

They called the Org, "The Rooks."

The monks told him his light had been severely damaged living inside the Pyramid of the Rooks. They told him he'd been brainwashed, yes, but perhaps more significantly, his light had been parasitized.

It had also been broken.

They broke it deliberately, in ways that would make it difficult for Revik to live without them. They didn't want him to leave, so they made it nearly impossible for him to do so on his own.

The Rooks "repaid" him for this rape by giving him the illusion of power, as well as a sense of purpose. The monks explained to him that most of Revik's "power" inside the Pyramid had been an illusion as well—accomplished only via the rape of every seer's light that stood below him on the rungs of the Pyramid's ladder.

This all felt true to Revik.

Moreover, he could see it, clearly, when they showed him light-diagrams of how the Pyramid actually functioned. In essence, the Rooks stole from him, and Revik stole from the seers below him on that ladder, and sometimes even those above him.

The monks told him he was suffering in part because he was rebuilding those pieces of his light they had broken in him.

He was rebuilding them so he could stand on his own.

In the meantime, they said, he was like a junkie screaming in pain from the hole in his light. He screamed because he missed the symbiosis of the Pyramid. He screamed because he'd forgotten how to live without it. He screamed because the separation from them hurt him.

They told him that his psychological pain stemmed mostly from this, as well.

Revik could feel the truth of this, too.

As much as it embarrassed him to admit it, he missed the power the Pyramid had lent him, even if that power was stolen. Perhaps more than that, he desperately missed the sense of purpose being in the Org had given to his life.

The monks assured him this was all part of the process.

They saw it as "necessary pain" to get him to the other

side of this "addiction" he had developed to the Rooks' light. They cautioned him that the Rooks had stripped away his true independence of mind while he'd been one of them. As a result, he'd lost the ability to really *know* his own mind, or make his own decisions.

They told him he'd lost confidence in himself as a result.

They told him he would get all of that back.

They promised him he would, if he did not give up.

As much as it annoyed the shit out of him, those things felt true to Revik, as well.

Still, he suspected some of these things were less about brainwashing, or his *aleimic* structure being damaged, and more about him genuinely missing being a part of the world. He missed being involved. He missed knowing what was happening.

Hell, he didn't even know if the last human war he'd been involved in had ended.

He didn't know if his favorite human bands got played on the radio anymore.

He didn't know if the same politicians were in office, or the same types of clothes were worn, or what scandals had broken, or what movies were out.

Then there was the mind wipe Vash had been forced to perform on him, as a condition of Galaith and the Rooks letting him go.

Because of that, Revik was missing pieces—black marks, where his mind had once lived, where *he* had once lived. Those empty, void-like spaces swirled with vague emotions and prejudices and wants, things that pulled at him but without any of the specifics that went with them, without anything for him to make sense of what he felt.

He could no longer remember good chunks of what he'd done since the end of the second world war. He'd stumbled across pockets of grief. He remembered faces, saw fleeting images that felt and tasted familiar.

He remembered the faces of some of the people he'd killed.

He even remembered happy moments, here and there.

He definitely remembered more decadent ones.

None of it lingered, however.

None of it stayed long enough for him to know what to *do* with any of what remained, or to remember which pieces of that belonged to him now.

He remembered Kali.

He remembered his flight from Vietnam.

The monks told him to let go of those memories, too.

They advised Revik to try and approach himself with new eyes, to relearn himself without allowing in any of those old ways of seeing himself. They didn't want those old illusions to warp and color and taint the accuracy of his self-knowledge.

They told him he didn't see himself clearly, either in the good or the bad. They told him he didn't see his abilities clearly, nor others clearly, nor how others viewed him clearly.

Revik didn't want to, though.

He didn't want to let all of that go.

Even when he tried to defy them, however, he couldn't hold enough of his own mind or emotions or memories for any of it to make a real difference.

He'd been in here for almost five years, according to Vash.

Five years, and no one had fed him a scrap of real news, not even on whether the American war in Vietnam had finally ended.

He didn't know if any of his friends in the Org were still alive.

He was losing his fucking mind in here.

He was starting to *really* lose his mind.

The monks, of course, called this "progress."

Revik had different words for it.

He'd been muttering and even shouting those words at

them for months now, but they didn't react to that much, either.

He wanted them to fucking react.

He wanted them to get *angry* at him now and then. He wanted them to shout back, punish him for being an asshole.

Hell, sometimes he wanted them to hit him.

But they never did any of those things.

They never gave him anything to push back against, which only made his frustration, confusion, and disgust with himself worse.

He wondered what they would do—what they would *really* do—if he just left.

If he just walked out of these cold, dry caves one night, hiked down the mountains to the nearest facsimile of civilization, got drunk as shit, did his damnedest to get laid as many times as his cock and light could handle it—would they care?

Would they even come after him?

Just thinking about it made his cock hard.

It made his skin flush, his light snake and spark like an angry, frustrated coil of electricity.

*Gaos.* He couldn't start thinking about sex right now.

He really couldn't.

He mulled the idea over, anyway.

He mulled it over, knowing he wouldn't do it, knowing *why* he wouldn't do it. Knowing penance was a condition the Rooks left him, too. Galaith left him with that, as a part of his agreement with Vash not to come after him after Revik defected.

Galaith had known the truth of him, just as Vash did.

The truth was, Revik wasn't cut out for living life on the run, any more than he was cut out for living as a monk.

Knowing none of that was the real reason, even now, just another bullshit story he fed his ego to keep it quiet.

He was still playing this nightly ritual with himself when he reached the door of his cave-like cell—

—and froze.

His light flickered out. It confirmed what he'd felt.

Someone was waiting for him.

Someone was inside his room.

Someone he didn't know.

## CHAPTER 3
# REQUESTED

He snapped into infiltrator mode. The shift happened fast—so fast, his mind didn't utter a conscious thought.

His light clicked into pure, clinical assessment.

He felt infiltrators inside those rock walls, not monks.

Revik's *aleimi* hardened into a more aggressive form of self-defense.

Of course, in doing so, he didn't miss the irony that even when he hated his own life, some part of him fought to protect it with a vigilance that bordered on pathology.

A few things calmed that hyper-vigilance relatively quickly.

Whoever waited for him in there, they made no attempt to hide from him. They made no attempt to hide their scans of him, either, which in seer's parlance was more or less the polite way to approach a stranger's light when you wanted to learn more about them.

It gave the other seer the opportunity to shield, for one.

Even so, the contact brought Revik's separation sickness back with a lurch.

Fuck. Whoever this was, they definitely weren't a monk.

The monks had figured out some way, around Revik at least, to keep their light from triggering the worst aspects of his deprivation.

It didn't really help, of course. He still found himself staring at some of them, depending on the specific frequencies of their light.

Even as he thought it, he wished he'd found time to jerk off that morning.

He wished he'd done it before he had to deal with whoever the fuck was in his room now.

Humor swept the Barrier space around him.

In it, Revik swore he heard actual laughter.

His face warmed as it sank in what the humor meant.

They could hear him. Even shielded, even though he hadn't yet made a sound that would have told them he was outside the door—they could hear his thoughts.

*It's quite all right, brother,* a voice murmured in his mind.

The seer behind it sent a warm, packed pulse of reassurance with the words.

*Believe it or not, I'm not entirely unfamiliar with such settings,* the male-sounding voice added ruefully. *I take no offense at your difficulties from living in a celibate environment for so long. Nor will anyone on my team. And whatever your issues on that front... for which I have nothing but the profoundest sympathies, my brother... I suspect I'm not really your type.*

Revik's jaw hardened.

There wasn't much he could say in response. The seer inside his room had already made it abundantly clear that he outranked Revik, sight-wise.

Still, Revik picked up a few things.

Middle-aged. Male. Military-trained.

Smart ass.

The other seer laughed again.

*Are you coming inside, brother Revik?* the same voice asked. *Or should I come out to you? I was told if I waited here long enough, you would eventually return. Or were those kind old monks lying to me, just to see if they could elicit an emotional reaction?*

Revik muttered under his breath.

He shifted his weight on his feet indecisively.

His hands rose from his sides. They clenched on his hips, maybe even to ground him, but his indecisiveness only worsened.

Then, realizing the monks probably didn't want him dead, no matter how much of a pain in the ass they found him, he walked the rest of the way to the door, making up the distance with swift but jerking steps.

He flung open the wooden panel, walked inside, and stopped again.

The seer who had spoken to him wasn't alone.

Three seers in total sat there.

Two males, one female.

The fact that he'd felt none of them specifically told Revik they definitely outranked him.

The one who let Revik feel him first, the same one Revik had spoken to from outside the door, smiled at him.

It had to be him.

Those gray eyes held the same humorous glint Revik felt in his mind before. The older male's light felt like what Revik first tasted from outside his door, too.

All three of them sat on cushions on the stone floor—cushions that someone must have dragged into the room to accommodate them, along with the thicker mats where the cushions had been placed, since neither thing lived in Revik's room normally.

They all sat with straight backs, like they were accustomed to sitting on the floor.

They looked up at him expectantly.

All three faced him in a disjointed half-circle.

Revik took a snapshot of the seer in the center, using his light.

He did it even as he looked him over.

The gray-eyed one was clearly their leader.

Those pale, far-seeing eyes stood out under chestnut-colored hair with some gray at the temples. Maybe three-hundred-and-fifty, four hundred years old. He was in good shape, not a spare ounce of flesh on him. He looked like a fighter, both from his muscle tone and the way his eyes flickered over Revik where he stood.

He had odd features for a seer.

His bone structure was almost human-European.

Coupled with those gray eyes, and his tightly-shielded, nearly invisible *aleimi*, Revik might have thought him human altogether, if the other hadn't already spoken in his mind.

He still couldn't see much of his light.

He strongly suspected he could only see as much of it as the male specifically wanted him to see. Even the pieces Revik managed to discern, he found himself pinning down only with difficulty. It honestly made him question if what he saw was all just another layer of disguise.

He had structure, this seer, but just how much, Revik had no idea.

Generally, that meant he had a hell of a lot.

"Who are you?" he asked, blunt.

The three seers looked at one another

They now appeared to be suppressing smiles.

Still, somehow, Revik got the sense that at least the two male seers were relieved at whatever they saw in him. Something in their faces and light hinted at that relief, as if they'd been bracing themselves to see something different when Revik walked through that door.

The male seer who wasn't the leader smiled at him.

He looked younger than his commander, maybe by as much as a hundred years.

He had light green eyes. Those irises, ringed with pale violet, held a strangely luminescent glow.

He also wore an even warmer smile on his lips.

Something in those eyes relaxed a deeper tension in Revik's chest.

The male seer with the green and violet eyes was almost preternaturally handsome, which was disarming as well.

Another voice jerked his eyes sideways.

"You are Dehgoies Revik?" the female asked.

Her voice sounded clipped, educated.

Revik realized only then that he'd been avoiding looking at her.

She had long dark hair she'd wound into a complicated braid, an infiltrator's hairstyle if there ever was one. Almost outside of his control, he found himself glancing over her body under the armored vest and shirt. He noticed she was tall even as he took in her high cheekbones, narrow waist, long legs.

His gaze stopped longest on her eyes, which were a strange mixture of light brown and green, with flecks of yellow and what might have been silver in them.

Those eyes were stunning, difficult to look away from.

Feeling her notice his stare, maybe even feeling the reaction behind it, Revik swallowed. He folded his arms tightly across his chest before he looked back at the middle-aged male sitting in the center of the three.

He considered saying nothing.

Then he realized he couldn't.

He couldn't say nothing.

"You might not be my type, brother," he said flatly to the gray-eyed, strangely human-looking male. "Although frankly, right now, that's debatable..."

The green-eyed male let out a grunt of amusement.

He grinned at the gray-eyed one, gave him a blatantly suggestive wink.

Revik glanced between them. Seeing the good-natured humor there, his jaw hardened more. He gestured towards the female with one hand, but he didn't look at her.

"...She is definitely my type. Does she need to be here?"

There was a silence.

"I mean it," Revik said. "I don't want her here."

The female clicked in obvious irritation.

She muttered under her breath in a language Revik didn't know.

When he looked at her directly, almost outside of his control, she shook her head, right before she clicked at him louder. A frown touched her sculpted lips.

"You're hardly *my* type, youngster," she muttered in Prexci.

That she spoke the same language he had meant she obviously wanted him to hear.

"Then consider this a favor," he retorted, his voice openly hostile.

"Maybe I don't want any 'favors' from you... *Rook.*"

"Then this meeting is over," Revik said. "Get the fuck out of my room. Now. All of you."

The gray-eyed seer raised a hand in a peace gesture.

Revik turned his head.

Once he had, he realized those light gray eyes had never left his face. He never saw those eyes lose focus—and yet, he distinctly got the impression he was being scanned, and that the probe came primarily from the gray-eyed male.

Revik couldn't exactly *feel* that scan, much less pick up on any details of what the other might be looking for, but the perception didn't dissipate.

If this seer could hide a scan that well—if he could keep it from showing in his eyes while staring straight at his target—he really *was* good.

A little too good.

The thought unnerved Revik, even as he grew conscious of how little he'd had to defend himself from such things in here. Ever since he'd left the Rooks' employ, most of his work had been in the opposite direction. They'd been trying to get him to *open* his light, to trust other seers, to relax his guard—things that went so far against Revik's previous training and instincts it was almost laughable.

Now he found himself wondering if maybe those monks made more progress with him than he'd realized.

Finding himself faced with three highly-ranked and better-trained infiltrators, Revik felt his paranoia ratchet up higher than it had gone in months.

Years, possibly.

His body continued to stiffen when the three seers in front of him didn't move. Revik continued to look around at their faces.

He lingered the least long on the female's, even now.

After a few more minutes passed, he refolded his arms, shifted his weight.

"You're not leaving my room," he remarked, colder. "Was I in any way unclear?"

The gray-eyed male lowered his hand to his knee without changing expression. When he next spoke, his voice bordered on gentle, but he didn't aim it at Revik.

"Mara. Wait outside, please," he said politely.

The female infiltrator, Mara presumably, gave the male a disbelieving look.

"Mara?" the gray-eyed seer said. "Please do as I ask."

Polite or no, Revik heard the order there.

He reassessed the hierarchy in front of him, even as it grew visible to him. The pecking order was fixed, and not based solely on sight-rank.

Military background? Some kind of special unit from the Seven?

After a long-feeling pause, the female seer pulled herself to her feet with obvious annoyance. Revik sensed no true rebellion in her, at least not towards the gray-eyed seer.

Her irritation appeared to be aimed at Revik himself.

In any case, clearly, the gray-eyed seer's authority was absolute.

The female aimed her steps for the outside corridor with athletic strides.

She gave Revik a hard stare as she walked past him. Those shockingly bright eyes of hers flickered over his body along with her light. He winced from the contact, stepping back, then clenched his jaw before he returned her look with a harder stare of his own.

He continued to watch until the door shut behind her.

Then he turned, once more facing the gray-eyed male.

"Was that absolutely necessary?" he asked.

The gray-eyed seer shrugged with one hand. "I confess, I felt it was. I wished to see what you would do."

"What I would do?" Revik felt his jaw harden more. "Meaning... what?"

"Meaning whether you would confess to an issue there or not," the other explained patiently. He gestured towards Revik's body. "...An issue we can all plainly see, my brother, if you'll pardon my saying it. I wondered if you would admit to it, warn us about it, or if you would deny it, and try to find some way to sate those urges later. Perhaps by some attempt to get Mara alone."

He said it lightly, with such obvious honesty, it took Revik a moment to comprehend his words.

"You thought I might *rape* her?" He stared at the other male, his anger hardening.

The other gestured vaguely, his expression noncommittal.

"Not necessarily. But I wished to gauge your response. And your honesty about your current condition, from being in here for so long." His eyes continued to watch Revik's, the gray irises calm. "I am quite satisfied with how you handled it, brother."

Revik's stare narrowed.

"This was a test?" he asked. "You brought her in here to *test* me?"

"Yes," the other said simply.

Revik felt his body tighten, but for a moment, he didn't know how to react, or how to push against the other, given what he'd said, and how he'd said it. The other male's words and light offered so little resistance they left Revik at somewhat of a loss.

Whatever this seer's true intentions, he at least wanted to *appear* to be honest and straightforward. Whether he was or not, Revik couldn't make up his mind.

"Why?" he asked finally. "Who the fuck are you?"

The gray-eyed seer didn't flinch.

Rather, he rose smoothly to his feet.

He moved silently, with a deceptive grace.

He also rose faster than Revik's eyes could track. Revik found himself stepping back in alarm, but only after the other had already straightened. Although Revik had moved in reflex and the other via intent, Revik still managed to be slower.

Once he realized that much, he just stood there.

His eyes locked on the other male warily.

It occurred to him he might be outmatched physically, too.

That hadn't happened in a long time.

"I am Balidor of the Adhipan," the other seer said.

Revik flinched.

Amazement filtered over his light.

Adhipan Balidor didn't wait for him to react.

"...I just signed your release papers, Dehgoies Revik," the gray-eyed seer added. He gave him a wry smile. "Thus making you, temporarily, at least, the direct responsibility of the Adhipan, and therefore of me. I will not take you without your permission, of course, but I will try very hard to persuade you to come with us willingly."

Revik stared at him.

He spoke before he knew he intended to.

"No," he said, blunt.

Once he'd said it, the answer strengthened in his light.

It hardened rather than softened.

"No," he said again. He shook his head. "No fucking way. Meaning no disrespect to you, of course, sir, but no matter who you are... no."

"You have not yet heard my proposition."

"I don't need to," Revik said. "It's not about you. It's about me."

"Meaning what?"

Revik stared at him, fighting incredulity. "Meaning what? Clearly, I'm not ready."

"To leave this place?"

"Yes."

"What makes you say that?" Balidor asked.

There was a silence.

Then Revik let out a disbelieving laugh.

"I just asked one of your people to leave the room because I don't trust myself with her," Revik said. "You felt the need to test me, to determine if I was a rapist... possibly a murderer of females, if I am reading your intent correctly. Do you really need me to answer that question?"

"You *did* ask her to leave," Balidor reminded him. "You did not hide your difficulties. You were honest about them."

"I may not be tomorrow," Revik retorted. "...or the day after that. I may not ask next time, brother Adhipan."

The gray-eyed seer smiled.

Those eyes turned shrewd once more, appraising.

Revik found himself thinking he was being scanned again, too.

"I believe you will," Balidor said, ending the pause. "Ask. Or tell us, if your difficulties become unmanageable. Is that not enough?"

"No." Revik stepped back unconsciously, physically and

with his light. "No, it's not enough. Again, no disrespect to you, brother."

He glanced at the other male in the room, who he'd almost forgotten, the stunningly handsome one with those strange, violet-ringed, green eyes.

That second male watched him intently too, a faint frown on his face, but more like he was concentrating, looking at something in Revik himself, something that either interested him, puzzled him, or possibly both. Revik felt himself flush at the scrutiny there.

He looked back at the human-like countenance of Balidor.

"Even if you are who you say you are," Revik said. "...I don't *know* you, brother. I'm not in the habit of trusting seers I don't know. And I don't know why you'd trust me."

"Would you like to see my credentials, brother Dehgoies?"

Revik felt his anger sharpen. "No."

The handsome, green-eyed seer sitting cross-legged on the floor let out a soft laugh.

"Then what do you need from me?" Balidor said.

Revik noticed that Balidor ignored the green-eyed male's amusement that time.

He kept his eyes on Revik's face. He held out his palms to either side, almost a position of prayer, but clearly one of submission.

"Will you not ask me, at least, what errand brings me here?" Balidor queried. "Or why I would want you with me specifically, brother?"

Revik hadn't wanted to ask that.

He hadn't wanted to ask because he feared some part of him might find that answer persuasive.

"I don't really want to know," he said truthfully.

Balidor smiled at that. He glanced at the green-eyed male, who chuckled again softly from his cushion on the floor.

Balidor returned his gaze to Revik's face.

His steel-gray eyes held a denser understanding, as if he wanted Revik to know that he had known that already.

Revik didn't think that the other's knowledge of his mind was put on.

In fact, he strongly suspected both males had already followed the main threads of his thoughts in more directions than Revik himself wanted to think about.

"Fuck." Looking between the two of them, Revik exhaled, unfolding his arms. "Fine. Tell me."

That time, Balidor let out a chuckle.

So did the male seer sitting on the floor.

Even so, Balidor's voice bordered on grim when he answered Revik's words.

"You have been requested, my brother. By name. By one with more pull than me."

"Requested?" Revik felt his shoulders stiffen. "By who? Vash?"

"By sister Kali." Balidor's eyes watched Revik's carefully as he said the name. "Since it is the only message she sent to us before she disappeared, we thought it wise to follow what she prescribed, before they—"

"Disappeared?" Revik cut in. "Kali disappeared? What the fuck does that mean?"

He stared at the other male.

He felt his light charge up around his physical form.

He felt the other notice, just before those gray eyes turned shrewd.

"Yes, brother." Balidor held his gaze, without so much as a twitch in the muscles of his face. "I am sorry to inform you, but she was taken from her home in the middle of the night."

Revik's pulse sped up.

"What about her mate?" he asked. "Where is he?"

"He is with her, of course. He tried to fight them off, and failed. They took him, too."

"Why would you want me?" Revik said. "Why would *she* want me?"

His voice came out harsher than he intended.

Balidor just stood there, unflinching in the face of Revik's hostility.

Revik subdued his words anyway.

"What am I supposed to do about it?" he asked.

"Help us." Balidor's gray eyes remained fixed on Revik's. "She asked for you, brother. She was quite insistent about it, from what Vash tells me."

Revik just looked at him for a moment.

Then he exhaled.

He shook his head, maybe in some vain attempt to clear it. As he did, he clicked his tongue sharply against the roof of his mouth, a seer's expression of regret, disagreement, disgust, disapproval, sometimes of annoyance or anger.

In Revik's case, it felt like all of those things.

"I can't," he said.

"Why not, brother?"

Revik stared at him. "I can't. I can't leave here." He gestured around the cell-like cave. He paused briefly on the male seer who watched them from his cross-legged position on the floor. "I can't leave."

He stared briefly into the male's green eyes and felt his jaw harden.

He said it anyway, even as he broke the stare.

His gaze swiveled back to Balidor.

"I'm not ready for this," he said. "Clearly, I'm not. Ask anyone here, if you don't—"

"I did ask," Balidor said. "As you can likely imagine, I was somewhat thorough."

Revik's jaw hardened more.

"Clearly you didn't speak to the right people then, brother Adhipan. Do you think I'm making this up? If you don't believe me, then—"

"—I disagree," Balidor interjected gently. He held up a hand. "Although I do *believe* you, brother. You understand that these are not equivalent?"

Revik stared at him.

He felt his embarrassment slide abruptly into anger.

"Well, you're wrong—" he began.

"—So does father Vash," Balidor cut in, interrupting him a third time, again holding up a hand. "...Disagree with you, that is. And the monks here seem to disagree, too, brother, since they have already acceded to my request. Kali clearly disagrees. Dalejem here disagrees." He motioned towards the green-eyed seer, still watching Revik's face. "So perhaps we do not see your condition as being quite the same as you do?"

Revik frowned down at the green-eyed seer, who smiled at him.

Revik's gaze shifted back to Balidor.

Balidor also smiled when their eyes met.

He never stopped studying Revik's face.

"Vash left the final decision up to your teachers here," Balidor added. "And ultimately, to you, of course. But he wished me to convey that he has full confidence in you."

The words stumped Revik.

They also silenced him briefly.

He dropped his gaze to the stone floor. He refolded his arms, tighter, as if trying to squeeze the air out of his chest. He could feel the green-eyed seer on the floor watching him. Somehow, the weight of that gaze caused his skin to flush more, without him really thinking about why.

He fought with the idea of going because Kali asked for him.

Could he really refuse her, given what she'd risked to help him?

He thought about what his life had been like, those last few months in Vietnam. He remembered the years before that, how those had felt, even though he could no longer recall all the details. It all felt so long ago now.

It wasn't really that long ago, though.

When images tried to accompany the thoughts, he winced.

He also pushed them forcefully away.

A flicker of disgust wound through his light, but he pushed that way, too.

"Her husband won't like it," Revik grunted, speaking aloud without meaning to.

From the floor, the green-eyed seer laughed.

When Revik looked over, annoyed, he saw the seer smiling at him again, warmth in his eyes and light, enough warmth to startle Revik. He couldn't quite wrap his mind around the way the other seer seemed to be looking at him.

He looked at him almost like a friend.

A comrade, at the very least.

Possibly an ally.

Whatever the precise meaning of that look, it was like nothing Revik would have expected, particularly given the conversation he'd been having with this male's boss.

When Revik looked back at Balidor, he saw the older seer smiling at him, too. The warmth in those gray eyes may not have been as prominent as the warmth in that younger, more handsome, more *seer-lik*e face—but Revik saw it clearly, irrefutably.

Again, he spoke before he knew he intended to.

Even he heard the surrender in his voice.

"Fine... fuck." He clicked as he exhaled. He looked between the two of them and his jaw hardened. "Whatever. When do we go?"

## CHAPTER 4
# THE GUARDIAN

They briefed him on the way down the mountain.
Revik sat crammed knee-to-knee and shoulder-to-shoulder between the male seer with the green eyes on one side, and Balidor on the other.

Five other seers sat on the same and facing benches, with four on each side.

Revik didn't recognize any of them.

He assumed they must be Adhipan, as well.

He couldn't help noticing all of them were male.

Even Mara, the female with those stunning hazel eyes, didn't ride down with them, not even in the front seat, so he had to assume the truck behind them contained all of the female seers in the group, including her.

He couldn't fail to take that as a message.

It crossed his mind to remind them that gender might not make a hell of a lot of difference to him right then.

The green-eyed seer snorted a laugh.

Revik glanced at him, frowning.

The other only smiled wider, clearly undaunted by Revik's glare. Reaching over with a grin, the seer Balidor called

"Dalejem" patted Revik's leg in a friendly way, letting his hand linger briefly to massage his thigh.

At that, Revik jumped nearly a foot.

Balidor looked over sharply when he did, then down at Revik's leg and the other male's hand. Balidor gave the green-eyed seer a hard look, one with a clear meaning behind it.

The handsome seer with the long, black and brown-streaked hair and those jade-green eyes removed his hand at once.

He made a gesture of apology along the lines of, *oops, I forgot.*

Revik waved it away, but not before his face flushed with heat.

Christ. This was going to be a shit-show.

He couldn't help thinking he wasn't going to be able to handle this, dealing with all of these non-monk seers. Infiltrators, as a general rule, were touchy and horny as fuck just in the normal course of their interactions. Hell, most *seers* were touchy and horny as fuck.

They wouldn't do it on purpose, and it definitely wouldn't be personal, but they'd probably be setting him off every few minutes.

And Revik hadn't even dealt with the females yet.

Female seers were generally more sexually aggressive than a lot of males.

That was doubly true for female infiltrators.

When Revik glanced around the back of the truck, he felt more eyes on him.

From what he could tell of their demeanor and light, he wouldn't have to worry about most of this lot making passes at him, anyway, at least not anytime soon. Unlike the green-eyed seer and their leader, Balidor, most of the seers crammed into the back of that Jeep appraised Revik like he was some kind of animal—one that would definitely bite them given the chance, if not try to kill them outright.

Revik supposed that shouldn't have surprised him.

They clearly knew who he was.

They knew he was an ex-agent of the Org.

If they all really were Adhipan, they likely had some awareness of his record while he'd been a Rook. They'd all know how close he'd been to the Rooks' leader, Galaith.

Balidor ignored their stares, so Revik did his best to do the same.

He didn't miss the off-and-on flickers and probes from their light, however, or the wariness that came off the snaking trails of their *aleimi.*

He also caught them exchanging words with one another about him, even though he couldn't hear the words themselves. They spoke about him in a private area of their military construct, a kind of "psychic channel" where they could speak without being overheard by anyone not on the same frequency.

Because of that, Revik only caught the vaguest flavor of what was being said, even though he sat right next to all of them.

It was just enough to make him paranoid.

He tried to focus on what Balidor was telling him.

He tried to ignore the others altogether, clenching his jaw against the pain in his light and wincing as the Jeep jostled and jumped over the uneven road down the side of the mountain.

"...As I said, her mate, Uye, got picked up by SCARB when he tried to stop them from taking her," Balidor was saying now.

He clasped his hands between his jostling knees, likely in part to keep them from knocking together.

"...He got hit with several additional criminal charges as a result, but we're negotiating with our contacts now to try and get him out of the high-security section of the camp where he's currently being held. They have him in a holding cell underground right now... separated from her. It will make it significantly more difficult to extract both of them."

Revik frowned.

Before he could speak, Balidor gave him a serious look.

"You should know another thing, too, brother," he said, lower.

Revik stiffened.

He couldn't help but see the hesitation in the other male's eyes.

"She is pregnant," Balidor said.

Revik flinched.

Immediately, he felt his chest constrict.

Balidor made a kind of conciliatory gesture with his hand.

"...More than pregnant," he added. "She is close to term. According to her husband, she could have her child any day now."

Revik felt a slow burn grow in his chest. It gradually shifted into a harder pain, until he found it difficult to breathe. It wasn't separation pain that time, but something else.

Without meaning to almost, he found himself thinking of Kali's husband.

He thought about if it had been him, stuck in a SCARB holding cell, being interrogated by Org agents, kept apart from his blind, pregnant, kidnapped wife, without having any idea what might be being done to her in the main prison yards—without being able to help her.

Just being separated from a pregnant mate would be enough to make most seers lose their fucking minds, much less having to think about hardened criminals doing gods-knew-what to their vulnerable mate in that condition.

For the first time since he'd met Kali, Revik found himself glad he wasn't her mate.

He also finally managed to focus totally on the debriefing, rather than on the current state of his own body and light.

"How the hell did they pick her up, if she is pregnant?" he asked, sharp.

Balidor shrugged.

He held out his hands, but the Adhipan leader's expression remained flat.

"That's completely illegal," Revik said, sharper. "How the fuck could they have arrested her and put her in a camp while pregnant? Did they not know of her condition?"

"They knew," Balidor assured him. "As I said, she is close to term, brother. There is no possible way they could not have known."

Revik stared at him. "How is that possible?"

"They broke the law," Balidor said. "Obviously."

"Under orders?"

"Obviously."

"And you think Galaith ordered this?" Revik frowned. He fought to think as he glanced at the other males in the back of the truck. "You think *he* took her? For the Rooks?"

"We don't know who did it precisely, but it is definitely possible it was Galaith."

"It is *possible?*" Revik stared at him. "Who the fuck else would it be?"

Balidor gave him another of those inscrutable looks.

Revik felt his jaw harden. "And the husband? You know where they are holding him?"

Balidor nodded. "Yes. We have his location. We are still not certain if they intended to take him initially, but in the end, they more or less had to."

"Why?" Revik growled. "Because he might complain to the authorities that they stole his pregnant wife from their goddamned marital bed?"

Balidor and the green-eyed seer exchanged looks.

Balidor looked back at Revik.

His voice grew mild.

"Well, yes... that is certainly *one* reason," he said. "Given the illegality of their actions, they could hardly let Kali's mate go free. He also killed a number of their agents when they broke into his and Kali's house. Hardly surprising, given his wife's condition. He killed a few more at the camp itself, when they touched his wife. That's when they threw him in solitary."

"They put him in solitary for that?" Revik growled. "And charged him with... what? Being mated? Being a rational fucking seer?"

A few seers sitting across from him grunted.

Revik heard agreement in their grunts.

He gave them a glance, then looked back at Balidor.

Balidor sighed. He clicked under his breath before answering in a tired-sounding voice.

"More or less, brother," he said. "It is likely they confined him partly in retribution for the killings... but the fact that they picked up a pregnant seer in the first place is so unprecedented, we have little to go by, in terms of what is 'normal,' or what rationales they might be using for their treatment of either one of them."

Balidor gave him a grim look.

"I will say, we no longer think Uye's treatment is being engineered from the outside... if that is what you are implying. It seems the Black Arrow and Sweeper guards at the work camp are unaware of Kali's true identity. There is quite a bit of chatter inside the camp about her 'condition' and how they are supposed to accommodate that, and keep her safe from the other prisoners. Arguments ensued from the moment she arrived. Mainly around the illegality of her arrest, and how holding her violates treaty with the Seer Nation, as well as World Court law. Our intelligence operatives tell us many of the seer guards are quite unhappy with her being there."

"Where do they have her?" Revik asked, frowning. "Which camp?"

*"Guoreum,"* Balidor said.

Revik frowned. *"Guoreum?* That's pretty extreme. What did she do?"

"She didn't do anything, brother."

"I mean... what are they *saying* she did?"

"As far as I know, they have not charged her with any crime. Which is why this worries us, brother. Even beyond the conditions in *Guoreum* itself."

Balidor re-clasped his hands and exhaled.

"There are a number of agents of the Org fighting to keep Kali's mate confined. We think this is partly in an attempt to pull intelligence off him. But we also think, based on intel we've received from the inside, that it's because of his sight rank, which is quite high. That's the good news, really. Better that, than because they know who he is specifically."

"Which is who?" Revik said. "Who is he, precisely? This Uye?"

"He is Kali's mate," Balidor said, giving him a flat look.

Revik frowned.

He opened his mouth, about to ask another question.

He got distracted when he felt eyes on him and turned, glancing surreptitiously at a particularly large male sitting on the bench across from him.

The seer was enormous—big enough to make Revik slightly nervous.

He was big enough to have Wvercian blood in him, despite his dark hair and complexion, and his bright hazel eyes. Despite his size, and his lingering stare, he watched Revik with noticeably less hostility than most sharing the Jeep with him.

If anything, the look there was curiosity.

Or possibly puzzlement.

Revik couldn't help noticing the giant wore a Nazi scar from the concentration camps across his face. It made him look a bit like a pirate.

Revik glanced back at Balidor when the Adhipan leader went on.

"...We think the Org's got Kali's mate targeted for recruitment," Balidor explained. "Which is why they won't release him back into the general population. His potential is statistically rare, and he's got a fair bit of training. Including some military, which they managed to discern, despite his attempts to hide it. Uye is also unreg'd with any of the agencies and has been for his entire life, so I imagine they are very curious about him. Both in terms of his reasons for being off-grid, and the fact that he managed it successfully for so long."

"How *did* he manage it?" Revik asked.

"With Kali's help, to a degree." Balidor motioned vaguely with one hand. "But Uye is a formidable seer in his own right. His marriage to Kali has actually made it more dire for him to hone his skills, not less. Simply being married to her has put his own life in a great deal of danger, of course."

Revik nodded.

He swallowed his questions that time, even though he still didn't really know what the "of course" meant, not exactly.

"So where are we going?" he asked finally.

"South America," Balidor replied. "*Guoreum* is north of Manaus. In Brazil."

"Yes." Revik's voice grew impatient. "I'm aware. And I understand the Org holding Uye if they have targeted him for recruitment. But why is *she* still there? Is she not yet sold? And if not, why not have your people buy her? If the Org guards do not yet know who she is—"

"Brother." Balidor cocked an eyebrow at him. "She is not for sale. There is no listing for her. On the *Rynak* or elsewhere."

Revik frowned.

The *Rynak* was the seer black market.

One of them, anyway, and the largest.

Any major sale of a seer would be listed there. A pregnant

female seer, close to term, would definitely be listed there, especially one with Kali's probable sight rank.

"Why the fuck not?" he asked.

Balidor clicked softly under his breath.

"There is really only one possible reason," Balidor said. "Clearly *someone* knows what or who she is. She never would have been picked up in the first place, if that were not so. As I said, she is *very* pregnant, brother. Both her and her offspring are worth a considerable amount... and they were taken illegally. The fact that she was not immediately sold and moved means she is already owned. They likely stuck her in *Guoreum* to hide her."

Revik's frown deepened. "But you said the guards—"

"—do not know of her, yes. But just because the guards don't know, doesn't mean no one does. We assume someone will come for her soon."

"Galaith?"

"Possibly Galaith. Yes."

Balidor frowned, making another noncommittal gesture.

"...Possibly someone else."

"Like who?" Revik asked again.

Again, Balidor made that noncommittal wave.

"We do not know," he admitted. "That possibility worries us more, frankly. Yet, it also seems strangely more likely. Galaith is usually pretty good about honoring treaties. It is difficult to imagine him picking up a pregnant female. Even Kali."

There was a silence.

Revik just stared at those unreadable gray eyes.

He fought with the conflicting emotions warring inside his light. He knew what lived outside of the human city of Manaus. Hell, he'd been there, on the ground, while it was being built. Maybe he couldn't remember all the details of those years, but he clearly hadn't forgotten everything.

He even remembered how the camp got its name.

It had been some flight of fancy of Terian's, Revik remembered.

Terian had been Revik's old partner in the Org.

Terry named it *Guoreum* after a mythological, crow-like bird, often equated to one of the Four in the seer pantheon. *Guoreum*—or "Rook," as the being was more commonly known—was said to live in the spaces between dark and light, good and evil.

It was the same being from which the Org itself got its nickname.

That name, Rook, generally wasn't meant as a compliment.

The being, *Guoreum,* acted as a kind of "Trickster" who played both sides of the fence. In the old stories, *Guoreum* was a liar, a thief, a conman, a killer, one who manipulated and distorted reality, often pretending to work for the "higher good" in order to twist people into giving him what he wanted.

Revik supposed most of the religious seers saw the Org that way, as well.

Naming a prison camp after a pantheon being, *any* pantheon being, never made much sense to Revik.

But then, Terian always had a strange sense of humor.

Whatever the name, there was nothing whimsical about the camp outside Manaus.

*Guoreum* was commonly considered the worst of the high-security camps built by the Org in the post-World War II period. It was designed specifically for hardened criminals in the seer world, and contained some of the most extreme measures of deprivation and isolation of any other camp its size, along with the most dangerous inmates.

The Org reserved the cells of *Guoreum* almost exclusively for terrorists and political prisoners of some rank, as well as other criminal threats to their "New Order."

Revik himself had sent seers there, not all that long ago.

The thought brought up a thick wave of nausea.

"How the fuck did they even find her?" Revik asked after that pause. "Why did Uye not take her into hiding, once she went blind?"

Balidor sighed.

He ran a muscular hand through his chestnut-colored hair.

"He did," he said, his voice heavy. "They were even protected by us to a degree. I do not know how they were found. Or why." He looked at Revik. His gray eyes held a more difficult-to-read emotion now. "You are aware of who Kali foresaw her offspring to be?"

Revik returned his look.

Then, swallowing as he remembered Kali's words to him about this, he nodded.

His voice turned gruff.

"Yes."

Something in Balidor's eyes relaxed.

When he next spoke, his tone grew almost gentle.

"There is something else I must tell you, brother," he said.

Seeing the knowing in the other man's eyes, Revik felt his jaw harden. He didn't look away from that steel-colored gaze.

"What?"

"I have been given a message. From her husband. To you." As if seeing something in Revik's face, Balidor hesitated, then made another of those nearly-apologetic hand waves. "We managed to communicate with him briefly, on the inside. We told him we were pulling you on his wife's request. We felt obligated to inform him of this development, if not necessarily to ask his permission. He had a right to know."

Revik nodded.

"I agree," he said simply.

He did, too.

He didn't really want the details of that conversation, however.

Balidor sighed. He clicked under his breath.

"Yet I must give them to you," he said, again apologetic. "Uye said to tell you that your role constituted one word... and one word alone. He said if you deviated from that role, if you tried to surpass or expand it in any way, with either his daughter or his wife, he would hunt you, brother."

Balidor hesitated, his eyes still holding that apology.

"...He said he would kill you, brother Dehgoies," he said, the apology audible. "Even if his family was unharmed."

Revik only nodded.

He couldn't say the words surprised him, but some part of his light retracted anyway. He definitely felt the threat more deeply than he would have from most seers.

Kali would have told her husband about him.

Of course she would have. She would have told him everything.

Revik nodded to himself. He felt his chest tighten.

It occurred to him that Balidor wouldn't continue until Revik voiced the question.

"What was the word?" he asked.

He looked at the Adhipan leader directly, and that time, sympathy shone from those pale gray eyes. Balidor laid a hand on his arm, in reassurance maybe, or maybe simply because he thought Revik needed the contact.

Hell, maybe he even did.

"Bodyguard," Balidor said. "The word he used was 'bodyguard,' brother. In point of fact, he said, *Hul-tare*, as in the ancient guardian of the Light."

Thinking about this, Revik nodded again.

He knew the myth of *Hul-tare*.

The part about that particular mythic guardian being celibate, asexual and willing to die for his charges could not have been unintended.

"I understand," is all he said.

He clasped his hands between his knees in an unconscious imitation of Balidor's own pose. He stared out through the window at the passing scenery. In some part of his mind, he catalogued pine trees, the distant flash of blue sky, white clouds intervening along with sunlight, contrasting the sharper edges of the Pamir range as they descended down the steep slopes.

He noted in that same part of his mind that they were heading south, so probably towards Kabul in Afghanistan, rather than Dushanbe in Tajikistan.

Ticking, ticking in the background.

The tactical part of his mind endlessly clicked on its own tracks, regardless of whatever emotions tugged at him on the surface.

Some days, it bothered Revik.

It made him feel like some kind of machine.

Other days, it was a relief.

When Balidor said nothing else, Revik only nodded again.

"If you talk to him again," he said. "Tell Uye I understand. I agree to this role."

Balidor nodded. He squeezed Revik's arm.

"I will," the Adhipan leader said.

Revik believed him.

When he glanced back towards the window, he paused on the green-eyed male sitting next to him, the same one who had been in his room in the monastery, the one Balidor called Dalejem. Revik realized only then that the other male was staring at him again, a thin veneer of puzzlement coloring those jade green and violet eyes.

The puzzlement was different on this seer than it had been on the giant one sitting across from him on the opposite bench.

Dalejem felt almost frustrated with what he did not understand.

Something new lived in the male's expression now, as well.

Revik discarded it as soon as it flickered past his awareness, if only because he didn't quite know what to do with it.

Even so, some part of his mind catalogued it anyway.

It looked almost like jealousy.

## CHAPTER 5
# RETURNING TO CIVILIZATION

They would be landing in São Paulo in approximately thirty seconds.

They would enter the São Paulo airport approximately twelve minutes after that.

The reality of both things had Revik in a state bordering on what he suspected might be an anxiety attack.

He had already reacted badly to Kabul.

Luckily, after Kabul, he'd had a chance to calm down.

Over the course of a very long plane ride, seated with a group of infiltrators whose light exuded more silence than noise, even when they spoke, he'd managed to calm down quite a lot. He'd even managed to meditate for part of the trip, sitting at the back of the plane.

He'd needed that calm, desperately.

He needed it even more now.

Given how he'd reacted to being in a human city for the first time in five years, he wasn't feeling all that confident of his coping skills. He knew São Paulo would be even more crowded, even more intense, and would involve even more humans ignoring his personal boundaries than what he had experienced in Kabul.

He also knew he had a better chance of being recognized here.

Under the Org, with only a few exceptions, Galaith kept Revik stationed in the West.

That meant primarily North, South, and Latin America, with some time spent in Europe and even less time spent in Russia and Ukraine.

Revik's time in Russia had been not long after the end of the second world war, so near the beginning of his time with the Org. It had more to do with operational priorities at the time, and the stint in Moscow only lasted about a year.

Without coming out and saying it explicitly, Galaith wanted Revik out of Asia.

From casual things his boss said to him, Revik assumed Galaith had been trying to put some distance between Revik and his family.

It was an idea Revik himself found quite funny.

There was no love lost between Revik and his adoptive family.

He wouldn't have sought them out for regular visits, even if he lived next door.

He wouldn't have done so even if he worked every tour of his career under the Org there.

He'd tried arguing that same point with Galaith a few times, but the Org leader remained immovable for some reason. He wanted Revik in the West. Other than those initial jobs in Moscow, and his tours in Vietnam, Revik never set foot in Asia, not once in almost thirty years.

Revik didn't try to voice any of his concerns about São Paulo to his new companions.

He followed along with them without speaking much at all, really.

He did notice that Balidor rarely left his side.

He didn't know if that was for his protection, or to ensure he didn't split at the earliest opportunity, but Revik found he appreciated the proximity of the other seer. He noticed the inhumanly handsome, green-eyed seer with the streaked brown and black hair didn't stray very far from him, either, which Revik also found strangely comforting.

Dalejem, or "Jem," as the other Adhipan seers seemed to uniformly call him, appeared to be making Revik a pet project of sorts.

He didn't talk to Revik much.

He'd cut out the worst of his staring, too.

He didn't call himself out as any kind of bodyguard, not specifically, or even as some kind of mentor or big brother within the Adhipan. He merely attached himself to Revik's side, and seemed to be shielding him almost constantly with his light.

He even shielded him from the other seers in their Adhipan group.

Normally, that might have irritated Revik.

Right now, however, given everything, Revik mostly found it a relief.

Something in the way the other seer's *aleimi* enveloped and held his would have made it difficult for him to mind anyway. He felt the protectiveness there, and couldn't help but appreciate it, even if Dalejem was a stranger to him.

Maybe he'd just been absent from that kind of warmth for too long.

Maybe that absence was making him stupid.

In either case, he let himself be escorted, even if it blinded him somewhat.

He didn't speak much.

He spoke even less to Dalejem than Dalejem did to him, and mostly just listened to Adhipan Balidor. Even so, he followed the two of them wherever they led. By the time they boarded that first plane, he'd already begun to follow them even when they didn't prompt him to do so specifically with their lights.

In the airport at Kabul, he felt like he'd been thrown into some kind of alternate reality.

He couldn't remember the last time he'd felt so alien, or so totally out of his depth.

The instant he stepped out of that Jeep—

Sounds battered him.

His light felt the wash of presences like an assault, as if he'd stepped out in the midst of a riot. It was only an ordinary human city, on an ordinary human day, but it felt like a war zone. Something about the clash of lights, sounds, presences, and other physical stimuli felt violent to him. He got completely lost in that chaos, overwhelmed by it.

The volume of everything shocked him.

The hardness of light, the intensity of emotions.

The loudness of their thoughts.

It was as if someone had, without warning, cranked the dial up on a radio, shattering a silence Revik only noticed in its absence.

He ended up standing in the middle of the street like some kind of time traveler from another world. He flinched from the horns, the shouts of pedestrians in markets, the people walking up and down the sidewalk and in forming crowds in front of the taxi stands of the airport. He ducked and flinched at dogs barking, music from open-air shops, feed stations running outside the larger stores, images and text flashing at him.

He felt like he might have a heart attack.

He felt like at any minute, he might be shot.

The contact with so many minds overloaded his seer's sight, effectively blinding him.

He struggled to filter, to screen and control the speed and volume of inputs.

He felt and heard them all around him, though.

He felt them not only in the more distant parts of his light, murmuring at the edge of his awareness, but so tangibly when they came physically close to him, it was as if he could see their thoughts with his physical eyes.

Those thoughts came at him like an attack.

Once he got close enough that some of those people actually began *talking* to him, wanting things from him, trying to sell him things, Revik basically hid behind the other seers, feeling some embarrassment for doing it, but unable to help himself.

To their credit, the seers closed ranks around him.

For the first time, he felt real understanding from most of them, and more compassion (and surprise, in some cases) than he did ridicule, which was a relief.

Even so, it was hard to take.

Hawkers and touts descended on them pretty much as soon as they hit the cold air.

Revik found himself staring up and down the dusty streets, lost in the sheer number of bodies, faces, and minds.

Even the animals completely freaked him out.

Truthfully, it felt like being on LSD.

For the first time since he left the Rooks, he felt high as fuck.

If it hadn't been for the lights enveloping him, particularly those of Dalejem and Balidor, he was pretty sure he would have had a full-blown panic attack. They probably would have had to tackle him in the street, shoot him up with some kind of tranquilizer.

Smells hit him particularly strongly for some reason, some of them extremely unpleasant, some mildly so, the rest just overwhelming in their frequency and intensity.

Petrol, exhaust fumes, spiced foods, sweaty bodies, dirty clothes, raw sewage, the chemical taste of perfume, animal urine, rotting vegetation from the stands, meat cooking, burning plastic from a trash fire, rotting animal meat, sulfur, cow shit…

He picked out each smell individually, but couldn't get away from any of them.

His eyes couldn't track all the faces that pulled him any better than his light. Some things stopped him harder than others, especially bright colors. He found himself staring at a group of women wearing full burqas of a sharp, lapis lazuli color.

He still barely comprehended what he was looking at when Dalejem pinged a warning at him with his light. When Revik's eyes swiveled to the other male, then followed the direction of his warning's meaning, Revik saw a group of male, Afghani humans watching him stare at the females in burqas, their faces openly hostile.

The connection between those male Afghanis, the warning in Dalejem's light, and the women fell into place, enough to get Revik to look away.

When he glanced at Dalejem, embarrassed, the other seer only smiled.

*Don't stare at the women here, brother,* Dalejem cautioned gently. *Not the human ones. No matter how hungry you are.*

Revik blinked at that, startled, but not offended.

Dalejem added, *It's less a morality issue than bad politics here, in this part of the world. We don't have time for a confrontation with the locals.*

His thoughts grew even more gentle, but still held a faint rebuke.

*We can push them, of course, brother Revik... but we are only supposed to do that in cases of absolute necessity, in areas that rightfully could be termed self-defense. We are not supposed to initiate or spark confrontations that might require us to unnecessarily impinge on their free will. It is part of the Adhipan code.*

Thinking about that, Revik nodded slowly.

It made sense.

The Adhipan would have a strict code about such things.

As he stood there, he continued to turn over the other's

words, wondering if he'd been staring at more than the color of the burqas after all, consciously or not.

He couldn't make up his mind.

Truthfully, he hadn't been aware of thinking about sex at all, not here. He hadn't even been fully aware of those humans in burqas as female until Dalejem pointed it out.

Now, Revik found himself overly-focused on the fact that there were female humans and seers around him, in addition to the rest.

Dalejem grunted, rolling his eyes.

*Figures,* he sent, nudging Revik's arm.

His light held humor, though.

Revik flushed.

Still, he did make a point of not looking overtly at the Afghani humans after that, especially the females, no matter how they were dressed. He also noticed that the female seers with them, Mara included, had covered their hair and in some cases their faces before they'd left the truck traveling behind theirs.

Revik knew that might be partly to obscure the truth of their race as much as adhere to local custom. Even so, he noted that things might be more tense in this part of the world than he remembered.

*Your intuition is correct,* Dalejem sent, apparently feeling enough of Revik's thoughts to feel compelled to answer. *Things are... heated... in this part of the world. Many social customs have become more rigid as a result. There is a resurgence of human religious fundamentalism everywhere right now, brother, among humans and seers.*

When Revik looked over, Dalejem shrugged.

*There are a number of radical sects following the seer myths, as well,* he added sourly. *Terrorism is on the rise. We have been trying to stabilize the situation, but most of it is symptomatic. Far deeper problems are beginning to manifest, brother, within both seer and human communities. The system Galaith set up to calm the humans following the wars is not really working. Where it does "work," it does so mostly through oppression.*

Dalejem flipped one hand eloquently, a seer's shrug.

Revik thought the other might say more.

He didn't.

Revik also wondered if Dalejem's words might be an accusation, in part.

If they were, he could not feel it.

Then again, Dalejem was Adhipan. There was a good chance Revik wouldn't feel it, not unless Dalejem wanted him to.

*There is no accusation, brother,* Dalejem sent, softer.

He squeezed Revik's arm briefly, then let him go.

Revik fought the flush that rose in his light, but only nodded.

He didn't ask for more information.

He would have plenty of time to learn about the current state of the world later. For now, he got the gist of what Dalejem was warning him about.

Mythers. Religious wars.

The scriptures were rife with predictions around this.

He let Dalejem and Balidor lead him towards the glass doors of the airport. He kept his light and his eyes within the group of infiltrators.

He still caught stares.

He found himself strangely self-conscious of his clothes. He touched his face to remind himself if he'd shaved, how long his hair was, what he even looked like.

It hit him, really hit him, that he hadn't left those caves in over five years.

At the thought, Dalejem and Balidor's lights wrapped more tightly into his.

It was strange to be protected by these two men, given who he was.

It was strange, but not unwelcome.

## CHAPTER 6
# THE ADHIPAN

Revik knew of the Adhipan before this, of course.

He didn't know much about them in terms of details.

Then again, apart from Vash and a handful of seers high up in the Seer Council, most seers knew nothing of the Adhipan.

No one was really supposed to know much about the Adhipan.

Well, not unless they were *of* the Adhipan.

Everything Revik knew, everything most seers knew, came in the form of rumors and quasi-myths. Most of what Revik had been told about the elite squad of infiltrators, he'd frankly questioned the accuracy of, if only because so many seemed to try and use sightings or encounters as bragging rights of one kind of another.

They joked about such things when Revik was with the Org.

They joked about every two-bit, wannabe seer having a lame "Adhipan" story.

Everyone assumed these stories to be lies.

Historically, the Adhipan had always worked in secret.

They trained in secret. They recruited in secret.

It had been that way for thousands of years.

All seers had *heard* of the Adhipan, of course, whether they believed in them or not. Revik heard stories of the Adhipan since he was a boy, growing up in the Himalayas.

Like most young seers, he'd heroized them.

Also like most young seers, he fantasized more than once about being invited into that elite cadre, being marked as one of the chosen.

He never had been, of course.

Balidor himself had been a quasi-mythological figure, even back when Revik was a child. Revik had heard myth-like rumors of Adhipan Balidor as far back as he could remember. It was said, by those who believed he existed at all, that Balidor was the greatest infiltrator alive.

Perhaps even the greatest of the past several generations.

It was said that his sight skills matched those of the Council Seers, and far surpassed them in any area utilizing a military or infiltration skill.

Balidor was a living legend, and not only because very few could claim to have met him or even seen him in the flesh.

Many believed it had been Adhipan Balidor who brought down the infamous *Syrimne d'Gaos*, history's only known telekinetic seer. They claimed Balidor, not Galaith, had been the one to bring Syrimne down during World War I, before Syrimne could more or less wipe out the entire human race.

Revik still entertained a few fleeting doubts that this human-looking seer could really *be* the famed Balidor.

Yet, as he watched him work and studied his light surreptitiously—or what he pretended was surreptitious, since the occasional puzzled and/or humorous look aimed his way by Balidor himself told him otherwise—Revik's doubt began to fade.

He felt no duplicitousness on any of these seers.

Even those who did not trust him, or did not like him because of what he was, did not hide those sentiments from him.

They were open about it.

They were really fucking open about it in some cases.

Further, Revik felt a frequency of light on Balidor similar to what he felt on Vash. Maybe because of that, he found it increasingly difficult to distrust him.

It rang of truth, somehow.

Truth, clarity, compassion, light.

Maybe even "reality" in the broader, philosophical sense.

At any rate, that high frequency of light didn't seem to be hiding anything from him, particularly not in terms of intent, or who and what they were.

For the same reasons, when Balidor named Revik as his responsibility, Revik hadn't taken those as idle words. The Adhipan not only followed Code, they considered themselves the protectors of that Code, its champions.

They did not lie. Not even in half-truths.

Moreover, they did not work against the free will of any being. It was one of the most basic tenets of Code, one that required absolute transparency.

So if Balidor was who he said he was, he would protect Revik, at least out here.

Revik hadn't yet asked if he would be returned to the caves of the Pamir once Kali's need for him had ended, but he assumed he would be. He therefore took Balidor's promise to mean that he would do everything in his power to return Revik to the monks in one piece so that Revik could complete the terms of his penance.

Which could also mean that Revik was a prisoner here.

In effect, at least, even if not explicitly one.

He forgot all of that, of course, as he walked off the plane in São Paulo.

He even forgot Kali, who he'd been trying desperately not

to think about since they'd first told him of her kidnapping—and her mate, who'd already threatened to kill him if he managed to fuck this up—and her unborn child.

Instead, he found himself once more struggling just to exist in the world.

He was also forced to face the fact that he really hadn't existed in the world, not on his own, not in years.

Possibly even decades.

He wasn't really doing it now, either.

He'd gone from being dependent on the Rooks, to dependent on the monks.

Now, he was dependent on brother Balidor and his famed Adhipan.

---

Within minutes, Revik found himself fighting not to...

Well, fight.

Hands pulled at him, tugging at his clothes.

He'd left the airport following close behind Balidor and Dalejem. His light and eyes tracked the positions of the other infiltrators as they left the enclosed area of customs.

Once the second set of glass doors opened them out onto the curb and into the tropical sunlight and dense, humid air, Revik let out an involuntary gasp.

Wet heat clung to his mouth and nose.

It sucked at his lungs, made it difficult to breathe. He broke out in a sweat, seemingly over his entire body. Shock hit his system as he realized again how few changes in environment he'd had to endure over the previous few years.

The weather reminded him of Vietnam, which didn't exactly calm him down.

Worse than that, he felt exposed.

He felt exposed even before a group of touts spotted their

group and surrounded them, offering him hotels, women, tours, food, stolen watches and illegal organic tech. They invaded his physical boundaries and his *aleimi* before Revik had come close to regaining his equilibrium.

Hell, they were all over him before he'd managed to adjust his eyes to the bright sunlight.

Fighting to control his reactions, he glanced around at the seers he'd left the plane with.

He found them all standing at the curb a few yards away.

They watched in apparent amusement as he alone among them seemed unable… or perhaps unwilling… to manage the crowd of humans, all of whom seemed to want something from him.

Unlike in Kabul, the Adhipan seers weren't helping him this time.

Even Dalejem wasn't helping him; he stood with the others.

The Adhipan infiltrators were using this as an acclimation moment for him.

They were deliberately letting him handle it.

Revik's mind could see the logic in that, in forcing him to adjust, but the realization made him panic at first. He hadn't fully realized how much he'd been resting on all of them until they ripped those training wheels out from under him.

He found himself in an island of humans, fighting to talk himself down, to not overreact, even as he shoved a pair of mirrored sunglasses clumsily over his eyes to minimize the chances someone might ID him as a seer.

"Dehgoies!" a female voice called out mockingly. "Do you intend to let them strip you naked? Or do you plan to join the rest of us at some point…?"

She sent him a snapshot as she said it.

Revik felt the meaning behind it, even as his skin warmed with more than just the heated air.

The Adhipan seers had thrown up a shield to protect him, despite his panic.

In that same cluster of packed images and meanings, Revik realized they were all waiting for him to use his sight to push the local humans away.

In that same cluster of packed information, Mara sent him more information and direction regarding the Adhipan Infiltrator's Code.

She explained that since the humans had approached him, it didn't break Code for him to push them with his light. It also didn't break code for him to paint illusions so the humans could not recognize him as seer, especially if such an illusion was important to the wider goals of the Adhipan charter, which required them to operate in secret, including among humans.

All of this fell under the category of self-defense, Mara informed him.

Like the rest of Balidor's team, Revik was allowed to do whatever he had to do to make his way through the city unmolested, as long as he used the minimum amount of persuasion, force, or illusion required to reach his goals.

Revik felt his light cringe with embarrassment, even as he sent a ping of acknowledgment back at the female infiltrator.

It had been a long time since he'd been forced to learn Infiltration 101.

At the same time, he appreciated them being clear about the rules, even if he was embarrassed that he *needed* that clarity, as if he were a Sark child, with no sense of inbuilt morality of his own.

The truth was, the Rooks didn't really have rules, not when it came to that kind of thing. Revik could not remember the last time he'd operated as an infiltrator in a way that required him to factor in anything approximating an ethical code.

The monks had rules, of course.

The monks were not infiltrators, though.

Their rules had been different.

Simpler, in most ways, but eminently impractical for operating in the human world.

Exhaling as he tried to push aside his embarrassment, Revik sent a gentle push out into the crowd with his *aleimi*, carefully turning the humans' minds away from him.

*He has no money. He is useless to us…* he sent softly.

He knew it was all right.

The Adhipan seers all but told him to do it, but something about impinging on their free will, even in this tiny way, still felt wrong to him.

Maybe he really had spent too much time with those monks.

Dalejem, who stood watching him with the rest of the Adhipan seers, let out a ringing laugh, clearly hearing him.

Revik gave him a hard look, in spite of himself.

*You are quite amusing, you know,* Dalejem sent, his clear voice warm with humor in Revik's mind. *You castigate yourself for having no moral compass… then in the next second feel guilty for even the tiniest push of a human mind. You probably wince at killing insects too, na, little brother? It is adorable, truth be told. But I cannot help but wonder… is this really the infamous and deadly Rook, Dehgoies Revik? The one we were all warned about? The one we were told to fear?*

Revik scowled at him a little.

He could feel no ill will in the other's words, so couldn't feel any real anger at him, but his skin warmed in embarrassment anyway.

*And you blush,* Dalejem noted, bemused. *You are a puzzle, little brother. A genuine enigma.*

Revik didn't look at him that time.

Anyway, by then, he had completed his push.

The human eyes in front of him glazed.

They slowly began to back away from him, almost as a group.

A man took his hand off Revik's arm, giving him an irritated look before shaking his head and walking back towards the glass doors. Revik could feel him already looking for a tourist with more to offer, and money to spend. The human female who had been closet to him in those few seconds backed away last.

She caressed Revik's thigh through his pants as her fingers left him.

Revik bit down on his tongue, hard.

Humor rippled the Barrier around him as he did it, and that time, Revik felt something closer to shame.

He fought not to let it turn into anger.

In the end, he shut his light down altogether.

Then someone had hold of his arm.

Before he could stop himself, Revik glanced over, meeting pale green eyes, a wide smile on a shockingly handsome face.

"Do not worry, brother," Dalejem said to him in English, smiling. "They are giving you shit. It is hazing, brother. They sent those humans at you, to see what you would do."

Revik felt his embarrassment turn into a more smoldering irritation.

Dalejem nudged him playfully with his shoulder.

"Do not be angry, brother," he said. Dalejem grinned wider. "It was not done in spite. Quite the opposite. It means most of them have decided they like you."

Revik rolled his eyes at that.

He snorted in spite of himself.

"They will not leave you behind," Dalejem added. He tilted his head for Revik to follow. "But we had better go."

*There is nothing to be embarrassed about, brother,* Dalejem added in his mind, softer. He squeezed his arm. *Truly. We are all surprised at how well you are doing with this. Surprised and impressed. Brother Balidor, especially. Personally, I think he is quite proud, as he is the one who really pushed to bring you along for this when Kali requested you. You are probably not shocked to learn a number of us tried to talk him out of it.*

Revik frowned at him.

He wondered why the hell Dalejem felt the need to tell him *that*.

*They have changed their minds since,* Dalejem added, gripping him tighter. *That was more or less my point, Revik.*

Revik didn't open his light, but he felt that tension in his chest relax slightly.

He averted his eyes from Dalejem's intent stare.

He followed the tug of those fingers and that light, fighting to ignore the fact that he'd gotten hard from the human's caress, and that Dalejem having his hands on him wasn't exactly helping. He knew the others had probably noticed his reaction already.

He knew Dalejem must have noticed, as well.

Clearly, the other male didn't care.

By the time Revik reached the curb, four SUVs had pulled up with tinted windows.

Modified, Revik guessed, perhaps heavily with organics. Likely bullet-proof and mine-proof glass composite on the sides and covering the lower chassis.

Dalejem smiled at him again.

"That tactical thing of yours," he commented, clicking softly. "It never leaves you. Does it, brother? It's like a nonstop commentary running in the background from what I can tell. No matter what you are doing, that part of you is working. Thinking. Noticing."

Revik blinked at him, surprised.

He didn't answer, but found himself thinking about the other's words.

Just how many of his thoughts could these Adhipan infiltrators hear, anyway?

He let Dalejem lead him into the last of those SUVs.

He closed his light even more when he found Mara in there, now grinning at him with a smug triumph in her eyes.

"Enjoy yourself, pup?" she asked as he took his seat.

When he glanced at her, he saw her staring pointedly at his crotch.

He covered it with one arm, almost before he knew he meant to.

He realized his mistake when she laughed in delight. Her laughter caused a few of the seers sitting around her in the cramped space to chuckle, too.

"Don't be ashamed." She smirked when he glanced up, winking at him. "From what I can tell, you have nothing to be embarrassed of on that front, brother. Quite impressive, in fact."

"Leave him alone, Mara," Dalejem said. *"Gaos."*

For the first time, Revik heard a harder note in the male's words.

He didn't know if he resented it or felt grateful.

In the end he decided not to entertain either thing.

He wiped the last of the thoughts from his mind and stared out the tinted windows with no expression on his face. He held his light as closed as he could manage, considering who he was with, and how fucked up his mental state was already.

He might not be as good at hiding his light as any of them, but he could still keep himself from thinking well enough to not give them too much ammunition.

At the thought, he felt a pulse of warmth hit his chest, strong enough and heated enough that he looked over in spite of himself. That time, when he met Dalejem's gaze—for it had to be Dalejem, since he was the only seer here who didn't seem to hate him entirely—Revik couldn't help but wince at the pity he saw in those green eyes.

He bit his tongue.

He looked back towards the tinted windows.

He wasn't here for them, he reminded himself.

He was here for Kali.

He was here because he owed Kali.

As he turned over the thought in the more bitter corners of his mind, however, he wondered if he might be lying to himself about that, too.

## CHAPTER 7
# I CANNOT ASK

"What are we doing out here?" Revik asked.

The other male didn't answer him at first.

Instead, he continued to push past branches, vines, and trunks in the jungle, a heavy, black, canvas bag wrapped cross-wise around his back.

Revik followed him. He matched the other's long strides without thought.

Even so, he felt a denser kind of pain hardening in his chest.

He could feel that the other seers were trying with him now.

They'd laid off on some of the teasing he'd gotten when they first landed in São Paulo, but he couldn't help but notice their eyes on him. They watched him more than they watched one another, and while he saw curiosity in some of those stares, not only hostility, the added scrutiny couldn't help but make him paranoid, if only because he couldn't read them at all.

They didn't seem to mind that, either, as far as he could tell.

Meaning, the power imbalance between him and the rest of them.

Anyway, Revik strongly suspected their more subdued air around him had more to do with Balidor chewing them all out than any change of heart, regardless of Dalejem's attempts to reassure him.

Still, the seer in front of him was maybe the only one Revik grudgingly trusted, apart from Balidor himself.

"Just come with me, brother," Dalejem said. He glanced over his shoulder at Revik. "I'm not bringing you out here to shoot you, I promise."

"Then what is this?"

Revik heard the wariness in his own voice. He flinched when he did, but since he couldn't hide the sentiment from his light, he supposed it didn't matter.

Dalejem clearly heard that suspicion as well. The green-eyed seer came to a stop in the middle of the jungle trail. He exhaled in amused exasperation, his hands on his hips as he turned to face Revik directly.

"Are you *always* this paranoid, brother?" he asked.

Revik thought about that.

He'd stopped when Dalejem did. Now he stood there, uncomfortable, as he wiped the sweat off his brow with the back of one hand.

"Yes," he said after a pause.

Dalejem laughed aloud. He shook his head bemusedly.

The long, brown and black hair he wore wound into a seer's hair clip had come down in pieces since they'd left the camp. Revik found himself looking at where it stuck to the male's neck, even as the other clicked at him in mock-reproach.

"It is a wonder they call the Org a 'Brotherhood,'" he said.

Revik thought about that.

He felt the truth behind Dalejem's words.

He'd noticed a number of those little ironies with the Org,

now that he was outside the Pyramid's construct and could see them more clearly. Before he could come up with a reply, however, Dalejem had turned back towards the trees. He hitched the heavy canvas bag higher up on his back and yanked a machete out of his belt with a scraping sound.

Revik eyed it warily until Dalejem swung it to clear their path. The muscular seer hacked at vines and broad leaves that disguised the game trail they were following.

"A hint, brother," Revik said. "Some indication."

Dalejem laughed.

He shook his head, once, a seer's refusal.

He didn't turn, or stop swinging the machete.

"I wanted to bring you somewhere we wouldn't be overheard," the green-eyed seer said after a pause. "No one else was offering, but we were all wondering, so I volunteered."

Revik came to a dead stop at that.

He stood there, unmoving, as his mind fought its way through the other's words.

Dalejem kept walking.

He only glanced over his shoulder long enough to chuckle.

"Gods. You really weren't kidding about the paranoia."

Revik only stood there, watching him.

He continued to watch as Dalejem moved away.

Realizing the other wasn't going to wait for him that time, Revik turned possibilities over in his mind, even as it occurred to him that some part of his light had reacted inappropriately to the other's words... meaning, he'd taken them as a sort of proposition.

But why would Dalejem have brought that heavy bag along, if all he was looking for was a blow job? No, that couldn't be what this was.

That was probably just wishful thinking on Revik's part.

If he were being honest, it was probably closer to a fantasy.

He frowned at the thought, even as his light reacted again.

He knew he probably wouldn't be able to hide *any* of his reactions for long out here, no matter how inappropriate they were, but after a few more seconds' hesitation, he shook his head. He clicked at himself in irritation—along with embarrassment, anger, and a number of other emotions he probably wouldn't have been able to put easily into words.

After a few more seconds, he shoved it all aside.

He began walking again—faster, that time—to close the distance between himself and the other seer.

When they'd been walking for another ten or so minutes, Dalejem led him to the edge of a wide clearing.

The space opened up so suddenly, Revik came to an abrupt halt.

He stared around at a view of marshy grasses and blue skies.

At the edge of the tree line, he receded back into the shadow of the nearest thick trunks, even as he held up a hand to shield his face from the sun.

He glanced over as Dalejem yanked the strap from around his shoulder and head. The green-eyed seer dumped the heavy black bag on the jungle floor.

Hands on his hips, Dalejem clicked at Revik softly when Revik lowered his hand.

Dalejem continued to just stand there, outside the shadow of the trees.

He just stood there, wholly visible in the bright sun.

"Gods," the other said, his voice still holding that friendliness. "You really are paranoid. Who do you think might shoot at us out here?"

"Humans," Revik said at once. "An outer patrol sent by the camp's guards. A SCARB scouting party, if they already felt us out here. Black Arrow. Drug farmers. Mercs."

Clicking bemusedly, Dalejem seemed to give in.

Revik could feel the near eye-roll in his light, however.

He wondered what made the other male so confident.

As if hearing him again, the handsome seer sighed.

He placed his hands on his hips and surveyed the surrounding hills.

"They cannot penetrate Balidor's shield," Dalejem explained.

He raised an eyebrow as he glanced at Revik.

When Revik didn't move, Dalejem turned. He walked back the way he had come and out of the tall grasses. He reached the place where Revik stood in the protective shadows of the tree line. He studied his face, and his eyes looked calmer now, warmer.

"It is all right here, brother," Dalejem said. "It is perfectly safe. I promise."

"I'm not afraid." Revik's voice carried an edge. "I just don't see the point of standing out in the fucking open if I don't have to."

The other gestured diplomatically. "It is smart to be afraid here. Especially for you."

"I'm not afraid—" Revik began.

"Of course you are," Dalejem cut in, matter-of-fact. "With good reason, brother. You are a traitor to them, are you not?"

Revik looked at Dalejem directly.

Although the other seer stood in the shade of several palm trees, along with a handful of Brazil nuts and floss silks, sparks of sunlight found Dalejem's green eyes. The light illuminated their color as well as the slightly darker ring of violet around each iris.

"I am a traitor to a lot of people," Revik answered.

He refused to look away.

Dalejem smiled.

He stepped closer instead. He laid a hand cautiously on Revik's arm.

"Did you bring your own gun?" he asked, seemingly out of nowhere.

Revik blinked.

Then, nodding, he reached for the holster under his left arm. He pulled out the Glock-17 Balidor had given him. He flipped it out, handle first. He started to hand it to the other seer, but Dalejem waved him off.

"No, no," he said. He clicked softly, as if impatient. "Don't give it to me. We'll start with that. Presumably, you know how it works. If you're carrying it."

He stepped out of the way.

When he moved, he opened up Revik's view of the grassy marsh that stood before them. Revik realized only then that the "field" was likely a product of deforestation. He wondered if it had been done to expand cattle grazing, or for some other reason.

He could see no cattle on it now.

He was about to ask Dalejem—again—what the hell they were doing out here, but the other spoke before he could.

Dalejem used a sharper, more business-like tone with him that time.

"Pick a target," he said. "One hundred feet. Mark it to me verbally before you try for it."

"What is this, brother? What are you—"

"What do you think I'm doing?" Dalejem stared at him, puzzled. "I'm trying to see if you can shoot. We're going on a live op tomorrow. You've been in a cave for *five years,* brother. Mostly learning *not* to kill things. We need to know if we can depend on you."

Revik blinked at him.

Then, putting that together with the rest of what the other had said to him on their walk out here, he let out an involuntary laugh.

"Are you offended?" Dalejem asked. His lips pursed.

"No." Revik shook his head. He raised the gun to more or less shoulder height. "No, brother. I'm not offended. Do you want a moving target? Or stationary?"

"Stationary." Dalejem gave Revik's light a rebuking nudge. "Did you think I brought you out here to harm defenseless birds, brother?"

"No," Revik said. "But maybe to bring back dinner."

Dalejem clicked at him, but Revik heard amusement there that time.

He felt more tension dissipate from his light.

"Do you have a target yet? You are very slow," Dalejem said, his voice openly teasing.

"I have one. I was waiting for instructions, brother."

"Instructions you already received."

Revik rolled his eyes in exaggerated seer-fashion. "The white leaf there. On the small cashew tree nearest."

"That's not a cashew," Dalejem said, squinting.

"Yes, it is."

Dalejem raised a hand. He shielded his eyes. "Okay, so it is."

"Do you want me to shoot?"

"Will it get you to stop talking?"

Revik let out a snort, then used his light and eyes to aim. Without belaboring it, he squeezed off a shot. He flinched a bit from the echo of the report, in spite of Dalejem's assurances of their safety out here.

"Satisfied?" Revik asked. He lowered the gun.

"Not yet."

Dalejem walked out into the open field.

Revik tensed as soon as the other seer left the protection of the trees, yet he remained where he was. He still gripped the gun, knowing he was covering the other male, although Dalejem hadn't asked him to do that, either.

Revik's light snaked out over the field as Dalejem walked.

He examined the nearby Barrier space for anyone who might be watching what they were doing. He focused especially intently on places where someone might have a clear shot at the two of them. Places he might have used as a sniper if he were the one hunting them.

As soon as he looked from his *aleimi*, he felt flavors of Balidor and the others, and realized he and Dalejem remained inside a protected part of the construct.

Dalejem had taken him to the edge of it, but not outside.

Revik's light mapped the boundaries of that construct as he watched Dalejem walk. He examined the edges and make-up of the lit border wall around the territory marked out by the Adhipan, which took up a few square miles of the Brazilian jungle. He watched how that light radiated outwards from the central camp he and Dalejem left about an hour ago. He followed it to the harder edge, where he and Dalejem stood now.

Then he realized there was a fainter version of that construct that stretched out even further, to the trees across the meadow, nearly all the way to the foothills he could see in the distance—

Revik let out a gasp.

His vision slanted out.

Everything around him grayed, darkened, even as his shoulder hit something—hard.

He grew aware of a distant voice.

Someone was shouting.

Someone was shouting at him.

He fought to come back, to answer them. He struggled against the pain that overwhelmed his light. He tried to claw his way back towards that voice—

A wrench in his gut nearly made him lose consciousness altogether—

Then he was looking up, blinking into dappled sunlight.

His chest had compressed into a hard knot.

He fought to breathe.

His fingers gripped his own shirt and vest in a sweated fist. He felt nauseous from pain, but he could see again; he could almost move his mind. He realized that some new kind of shield constrained his *aleimic* light.

Whatever it was, it held Revik's light tightly to his body.

He felt Balidor in that, along with flavors of the man standing over him, his tall form and broad shoulders and chest blocking the sun.

Revik was still looking up, fighting to focus his eyes, when the sound came back on, even as the man fell to his knees in the cluster of tree roots over which Revik lay.

As soon as Revik realized that much, he found himself understanding a few more things.

He was lying on his back, and his back hurt.

It likely hurt because he'd connected hard with those tree roots when he hit the ground. He let out a low gasp. Then he was fighting to get up, to pull his light even closer to his body. Before he could manage it, Dalejem laid a hand on his chest.

The green-eyed seer gripped Revik's arm with his other hand.

The male seer flooded Revik's light with warmth, with his own light, and Revik groaned.

He writhed under the other's touch.

He fought him off, hitting out almost violently before he'd made a conscious thought.

"Fuck," he gasped. "No. No, goddamn it."

Dalejem immediately withdrew his light.

As if to make his intentions clear, he also raised both of his hands.

Once he had, he stared down at Revik, his expression bordering on wary.

After a long-feeling pause, Revik's eyes clicked into focus.

He realized only then just how completely he'd closed his light off to the other male. It wasn't wariness he'd seen in the other's face, but something closer to caution—laced with a sympathy that stood out prominently in those jade and violet eyes.

"Are you all right?" Dalejem asked.

Revik realized he continued to clutch his own shirt over the front of his chest. He continued to struggle for breath, sweating and gasping like he'd been running. He felt light-headed, overly warm, yet also like he had a chill.

It felt like his blood was low on sugar. He felt like he'd fainted.

He *had* fainted, he realized.

Fuck.

"Yeah. I'm okay." He wasn't looking at Dalejem now, but down at his own hand, the one holding up his body on one of the exposed, rounded roots of a Brazil nut tree. His hand still gripped the Glock somehow, and it occurred to him the thing was live, and still had ammunition in it. He clicked the trigger safety in rote, then set the thing down on the ground.

It was a miracle he hadn't shot himself.

It was even more of a miracle he hadn't shot Dalejem.

"I'm okay," he repeated numbly.

He sat up, and stopped again, immediately light-headed. He wiped sweat from his brow, and realized only then that his hands and arms were shaking.

"Sorry. Gods." He looked up at the other male, his voice reluctant. "Are you all right? I didn't... I didn't, you know... do anything. Did I?"

Dalejem gave him a wry smile. That worry remained prominent in his green eyes. "You fell like a stone, brother. Does that count?"

Revik didn't answer. He continued to fight to gain control over his light, and his body. He wondered if he should risk trying to stand.

"I should have warned you, brother," Dalejem said, his voice gentle. "Balidor connected our construct to her last night."

Revik didn't speak, but he felt his body stiffen.

He fought with the part of himself that wanted to deny

that as the cause for what he'd just done, how crazy he was acting, but he couldn't do that, either.

Unfortunately, Dalejem didn't seem willing to let it go so easily.

"Balidor is right, then? You are fixated on her?" he asked.

The other male's voice remained deceptively casual.

Revik felt his jaw harden more, enough to hurt his face.

"I'm not trying to embarrass you, brother," Dalejem said. "But we should talk about this. Balidor had concerns about this with you. So we can either talk about it here, you and I... or you can go back to camp, and Balidor can examine your light himself. You can discuss it privately with him. Or the three of us can talk about it together, if you prefer."

Revik glanced up.

He felt the light in his chest grow dimmer.

"Is that the real reason you brought me out here?" he asked.

His voice came out cold. He regretted his words almost the instant he said them, but he couldn't seem to make himself take them back.

Dalejem shook his head. "No, brother." He continued to gauge Revik's face, and seemingly his light now, as well. "Are you not going to talk to me, then?"

Revik stared at the trunk of the tree without seeing it.

He fought back his emotional reactions, the shame that still wanted to take over his light, the deeper feeling of anger and resentment.

Why the fuck hadn't they left him in that cave? He shouldn't be here. He shouldn't fucking *be* here, and he'd told them that. But they dragged him out here anyway, and now they wanted to give him shit for not being able to handle it?

"No one is blaming you, brother," Dalejem said, quieter. "I am only asking. Do you not want to admit that much? You are fixated."

Revik shook his head, but not in a no.

Dalejem frowned slightly anyway. He looked over Revik's body, then conducted what must have been at least a quick pass over his light.

"You are not fixated?" Dalejem asked.

Revik exhaled. He felt that anger sharpen in his light, even as he forced his fist to open, for his fingers to release his own shirt. He stared down at where sweat had dampened the front of it from his hand, twisting it into an odd pattern from the intensity of his clutching.

He felt that shame twist deeper in his gut, even as he forced himself to speak.

"I honestly don't know," he said. "I don't know what it is."

"You have been fixated before?"

Revik looked up. He bit his tongue, hard enough for it to hurt. "Yes."

"When?"

"My wife," he said. He looked away again. "During the war."

He slid back on the mud and ferns, but stopped when he got light-headed. When his eyes found Dalejem next, the other seer only nodded.

"This is different?" he prompted.

Revik nodded. "Yes."

"In what way?"

Revik exhaled another breath. He let his irritation be audible. "I don't know. I fucking don't. This is more about light. It's worse this time. Worse than it was when I met Kali the first time, in Vietnam. I didn't react like this before." He stared down at the mud and let out a humorless laugh. "Fuck. I didn't do this before. I just wanted her."

"Sex, you mean?"

Revik glared at him. "Yes. Sex. I nearly raped her. I told her to leave Saigon, or I *would* rape her. It wasn't an idle threat."

Dalejem didn't blink at the news.

"Would you rape her still?" he asked neutrally. "Even with her pregnant?"

Revik felt a sick horror at the idea.

He recoiled, physically and with his light. Nausea came with it, a feeling that had nothing to do with separation pain, and everything to do with revulsion. It didn't come with a conscious thought, but when he glanced up, he saw relief in the other male's eyes.

"Well, that is good," Dalejem said. He exhaled a held breath. He rested back on his heels, so that he was more or less kneeling in the mud and bracken. "So what happened just now?"

Revik glanced around.

As he did, he realized that it wasn't only Dalejem asking this.

He could feel the rest of the Adhipan squad with which he'd been traveling for the past two days. He felt Balidor's light the most prominently, but he felt the others there, as well. He felt their eyes on him, their *aleimi*.

He felt them weighing him, trying to decide if they could trust him.

Trying to decide if he belonged with them in this fight after all, no matter what Kali had said, or that she had asked for him by name.

"Kali thought it wasn't *her* I was reacting to," Revik blurted.

He said it without thought, before he'd decided if he wanted to tell them that, either.

Still, it was too late to pretend nothing was wrong with him.

Maybe they could even help, if they knew what caused it.

He forced another breath. He fought to open his light, to show them, at least in some part, where he was speaking from, what he was remembering.

"...I don't remember a lot of things well," he admitted. "Vash and the Org erased a lot when I left. But I remember how I got back to the compound in Seertown. I remember what happened in Saigon, before I defected."

"So tell us about that, brother."

Revik shook his head, but again, not in a no.

"I *have* told you. I wanted her. I told her to leave Saigon. But then fucking Terian and Raven took her, after I tried to let her go. They tied her up, and Galaith wanted me to kill her. They wanted me to rape her, too. So I defected... and brought Kali with me. For part of it, at least. I brought her most of the way to Phnom Penh."

"Did you hurt her?"

Revik shook his head. "No."

Another silence fell after he spoke.

Revik felt the Adhipan infiltrators conversing in the Barrier space around him, but he couldn't pick out anything of what was said. He lay there in the mud, half propped up on one arm. He could feel them looking at him, assessing and discussing his light. He got the feeling at least some of them worried he was unstable—a half-feral animal that might go on a violent rampage if they didn't chain him at night.

He didn't feel any maliciousness in their assessment, though.

If anything, it felt totally detached.

Borderline clinical, really.

"What did Kali think you were reacting to?" Dalejem asked next. "If not her, what?"

Revik felt his jaw harden more.

He didn't meet Dalejem's eyes, but felt his chest close a second time.

It wasn't so much in anger that time, or even shame, but rather in an almost overwhelming feeling of privacy, of not wanting them that close to this part of him, of not wanting them to know anything about this.

"Brother," Dalejem said gently. "We must know. Surely, you must see that?"

Revik thought about his words.

After another pause, he exhaled in defeat.

He knew resentment still seethed off his light.

He also felt defiance there, for the first time really, at least since he'd tried to order them out of his room.

"Kali thought I was reacting to her daughter," Revik said, his voice cold. "She thought it was her daughter that caused me to fixate on her. She wasn't pregnant then, but she knew she would be. She claimed her daughter's light already hung around her person."

Revik looked up.

He knew his eyes held an open challenge now, if not an overt threat.

"She seemed very certain that was the source of my confusion. She said her daughter and I knew one another. That we were..." His jaw hardened. *"...connected.* In some way."

Dalejem nodded, silent.

Even so, Revik saw a kind of flinch in the other male's eyes, as if Dalejem saw something in Revik's face that made him cautious.

After another few seconds of what felt like the rest of the Adhipan conversing with one another in the space around Revik's light, Dalejem's legs straightened smoothly. He rose gracefully back to his feet, so quickly Revik flinched. Once he was upright, Dalejem held out a hand to Revik.

His face held no readable expression at all now.

Revik looked up.

He didn't take the offered hand, not at first.

He continued to gauge the other man's face instead. He tried to discern where things stood with them now. It felt important to know.

Seeing the look there, Dalejem's expression relaxed, all at once.

"It is all right, brother," he smiled. "We will not send you to the firing squad on this day. I promise you."

"Then what?" Revik's voice came out blunt, unmoved by the other's attempt to lighten things. "Will you send me back? Back to the Pamir?"

Dalejem shook his head at that, too.

He clicked softly, but with a smile as well.

"No, brother," he said. "Nice try. But no."

Feeling the pain worsen in his chest, Revik didn't answer.

He did take the offered hand that time, however.

Once he was upright, Dalejem clapped him on the shoulder. He continued to gauge Revik's face, maybe worried he would pass out again. He continued to hold him there for a few seconds, as if trying to determine if Revik could hold himself up under his own power.

"Stay away from her light for now, brother," he advised. "We can't have you cracking your skull out here. And we still intend to make a move for extraction tomorrow."

"Tomorrow?"

"It cannot wait," Dalejem said, his voice businesslike. "She is very pregnant, brother. We cannot wait even for one more day."

Revik was already shaking his head. "I can't go on that. Extraction. I can't—"

"We will work that out," Dalejem broke in smoothly.

Dalejem startled Revik then. He slid his fingers into Revik's hair. He gripped him tightly, right before he raised his other hand to his face and began caressing his jaw and throat. He slid his hand lower when Revik didn't resist or pull back.

He massaged Revik's shoulder with strong fingers.

He continued to stroke and massage his skin as Revik felt his light react.

Then he was more than just reacting.

Revik felt himself start to open under the other male's touch.

He fought to control it. He tensed under Dalejem's fingers, but he didn't move, or try to evade his hands. He found himself leaning into him instead, opening his light. His breath started coming harder then. His heart hammered in his chest. His skin grew warmer.

*Gaos. Gaos,* he was going to fucking lose it.

He was going to lose it if the other didn't stop.

Dalejem must have heard him.

He released Revik at once and stepped back.

"Sorry, brother," he murmured.

His green eyes shifted away.

His mouth thinned to a line, but Revik couldn't read the exact expression there, if it was anger, frustration, irritation that Revik had taken the affection how it wasn't intended, or even embarrassment that he'd been misunderstood.

Revik fought not to react to his own uncertainty. He was still searching for words when the other male looked at him directly.

"I cannot ask," he said. "I cannot. You understand this, brother?"

Revik nodded. Truthfully though, he didn't understand.

Was Dalejem saying to leave him alone?

Had he been pulling on Dalejem with his light?

Fuck. Of course he had.

He was pulling on him even now.

He was hard just from five seconds of ordinary seer affection.

More than that, he was struggling to control himself.

He felt his skin warm more at the realization, but he didn't look away from Dalejem's face. He clenched his jaw as he fought with words, some way to diffuse this. He couldn't trust himself to speak rationally to the other male's words—he couldn't even trust himself to ask a coherent question right then—but he didn't want Dalejem to be angry with him, either.

Confusion continued to shift around his light as the silence grew awkward between them. Revik felt the other male waiting for him to answer in some way, but he had absolutely no idea what Dalejem expected him to say.

He got the main message.

*Gaos*, he got it in neon lights.

Wasn't that enough?

"I won't rape you either, brother," he said finally.

He tried to say it lightly, to make it a joke.

He knew it fell flat, even as he said it.

When Dalejem arched an eyebrow at him, his eyes an obvious question, Revik felt his embarrassment worsen.

After another awkward pause, Revik added, "...Although brother Balidor is welcome to post a guard by my tent, if it helps with camp morale. I won't be offended."

Dalejem gave him an almost annoyed look at that.

His annoyance mixed with puzzlement, mixed with a frown, like he couldn't quite comprehend what Revik had said... or why... or even what language Revik was speaking.

He didn't say anything, though.

Dalejem just looked at him, and Revik couldn't read his face.

Frustration warred in Revik's light and chest as the silence stretched, as he continued to study Dalejem's high-cheekboned face, the long line of the other male's neck, which didn't seem to move, in emotion or anything else.

He felt blind.

He felt *blind* with these fucking Adhipan seers.

He felt blind with all of them, not only Balidor.

Not only Dalejem.

Still, he supposed he understood enough.

When he refocused on Dalejem's eyes that time, the other male's expression had changed again. That time, Revik saw only sadness there.

He couldn't look at that for very long, either.

## CHAPTER 8
# ARGUMENTS IN THE DARK

Dalejem kept him there for a few hours longer.

Revik wondered afterwards if that had been mostly for his, meaning Revik's, benefit—to allow him to put off having to face the others.

Still, Dalejem made good use of the time.

He tested Revik on more weapons.

Dalejem had Revik go back to the handgun before continuing on to automatic rifles, which turned out to be part of what he'd lugged through the jungle in that black, canvas bag. He'd also brought a number of laser-scoped things, as well as two organics-only guns that Revik had only ever used under the Rooks.

When they'd gone through the entire weapons cache the older seer brought, Dalejem instructed Revik to sit with him, on a blanket on the jungle floor.

For the next four-plus hours, the green-eyed seer assessed Revik's sight abilities.

He tested his shielding first.

Then his ability to discern different types of Barrier attacks.

He moved on to complex offensive sight skills after he'd

conducted a methodical spot-check of the basics, then ended on another set of defensive skills, primarily Revik's ability to scout his environment while under the constraints of a hostile security shield.

Through all of it, Dalejem kept Revik's light far away from where he'd ventured just before he passed out.

Presumably, *Guoreum* lived out there, along with a thread to Kali's light.

Dalejem also filled Revik in on the basics of their extraction plan.

They would be leaving tomorrow morning.

Before dawn.

Revik would be with Dalejem's team, so the green-eyed seer would be right beside him for most of it. Revik wouldn't be one of those to go in for the extraction itself, Dalejem assured him. They'd keep him stationed at a rearguard position, on the other side of the fence. Revik wouldn't be asked to go inside *Guoreum's* main security grid at all. He would not cross the military-grade Barrier perimeter, much less venture into any of the slave paddocks.

Revik couldn't overstate his relief at that information.

The idea of being inside *Guoreum* fucking terrified him.

Given his previous connection to the Rooks and their Barrier frequencies, it made him feel sick to his stomach.

Even now, with those safeguards and assurances in place, Revik's throat closed as Dalejem laid out the timeline. His mind began immediately to calculate how many hours remained before the op went live.

He kept that clock running in the back of his mind for the rest of the afternoon.

It was still running down now.

The lower those numbers grew, the more his anxiety ratcheted up, until it started to affect him physically. He struggled to think in straight lines at all by the time he and Dalejem emerged back at the main camp a few hours later.

By then, it was dark out.

Revik knew the push was largely because of Kali's condition. He felt something else driving their timeline as well, something that felt more nebulous, although he suspected it only felt that way because he could only see parts of the construct they were using.

At base, Revik was still a tourist here.

"What role will I play?" he'd asked Dalejem as they trekked back through the jungle.

"Kali asked for you," Dalejem reminded him.

"I get that," Revik said. "But what role will I play? With your team?"

"Kali asked for you," Dalejem repeated, as if that explained everything.

More and more, Revik was beginning to think it did.

He couldn't imagine why the Adhipan would have brought him out here otherwise.

Still, he struggled to let it go.

"Do you know *why* she asked for me?" he pressed. "Did she give any kind of reason? Anything that might tell me what I'm supposed to be doing?"

He knew he likely wouldn't get a satisfactory answer.

Even so, Dalejem's laugh frustrated him.

"You will have to ask her that yourself, my brother," the other seer said.

That time, he glanced over his shoulder with a grin.

Revik didn't press him again.

Still, the silence on that front made his anxiety worse.

Now, as he sat with the rest of them in the dark, around an organic heater in lieu of a fire, Revik wondered again why they'd brought him out here. He was unable to shake that feeling of utter uselessness, of being far more of a burden than an asset. Moreover, the idea of holding a gun in a live op, of shooting that gun at actual people, made him feel sick.

He felt nauseated even thinking about it.

The fact that the idea scared him so much struck him as ludicrous, in a way.

He'd spent most of his adult life in some kind of military capacity.

He'd carried a gun most of his life, too.

Now he felt like he'd stepped from one completely unreal world to another, with no transition space between the two states.

He was pretty sure, out on the ground, in a live op, he'd freeze.

"You won't freeze," the giant seer said from next to him. The same seer patted him companionably on the knee. "It's like riding a bicycle, brother."

Revik recognized him as the large male seer from the Jeep ride down from the mountains, the one with the Nazi scar on his face, with the dark hair and hazel eyes who looked like a pirate. The broad-faced seer smiled at Revik. He handed Revik a bottle of what turned out to be *churek,* a seer drink with calming properties.

Revik downed a few swallows of it.

He gestured a heartfelt thanks, and the big seer next to him grinned.

"You'll be fine," he said encouragingly.

He smacked Revik on the shoulder that time, hard enough that Revik flinched, falling forward slightly, towards the stove.

He listened to the others joke and talk quietly amongst themselves, even as he overheard some tactical discussions in the corners and edges of his sight.

None of them bothered to try and include him in those more serious discussions.

He didn't mind—at all, really—but again, he wondered why he was there.

He was still sitting there, more or less spacing out as he

stared at the stove, finishing off the bottle of *churek*, when he heard his name, and turned.

He stared into the dark, in the direction from which the voices had come, only to see Dalejem and Mara standing there. They huddled in a shadowed spot between two of the waterproof tents, which had been strung up beneath the trees.

The two of them weren't speaking to him.

They talked quietly to one another but with some agitation.

Both of them gestured a fair bit, but not in seer sign language.

Revik had examined the tents earlier, mostly to distract himself, and to give his mind something to do as the others worked and prepped for the op. The tents used a rigging he'd never seen before. They also stood taller than other tents he'd used in the field. They were tall enough that most seers, even him, should be able to stand up straight inside one of them.

When Revik continued to stare, eventually Mara and Dalejem noticed.

They turned, nearly in unison, and stared back at him.

Revik realized only then that the two of them had been arguing.

Feeling his face flush, Revik swiveled his head back towards the organic heater.

He made his expression as still as stone.

He wanted nothing more than to rise to his feet, to retire to his tent for the night.

Unfortunately, the tent he'd been assigned to share with four other seers happened to be the one right next to where Dalejem and Mara now stood.

For the same reason, Revik remained where he was.

He stared into the glowing coils of the heater and pretended he could not feel that they were arguing about him. He had no idea about what. He strongly suspected he did not want to know. His *aleimi* followed the whispers of charge and anger as they trembled his light; pain coiled around him the instant Dalejem and Mara resumed their heated discussion.

He never thought he'd miss those caves, way up in the Pamir.

He would have laughed at the idea, even a day earlier.

Even so, in those long-feeling minutes while the argument persisted, he did.

Miss them, that is.

## CHAPTER 9
# SPLINTER

Revik stood by a cluster of green-brown roots belonging to a dense grove of walking palms.

Sweating.

Fighting to keep his focus, to keep his light close to his body as he scanned the nearby trees. Fighting to keep his mind locked to Balidor's, who told him he'd act as Revik's anchor to help stabilize his light out here.

The reality of that blew Revik's mind when he let himself think about it.

Balidor was with the forward extraction team.

That meant the Adhipan leader was probably two miles away from Revik right now, physically. That didn't even get into the fact that Balidor would be protecting Revik's light from *inside* the Rook construct around the slave camp.

They'd left him behind, just like Dalejem told him they would.

Not by much. Not by very much at all, really.

He still felt too close.

He now stood less than three clicks from the perimeter fence, and well under two miles of the forward extraction team and the first of *Guoreum's* main buildings.

Revik knew from the smatterings of memory he had of this place, as well as the satellite images he'd seen on the way down here, exactly where those buildings were located. He even remembered with a decent amount of accuracy which buildings were used for what. In checking his memories against the Adhipan intel, he'd remembered where the C.I.C. lived, along with the medical labs, the high-security holding center, the guard and military barracks.

Even out here, the familiar flavors of the Org construct clung to his light.

It pulled on him in ways that made it difficult to think.

It sickened him and drew him and scared the fuck out of him. It also left a metallic taste in the back of his throat that simultaneously made him feel manic and reminded him of doing drugs, especially in those last few months in Vietnam.

In Saigon, he and Terian had been high pretty much from the moment they dragged themselves out of bed in the morning until they passed out at night.

Worse than any of that, Revik felt lights he recognized.

Actual beings. People.

Maybe even seers he'd been friends with.

He knew it came from more than just the construct structure itself. It wasn't just a familiarity from the flavor of the security grids, the Pyramid network, the overall taste of Galaith and the Barrier beings behind him—Revik recognized actual *beings* inside that grid.

Despite his more conscious paranoia and anxiety, it hadn't fully sunk in that he might run into seers he used to know out here.

It hadn't fully sunk in he might be shooting at people he used to consider friends.

He could feel Balidor shielding him from a lot of that, even now.

Even in the middle of an extraction op, Balidor was helping him.

That fact both reassured him and ratcheted up his nerves.

The pull from that silver light was fucking strong, even now.

Even with such a highly-skilled seer as Balidor protecting his light.

Being out here alone both calmed him and made him more nervous too, in more or less equal amounts. He didn't fully trust himself alone. At the same time, he worried he had a target on his chest from his resonance with the Org network. He didn't exactly want other seers in harm's way if he was as visible out here as he felt.

Revik knew he was well outside the furthest edges of the main construct perimeter, but he still felt too much, which made him even more nervous about the inevitable pursuit they'd face once Balidor got Kali out.

They'd been gone for over two hours.

Revik could taste sunrise in his light.

He couldn't yet see any shift in the colors of the night sky, but the sun would be coming up soon. His internal clock told him they were less than an hour from sunrise now.

They were cutting things close if they wanted to get through that security grid before it got light. At this point, they were cutting things damned close.

Then again, dark or light—it didn't matter much with seers.

The thought had just left his *aleimi* when something shifted.

The change was fast, soundless.

Alarms.

The tremors hit Revik's light through Balidor first.

Then the actual shockwave expanded over him.

It hit directly into his *aleimi* from a nearer source.

Before he'd regained his equilibrium, or even made sense of what he'd felt—

Dalejem appeared in front of him.

The green-eyed seer flashed into being like a ghost from between the trees.

The seer's sudden appearance among the walking palms, his face pale and sheened with sweat, nearly gave Revik a heart attack. He hadn't felt the other's approach in any way. He hadn't expected it at all, and the knowledge hit him, hard, how vulnerable he was out here, even as Dalejem walked directly up to him.

The dark-haired seer had his hair clipped back.

Covered in body armor, he carried a heavy, semi-organic gun as he walked right up to him. He spoke aloud once he was close enough, not in Revik's mind. He used a low whisper, presumably to avoid being heard in the Barrier.

"Come with me, brother," he said. "Now. Balidor is bringing her out."

He had ahold of Revik's arm before Revik had recovered from any part of this.

Revik nearly fought the other male before he abruptly brought his light back under control. He bit his tongue, forced himself to relax.

He forced himself to do as the other said.

By the time Dalejem released him, he'd almost succeeded.

Revik pulled his mind back into that well-worn track in his mind, the part of him that knew how to follow orders, that understood the chain of command. He clicked fully into that harder military mode and walked as fast and as silently as he could after the other seer.

Dalejem himself moved without making any sound at all.

Revik had never seen anyone pass through complex terrain, in the dark, so silently. Dalejem moved like a spirit through the dense jungle, so quickly Revik had to increase the lengths of his strides just to keep up and not lose him in the trees.

He tried his damnedest to follow as quietly, too.

He winced when he heard the sounds made by his feet or

body. He rubbed against branches, stepped on pieces of the jungle floor that made noise, breathed too hard, slipped on leaves and mud.

Dalejem's his light wound deeper into Revik's after he snapped a particularly loud branch under his boots. Without a whisper of rebuke, the older seer began showing him with his light how to navigate the undergrowth more quietly.

Embarrassed as he was, Revik took the instruction, and gladly.

Within a few minutes more, both of them were making scarcely any sound at all as they walked through the trees.

Revik's mind continued to churn as he followed the prodding of Dalejem's light.

Why had they sent Dalejem ahead to get him?

Was it to keep him away from Kali's light?

"In part, brother," Dalejem said. His voice stayed low, like before. "They also want protection on several sides, and to split our parties. Balidor tripped the alarms on the way out. As a result, we were forced to improvise. It made sense to pull you into the first splinter."

"How?" Revik asked. He kept his voice as soft as the other's. "With the alarm?"

"A trigger they missed," Dalejem shrugged.

Revik didn't answer.

He wasn't surprised, though.

Balidor intimated more than once on the flight to São Paulo that his team hadn't been allotted adequate time to prepare for this op. Given their need to pull Revik, and their efforts to get Kali's mate out of solitary, they'd had almost no time at all.

Then there was the pregnancy, of course.

That added a layer of complicated urgency to everything connected to this mission, in addition to upping the ante on time constraints for going live.

Unsurprisingly, they'd cut corners on planning time, and

likely on double-checking all of their intel on the camp. This whole venture had a somewhat "spontaneous" feel to it that exhilarated Revik in a strange way, even as it worsened his nerves.

Dalejem's teeth shone white in the darkness in front of him.

"You like this kind of work, yes?" the other asked. "I have felt this on you."

Revik didn't answer.

He didn't answer partly because the question annoyed him for some reason, but also because speaking unnecessarily out here didn't strike him as a particularly good idea.

Ahead of him, he heard Dalejem chuckle.

"You really are a soldier, aren't you?" the other man teased. His voice remained quiet, only audible because the jungle was quieter. "A highly paranoid one, yes, but a soldier nonetheless. At least they didn't lie to me about *that* part of your make-up."

Revik didn't answer, but he frowned a little.

He wasn't sure if he really wanted to know what the other meant about lies he had heard about him, or what Dalejem now thought might be true about him instead.

Revik could feel the other seer pulling on him lightly to ask.

Revik could feel it intensely a few seconds later, and while the warmth there mainly confused him, Revik felt himself reacting to it in a less closed way, as well.

Some part of him *wanted* to ask.

But yeah, he didn't.

---

THEY MET UP WITH THE REST OF THEIR SPLINTER GROUP LESS THAN twenty minutes later.

## THE EX-ROOK • 101

Once there, Revik was surprised, and not particularly pleased, to see Mara among the others assigned to his group.

Others included the giant, half-Wvercian looking seer with the scar on his face who'd given him a drink the night before.

Revik now knew the big seer as Garensche, or "Gar."

Garensche was the only one who smiled at him, raising a thick hand in greeting. The five others, three males and two females, didn't look at him with hostility, but they didn't exude a lot of warmth, either.

Mostly, they ignored him.

"Balidor was shot," the first one said to Dalejem as soon as they emerged in the clearing. She went on, her accented voice neutral. "They got out cleanly, however… and otherwise in one piece. The primary target is unharmed. So is her mate. They have ten in the main extraction team now. Plus ours and another splinter flanking them to the west. They currently are located about five clicks west of here, maybe half a click north."

Dalejem nodded. He made a short, acknowledging salute as he bowed.

Revik looked at female who had spoken.

He studied her face in the half light.

Clearly, this seer was in charge of their smaller group.

She had a distinctive look about her, so he remembered noticing her before, when she'd been part of the planning sessions with Balidor and the rest.

Her name was Yumi.

She had a beautiful and somehow savage face, one that belonged to almost the caricature of a seer hunter. Something about her made her look imminently dangerous—whether it was the high, sharp cheekbones, the intensity of her dark eyes, the muscles of her shoulders and arms, or the unusual and very traditional-looking tattoo pattern that covered most of her face.

He wondered at her age, given that tattoo.

The markings, which shone dark blue, made of symbols he knew mostly from religious texts, looked unlike anything he'd ever seen before.

He wondered where and when she'd gotten it.

Those markings would definitely make it difficult for her to blend in with humans.

But then, maybe that had never been a big priority for this particular seer.

It also may not have been a possibility, given her distinctly seer features and eyes, not to mention her height, which dwarfed that of most female humans.

Despite her severity of features, the intense markings, and the fact that she utterly ignored him, Revik couldn't help noticing she was attractive. That feral beauty of hers drew at his eyes. It caused him to stare until he literally had to make himself stop.

His light found her light interesting, as well.

Possibly more than interesting, if he were being honest with himself... and if he had any intention of letting himself go there... which he did not.

Certainly not during a live op.

She was tall, nearly as tall as him.

He didn't know that from now; he knew it from before, when he'd watched her surreptitiously during planning sessions with Balidor back at the camp.

Currently, she hunched over a holographic map that covered the floor of the small clearing. Revik's eyes followed hers to the topographical depictions. He noted the three clusters of living lights that made up the main extraction team under Balidor, plus the two splinter groups more or less flanking them, including the one to which Revik now belonged.

The map was fascinating to look at, and reminded him of similar toys he'd used while working for the Rooks. Its level of detail included the cluster of trees in which they now stood, and even the strange, glowing violet light exuded by the map itself.

The holograph currently covered a six-by-six square of the clearing floor.

The prominence of that light unnerved Revik a little.

Apparently these Adhipan infiltrators didn't care that it might get picked up by Org sensors as well, whether the device generating the map had organic shielding or not. Not to mention the fact that the map could be seen physically if one of the Org teams got close enough. All it would take is one agent spotting the illumination through the leaves and trunks. The flickering images would inevitably pull eyes and light.

The seer with the tattooed face gave him a withering look.

"We know where the enemy is, brother," she said.

She highlighted the relevant area of the map. She pinged Revik a little harder than necessary to look at the associated segments.

"...A little faith, if you would. And perhaps some small amount of respect for the training we receive under brother Balidor."

Revik felt his face warm.

He knew the sky was too dark for them to notice.

Probably.

"Is he all right?" he asked. "Balidor."

"Of course," Yumi replied, dismissive. "They are slowed mainly by the target's condition, not by brother Balidor's. He assures us it is a flesh wound only. Still, he has assessed that they need help in getting a safe distance. We are to loop around behind them. If possible, we are also to divert the team of *Rook scum* following them."

Revik felt the jab directed at him from her emphasized words.

He only nodded.

He continued to stare at the map as he turned over what she'd actually said.

"Do you approve, pup?" she asked scathingly. Her dark eyes lifted to his.

He nodded again, and pretended he didn't hear the sarcasm.

Hesitating, he almost didn't say it, then did.

"Well," he said, cautious. "There is one thing, if you'll pardon my thoughts on this. Since we're so close to the perimeter, we have an easy diversion available to us... assuming I am hearing you correctly, and our current priority is to gift brother Balidor time."

Revik swallowed.

He nodded towards the holographic map.

"If you allow me to cross that security line... long enough for them to ID me, I mean... they'll follow us. I can pretty much guarantee it." He met her gaze. "It would buy Balidor minutes, at least. Possibly a great deal more than that, if we can convince camp security the extraction targets are with me."

He glanced at Dalejem, then back at Yumi.

"You must realize you are a myth to them," he said, when neither spoke. "They won't think Adhipan. Not until Central gets involved, and even then, it won't be the first place their minds go. They definitely won't be looking for brother Balidor. They'll think bounty. The *Rynak*. Private security team out of Asia. Desperate family members. Family members with enough cash to hire mercs. If they feel me out here, they'll assume I'm running with a private outfit now. They'll also assume I'm the highest ranked, and probably leading my own teams. It wouldn't be hard to convince them Kali was with me."

All eight sets of eyes had turned.

All stared at him now.

Their eyes glowed strangely in the light of the holographic map.

Revik could feel the *aleimi* of each seer dart around him. He felt them measure him openly in the silence after he spoke. He felt wariness there, but also no small amount of surprise.

"You'd be willing to do that?" Yumi asked, after a beat.

Some of the acid had dropped from her tone.

Revik barely hesitated before nodding again.

He glanced around at the rest of them. He felt his shoulders tense even as he bounced a little on his heels, almost without noticing he did it.

"I'm here, aren't I?" He gestured expansively with one hand. "There must be a reason. By now, you all know it's not for my sight skills."

That actually brought a smile to her face, and a true relaxing of her expression.

A few of the others chuckled, too, including the giant seer, Garensche.

Revik saw Dalejem frown, though, even as the green-eyed seer turned to give Yumi an irritated look. Yumi gestured at him, using a number of signals Revik didn't know, something that must be specific to the Adhipan.

Then she faced Revik himself.

Still smiling, she straightened to her full height.

She motioned around at the rest of the team.

"Do you know all of us, brother?" she asked politely. "By name, I mean? Are you familiar with each of our lights? We will need to remain close to you, if you are really crazy enough to do this thing you are offering. You should be able to tell us apart... *na?*"

Revik looked around at faces. "I think so. By name, that is."

"You think?" Yumi quirked an eyebrow. Her voice

remained friendly, even as she motioned around the circle. "Show me, brother."

Revik exhaled a little, then pointed.

"Gar, Poresh, Mara, Dalejem." He pointed at Yumi's own face when he looked directly at her. "Yumi." He shifted his gaze to her right. "Ontari. Vikram. And you are Dalai, right?"

The shorter female with the dark brown hair nodded.

She gave him a warm smile, too.

"Very good," Yumi said approvingly. "Now we will talk about the how, yes?" She glanced at her watch, an organic-component band that looked like it might have holographic capabilities of its own. "We do not have much time. Can you improvise, pup? For that matter, can you follow instruction? Outside the Pyramid of your former masters, that is?"

The words held less bite that time.

They may have even held a measure of sympathy.

Somehow, Revik felt the sting of them a lot more, though.

"I can manage," he said.

He stripped all emotion from his words.

She measured him again with her eyes, then nodded, once, an infiltrator's nod.

"Good," she said. "Stay by me," she added.

Her voice was all-business now.

She clicked off the map, leaving the clearing in relative darkness, although the band around her wrist continued to emit a blueish glow of light that illuminated her face and a small ring around her, which included Dalejem, Poresh, and Ontari.

"We will talk, you and I," Yumi said. She still spoke to Revik. "As we make our way back behind Balidor and closer to the perimeter fence."

She already moved fast across the jungle floor.

Revik found himself loping to catch up with her long legs and strides. She walked past him and into the trees without slowing or looking back.

He noticed she aimed their party more or less due south.

He felt the other seers close in on the two of them from all sides once he walked directly alongside her. A few seconds later, he realized he'd been inserted into a mobile construct, too, almost without him realizing they had done it.

Mobile constructs of this type were advanced Barrier tech, Revik knew.

It was Barrier tech he was only vaguely familiar with outside the confines of the Rooks' Pyramid. Meaning, he knew how it worked within the Org network, but outside of that context, he understood the mechanics only a small amount, and possibly not at all.

The Rooks utilized a very specific, non-physical anchor via Galaith and the beings he worked with to ground mobile constructs. Given the lack of integrity of those beings, it was a method the Seven and Adhipan would not (and possibly could not) replicate.

Revik had no idea how the Adhipan accomplished a similar effect outside of those spaces. He knew the Barrier connections that the Adhipan utilized were very different than what he'd been trained on under Galaith. They differed in functionality, in form, and, more importantly he suspected, they differed in how they interfaced with the material world.

In simple terms, the beings utilized by the Adhipan were far less entangled in the physical world than the beings the Rooks used. The Rooks used the Dreng for such things, parasitic beings who operated close to Earth.

Vash and the Seven, and presumably the Adhipan—did not.

Therefore, Vash and the Seven, and presumably the Adhipan, didn't generate Barrier constructs the way the Rooks did in general, much less out in the field. Revik knew such non-stationary constructs were possible *in theory* outside the Pyramid.

He'd simply never been a part of one himself.

Tactical nets of various kinds, sure, but not an actual mobile field construct.

He tried to get a feel for this one as he walked.

He surmised, from his knowledge of directed shielding and how it connected with constructs of this kind, that the mobile was likely not strong enough for all of them to sleep inside it without risk of a Barrier attack.

Therefore, they must still use sentries for longer ground ops, just like Revik had under the Seven, with a few seers guarding the rest and rotating for sleep.

Limitations aside, the construct he felt remained dense enough and multilayered enough to catch his breath.

He felt Balidor in those strands.

Moreover, the longer they walked, the more tightly the construct wrapped into and around his *aleimi,* like threads in a heavy cloth.

As Revik struggled to adjust to it, and to the feel of being inside it, he found Yumi looking at him. He realized he'd kept pace with her in spite of the distraction.

"Are you all right, pup?" she asked.

"Can we dispense with the 'pup'?" he grumbled at her. He slid past another set of gum tree branches and caught his sleeve on one as he did.

He jerked it free, but not without some embarrassment.

She smiled. She clapped him on the back in a friendly way.

"Of course, youngster," she smirked. "You can stay hidden? Until we need you not to be hidden?"

"I think so."

"Because you are very loud," she added. She motioned around at the trees. "I am worried you will get shot out here, and Balidor made me promise I would not leave you in the jungle with a bullet in your brain. Even if you annoyed me greatly."

Revik let out a low snort, in spite of himself.

Even so, the comment about his "loudness" got to him a little, maybe because he knew it was true, even with Dalejem's help earlier. Or maybe he'd just spent too many hours standing out in these fucking trees.

Too many hours waiting to get shot at for being a traitor, by one side or the other.

"Tell him it was an accident," he suggested, his voice flat. "You mistook me for one of them."

Yumi grinned at him.

She didn't answer him aloud.

Instead, once the mobile construct finished formulating around the two of them and the rest of the splinter team, she spoke directly into Revik's mind.

*I checked with Balidor on this, and he approved your plan, brother Dehgoies,* she sent.

She gave him a more appraising look, one that contained a lingering friendliness.

*He doesn't want you getting too close though, brother,* she added in warning. *He's stipulated that we let them have a bare taste of your light and then immediately go. We are to loop to the north and east for at least thirty clicks before pausing to assess their response, and to check in on the status of our own teams. From there, we will determine when and how to rejoin the others. Assuming we are not still in open flight.*

*Won't they be gone by then?* Revik sent, puzzled. *Balidor and the main extraction team? They have an airlift coming, I would assume?*

She cocked an eyebrow at him. *Why do you ask?*

*What you just said,* he returned at once. *Why would we need to determine how to rejoin them? Why not simply have the exit transport meet us wherever we are?*

She rolled her eyes.

That time she clicked at him with a touch more irritation.

*It's a little early to concern yourself with our own extraction, brother Dehgoies,* she sent. *Focus on what we are doing now. It is*

110 • JC ANDRIJESKI

*quite dangerous... in case you were unaware. As I said, I'd prefer if you didn't get shot.*

Revik frowned.

He could feel there was something they weren't telling him.

*Why are they going north at all?* he sent, still thinking. *Why not just head back for the airstrip in Manaus? If we manage to get the Org units to follow us, they could possibly take the river to circumvent the Sweeps, or—*

*You don't need to know any of that yet,* she sent. Her thoughts grew abruptly warning. Without slowing her pace, she gave him a look. *And before you have another of your paranoia attacks, brother Revik... none of us traveling with you knows. We are following orders. All I know for certain is that we aren't going back through Manaus.*

*But why not?* Revik felt a kind of frustration building in his chest, and realized it was probably fear, and not for himself. *Surely Balidor must know how risky it is, to go deeper into the jungle? The next town with a decent airport might be Bogotá, for fuck's sake. The Org will have transport helicopters out here soon, assuming they don't already. They can drop right down among us. With Kali that pregnant, we won't be able to keep a lead in any case, even if they only come after us on foot—*

*Brother,* Dalejem sent softly. *Calm yourself.*

Revik turned. He frowned at Dalejem where he walked behind them.

Dalejem only met his gaze, his own unapologetic.

Eventually, Revik looked away.

When he glanced back at Yumi, she rolled her eyes at him, but strangely, her thoughts grew more patient, not less.

*Jem is right. Do not worry about this now, little brother,* she sent reassuringly. *I promise you, we'll tell you the details when we can. In any case, I assure you that brother Balidor is not foolhardy. He is anything but a risk-taker by nature. So he must have good reason for deciding the course he has. I trust him. I suggest you try to do the same.*

She gave him a faint smile.

*Focus, okay? Your responsibility is to your part of the plan. That is standard military procedure,* na? *Even for the Rooks?*

After a pause, Revik nodded, reluctant.

Yumi clicked at him again, in amusement that time.

*You are too used to being in charge yourself, maybe?* she suggested coyly.

Revik gave her a harder look.

Yumi laughed as silently as before.

*Relax, brother,* she sent. Her voice grew coaxing, threaded with warmth. *Balidor says their on-site infiltrators, whatever their ranks, will have imprints of your aleimic signature in their files, both Barrier and electronic. You will not need to be recognized by individual seers if that is the case. He said that further, given who you are, they might even have those records flagged with some kind of high-priority status…?*

She glanced at him.

"Is that true?" she asked aloud.

Revik nodded, once. "Probably. Yes."

Nodding back, the same decisive way he had, she resumed speaking inside his head.

*In that case, it is much simpler for us,* she sent.

She exuded another pulse of warmth in his direction.

While that warmth was obviously meant to reassure him, Revik tasted her own emotion in it. That emotion felt very much like relief.

*This is very good,* she sent, as if to confirm what he'd felt. *We do not have to risk you very much. Or ourselves, for that matter,* she added, winking at him and smiling in the blueish glow of her wrist-band. *We will simply find a place in their construct, brother, where they have no guards or patrols nearby. This should not be difficult since they have deployed a relatively small percentage of their people to watch over the remaining pris-*

*oners while they focused on pursuit of Balidor and your friend, Kali. The vast bulk of their military back-up was already sent after the extraction team. So we will put you in their range only just. Then we will go, and assume their security measures can handle the rest.*

*And if they don't?* Revik grumbled.

Yumi shrugged.

*If they do not divert an adequate number of their team towards us, we will revisit our strategy. Perhaps we shall even attack them directly. From behind, of course, and likely with support from the other splinter group.*

She gave him another small smile.

*They will likely know what we are doing,* she added. She quirked an eyebrow. *I doubt they would believe you so sloppy as to cross that perimeter line by accident.*

Revik glanced up. He heard the compliment woven into her words.

She didn't bother to return his look.

Instead, she shrugged with one tattooed hand.

*But we must assume you will be sufficiently tantalizing bait, brother,* she added with a smile. *Regardless of why they believe you to be here. Hopefully you will be more tantalizing than whatever they think they are following in brother Balidor and sister Kali. Although Balidor plans to support our distraction with Barrier illusions and a few tricks of his own.*

Revik nodded.

He fought to think, but mostly he let it go.

He was still trying to walk more quietly, but without Dalejem's direct help, he knew he was only having minimal success. Even so, he found himself relaxing somewhat as he turned over some of the meanings behind Yumi's words.

Her logic made sense.

Balidor's logic made sense.

The instant Revik's light hit the Org construct, alarms would ring all the way to the top of the Pyramid hierarchy.

Once they confirmed his ID, it would change the status of this extraction, and fast.

It was a calculated risk, and not only for him.

Based on that, he couldn't help but be relieved at Yumi's and Balidor's determination not to push on that too much. In and out. Let the Org feel him, and bolt. If the tactic lifted only some of the pressure off Balidor's team, it would be worth the risk.

When he glanced over again, Yumi smiled at him.

*Perhaps you are not so dumb after all, Rook,* she sent softly, where none of the others would hear it. *I am thinking now that you will be very useful to us, brother.*

Revik suppressed a low surge of anger, a real one that time.

He controlled it by biting his tongue.

He found himself thinking about her words, even as doubt nagged at him. Who really wanted him here? Was it really Kali? Or someone else?

Someone inside the Pyramid, maybe?

Why had the Rooks taken Kali in the first place?

Balidor hinted more than once he didn't believe Galaith to be behind this, but Revik had trouble believing it, even with who Balidor was. To Revik's knowledge, no one inside the Org besides Galaith could pull something like this off. Who else could control the Sweeps?

Who else could use *Guoreum* as their own private dark site?

It still felt like the question no one wanted to answer.

Yet it was the only *real* question around any of them being here at all.

Revik glanced at Yumi, conscious suddenly of the silence between them.

She winked at him, laughing silently yet again.

*Don't be angry with my teasing, brother. I'm just testing your reflexes, which is a part of my job here, too. I need to know if you can reign in your emotions, if need be. We can't have you freaking out in the field, can we?*

*Freaking out?* He gave her a disbelieving look. *Is that a serious concern?*

She shrugged, clearly indifferent to his anger.

*As I said, brother Balidor is a cautious man,* she sent.

*If that were true, he would have left me in the Pamir,* Revik retorted. *As I wanted. And requested. Repeatedly.*

She only smiled wider.

She nudged him with a muscular, tattooed arm.

*From what brother Jem tells me, you're a bit paranoid, Rook,* she said, still smiling. *A bit hypersensitive, too. Of course, he finds it all quite charming. But he's a big softie, our Jem. He's also prone to taking in strays. Of all shapes and sizes.*

Revik didn't answer those words, either.

Still, they irritated him.

Maybe because he could feel her trying to nudge his mind overtly that time, to get him to see something, or understand something, perhaps… something he either didn't want or didn't need to see or understand any more clearly than he already did.

Or maybe she was just jabbing at his emotions again.

Testing his reflexes, as she'd said.

He didn't try very hard to untangle it, whatever it was, mainly because the only real possibilities had run through his mind already.

Besides, Dalejem already drew a line in the sand where Revik was concerned.

It was a line Revik probably hadn't needed pointed out to him so explicitly, but one that hadn't left a lot of room for ambiguity.

Revik's thoughts grew even more irritated when he remembered Dalejem and Mara outside of his sleeping tent that night, talking about him where they must have known he would feel it.

For some reason, something either in his thoughts or his expression made Yumi laugh again, harder that time, but still almost soundlessly.

Before Revik could give her an appropriate glare in response, she shut off the light glowing at her wrist.

The action left them in total darkness.

It also effectively ended their conversation.

## CHAPTER 10
# QUOREUM

"Are you ready, little brother?" Yumi asked.

She kept her voice low despite the distance between them.

He glanced back at her, at all of them where they stood in an uneven line, broken by the dense jungle trees.

He saw rifles raised, hands by triggers, and a darker humor invaded his light.

He had a sudden image of them opening fire on him, rather than covering him.

*Nice try, little brother,* Yumi murmured in his mind. *You won't get out of this that easy.*

Revik remembered Dalejem saying something similar to him the day before.

He smiled grimly, in spite of himself.

*I am ready,* he told her, equally quiet.

*Then go,* she sent. *Just be careful, brother. This is not the time to hurry. It is not the time to act the hero, either. If you feel anything that worries you, get out. At once. We will feed your light to their sentries some other way, if Balidor decides it is still needed.*

Revik nodded to that, too.

There wasn't much left to say.

He paused a few seconds more. He crouched behind the last lines of jungle trees and undergrowth, in the shadow of the same as he gazed over the grounds of *Guoreum.*

It was the closest he'd been to anything of the Rooks since he defected.

His eyes scanned the uneven landscape, most of which had been cleared almost entirely of jungle. He fought to keep his heart rate down, and to do as Yumi said: to exercise caution, to neither rush nor unduly hesitate.

He couldn't afford to rush.

Trying to get this over with faster wouldn't be any safer than dragging his feet in some unconscious effort to avoid doing it altogether.

He worked to ground himself in the physical.

He worked to calm himself with breathing techniques the monks taught him.

As he did, he continued to map his environment.

The clear-cut around the edges of *Guoreum* left a scar of black earth and uneven trunks, broken by rutted roads for military-style vehicles around the perimeter of the metal fence.

Inside that fenced area, Revik saw clumps of trees here and there, most of them in the distance, and most situated near cement block barracks and other structures.

Those trees were probably left as shade for the camp's employees.

Uneven stretches of grass also bordered segments of the road. The road itself consisted of mud ruts and hard-packed earth. The nearest of those ruts passed only a few meters in front of where Revik currently hid.

No trees seemed to have survived in the immediate area of the fence itself, which made sense. The guards definitely would have chopped those down. Revik had a clear view down a gentle hill that made up much of the open pasture in this segment of camp.

Behind him, the jungle clung around him as if in spite.

Or fear, maybe, that it would face the ax and tractors next.

Revik didn't see any guards in the area in front of him, or on the stretch of road along either side of the fence as far as he could see. He heard no vehicles nearby either, only a distant hum of a combustion engine, which could have been a generator for the camp itself.

Further away, he caught snippets of what might have been the speaker system to the main camp grounds. He heard the distorted sounds as they called out some instruction or other to the inmates or guards.

Revik couldn't make out the words.

Even so, just that small glimmer of prison life reminded him.

It brought back a rush of images and feeling, a reality of this camp and others like it, of places he'd been, places he'd helped design and build, places where he'd walked alongside those guards and told them what to do. It evoked even less pleasant memories that were more personal to him, such as questioning traitors under the Rooks.

Even before that, really.

It brought back flickers of memory and feeling from his time with the Nazis.

Smells. He could fucking *smell* it all again, the burning towns surrounded by mud-rutted and snow-covered fields. Stretches of winter and freezing cold, dead peasants and German troops huddled in rags. He remembered months of this: Russia, Ukraine, Poland, Slovakia, Prague, Belgium, France, Belarus—

But he didn't want to think about that now, either.

Sweat broke out over his body, somewhere in all of this.

He wanted to blame the heat, but it wasn't that hot yet, not with dawn's light still inching slowly and gradually over the field. He stared down the dirt road, and Revik bit the inside of his cheek. He fought to keep his *aleimi* in check, his emotions in line.

He did that mostly by trying his damnedest to blank out his mind altogether.

He was just outside the perimeter fence.

Less than ten meters.

The construct began before that, though.

The construct started maybe half that distance away.

He could feel the seething Barrier light even as some part of him tried to ignore it, at least in terms of its familiarity.

Those more familiar flavors lingered the loudest though, flavors he could feel some part of him wanting to resonate with, to immerse himself in, even from here. It was like the buzzing hum of a radio, played just at the edges of his awareness, sometimes quieter, sometimes louder. His ears strained for it, strained to pick out the exact melody, the exact voice, even as other parts of him were repulsed by the neediness in that part of his light.

He was like a fucking junkie.

He was like an addict watching someone do a drug deal from across the street.

He clenched his jaw. He fought to redirect his obsessive thoughts back to the physical aspects of where he was.

He stared first at the fence, if only as a place to focus his light.

The fence was clearly electric from the insulators he could see jutting out at regular intervals along its length on the outside, and the grounding pole poking just above the earth on the inside of the rutted road.

The top part of the fence was also covered in razor wire.

His attention shifted next to image captures, which seemed to live on every fence post he could see down the entire length of road. They sat atop narrow poles, small and insect-like, with a bubbled eye a good ten meters above the ground. The cameras significantly cleared the loops of razor wire and electrified fence, giving them an unobstructed, 360 degree view.

He knew when he moved forward, even just a few meters, the nearest three cameras would pick up his outline.

The construct alarm would likely go off even before that.

He hadn't seen any more offensive weapons in the fencing mechanism, but given the green-tinted shine of the fence posts, betraying their organic components, he couldn't rule it out. If nothing else, that green glow told him that anyone attempting to *cross* that fence from either side would likely get more than just a shock.

It was probably tied to their collaring and implant system, as well.

He glanced up at the harder gray of the dead-metal razor wire and the heavy bars that hung on thick chain links.

He couldn't help seeing those as almost redundant.

Whoever they held here would never get that far.

Not on their own.

He was wasting time, though.

The sun hadn't yet risen above the horizon line, but it was about to. The predawn light was slowly turning the sky a dark pink and cobalt blue. The early beams illuminated most of the field east of where he crouched, just behind the last line of trees leading into the jungle.

That same light extended south where the clear-cut continued, but stopped short before it reached where he stood, blocked by the dense trunks and undergrowth. Even so, when he glanced back a second time, Revik could see the outline of the Adhipan infiltrators where they watched him, their postures tense, from about ten meters away.

*Brother?* Yumi sent. *Are you going?*

Revik let out a sharper exhale, then a nod.

*Okay,* he sent.

He didn't hide his reluctance.

He rose slowly from his crouch. He stepped out from

behind the trees, moving with a purpose he couldn't make himself feel.

Immediately, he felt the construct of the work camp.

He could almost *see* it, writhing in the space in front of him.

He hesitated right at the periphery.

Almost without knowing he did it, he winced, closing his eyes...

Then he stepped over that line.

---

Alarms exploded inside his mind.

Deafening, raw.

Like a scream inside his head.

Revik felt the division as tangibly as if he'd just stepped his whole body into a full tank of water. Silver strands like metal teeth and razor wire slid invasively into his light.

They entered him so cleanly, so totally without resistance, he couldn't begin to think about defending himself.

Those same Barrier strands wrapped into structures he hadn't touched in over five years.

Those structures and resonances that still lived inside his light, invisible when dormant, now vibrated with a sick, metallic, silver hum.

It felt so familiar, so intensely familiar, he let out an involuntary groan.

He stood there, fighting to breathe.

His whole body clenched into a hard knot. That silver light paralyzed him, locked him to the spot where he stood. He was blind. His body was concrete.

His feet felt buried in the earth.

The alarm continued to go off.

It was so loud now, he thought it might shatter his skull.

The silver strands wrapped into him tighter and he let out a cry.

He fell to his knees on something hard.

They continued to invade his light. Now it felt like toxic sludge dumped down on him, blinding his sight. They poured that sick shit into his *aleimi* without pause, without stopping when it felt like it might kill him.

It nearly knocked him unconscious, but the Org construct didn't stop.

Nausea rose so quickly Revik couldn't work his throat or stomach to deal with it.

He fought to get back to his feet.

He fought with all his being to move his hands, his legs, his knees.

He knew he was down, but he couldn't stop fighting.

Every part of him fought to escape.

Terror exploded in his mind, his light. They were coming. He could feel them coming for him. They knew who he was. They knew who he fucking was.

He had to get away… crawl away, if he had to…

Hands abruptly grabbed him.

Immediately, his terror exploded outward, making him cry out.

*They had him. They fucking had him.*

He tried to fight them off—

"Brother," a familiar voice said through gritted teeth. "Brother, stop fighting us! Let us get you out of here! They're closer than we thought. They're coming!"

Even as he said it, another sound ricocheted through Revik's mind.

He didn't know how he heard it, given the blindingly loud siren, the screaming behind his eyes, the voices of the uniformed soldiers who were trying to drag him to his feet.

That sound somehow lived in a near-silence behind all the rest.

Perhaps the sheer physicality of it simply overrode the Barrier noise he couldn't think past.

That, or the familiarity.

Something about that pure familiarity, of muscle memory, of years and decades of ingrained habit, lurched Revik back into motion, even when nothing else could.

He moved in spite of the paralysis, in spite of the silver strands, in spite of the pain that wanted to shatter his skull, in spite of the mercury light shaking of every muscle in his body.

It wasn't even that loud, that sound.

Not at first.

Revik knew exactly what it was though, and what it meant.

It was gunfire.

## CHAPTER 11
# NO ONE WILL LEAVE YOU

*Run!* Yumi commanded. Her light vibrated their small construct. *Flee! Now! All of you! Do not worry about the construct. Head at once for the rendezvous!*

*Rendezvous?* Revik thought, his mind numb. *Where the fuck is that?*

Panic invaded his light, the realization that they intended to leave him behind—

"No, brother," a voice said firmly from beside him.

Revik looked over at the man half-jogging next to him.

He realized only then that the same seer still clutched his arm in a death-grip.

Dalejem. Always Dalejem.

Revik felt a relief so profound, he could have hugged him.

Not just could have—wanted to. He wanted to hug him, to wrap himself around him, lose himself inside that light—

He couldn't think about that, either.

Confusion fought with the pain throbbing behind his eyes. It made him question everything, even his own eyes, what he felt with his light.

Was it really Dalejem there? Or was that just who he wanted it to be?

He couldn't fucking see. He couldn't fucking see anything now.

The male beside him didn't look at him.

He continued to pull Revik forward into the jungle. He urged him faster with his light and that iron-like grip on his arm, even as he spoke reassuringly to Revik in hurried pants.

"Don't worry, brother... I beg you. We would never intentionally let harm come to you. I promise you." He glanced up at Revik then and jumped.

He stared at him, as if shocked at something he saw on Revik's face.

Revik fought to see him, to focus his eyes, but he couldn't.

"...We couldn't risk giving it to you," Dalejem explained.

For it was Dalejem, it had to be Dalejem. Who else would it be?

Who else wouldn't have left him there in the dirt?

Couldn't risk giving it to him?

Couldn't risk giving him what?

"...We had no idea what the construct would do to you," the other seer continued. He still gripped Revik's arm in that iron hand. "We didn't know whether you would be able to shield any information from them at all. As it is, they might have killed you. They almost *did* kill you, even with us shielding. We should have foreseen this. We shouldn't have let you go—"

He looked at Revik again.

That time, the green and violet eyes looked fierce.

"I'll get you there, brother." His voice grew cold, uncompromising. "I promise you I will, or neither of us will get there. I won't leave you. I promise I won't leave you. Okay? Stop thinking that I will, or I will be deeply offended, brother."

Revik nodded. He bit the inside of his cheek.

He fought not to throw up.

He could feel other lights around him now.

He felt sympathy, whispers of concern.

He even felt guilt.

It confused him more than anything.

Who were these people? Why did they care about him at all? What did they want from him? The question made his head hurt, his gut churn.

No one was ever nice to him for no reason.

He'd learned that years and years ago. It was always a trap.

It was always a fucking trap.

There was always a price.

The silver light continued to slide around him. It pulled at him, made his nausea worse, made him fight to keep down his bile, to keep his legs moving, his body lurching forward.

That same metallic light found an entry point, somewhere outside Revik's awareness.

It found him through some structure that lived in his light, above his head. Before Revik could stop it, or even send out a warning to the others—

It funneled down through that same structure, blanketing him in iron.

The pain of it made him stumble.

It nearly dropped him to his knees.

The nausea worsened, until his whole body heaved.

He had no idea if anything came up. His vision blurred for real, bringing on a disorientation and fatigue so intense he stumbled a second time. That time he fell... into a tree. He grabbed it briefly, gasping, but those fingers tightened on his arm even more.

He could barely feel them now.

The silver light still rained down on him.

The pain in his head and chest started to get worse.

Then a lot worse.

Then it was so bad Revik realized Dalejem was right.

He was already dead.

The Rooks would kill him out here.

There was no place left for him to go, nowhere far enough that the Rooks and Galaith wouldn't follow. They'd found him. They'd found his light again.

To them, it wasn't Revik's light at all.

It was theirs.

Maybe they were even right. Maybe it *was* theirs.

They'd likely done more to change it and grow it and cultivate it and mold it than he had, whatever he'd told himself at the time. When it came down to it, you owned what you used. When you forfeited that ownership, there was no one left to cry to.

Now they'd just finish the job.

They'd break everything in him. Cover him over in molten metal and cold fire.

It was already too late. They already had him.

If the others stayed, they'd only be caught as well.

If they tried to carry him out, they'd be caught.

If they tried to fight the Org, they'd be caught.

Anything they did to stall their flight out of here, and they'd be caught with helicopters filled with Black Arrow operatives, with the weight of the World Court and all of SCARB and the Sweeps and the camp authorities raining down on them.

They'd be caught and they'd be disappeared.

They'd be lost.

It would be Revik's fault.

The Org's infiltrators who would descend like vultures in the dark.

Dalejem said he wouldn't leave him.

At the time, the words reassured Revik.

Now, the memory of them panicked him.

Thoughts jumbled and jerked inside Revik's brain, so intensely he couldn't speak, not even to tell them to leave him, to leave him there—

Then, out of nowhere, something else intervened.

Not something.

Someone.

Someone who suddenly felt an awful lot like—

"Balidor," Dalejem muttered next to him.

Revik could hear him.

He could hear the other seer again.

He could hear him, and feel his hands on him, the articulation of his fingers.

It was such a relief he could only close his eyes.

The seer next to him continued to mutter under his breath, his words warlike, close to angry, yet exuding a relief that was almost physical.

"—It's about fucking time," Dalejem growled. "We've been trying to reach him since you fell in that road. They will help you, brother. Him and the woman. They have Vash looped into the construct, too. And Tarsi, our old leader in the Adhipan. At the very least, they'll keep those Rook fucks from killing you from the Barrier before we can free your light—"

It confused Revik somewhat, how angry the other male sounded.

It crossed his mind that he might be angry at him—

"No, brother." Dalejem's grip on him tightened. His voice grew lower, even as warmth swam over Revik's light. "No one is *mad* at you, brother. Trust me on this."

He yanked harder on Revik's arm.

Worry bled through his fingers.

Revik followed mindlessly, conscious suddenly that he had his other hand on the butt of the Glock strapped to his right thigh. He gripped it compulsively, but didn't try to draw it. He wasn't trying overly hard to be quiet at that point, either, although he followed the prodding of Dalejem's light and the pull of his hand.

For a few minutes, that's all he was aware of.

Light, that grip of fingers, the sounds he made through the jungle.

Then, it struck him that something had gradually begun to change.

He could almost see again.

He felt flavors of Vash in his light now, as well as Balidor.

He still felt Balidor most of all, but he pulled on Vash compulsively, and felt the other seer's presence grow even stronger. He had to bite his lip to keep from trying to talk to the older seer. He found he wanted to talk to him, even though the words weren't really there, nothing coherent, nothing that made any sense.

*I love you, my son,* a voice murmured.

Tears came to Revik's eyes.

It felt so far away. Vash felt eons away, lifetimes away, but Revik knew that voice. He would have known it anywhere, even if the distance was thousands of times what it was.

The voice grew fierce.

*I love you, my son,* Vash repeated. *No one will leave you there. No one. I love you. Your aunt loves you. They would not dare leave you there.*

Revik nodded.

He nodded, and that compulsion to speak, to have the other hear him, faded slightly.

Tears blinded him instead.

Relief flooded over him as the tears fell, even as a part of him felt embarrassment, even shame for how badly he'd needed to hear that from the old man. He'd needed to *feel* that from Vash, more than from anyone out here in the jungle, despite the fact that his life was in their hands, despite the fact that Balidor himself, famed leader of the Adhipan, had sworn to protect him, to personally keep him safe.

In the end, it was always Vash.

It was Vash who was there for him. Who never gave up on him.

Even when everyone told the old man Revik was evil, that he was beyond saving, Vash remained with him, in his light. He didn't seem to care what any of them said.

Revik didn't know why the old man loved him.

He only knew that he did.

He also knew that love was probably the only reason he was still alive.

"That is beautiful, brother. Truly."

Revik turned his head.

He found Dalejem there, still pulling him along, his hand still gripping Revik's bicep like an iron vise. Dalejem seemed to hold him up through sheer force of will. In blurred greens, blues and yellows, the jungle and sky grew faintly visible again, although Revik had no idea where he was, or what direction Dalejem was leading him.

Seeing the warmth in the other male's eyes, Revik could only nod.

His embarrassment returned in a heated flush when he realized the other seer had heard everything he'd been thinking, every childlike, illogical word that had gone through his head.

He fought to relax.

He took a deeper breath, fought to move his muscles more under his own will, but Dalejem resisted him slightly. The green-eyed seer used his light to continue to guide Revik's own, as well as Revik's physical body.

"Let me do it," Dalejem said. "Relax, brother. Try to trust me."

Revik heard relief in the other male's voice.

"Just be as open to them as you can," Dalejem added. He renewed his grip on Revik's arm. "Stay with Vash... and with Balidor. They have a better shield around you now. Let them try to pull some of that shit out of your light."

Revik fought to make sense of his words.

In the end, he only nodded.

Dalejem had already looked away by then.

He began pulling Revik along faster, even as the Adhipan seer's *aleimi* grew more gentle within his, more coaxing than demanding, more guiding than yanking or forcing. Dalejem's green and violet eyes focused ahead, on the path in front of them.

Revik found himself doing the same.

He could almost see for real now.

Not only had his vision started to clear, but the trees had grown visible around him, enough that he knew the sun must be significantly higher in the sky than he'd imagined. That meant more time must have passed than he'd imagined, too. It had to be well into morning if this much of the star's light reached them through the thick canopy.

He realized for the first time that Dalejem held a machete in his free hand, not a gun, and that he was hacking them through the jungle, moving faster than Revik would have thought possible, given the terrain.

"They knew it was me," Revik managed, a few minutes later.

Dalejem let out a humorous laugh, nearly hoarse.

"Yes, brother," he said, that darker humor still in his voice. "They most certainly did know it was you."

"Are they following us?"

"Yes," Dalejem said.

"Just the ones at the camp? Or the ones who had been following Balidor and..." He hesitated on her name, even now. "...And Kali?" he finished. "Those seers, too?"

"About half of them, yes. The plan exceeded our expectations in that regard." Dalejem glanced back at him. "They really want you, brother."

Revik wasn't sure how to respond to that.

In the end, he only nodded.

Dalejem likely didn't see that nod, either.

As before, the older seer had already turned his attention

back to the not-path he hacked for the two of them through the jungle. Revik found himself watching in fascination as Dalejem moved them forward at a near-steady pace, guiding them around larger trees and stumps and even boulders as he found openings through the dense greenery. He moved with the grace and precision of a dancer.

He wielded the long knife as if it were a sword.

Neither of them spoke for what felt like a long time.

Dalejem hacked through the undergrowth, and Revik watched. He followed close behind Dalejem and to his right. Dalejem's hand never left Revik's arm, yet the blade never came close to him or hesitated in one of its perfect swings carving a path through the dense green.

The other seer was left-handed, Revik realized suddenly.

Not like it mattered all that much with most seers.

Living as long as they did, most became ambidextrous to one degree or another; but Dalejem clearly favored his left hand and arm for this kind of work.

Eventually, Dalejem seemed to sense Revik was more or less "back" with him and released his arm.

Revik immediately slid into the empty space behind him.

He stepped almost directly in the other's footsteps, remaining at least halfway in his light as he followed him through the vines and leafy plants.

His mind went nearly blank as he watched the other work.

Fatigue tried to slow him down, to make his legs move more clumsily, but whenever his eyelids drooped too much, Dalejem would jerk him back from that edge with his *aleimi*. Whatever he did to Revik exactly, it brought Revik's mind back into sharper focus.

Revik could feel the Org seers pursuing them now.

He fought to keep his light away from theirs.

Even so, he couldn't help but feel it when those silvery, mercury-like threads tried to find ways to resonate with his.

He felt them working in teams. He felt them trying to penetrate his shields, looking for dark spaces in his light where he might be less conscious.

Revik also felt Vash there, working with Balidor and the others.

He felt Vash ease Revik's own light back patiently a few times, warmly reminding him to let them handle it.

Revik tried.

He tried his damnedest to ignore everything happening in different parts of his light, but he couldn't quite succeed, not totally.

Fear kept him watching the edges of his *aleimi*.

The fear made his own light act compulsively, which turned into a kind of self-reinforcing loop, where he resonated with them more the longer he watched them. He would see the Org seers get closer then, see them trying to actively take over his light, and his paranoia would shoot up, causing him to focus too much on the Barrier attacks... and then on the actual Rooks chasing them.

Then Vash, or Balidor, or Tarsi... or all three of them... would be forced to focus back on Revik, to get him to let go of the whole thing, to turn away.

Within minutes, sometimes seconds, the cycle would begin again.

He knew he was only making it easier for the Rooks to find him.

He knew that, but fear would take over his light, and he wouldn't even know he was doing it until Vash shook him again inside the Barrier construct, reminding him.

He did wonder—again—what the fuck he was doing out here.

He wondered why anyone would think him coming out here was a good idea, why he'd been stupid enough to offer to approach *Guoreum* on his own, why he'd put everyone in his unit in mortal danger, why he'd walked into that construct with little or no shielding.

It was pure ego.

Hubris maybe, or maybe an even more childish attempt to prove himself to the rest of them, to try and feel useful, to try and prove Kali wasn't wrong to ask for him.

Kali.

For the first time, he let himself remember she was out here.

She was with Balidor, right now—

That time, there was no warning at all.

Everything went black.

He lost touch with his body, the jungle, his fingers, his hands, the rhythm of Dalejem's swinging machete, even the pain in his head and chest, the shakiness of his muscles and joints.

He lost all of it before he could take a full breath.

It happened so fast, the fear never touched him.

Some part of him pulled a switch, and everything went dark.

The higher parts, the parts of him that always remained awake in some way, conscious in some way, vacated his body without an ounce of friction between himself and some higher place in the Barrier.

The lower parts of himself...

Well, to them, he simply disappeared.

## CHAPTER 12
# BONES OF IRON

When Revik opened his eyes, he was being carried.

Not by one seer that time, but by many.

At least three different presences he could feel surrounded him, although there may have been more. They had him on some kind of stretcher.

"*Gaos*, this fucker is heavy," someone muttered under him.

"It could be worse," another voice said humorously.

"How?" the first one grumbled.

"It could be Gar you're carrying," the other said.

The words brought peals of laughter, if somewhat muted laughter, from more than one side. One of those came out in a near-wheezing voice, deeper than the others.

"Fuck you all very much," the deeper voice said cheerfully.

Revik fought to move, to turn over.

Maybe even to climb off the bouncing stretcher.

Immediately, several voices shouted him down from where they held different sides of the organic metal frame.

"Wait, brother! Wait!" Dalejem's voice came out louder

than the others. "We are nearly to the rendezvous. We will set you down there. Patience!"

Revik froze.

He fought to think, couldn't really.

He stared up at the green-leafed canopy of the jungle. Then, realizing Dalejem's words made sense, Revik did as they instructed him. He relaxed his muscles entirely into the padded material of the stretcher.

Still, the reality of being carried was strange, to say the least.

He continued to stare up.

He fought to clear his mind, to think past the pounding of his head.

Sunlight wafted through broad leaves. It spun down lazily past green-mossed branches and ferns growing out of dark trunks. Revik glimpsed slices of blue, but most of the world was green: a soft, cathedral-like green he felt to be growing around him. He absorbed that sensation of growth almost tangibly despite the dense heat and wetness in the air.

He saw faces a few times in those branches.

A few were definitely monkeys, but a number he couldn't identify for certain.

Sloths, maybe?

He saw birds, too.

They winged and flitted between moss-covered trunks.

Some were so colorful, with such long tails and broad, fingered wings, he couldn't help but follow them with his eyes, entranced with their beauty.

"Maybe you are right, Jem," one of the seers huffed under him. "He is a big softie, our Rook. He is looking at birds now, waxing philosophical while we carry his heavy ass."

Laughter broke out among the other seers nearby, even as Revik's face warmed.

Still, he couldn't help but hear and feel the relief in their laughter. The tangibility of that relief relaxed a tension he'd carried in his chest.

It also bewildered him.

"Of course we are relieved!" another familiar voice scolded, female that time. *"Gaos,* brother. We thought we'd killed you. You fell like a fucking corpse in that road. Then, after we managed to get you out of there, you fell *again,* and we thought you were dead for real. We thought your fucking brain had popped—"

"That, or your *aleimi* decided we were nothing but a bunch of *dugra d'aros* and fled—" another voice added cheerfully.

"That, or you let your heavy ass drop, just to spite us," another female muttered, more grumpily than the others, but still exuding flavors of that relief.

Revik's mind had cleared enough that he knew most of the voices now.

The first female to speak had been Yumi, the last Mara.

The one to tease him for looking at birds had been Poresh.

They had all been teasing Garensche, the giant with the Nazi scar on his face.

"You should be kissing brother Gar's ass," Mara muttered.

She huffed a little from where she held her part of the stretcher.

"...He managed to fry part of the net they'd brought down on us, trying to pinpoint your location. He hacked their organic machines, got them to turn on their Rook owners. It took them over an hour to pull their organics out from under Gar's control. They were pretty pissed, let me tell you. But by then, we'd lost both of the ground teams they sent after us."

Revik thought about all that, puzzled.

"Really?" he asked.

More laughter erupted under him.

"Brother Gar is a bit of a mystic with the machines," Dalejem explained. His voice contained a smile when he went on. "It is quite beyond our comprehension, really. We have learned it is better just to let him do his thing and not try to understand what he does. None of us *really* wants to know what he promises them, to get them to do his bidding."

More chuckles rose from Dalejem's words.

Revik heard Garensche's laugh among them.

Clearly this was some long-standing joke within the military unit.

Revik relaxed more deeply into the stretcher.

He folded his hands on his abdomen and looked up at the looping vines and thick-fingered leaves that blocked and unblocked the sun above his eyes. He saw more palms than any other kind of tree out here, but gum trees also littered his vision, along with banana trees and papaya and a number he couldn't identify.

He found himself thinking they were higher than they had been, elevation-wise.

They still walked up a noticeable slope.

He considered trying to use his light to determine more.

After a second of contemplation, he thought better of it.

He found himself remembering what he'd been doing right before he passed out, and pulled his light even tighter around his form.

He wanted to ask, though.

He wanted to ask badly enough that he bit his tongue as he looked up at the sunlight-banded trunks.

"She is fine, brother," Dalejem said, his voice more gentle than the rest.

"Did she have her baby?" Revik asked.

"No."

"You are sure?" he blurted.

Revik asked it before he could stop himself.

Once he had, he felt their living lights flicker around him, more invasively that time. Most of those light probes felt good-natured still, but Revik felt curiosity there, mixed with a faint flavor of assessment, one that indicated at least a few of them were monitoring his mental state for stability and/or rationality. He also felt flavors of amusement, particularly from those who seemed to think they knew *why* he asked the question.

Feeling his defensiveness worsen, Revik spoke again without thinking, breaking the silence when no one answered him.

"I felt something."

Yumi chuckled a little at that. "Well, clearly. Since it nearly killed you."

"No." Revik shook his head. He felt his face warm more. "No, I mean I felt—"

"We know what you felt," Yumi broke in. Her voice grew gentle, more like Dalejem's. "It is true that she is very close. Very, very close, perhaps. Balidor has already said that she instructed him to go deeper into the jungle for that reason."

"What?" Revik turned his head on the stretcher. "Why?"

Yumi met his gaze when he turned. She shrugged. The dark blue of her tattoo looked closer to green under the jungle canopy.

"I do not know that, brother," she said frankly. "Balidor might not even know that, not for certain. Clearly, she has her own reasons for wanting to be away from the vast majority of human and seer lights when this child is born."

Revik fought to think about that.

He fought to make sense of why she would risk such a thing.

Eventually he only nodded, unable to make sense of the threads of meaning that came to him, mostly in whispers of presence and light.

He felt almost like he *knew* something, which in some ways disturbed him more than what he didn't know. He felt familiarity there, some whisper of understanding that didn't come from him, at least not directly—at least not from his conscious mind.

Whatever it was, it wouldn't stay with him, and he didn't dare look closer than he had already.

Kali was leading them into the jungle.

Out of nowhere, a hard coil of pain wound through his light.

It brought up a sickness that made him writhe on the stretcher. He had to bite his tongue to keep from making a sound.

Even so, he exhaled a near-gasp once he could breathe at all.

He felt at least a few of the other seers react to the pain coming off him. He even heard some of them suck in breaths nearly at the same time he did. The wave hit them hard enough that their steps faltered around him. They were never in danger of dropping him, not that he could feel, but it felt almost as if they paused on the same note and regained motion in the same breath.

"Shield your light, brother," Yumi said from next to him.

Her voice came out low.

It was clearly a command, however.

Revik opened his eyes, and realized only then that he still had his head turned towards her. He met her gaze and nodded. He fought back another swell of pain and embarrassment that struggled in his chest as he did.

None of them spoke again until they reached the rendezvous point, just past the crest of the mountain.

## CHAPTER 13
# DESPISED

It was nearly dark by the time they arrived.

The rapid change in light confused Revik at first.

He thought a storm must be rolling in.

He thought clouds were blocking the sun above the canopy.

Then he saw pieces of sky, saw them changing colors to pinks and oranges and reds, and realized he must have been unconscious for most of the day while they traveled.

He'd lost nearly a whole day.

He doubted they would have the luxury of staying in the new camp for long.

He also knew he should take his turn at sentry given he'd already spent most of the day sleeping and none of his companions had that luxury. Before he could voice even a part of this, however, Yumi informed him he would need to get more sleep, and that he would be required to accept help in replenishing his light in the process.

He wasn't given the choice.

When he climbed shakily up off the stretcher after they put him down on the ground, Yumi and Dalejem had ahold of him on two sides as he straightened.

It was a good thing they did.

Revik's knees buckled as soon as he'd pulled himself up to his full height.

It happened suddenly enough and violently enough, he likely would have fallen straight to the dirt without the two of them there.

They continued to stand there with him, supporting a percentage of his weight and most of his balance while four other seers swiftly erected a rough circle of those odd, hanging tent-structures. They used thick, low-hanging branches from the nearby trees and an organic wire of a type Revik had never seen before. He watched, dazed, as that same wire sought out connecting points and weighting on six sides.

Then it pulled the semi-organic tarp taut above the ground.

They managed it all in what felt like a handful of minutes.

Interior mats were already being inflated as the last wires got secured and locked in place. Then Revik was informed that he'd be using the first of those tents, and that he had his choice of connectors to feed him light.

He didn't hesitate.

He was too tired to hesitate, or to pretend he didn't have a preference.

"Dalejem," he said.

The male seer flinched.

He didn't speak, though, or protest with his light.

He didn't even change expression really, although Revik saw a frown touch the mouth of Mara, who looked over when Revik spoke.

Dalejem either didn't see that or chose to ignore it.

Instead, he grew abruptly businesslike.

Without waiting, he gripped Revik's arm tighter.

He took what remained of his weight and balance away from Yumi and led him straight into that first tent they'd erected. Once inside, Dalejem released him and began unhooking the armored vest from around Revik's chest with deft fingers. He had that and the gun holsters off him with an efficiency that only disoriented Revik more, although he made no move to stop him. He simply stood there and let the other male undress him.

His arms hung soft and useless at his sides the whole time.

When he finished, Dalejem ordered Revik to lie down.

Revik didn't argue with that, either.

He barely paused long enough to pull the armored shirt over his head, and then only because he was so fucking hot—too hot to want the dense fabric next to his body, even with it getting dark outside. He felt more than saw Dalejem suck in a breath when the other male got a look at his back.

Revik pretended not to notice.

Then he fought not to care.

He deliberated tried to blank his mind but didn't fully succeed.

*Gaos.* What was wrong with him?

He was used to seers reacting that way to his scars.

The reaction was a natural one. He had little cause to be offended by it. Very few seers had scars like him. Revik was used to the stares they evoked whenever he exposed that part of his skin to another seer for the first time. He was equally used to the questions he inevitably got about how and where he'd obtained the scars... questions he couldn't have answered even if he wanted to.

The truth was, he didn't remember.

He supposed that was part of what had been taken from him when he left the Rooks.

Possibly, he hadn't remembered even before he left the Rooks.

For some reason, the blank spot there felt different from the others in his light.

It felt older. It also felt more impenetrable.

Still, it could have been from him leaving the Rooks.

They'd erased a lot of his memories in those early months, including ones he'd had before he joined the Org, which apparently happened at some point during World War II. Vash told him that the forfeiture of memories was part of the agreement the Seven made with Galaith when Revik defected.

Revik hadn't asked why that was.

Hell. He *knew* why.

There's no way Galaith would let him share Org secrets with the Seven or the Adhipan. Given how high up Revik had been within the Org hierarchy—and Vash assured him, it had been high—Revik must have known things even most Rooks didn't know.

Given that, the source of his scars struck Revik as relatively trivial.

Whatever caused them, Revik supposed it didn't really matter.

It wasn't likely to be a pleasant story, in any case.

He'd learned to ignore both the stares and the questions over the years, but he wasn't immune to them. Moreover, for the first time it occurred to him that it might be harder to evade those questions outside of the Rooks' Pyramid than it had been inside it, at least with other seers.

Luckily, most humans didn't attach as much importance to how his back looked.

They found the scars fascinating, sure, and still an anomaly, but scars weren't as rare on human bodies as they were on seer bodies.

Dalejem didn't ask.

He waited until Revik was down, then laid down next to him on the same mat.

He didn't touch him at all as he stretched out on his back next to where Revik lay sprawled on his stomach. Revik turned his head to avoid the awkwardness of having his face aimed towards the other male, but he still felt the other's eyes on him, especially on the scars that covered most of his back.

He was thankful for the lack of questions.

Even so, he could feel the seer wanting to ask.

More than that, he felt sympathy there, a heavier weight of empathy that bled understanding between them, even though no part of the male's skin touched Revik's own.

In some ways, that was worse.

He couldn't help feeling strangely guilty for making the other seer feel bad about what some unknown person or persons had done to him.

Thinking about what Dalejem might see of him in the light exchange didn't make him feel any better. Sharing light meant sharing memories, at least to a degree. Most of those memories came up as a product of the resonance between both seers' lights, and the relative trust between them, and the relative affection there.

For the same reasons, the exact memories that surfaced were more or less outside of either seer's control.

Forcing that uncomfortable fact out of his mind, Revik went back to trying to blank out his thoughts entirely. He couldn't refuse the light, and he couldn't control the process, so he just had to let it go.

It wouldn't make any difference at this point anyway, he told himself.

He didn't stay awake long enough to remember the connection being made.

His dreams, once they came, were of him running through a different jungle, with steeper hills, more rocks, denser trees and harder plants... with different Rooks chasing him.

It felt like a memory.

Some things that came to him as dreams felt like fears, or abstractions, means of his mind chewing through some problem or anxiety. Some things came through as nearly prophetic, as originating in some Barrier space or Barrier presence that was trying to tell him something, whether for his good or not.

This didn't feel like those.

It came through as immediate, dark, filled with denser emotions he could almost taste. It contained a physical immediacy that stuttered his heart in his chest.

He fought to breathe.

He launched his body up a near-vertical hill.

He stumbled, face-planted into the peat and roots at the base of a heavy-trunked tree. He slid down the hill a few yards until he dug the toes of his boots into the soil and stone.

He dragged himself back to his feet.

He bled from a gunshot wound. Maybe more than one.

His arms, hands, face, and neck stung, littered with cuts and nicks from the trees and bushes as he ran.

He'd lost his jacket somewhere.

He was out of water.

The dark forest loomed around him behind his eyes. It never seemed to end. He had been running here for weeks, it seemed. Months.

Years.

The same thoughts looped in his mind, through all of it.

They wanted him dead.

They all wanted him dead.

He would be despised now.

Not only by the Rooks chasing him, but by all of them, on both sides of that line.

He would be despised.

---

He woke up in pain.

Not physical pain, despite his dream.

Separation pain.

That shouldn't have surprised him, either.

It didn't surprise him, not exactly, but it still managed to embarrass him.

He controlled it in reflex, even as he fought to bring his mind back on line, to ground himself in his body.

He knew one thing almost at once.

He didn't wake up on his own.

As he thought it, his eyes slid to the open flaps of the tent, and the silhouettes that stood there, blocking the light from what must be another organic heater.

Yumi face and body stood directly in the opening between the flaps. She talked and signed to Dalejem, who remained just inside the tent and wore full armor.

Revik could feel two others waiting just outside the tent as well.

Poresh and Mara, from what he could tell.

It was pitch dark out there now. He could feel tension in the construct of the camp, even beyond how Dalejem was dressed. They'd be on the move soon.

Dalejem glanced over at him, his pale eyes visible in some outside light.

"Yes," he said. "We have to move. As soon as you're ready."

"Where?" Revik asked. He fought a yawn, in spite of himself.

"Balidor wants us to take up a flanking position behind them," Dalejem said.

He continued to look Revik over, as if assessing his condition.

"...A new group was sent by the Org," Dalejem added. "This one looks dangerous. Not guards. More like a professional extraction team. They took helicopters to a site only a few minutes ago, landing a few clicks from Balidor's people. He expects to be under hard pursuit soon, and they are in no condition for it—"

"What time is it?" Revik asked.

"Oh-five-thirty."

"What?" Revik's eyes opened wide at that, even as adrenaline shot through his system. His internal clock hadn't prepared him for that answer at all. It must have gotten broken along with half the structures in his *aleimi*.

*"Gaos di'lalente.* How is that possible?" he muttered.

Dalejem didn't answer.

Yumi, on the other hand, let out a disbelieving snort. She folded her muscular arms across her chest before she glanced at the seers on the other side of the flap.

"You are very good at napping, Rook," she said. She quirked an eyebrow.

Revik heard the teasing there, but still felt himself frown.

Dalejem's voice came across mainly as impatient.

Revik couldn't quite tell if that impatience was aimed at him or at Yumi.

"Balidor has been re-routing the flavor of your light for most of the night," Dalejem explained. He looked only at Revik. "Mostly using key imprints from your *aleimi* the Org seems to be targeting, and bouncing them through the other splinter's construct. He did it to give you time to recover, but they need us now. This new group of professional hunters is gaining on them. That situation will not improve, given Kali's condition."

Dalejem hesitated, as if he wanted to say more.

He looked about to speak when his eyes shifted abruptly to Yumi.

It looked to Revik as if she'd pinged Dalejem's light, warning him silent.

If she had, Revik felt none of it.

He frowned anyway.

"What?" he said. "Just fucking tell me. Jesus."

Yumi answered him. She spoke before Dalejem could.

"Kali asked for you, pup. She thinks they will need you soon."

"For what?" Revik asked.

He pulled himself up to a seated position.

He winced and wrapped an arm around his chest once he had. He fought to control his separation pain as he blinked up at the other seers. He realized only then that he was still shirtless, and then mostly from Yumi's eyes on him.

"I do not know," Yumi said, matter-of-fact. "But as you likely know by now, your friend Kali often knows things most of us do not know. Therefore, brother Balidor does not usually bother to try and second-guess her."

Revik nodded.

He was still fighting to wake up, but worked at it more consciously now.

He pulled his shirt off the mat when he saw it balled up on the side of the tent next to where he'd been sleeping. He untangled it clumsily and yanked it over his head. He tried to remember what he'd done with the armored vest.

Then he remembered Dalejem had taken that off him.

He glanced towards the tent's door, and saw his guns and vest sitting there in a neat pile. He couldn't remember if Dalejem had done that at the time, or sometime since.

He didn't look at the either of them as he pulled himself to his feet.

He paused only long enough to assure himself he could keep his balance, then walked with more purpose towards the small pile of armor and weapons. He still wasn't looking at them when he reached it and began promptly to dress and equip himself.

He'd just finished buckling the holster back around his waist, the vest open around his chest, when someone handed him a canteen of drinking water. He barely looked at the hand holding it before he took it.

He drank down probably a third before it occurred to him to come up for air.

When he handed it back, someone handed him food, too, a plant-matter and protein-base wrap that served as basic req out in the field.

He took a bite from that without thinking, too.

While he chewed, Dalejem finished doing up the front of Revik's armored vest.

Revik ate the entire wrap in about thirty seconds flat, and his stomach only protested that there wasn't more.

As if he felt that, Dalejem laughed. He punched Revik lightly on the arm.

"There is more," he said. He smiled for the first time Revik remembered since they'd left for *Guoreum.* "But you will have to eat and walk, brother."

Revik only nodded.

He left the tent behind the other seer. He only paused to reach down and tie the organic strap around his thigh, holding the lower holster to his leg.

They were already dismantling the tent as he left out the front.

He felt better, though.

A lot better.

And strangely ready for a fight.

Dalejem must have felt some smattering of that, because he laughed, even as he motioned for Revik to follow him.

The front end of the group had already begun hefting packs to their shoulders. They entered in a single line through an opening in the jungle at the far end of the clearing.

It hit Revik again that they hadn't been kidding. The whole group really had been waiting for him. Once the realization sank in, Revik sped up his pace. He took a second wrap from Garensche when the tall seer handed it to him.

He unwrapped it quickly without slowing his steps.

He took a bite out of the end, as much for the energetic

boost as out of hunger. He never stopped following behind Yumi and Poresh as they disappeared into the trees after with the others. All of them wore heavy packs strapped to their backs.

Revik glanced back just long enough to see the last two seers of their group, Ontari and Vikram, stuff the collapsed tent and mats into their packs and heft them onto their shoulders to follow the rest of them into the jungle.

And just like that, they were a military unit again.

## CHAPTER 14
## SACRIFICIAL LAMB

They hiked through the jungle for two more days.

During that time, Balidor's team and the Rooks sparred back and forth between constructs in the Barrier. They also crossed lines and followed resonances into Revik's group and the other splinter.

At the end of the first day, Balidor broke his own team into smaller fractions yet again, likely in a further attempt to keep the main Org extraction team away from Kali.

Yumi's team—as Revik had come to think of their group—now stood between the smaller group being led by Balidor, and that same Org extraction team.

It took them almost twenty of the last forty or so hours to position themselves there, with Yumi, Gar, and Vikram mapping the area of the Org's mobile construct warily, and then skirting carefully around its edges to avoid direct contact.

Revik knew that caution, in large part, was because of him.

He also knew more than a little uneasiness remained around their position because of him, and not only from within his own group.

Everyone monitoring their construct, including Balidor and those helping remotely from the Pamir and Seertown, worked to keep Revik's light as far from that extraction team as they possibly could. Where they could, they projected Revik's light elsewhere, as a distraction and a means of confusing the team's priorities.

By then, they were pretty sure the team of Org hunters knew it was Adhipan they were chasing, not Revik running some private-sec merc group. Given the sight ranks of the seers in that new group, and the support they appeared to be getting from multiple, remote locations, Balidor warned them to assume they could see a lot more about our team than most SCARB or Black Arrow teams, even the highly ranked ones.

Revik had been told by Yumi and Dalejem that their constructs were now being overseen primarily by Vash and Tarsi.

That was almost unheard of for ground operations, apparently even for the Adhipan. Dalejem told Revik he had never heard of such a thing before, particularly not when Balidor himself led a ground mission.

But there was a lot unusual about this op, Revik sensed, just from the way the Adhipan seers were acting, and the whispers of surprise and raised eyebrows Revik had witnessed a number of times when Yumi updated the group on new developments.

Dalejem warned Revik that a team was also assigned to his light, specifically.

Apparently Vash and Tarsi were overseeing that particular construct, as well.

Revik's own eyebrows went up at that.

He didn't try to probe closer, however.

He didn't even ask many questions.

He also did nothing to test those boundaries, or do anything but try to keep his head down, even within his own unit.

Even so, he felt flickers of recognition, of familiarity, at times—and not always from the Adhipan or Vash side of the Barrier shield. His aunt Tarsi had always worn her *aleimi* like a diamond wall, so he didn't feel her at all. He knew he *wouldn't* feel her, not unless she specifically wanted him to for some reason.

That left the Org.

At least some of the familiarity he felt had to come from them.

The longer they spent out here, the more Revik suspected he knew at least one of the seers following them in that advance hunting team.

He even thought he knew which one.

He chose not to think about that too closely, either.

For one thing, the idea deeply disturbed him.

The idea of seeing Terian out here, given their last interaction in Vietnam, was more than his mind could truly process with any kind of rationality. The last time he'd actually *seen* Terry was in Calcutta, when the other seer was shooting at him.

Terry had hit him, too.

Twice.

But then, Terry was always a good shot, even when he was drunk.

Just thinking about his old partner made his adrenaline spike.

It had been five years.

Five years that stretched into infinity in those caves of the Pamir. Those years of meditation left Revik's memories of his time with the other Rook seer hazy at best.

He knew he'd been high for a lot of it, but that definitely wasn't all of it.

For some reason, Galaith erased a hell of a lot when it came to Revik's memories of Terian. Revik could feel the gaps there. He felt them tangibly, like black holes in his light, empty spots in his structure.

He supposed that made sense.

After all, Terry was his partner.

They'd done a lot of jobs together.

Most of what Revik had known, Terry had to have known, too.

Hell, Revik couldn't even be certain what their last interaction had *been,* precisely. He remembered Calcutta, but his last conversation with the other seer in Saigon was more than a little hazy.

He tried to remember what he'd done to Terian, when he took Kali out of Saigon.

Had he hurt him? He must have disabled him and Raven in some way, but Revik couldn't remember the specifics of that last encounter well enough to know for sure how he'd done it. He couldn't have just knocked them out with his light; they were both too highly trained for that.

He must have hurt them.

He must have hurt them pretty badly, to keep them from coming after him.

It was the only thing that explained how he hadn't been caught, or stopped before he reached India. Given the head start he'd given Kali, and then himself when he began making his way to Cambodia and then Thailand, he must have hurt them.

He never would have gotten out of Saigon, otherwise.

He especially never would have eluded Terian, who could be as dogged in his own way as those monks up in the Pamir.

More so, maybe.

Terian's particular brand of crazy tended to come with a form of obsession that Revik hadn't seen matched in many seers. All seers had a biological and psychological tendency towards fixation and obsession, especially when it came to sexual and romantic connections, but Terian was in a whole other category.

For all his short attention span and strange otherworldliness in the normal day-to-day, when Terian really got his mind set on something, he could be frighteningly focused.

He could be focused to the point of full-blown self-destruction.

But Revik didn't want to think about Terian.

His body had finally more or less adjusted to the heat and humidity by the third day they'd been out there—meaning, the third day following the go-live for the op, which to Revik started on that predawn morning when Balidor first broke Kali out of *Guoreum*.

He hadn't heard anything specific about Kali's condition in the last twenty-four or so hours. Really, not since he'd asked Dalejem and Yumi about her from that stretcher as they carried him up to the make-shift camp at the rendezvous point.

He took a few swallows of water without slowing his pace.

He walked with the others in his team (...*pod*, his mind whispered, inserting the Org term for a basic ground unit before he could restrain himself...) and wiped sweat from his forehead with the back of his hand.

Like he had been for days now, he did his best to keep his mind only on the immediate terrain, and on the seers around him. He and the others currently formed a broken line up the hill, distributed more or less like a guerrilla fighting force, but Revik could tell they still formed more of a diversion and a buffer for Balidor's group than an offensive fighting team.

That could flip on a dime, of course.

If Kali needed them, the team's focus could do a full one-eighty.

Revik knew that. Some part of him waited for that, and

waited for the order that would turn them back into a forward unit, not simply a support team.

He could feel how close that order was at times.

The particular slope they traveled up now angled steeper and higher than the last few. The ridge of jungle-covered mountain formed most of one wall around a low, bowl-like valley filled with more grazing land.

When Revik stopped and stared long enough, he could see scattered shadows covering that field, especially under the trees and by the river tributary that ran along the valley's far wall. Revik knew from the way the shadows moved, they formed a good-sized herd of grazing cattle.

He could feel the Org construct getting closer to them.

Now that the sun had begun to sink behind the hills to his left, Revik found the tension in his body worsening. The nights were more difficult for him for some reason, in terms of the *aleimic* side of things. He had a tendency to resonate more with the Org constructs late at night, possibly because he was tired and controlled his light less well.

He watched the sun dip lower towards the horizon and fought to prepare himself mentally to spend another night out here, and to keep his light focused on Vash and the other Asian seers as much as he possibly could.

Still, he knew the attacks would come as soon as the darkness settled.

Those attacks would worsen in the early hours.

They would worsen not long after midnight struck.

As far as sleep went, Yumi usually stopped their group not long after the Org team stopped, which only happened for a few hours at most, and often less than that.

Each of them in Yumi's unit would be lucky to get thirty, maybe forty minutes of sleep in a stretch, as they rotated through some combination of guard duty—both the Barrier variety and the physical kind—and catnaps with the other infiltrators.

Revik knew that was part of their psychological sparring with the Org, too.

The Rooks would make certain they always got more sleep than their quarry.

They would also try to make them want it.

They would push every individual seer to work around their own infiltrators to get it. Knowing it was a power play didn't really help to combat the effects. Sleep deprivation was harder on seers than humans in some ways, in that it depleted their light, making them weak in more than simply the physical.

That was part of their role as quarry, though.

They could only do what they could to maintain a safe lead, to protect Balidor, and to buy the seers ahead of them time—time for whatever it was Kali needed time for.

The seers ahead of them were probably carrying Kali by now.

The thought brought a low stab of pain that caught him off guard.

Unfortunately, Revik wasn't the only one to feel it.

A few of the nearby seers jumped a little, glancing at him.

It wasn't sexual pain, at least—not that time.

It was more like worry mixed with a deeper, sharper, less-specific anxiety around the flavor of the Org's construct following them.

He knew Terry would want to kill Kali.

He remembered his partner well enough for that.

If Terry was really out here, and Terry knew who Kali was, and knew she was the escaped prisoner he and his people chased, he would definitely want to kill her.

Knowing Terry, he would be obsessing on killing Kali.

He would be obsessing on making Revik *watch* him kill Kali.

Terian being involved in this mess might even explain why the Rooks took Kali in the first place. It explained why

Balidor doubted Galaith was the one who ordered his people to bring Kali here. Knowing Terry, he could have done it on his own—outside the chain of command, even against Galaith's orders.

It wouldn't be the first time.

In fact, the more Revik thought about it, the more he could very easily picture Terian doing exactly that, especially if he somehow found out where Kali was.

He'd do it out of spite. He'd do it out of revenge.

He might even do it to lure Revik out in the open.

Assuming the Org continued to track Revik's whereabouts after he left their employ, and Terry got ahold of that information somehow, Revik's old partner would likely do anything he could to get Revik out of those monk's caves. The very idea of Revik being in there, meditating around a bunch of "kneelers," would have driven Terry either into paroxysms of laughter—or rants born of disbelief and fury—or both.

Likely both.

The pain in Revik's gut sharpened a second time at the thought.

It wasn't as bad that time.

Even so, it was intense enough that Revik found himself wishing Kali's damned mate would get her out of here already.

Why the fuck would *anyone* choose to have a baby out in the jungle?

Why didn't they have more backup at least?

Not just in the Barrier, but *down here,* on the ground. They should have five times this number of infiltrators helping her, given who she was.

He saw a few seers in the team glance at him, curiosity in their eyes.

"Why are we going this way?" he muttered to himself.

He wiped sweat off his brow with the back of his forearm as he said it. He gazed up the tree-filled slope and felt his jaw harden. He'd been talking to himself mostly, barely muttering really, but Mara surprised him by answering, speaking in an almost normal tone of voice from where she walked slightly behind him.

"We're going this way because your wannabe girlfriend is an intermediary, Rook," the female seer said, a thread of humor in her voice. "...and apparently, she's calling the shots right now, not brother Balidor. So stop your whining, Dehgoies."

"Is whining against the law, now?" Ontari asked. He winked at Revik. "I think someone should tell sister Dalai that, if so."

"Bite me," the same seer said sweetly.

Dalai trudged up the hill on Revik's other side, an expressive frown on her fine-featured face. She looked about as seer as she possibly could, with the distinctive Asian-seer features and dark, purple-blue irises with orange rings.

"...Is it *my* fault these wretched swamplands don't agree with my delicate constitution?"

She sniffed expressively, and gave Ontari a flat look.

Ontari snorted a laugh. He rolled his eyes towards Revik.

"Don't believe her for a second, brother Dehgoies. I've seen her chop the heads off rats and eat them, when we were hungry enough."

Revik smiled a little in spite of himself, clicking softly.

"Should I tell him about our last job in Afghanistan, brother?" Dalai asked, her voice even more mockingly sweet. "I'm sure he would *love* to hear that story, Oni."

"No," Ontari said, laughing again.

Mara gripped Revik's arm.

It caused him to jump, then to look down at her face.

"I know," she said conspiratorially. She gave him another grin, a glint in her light eyes. "Why don't you use the time we have out here to try and learn how to walk quieter, Rook?

That, or we can help Gar lose weight like he said he wanted, and make him carry you up the hill?"

Revik glanced at Garensche.

He didn't slow his pace as he hiked up the slope.

The big seer probably carried half the camp requisitions on his broad back already.

Garensche looked at him in the same set of seconds, a frown on his thick lips.

"The hell I will," he said, his voice a louder mutter than Revik's had been. "No one wants to lose weight that badly, sister Mara."

On Gar's other side, Poresh broke out in a laugh, as did Dalai.

"Come on, brother Gar," Poresh teased. "You know you want to. Any excuse to get our youngster Rook alone."

When Gar looked over at the two of them, Dalai slapped the big seer playfully on the shoulder.

"You *did* say you wanted to lose weight. I heard you. Same as Mara."

"Not by giving myself a hernia," Garensche retorted. He clicked and smiled despite his tone. "Are you all forgetting how fucking heavy that damned Rook is? He may look narrow, but he has bones made of iron, I swear it. That, or—"

"Are you sure those were his bones?" Dalai teased.

She gave Revik's crotch a pointed glance.

"Shut up, all of you," Yumi cut in.

Her voice came out quiet, but still managed to penetrate the banter. She gave Dalai, Mara, and Poresh particularly hard stares. "Are we on a job here, or flirting with the ex-Rook? Which is it?"

"Can't we do both?" Gar asked, grinning at her.

"No," Yumi said, her voice colder.

A few more of them chuckled, even Vikram, who was normally quiet.

Revik felt flickers of humor from the group more generally, along with wise-ass remarks a number of them seemed to think better of and suppress, given Yumi's threatening looks.

As for the jokes themselves, Revik didn't take any of it personally. He was used to that kind of thing. Being a smart-ass was kind of a military staple.

It was just one of many ways of whistling in the dark.

When Revik glanced forward, he saw Dalejem frowning back at the rest of them, too. He looked even more annoyed than Yumi. Revik saw his light green eyes settle the hardest on Mara, but he couldn't get a sense of what that was about, either.

Or maybe he just didn't want to.

He brushed it from his mind.

He gripped his rifle a little tighter and hitched the backpack higher on his shoulders in the same pause it took him to rearrange the gear. He'd been pulled into the rotation with equipment and camp set up and break-down like the rest of them. Although really, he'd put himself into that rotation, without being told, or even asked.

As soon as he finished adjusting his pack, he felt another thread of recognition whisper around his light. Someone monitoring the shield around Revik's *aleimi* knocked the thread away, but the proximity of that familiar light, which felt more and more like Terian, brought a rush of adrenaline back into Revik's blood.

It also got his legs moving faster.

They hiked in silence for what felt like another few hours.

Throughout all of it, Revik felt probes like that, only to have them pulled away by one of the Adhipan or Pamir seers, and once by Yumi herself. She glanced at him when it happened that time, frowning slightly, although it felt more like worry than an accusation.

The realization reassured him.

But truthfully, not a lot.

He'd gone back to more or less spacing out, focusing blankly on the jungle, when another... *something*... hit into their Barrier construct.

That time, it wasn't from the Org.

Revik felt it through the others first.

Eventually the original impulse reached enough of his light that he could pinpoint direction, if not the exact flavor or presence from the Barrier. Once enough of it filtered over his *aleimi* for him to get a sense of where the order originated, understanding caused his breath to suck in, even as every seer in his group came to a dead halt.

None of them spoke.

They stood, listening.

Their lights went utterly still.

It was so quiet, Revik could hear Dalai breathing beside him.

He saw her small white fingers knuckle into a clench around the straps of her backpack, even as she glanced at him. He also felt the question in her light.

He sent back an impulse, no words.

The impulse essentially meant, *I don't know.*

He was still standing there, breathing into the silence of the trees, when Yumi spoke, causing all of them to jump a little.

She spoke to Revik.

"Looks like you got your wish, pup," she said, her voice holding a thread of humor. "I guess your friend isn't as reckless as you'd thought."

Ontari answered instead of Revik.

"Which wish was that?" he asked, his voice joking. "Or do we want to know?"

Despite the male seer's words, Revik felt the tension in the group deflate, even as relief swam through the mobile construct as a whole.

Revik understood the why of that, too.

Whatever he had felt up ahead, it definitely didn't belong to the Rooks.

Yumi exhaled in a series of soft clicks along with the rest of them.

"His wish for Kali to have called in more of the cavalry," Yumi said. "To not depend solely on us... the lowly Adhipan."

Revik could hear the smirk in her voice.

He also felt and heard the relief there.

Despite her teasing, and the open eye roll, Revik felt relief on her much more strongly. He felt it in the others as well, as soon as her resonance with the other infiltrators rippled through the rest of their group's light.

Feeling somewhat emboldened by it, Revik reached out tentatively with his *aleimi*. For the first time in days, he actively scanned for a specific frequency in the Barrier he'd felt, rather than letting it trickle through the shields the others held around him.

Once he'd aimed his light in the right direction, he could immediately see what Yumi meant... partly because Yumi herself caught him in the act.

Once she had, she plugged him directly into the new influence in the construct.

Presence washed over him.

New living lights exploded into Revik's awareness. They popped up all over the hill in front of him as they appeared in Balidor's construct. Revik watched in a kind of awe as more and more of them grew visible.

They grew into a shimmering sea of light in the dark.

As he looked over them all in wonder, Revik realized they'd been deliberately concealed from view until they got close enough to provide an effective message.

That message wasn't meant for him, or for anyone in Balidor's team.

It was a direct, unambiguous, billboard-sized message to the Org teams chasing them.

Feeling the strength represented there, behind that distinctive flare of light, Revik felt his shoulders abruptly relax.

He hadn't noticed how tense he was.

Not until that tension lifted.

"Reinforcements," he muttered.

"Yes," Yumi said, smiling at him. "It looks like the group Kali's husband told us about has finally arrived."

Revik frowned faintly, but didn't comment.

Kali's husband was behind this? These were *his* people?

The thought bewildered him more than a little, and made him wonder again who this Uye really was. He didn't say anything though, or even bother to tell Yumi that was an intelligence briefing he clearly hadn't been privy to.

*We couldn't tell you, brother,* Dalejem murmured in his mind. *Not until now. Not with the Rooks' infiltrators attacking your mind every few seconds. You should not take this personally. It is not an indication of distrust.*

Revik glanced at him.

He flushed a little to realize he'd once more been overheard, but relaxed at the other's words. Holding that still, pale-green gaze, he nodded, once. He gestured briefly in seer to acknowledge his words, and to tell him he was not offended.

Once Yumi finished showing them the full strength of their new allies, she once more closed down the specific thread hooking their group to Balidor's construct. Revik figured the caution remained due to their physical proximity to the Org extraction team.

"Brother Uye speaks for this team, as I told brother Revik," Yumi said.

She glanced around at the group as a whole.

"It is a large number of infiltrators," she explained. "Most of them highly ranked. Quite a lot of reinforcements, my brothers and sisters. But we cannot afford to drop our vigilance. There is a good chance the Rooks will call for reinforcements, as well."

"From where?" Vikram asked in heavily-accented Prexci. "This team of Uye's. Where do they come from?"

Revik glanced at him, surprised.

Apparently he wasn't the only one to wonder this.

"Unknown," Yumi said. "They are not Adhipan. Nor Seven."

"They are friendly, though?" Ontari asked, his voice wary.

"Very friendly. They are here for the Bridge," she smiled.

Revik heard a few sighs next to him, with more relief in them than he would have guessed. He hadn't realized how much their precarious situation between the extraction team and Kali had been stressing all of them out.

He alone seemed stunned by the rest of her words.

"The Bridge?" he said into that silence. "Is that known then? For certain?"

Yumi gave him another direct look.

She didn't answer his question, however.

"Balidor is coming here," she said instead. "We are to wait for him to reach us. He says they're only about fifteen minutes out, and that we should remain ready to move, if need be. So packs on the ground, but stick with field reqs if you're hungry."

Revik glanced around as other seers began shrugging heavy packs off their shoulders.

They set them on the ground where they stood or leaned them against trees.

A few had canteens out already, and were drinking from them freely, heads tilted back. It didn't really cool down very much out here at night. Not enough, anyway, not for the pace they maintained, or how much gear and clothing they wore and carried.

Still, Revik felt some surprise in the others, at Yumi's revelation about Balidor.

Then it seemed like they were all looking at him.

Meaning Revik himself.

"Yes," Yumi said, answering some question Revik hadn't heard. "It is for him. I'll let brother Balidor explain in full."

"Is that such a good idea, sister?" Vikram's voice sharpened. "Given what happened last time? It strikes me as... unwise."

"We will let Balidor explain."

"But sister—"

"Again," Yumi broke in. Her voice grew harder, less compromising. "That is between him and his gods. He will have to decide for himself."

Realizing they were talking about him again, Revik looked over at her, seeing the bare outline of her face with his combat-trained night vision. The female seer smiled at him, but that time, Revik didn't feel a lot of humor in her light.

In fact, what he felt came a lot closer to sympathy.

"Looks like you've been requested again, pup," she said only.

Before he could say anything, Yumi shrugged off her own pack.

She promptly sat on top of it and tugged a piece of jerky out of a pocket in her vest. Revik watched her chew on it. He tried to decide if he wanted to ask one of the dozen or so questions now hovering over the construct they all shared.

He decided he didn't.

He shrugged off his own pack instead.

He let it fall to the ground pretty much where he stood, then bent his knees to sit on it, as Yumi had done. Tugging the canteen from his belt, he took a long drink.

He let the canteen fall to his thigh a few seconds later with a gasp, and pulled out a piece of jerky. He chewed on it mechanically as he slowed his breathing.

He deliberately let his body rest.

He continued to bite and chew as he aimed his eyes up at the dark canopy and the few stars he could see past it, twinkling like sentries from between the dark leaves.

Whatever was coming, whatever they were about to ask him to do, he already knew he'd likely say yes.

He'd say yes, even if there was a good chance it would get him killed.

He had his doubts Balidor didn't already know that.

He had even fewer doubts that Kali herself didn't.

When he sighed, letting his gaze drop back towards the camp, he saw Dalejem watching him, sitting on his own pack a few meters away. The seer frowned with his perfectly-formed mouth, his handsome features hard, his canteen gripped in one hand. He stared directly and unambiguously at Revik with those light-green and violet eyes.

His sculpted lips hardened in what had to be anger.

Revik hesitated on that unblinking stare, startled by the depth of feeling he saw there.

He didn't know what it meant.

He honestly wasn't sure he wanted to know.

Taking another drink of water, he looked back up at the night sky.

He swallowed as he tried to push that from his mind, as well.

<hr />

They didn't have to wait long.

Fifteen minutes ended up being conservative, despite the distance Revik had felt between them and Balidor's main camp, back when Revik first looked for them.

Either Balidor and his people were already on the move when Balidor sent advance notice of his arrival, or they navigated their way through the dark jungle a hell of a lot faster than Revik could have imagined.

Revik could feel by then that the Org extraction team had halted, as well.

He didn't let himself dwell on how those two events likely tied together.

When Balidor entered the clearing he didn't hesitate, but walked directly up to Revik. The Adhipan leader approached him so surely, it might have been broad daylight, not pitch black under the jungle leaves and branches.

Once Balidor stood over him, he spoke aloud, seemingly to the entire group.

"Galaith has agreed to a parlay," he announced.

Revik's eyes and light twitched towards the periphery of their circle.

He felt Zula and Tobe out there, along with four other seers whose names he had never learned, but whose lights he recognized from the planning camp outside of *Guoreum,* and from the Adhipan construct more generally.

At least one of them was part of his protective detail inside the Barrier.

"...Galaith has a stipulation," Balidor said, at the end of his long pause. His eyes swiveled to Revik. "He will only deal with you, brother."

Revik just sat there, on his pack, looking up at him.

He wasn't surprised by the Adhipan leader's words.

Frankly, he didn't know why anyone would be.

Regardless, he felt the seers in his unit staring at him.

He also felt them talking amongst themselves, just outside his hearing.

He felt those whispers more strongly from some in the group than others, but the overall feeling was more or less consistent, at least from those in Yumi's unit. They considered him one of theirs now. They'd seen him collapse in the road outside *Guoreum*. They'd risked their lives, been shot at, carried him for miles, all to save his life.

They thought this was a trap.

They didn't want him to do it.

They wanted him to say no.

In all of that, Revik felt Dalejem especially strongly.

The green-eyed male wished an especially amplified version of that hard "no" at him so strongly, Revik had to disentangle himself from the other seer's light, and from the imperative behind it, to even see his own thoughts. After he'd more or less succeeded in doing that, he still struggled to think logically about Balidor's request.

He could see what his unit saw.

He could see the lack of transparency there, in the Rooks' light.

He could feel the duplicitousness of it… and especially of Galaith.

They could see a teacher who craved contact with his former student.

They didn't like it. They didn't like it at all.

Truthfully, Revik didn't like it, either.

Again, however, he'd already known what he would do.

"Yes," he said.

He didn't realize he'd been staring at the ground when he said it, not until he looked up. He met Balidor's gaze, which he could only just see in his adjusted night vision.

"I'll do it," he said. "All right."

He felt a stab of angry light at him, and turned his head.

Dalejem stood there.

Revik's *aleimi* picked out more details than his eyes. He felt the Dalejem's arms taut at his sides, his hands clenched into fists where they rested on his gun belt. Revik felt another pulse of anger from the other seer and winced, in spite of himself.

*I'm sorry*, he sent to him quietly.

The other seer only sent another plume of harder anger.

"I'm going," Dalejem said aloud to Balidor, his voice cold. "If you're bringing him to them, like a sacrificial-fucking *lamb*, then I'm going, too."

Balidor gave him a long-seeming stare, then nodded.

"Agreed."

The Adhipan leader looked around at the rest of the group, his expression unmoving. His living light didn't so much as ripple from what Revik could feel.

"We can take seven, including Dehgoies," Balidor said, still looking around. "That leaves spots for four more. Volunteers?"

"Me," Vikram said, surprising Revik.

He glanced at the Indian-looking seer, who smiled at him from the dark. The seer's white teeth shone at him, strangely reassuring.

Then next voice that spoke surprised Revik even more.

"Me," Mara said. She stepped forward. "I am coming."

"Me, as well," Yumi said.

"I will go, too," Dalai added.

Balidor nodded. He looked around at all of them.

"That is seven." His eyes returned to Revik. For the first time, his light exuded a faint worry, even as he adjusted the rifle slung over his shoulder.

"No packs," he said, his voice still expressionless. "We leave now." Balidor looked at Garensche. "You are in charge of the remainder of the group out here, brother. My people, too. I would like all of you to stay here, in roughly this area, until we come back. Use sentries. And be ready to move, if I call for reinforcement."

The big seer nodded. He glanced at Revik with those hazel eyes.

Revik felt worry ripple off his light, too.

It occurred to him only then that at least half of the seers here didn't expect him to come back. Not alive, anyway.

The other half seemed to think he would at least come back damaged.

Revik swallowed, but shoved the thought aside.

He found himself standing with the small group of volunteers. He arranged the gun strapped around his shoulder not unlike Balidor had just done, but more in a kind of nervous patterning than out of any real need. He was still standing there when his self-appointed personal bodyguards and Balidor started to move.

They aimed for the opening between the trees to the south of where they now stood, so back in the direction they'd already walked.

Only Dalejem stopped beside him.

Before Revik realized what the other male intended, Dalejem formed an *aleimic* link, just the two of them. As he did it, he shielded them from everyone else.

More than that, he pushed the rest of the seers' lights out.

*You don't have to do this,* he sent. Dalejem barely paused before his light grew fainter, becoming the barest trace of a whisper. *Don't do it, Revik. Please. We'll find another way.*

Revik felt a strange jolt in his chest.

He realized it was because Dalejem had used his given name.

He looked at him, and found the other male wouldn't meet his gaze.

*I have to,* Revik sent simply.

*Why?* Dalejem demanded. His light sparked with real anger. *Why do you have to?*

Revik sighed. He clicked softly under his breath. *Because Balidor wouldn't have brought this to me, if there was another way.*

He didn't say the other thing he thought.

He didn't say what he felt, without knowing how he felt it.

Kali was having her baby.

Revik felt Dalejem frown. He sent the green-eyed seer a pulse of warmth.

*Don't worry, brother,* he sent. *It'll be all right. I have all of you there with me. We aren't going in blind.*

Dalejem didn't answer.

When the older seer moved away an instant later, he severed the link between them and stepped deliberately out of Revik's light.

Revik felt his chest tighten again, for a different reason that time.

Still, he managed to keep it off his expression.

He gripped the rifle he wore more tightly.

He followed the small group of Adhipan into the gap between the trees. By the time he'd more or less caught up with Dalejem and the others, his mind had fallen mostly blank. He deliberately focused on the sounds and smells of the jungle, and nothing else.

He barely noticed as Vikram and Dalai took up position behind him.

## CHAPTER 15
# PARLAY

Revik felt the panic start in his chest before they were halfway there.

It worsened exponentially as they approached the edges of the mobile construct of the Org extraction team.

He was remembering now, viscerally, nearly physically, what *Guoreum* had done to him, like an animal remembers being burnt in a fire. The memory flipped a panic switch in the back of his head. It caused his heart rate to speed up, his breathing to tighten.

They were still at least a hundred yards from the clearing Balidor told them about, but Revik could already feel them.

He felt the Org pod up there, waiting for them.

Waiting for him.

No one in Revik's group apart from Balidor had spoken a word since they left the others, not where Revik could hear it, anyway. He couldn't recall a single whisper of speech or meaning for at least the past half-hour. He hadn't felt anything at all inside the construct, not even directed at someone other than him.

Balidor briefed them on their way back down the hill.

He'd mainly used nonverbal, packed intel inside the construct.

After that, silence descended over their group.

Revik felt a keening kind of nausea in his belly the closer they got to the rendezvous, one that—for once—had absolutely nothing to do with separation pain.

It was fear.

Pure, unbridled fear.

He felt the seers around him react to that fear.

They drew closer to him physically even as they enveloped him in more of their light. Unfortunately, none of what they did really helped to mitigate the fear itself. Revik started to worry he wouldn't be able to handle this. He might freak out for real, even apart from what the construct would do to him when he crossed that line—

*Brother,* a voice spoke gently into his mind. *Calm yourself. There is more than just me protecting you out here.*

Revik jumped a little, glancing to his right.

He found Balidor walking beside him, watching him through the dark.

The older seer smiled at him reassuringly.

He glanced briefly at Dalejem as he walked.

*I know you only said it to calm your friend,* the Adhipan leader added. *But you spoke truth to him just now. We won't let anything happen to you, brother Revik. I promise you.*

He smiled more broadly at Revik's frown.

His thoughts grew a more prominent thread of humor.

*Vash would skin me, for one... not to mention what your aunt would do to me. Trust me when I say this. You will be all right. I will make sure of it. So will those aiding us. So will Kali. She has her people involved with this, as well.*

*It's not you I don't trust,* Revik began. He knew his panic was spilling out over into his thoughts, but he couldn't pull it back. *It's not any of you I don't trust. It's me. I can't handle this. I dropped like a dead person outside of Guoreum. You saw it—*

*That was my fault, brother Revik.*

*No,* Revik sent, exasperated. *It wasn't—*

*Yes. It was.*

Balidor's mental voice grew an edge, but it didn't feel aimed at Revik.

*That was a mistake I haven't come close to apologizing for deeply enough, brother,* Balidor added grimly. *...and likely never will. I am truly sorry, Revik. That was completely and utterly my fault.*

*It really wasn't, though,* Revik sent, unable to let it go. *It wasn't your fault—*

*It was,* Balidor cut in. He gave him a hard look through the dark. *It was entirely my fault, brother Revik, and trust me, I do not speak only my own opinion in saying it. I thought your Aunt Tarsi would fire me as head of the Adhipan for what I did there. If she did not have me banished from the Pamir altogether.*

The thought brought Revik's mind to a brief halt.

Fired from the Adhipan?

Was that even possible? Or just a term of speech?

Balidor surprised him.

He chuckled in the recesses of Revik's mind.

*Oh, it's possible, brother. Believe me. Tarsi might have had to persuade Vash, if that had been her decision, since he is the official head of the Council of Seven. But truthfully, I don't think that would have been overly difficult to do. Vash was as angry with me as she was, even if he expressed that anger far less explosively than your aunt.*

Revik didn't answer, not directly.

Even so, Balidor's words that time surprised him even more.

Vash... angry? He couldn't even imagine Vash angry.

He'd assumed the Adhipan leader had been teasing him when he joked about Vash skinning him or even berating him, especially out here.

Balidor chuckled again, softer.

Before Revik could think of a response—

His *aleimi* lit up violently.

The same sensation brought his nausea forward in a harsh wave.

His breath stopped abruptly in his chest, so hard, so fast, he choked on it.

It only occurred to him a few seconds later that Balidor had been distracting him.

They had reached the edge of the Org construct.

Before Revik could even think about halting the forward motion of his body, or even slowing his feet as his living light screamed in protest—

He had crossed that line into the Pyramid's wave.

He didn't feel it as strongly that time.

The light around him shifted.

He felt that line, yes… but he felt his connection to Balidor more.

He felt his connection to the rest of the seers who more or less encircled him now, too. He glanced around in near-wonder as he felt them protecting him on all sides, their lights hardening into dense, nearly opaque shields that cushioned his light, forming a solid barrier between Revik and the structured, fast-moving, metallic light of the Org.

Feeling that wall, Revik forced himself to breathe.

He kept walking.

He breathed more regularly as he adjusted to the shift.

As they approached the clearing he could feel up ahead in the jungle—a clearing he felt only via the *aleimi* of the seers around him—an actual, physical light ignited between the trees.

As it did, Revik realized they were even closer than he'd realized.

He recognized the peculiar, greenish glow of multiple organic *yisso* torches even as he watched Balidor enter the last row of trees before the clearing itself.

THE EX-ROOK • 181

Dalejem and Yumi followed without hesitation.

The three of them left Revik to be the one to hesitate, right at that edge, even as he felt a flush of warmth and reassurance from Vikram and Dalai, who walked directly behind him.

*It's okay, brother,* Vikram told him softly. *It's not only Balidor and the Council. We won't let those* endruk et dugra *bastards touch you, either.*

Revik glanced back, even as he saw Dalai nod.

She gestured her agreement with Vikram emphatically with one hand.

It hit Revik again that they felt responsible for him.

However it was they actually felt about him, or what he'd once been, they felt responsible for him now. They'd adopted him as one of their own.

The thought touched him.

It touched him more than he could fully feel at first, even without knowing exactly what it meant.

He took a deep breath. He forced himself to move forward. He walked, blinking, holding a hand up to the light, into the lit clearing behind Balidor and the others.

For a moment, a scarce instant, it felt as if he'd been transported into another world.

Maybe a whole other version of himself.

It was one he'd rather have forgotten, frankly.

※

AFTER THE BAREST PAUSE, HE WALKED OUT PAST THE OTHERS, into the center of the clearing.

He did it partly to prove to himself he could.

He did it partly out of posturing.

He did it partly to normalize this in some way.

He was supposed to be the emissary, after all.

Something about being inside an honest-to-gods Org

construct and still on his feet—of being cocooned from all but the barest tastes of that Dreng-soaked light—turned off the panic switch that nearly incapacitated him when he stood outside those construct walls.

It flipped him into pure infiltrator mode, instead.

His shoulders straightened. His gait shifted into a pure military, fighter's stalk, almost before he realized he'd made the change.

He felt the seers around him react to that change—meaning those on his side.

Some, like Balidor, reacted with pure relief.

Revik felt flickers of other reactions too, everything from surprise to a faint unease as they adjusted to this other side of him, and of his light.

During the debrief down the hill, Balidor informed Revik of the basic strategy. He'd asked Revik's opinion of that strategy, given his familiarity with how the Org operated, but Revik hadn't a whole lot to contribute, really.

It was clear Balidor understood the Rooks well.

Moreover, the Adhipan's intelligence was good.

It was scary good, although Revik had to remind himself that he, meaning Revik himself, wouldn't remember anything truly sensitive about the way the Org functioned anyway.

Balidor's instructions were specific, down to how he wanted Revik to stand.

He asked Revik to show no visible signs of weakness if he could help it, in the event the temptation might prove too much for the Org pod. He instructed Revik to ignore any hits at his *aleimi*, to let Balidor and his protection detail handle that end of things. He warned Revik to stay out of his emotions and reactions as much as he could.

Balidor told Revik he would need to stand in front, as emissary, just as Galaith requested.

Revik would hold onto his guns, but not hold any in his hands.

Remembering all of that now, Revik entered the clearing with his rifle slung behind his back, his handguns in their holsters. He kept his hands visible, to emphasize the fact that they were empty. He found himself sliding into even more of a fighter's walk as he approached the line of Org infiltrators.

That was habit, too, he supposed.

His mind remained more or less blank after he broke the circle of light that bled into the jungle trees from the two *yisso* torches. He could see now that each of those torches was held by a separate Org agent, one female and one male. The torch-bearing agents stood on either side of the ring of trees, so that most of the area was lit, along with every face.

All of the Org agents were armed, of course.

All but the torch-bearers held weapons in their hands.

Revik noted that fact, even as he deliberately ignored it.

He walked to the center of the clearing, all while maintaining that strangely empty mental space. If anything, the clarity and silence of that space heightened, the more faces of Org infiltrators he could see. The reality of them—as fellow seers, as physical beings—snapped him into a totally different headspace, turning them from bogeymen to tangible targets, something he could wrap his arms and mind around, something he could comprehend as real.

That simple shift of perspective sent him into an even deeper calm.

Instead of fearing them, he measured them, like he would adversaries on any op.

Or hell, like he would any *seers* in a situation where he couldn't predict the outcome, particularly if he found himself heavily outnumbered.

His *aleimi* found twenty distinct infiltrators.

He found them fast, then confirmed the number with a flickering gaze.

Some were more visible than others, but he didn't doubt the count.

His *aleimi* took snapshots of the light-markers on a few of them for future reference. Apart from their leader, he didn't recognize any of those lights specifically.

Well, at least not that he could remember.

He suspected more Org agents watched them from the jungle.

He felt flickers of a separate construct, along with the barest markers of some kind of formation to the east and the west of where he stood.

His military mind made those wings wrapped around the main unit.

Protection, but also with offensive capability.

Not a dumb move, "parlay" or not.

But then, Terian was never dumb.

Nor were the Org military planners, whatever their other shortcomings.

Revik's mind told him a minimum of twenty-four additional infiltrators he couldn't see. Maybe as many as thirty.

*Twenty-five,* a voice murmured in his mind.

Revik glanced behind him.

His eyes met Balidor's. He felt his shoulders lose a fraction of their tension when he realized it was the Adhipan leader who had spoken. The two of them were still connected tightly enough to communicate, even in here. The thought relieved him enough that he dared to answer back, hoping it stayed inside the construct-within-a-construct.

*They have us flanked. They could cut us off,* he sent, soft.

*I know,* Balidor sent back. He pulsed reassurance at him. *They've got some unusual qualities in this construct, brother, so stay alert. I sense close to ten out there, on either side of our exit path... with some of the nearer lights being mirrored decoys to give us close to accurate numbers while obscuring their formation. So we know how many, but not where, precisely.*

*They've got three times our number,* Revik sent. *Probably more that could reach us by air in a handful of minutes.*

*I know that, too, brother.*

*My point is, what if they won't let us leave?* Revik asked.

*Then it's war,* Balidor replied. *Galaith knows that.*

*But does Terry?* Revik murmured, quieter still. *More to the point, will he care, even if he does know?*

Balidor didn't answer him directly.

Instead, he directed Revik's attention to a different seer in the main group.

*That one knows,* he told Revik, equally soft. *I suspect he cares, too. Moreover, he knows who I am... and that I can hear him. I suspect he has a direct line to Galaith.*

Following Balidor's mind's nudge, Revik's eyes found an unusually tall, violet-eyed seer. The male lived somewhere in the five-hundred-year range, with iron gray hair and a Nazi scar that nearly bisected his long, angular face.

Even from across the clearing, Revik could feel the intensity of the seer's light. With that charged frequency came flavors of structure that felt unusual to him.

Balidor was right.

That seer was formidable.

Exceedingly high sight rank. Likely high not only in potential but in actual, particularly given his age and the level of training Revik could sense on him.

But Revik knew he couldn't avoid looking at his ex-partner for much longer.

He couldn't avoid Terry forever.

After he finished measuring that older, gray-haired seer, after he tasted a harder snapshot of the fast-moving structures above his head with his *aleimi*, Revik's eyes swiveled back to the space directly in front of where he stood.

The seer who stood there was significantly younger than the one with the violet eyes.

He was also shockingly, disconcertingly more familiar.

Revik felt his breath get lost somewhere in his chest as he stared at his old partner.

They'd been more than partners, in the work sense, that is.

They'd been closer to brothers—*real* brothers—as close as anyone could be to that, while living inside the silver light of the Org.

At the very least, they'd been friends.

Revik didn't move for what felt like a long number of minutes. He couldn't move. He could scarcely breathe normally, or blink his eyes. Even so, he felt his body and light fighting to control themselves, to keep from showing any sign of strain.

He stood there, frozen in the amber-eyed stare of Terian.

For a long moment, neither of them spoke.

Revik looked over the handsome seer. He recognized the body he wore, recognized so many things about his light. He traced every element of the familiar features: the high cheekbones, the dark auburn hair with streaks of highlight from the sun, those weirdly intense and penetrating amber eyes. Revik looked over Terry's state-of-the-art organic uniform, the gun he held in long-fingered hands.

Revik knew how dexterous those hands were.

He knew it in the good and the bad sense.

He knew how fast Terian could move.

He would have knives on him, at least four, but likely closer to ten.

Revik's gaze took in his lean, muscular form, the strange tilt he felt on Terian's light, the intense and weirdly beautiful geometries that went with that tilt.

Silence from Terry was more than he could really deal with, though.

Maybe it was the amount of time Terian let pass, or the pure anomaly of this particular seer remaining quiet for any amount of time at all, but Revik ended up being the one to break that impasse. The fact that it was him who spoke first, and not Terian, caused a number of seers on both sides of that line to jump perceptibly where they stood.

"I am told you agreed to this," Revik said.

His voice came out low, deep, with more accent than usual.

When Terian didn't speak, Revik gestured vaguely with one hand. He wasn't entirely sure what he meant by the motion, or if it came purely from nerves.

"Terry?" he queried. He hit the words a little harder. "Is this true? Did you agree to act as go-between for Galaith on this thing?"

Again, the amber-eyed seer didn't answer.

As the silence stretched, nerves bled back over Revik's light. He clamped down harder on his *aleimi* when he noticed. He glanced around at the faces of the other Org infiltrators, maybe to distract himself. Or maybe he did it instinctively to collect more information.

In any case, he found himself stopping on one face in particular.

Once his eyes fully landed there, disbelief stole over Revik's light.

He stared at the strange seer, noting the line of light he could feel between that seer and Terian. The longer Revik stared, the more he felt flavors of Terian coiling around the younger seer's *aleimi*, strangling that *aleimi* in obviously intimate ways.

Jesus.

The seer was tall. He stood at nearly Revik's height.

Black hair.

Pale gray eyes, but nothing like Balidor's.

Instead, they appeared closer in color and shape to Revik's own, only with a more opaque tint, one that might even look blue in the right light. Under the *yisso* torches, his irises shone almost white.

Angular face. Narrow mouth.

The similarities were too obvious to ignore.

This fucking seer looked like him.

And Terian was sleeping with him.

Terian was screwing a look-alike of Revik himself.

Something in that understanding brought a sick tilt to Revik's mind and light. It flooded him with whispers and tastes of memories he no longer wanted anywhere near him, or anywhere near his light. He couldn't stop or suppress his reaction entirely, but managed to shove the worst of it aside, long enough to tear his eyes off the male with those pale, nearly colorless eyes.

He found himself looking at Terian.

Without knowing he meant to, he found himself speaking.

"New pet, Terry?" he asked.

He regretted the words, as soon as he'd said them.

He also heard the anger in his own voice.

Terian let the barrel of his rifle drop, right before he slung it behind him, over his shoulder. Revik didn't know if Terian did that to mirror how Revik wore his own rifle, or just to make it clear he didn't see him, or any of the Adhipan seers behind him, as a threat.

Knowing Terry, it was likely the latter.

Regardless, Revik felt himself tensing again. He felt something shift in the light of the male seer standing in front of him.

Revik already managed to set him off somehow.

Maybe he'd simply ignited some part of Terian's crazy by pointing out Revik's obvious physical resemblance to Terry's new lover. Remembering how unpredictable Terian could be, especially when he was pissed off about something, didn't exactly help Revik assess the situation calmly. Remembering bits and pieces of how Terian used to screw with *him*, Revik specifically, when he felt wronged by him, or angry, didn't help, either.

Nor did the fact that Revik couldn't remember the last thing he'd done or said to his ex-partner. He suspected telling

Terry that wouldn't exactly calm the other male down, though.

"Something like that, yes," Terian answered belatedly.

A smile toyed at the edges of those sculpted lips.

Revik found himself getting more flashes of memory that didn't relax him.

"...Do you approve, Revi'?" Terian added in that lilting voice of his. "He's quite handsome, don't you think?"

Revik frowned. Again, he knew he should drop it.

Yet somehow he didn't.

"Is it for my benefit?" he asked.

"Not entirely, no." Terian's smile grew into a smirk. He glanced back at Revik's look-alike. "He's quite... accommodating."

Revik fought a frown out of his expression that time, too.

He felt the thread of light Terian aimed at him when he said it. He felt Balidor block and then deflect it, but not before Revik got the barest taste.

Terian wasn't going to let this go.

It might not have mattered what Revik did or said, but Revik's opening words to the amber-eyed seer definitely hadn't helped.

Revik's light hardened instinctively at the thought. He closed off more of it to the Org pod in front of him. Once he'd closed his heart, especially, the feeling that came up in his light edged closer to disgust.

Maybe even contempt.

Something in that felt familiar too, and at the moment, not entirely unwelcome.

"I'm happy for you." Revik gave the tall, gray-eyed seer an openly dismissive look, even knowing he might be inciting Terian more. "...For both of you."

Terian grinned.

Great. Revik already managed to make this a game for him.

"Oh, no need to chime the bells yet, old friend," Terian smiled. "There's always room for more to play, yes? Back in the day, we could have violated him together. He would have liked that, I think. He's got a bit of your masochist's edge."

Revik felt the remark like a punch.

Nausea rose in him, again only marginally related to separation sickness. He caught a glimmer of the images Terian fought to throw at him, even as it crossed his mind that the Adhipan seers—Balidor at least—could see all of it.

The silence stretched.

Revik didn't drop his gaze. He saw the delight dancing in Terian's amber eyes. His old friend could clearly see that his words had gotten to him.

Terian smiled wider.

He aimed that smile at the tall, Revik look-alike he was currently fucking, then looked back at Revik himself.

That smile still danced in his eyes and the edges of his mouth.

"He gets a bit possessive, though, Revi'," Terian said next, lightening his voice. "You'd have to fuck him a *lot*, Revi', to get him over that. Until you broke him, maybe, got him to say uncle. I think he'd like that, too, though, Revi'… as I said, he likes a little pain with his sex. Not as much as *you* do, of course, but then… not many do."

That time, Revik couldn't hold eye-contact.

He averted his gaze. He felt his hands tighten into fists.

His face warmed too, even as he fought not to look at the row of Adhipan seers standing behind him.

Terian chuckled. He clicked at Revik in mock surprise.

"*Gaos.* Did you just blush, Revi'? It used to take considerably more than that, to get such a reaction from you…"

Terry clucked in mock consternation.

"What have they *done* to you, my brother?" he said, still clicking. "And are you as celibate these days as you feel? Perhaps you only fuck Council-approved whores now, and are finding the willing ones difficult to come by? I imagine there are few, if any, who would deign to touch you, given your unsavory past…"

Revik didn't answer that either.

Still, his light coiled into and around the words.

Terian always had that sick insight of his, the ability to see past the surface, even more than most seers. Maybe because he was a sociopath, he was less likely to reinterpret what he saw to fit his own emotional needs. He had few emotional needs—at least for the usual things, for others' approval, love, affection, or whatever else.

Instead, Terry saw things as they were, at least in that more limited sense.

He saw them that way because he needed to, to better manipulate those base reactions to his benefit, or simply to bend those things more easily to his will.

Because of course Terry was right.

Revik knew he was right.

It was a knowledge that had sat with him the whole time he'd been in those caves, although up there, it had been easy to avoid that truth… and to pretend it didn't matter to him.

But he knew the truth.

None of the seers of the Seven or Adhipan would ever want him, not really.

Not after what he'd done.

Not after who and what he'd let himself become under the Rooks. Not after everything he'd done in all those training and interrogation sessions, much less what he'd done during the wars and ops he'd conducted and designed and fought for Galaith. Revik's disconnection from the Org Pyramid had been public. It occurred inside a quasi-public construct at Vash's temple in Seertown, and it was part of the public record now.

All of those in attendance would have talked.

Moreover, many of those who attended didn't strictly need to be there.

Now that he was officially in penance, Revik's years in the Pamir were also public record. That meant any seer could access that information about him if they wanted.

Revik would be paying seer whores the rest of his life.

If he wanted to lie with any of his own kind, he would have to give up on finding willing partners. He would have to pay them. He might even have to pay them a lot.

Unless he found another seer as fucked up and dispossessed as he was—one he happened to want, and who also wanted him—Revik would spend the rest of his life alone.

His future life once he left those caves suddenly felt crystal clear to him.

Apart from Vash and Tarsi, who were old enough they couldn't have more than a hundred years left between them, he'd have no one.

He'd be even more alone than he had been inside the Org, likely for the rest of his life.

Balidor's light swam more deeply into his.

It filled him so completely, it caused Revik's face to heat.

*You don't know that, brother,* Balidor murmured softly.

Warmth pooled in Revik's chest, a denser sympathy.

*…You don't know everything, brother. Not even about yourself.*

Revik glanced behind him, in spite of himself.

He looked over the faces of the Adhipan seers standing there. He avoided Dalejem's green eyes, not wanting to see the expression there, or to know if he'd heard everything that had just passed through his mind. He paused on Balidor's face, instead.

He knew the older seer meant well, at least.

Revik knew he should nod to him, acknowledge his words somehow, but he couldn't seem to make himself do that, either.

Terian took a step towards him.

Somehow, the movement snapped the connection Revik had felt there.

He flinched, swiveled his gaze and full attention back towards the Rook.

He felt his infiltrator's mask return as his mouth hardened.

He couldn't be having emotional moments right now, whatever the cause.

"You really do look... housebroken," Terian said.

That smile grew even more audible in his voice.

"What happened to your light, my friend? Is it true that they stashed you away in Himalayan ice caves after they cleansed your mind? Forced you into penance to plead forgiveness for your sins? I wouldn't have believed it, myself, but all I can feel on you now is the stink of kneeler's mantras and incense."

He paused, waited to see if Revik would rise.

When he didn't, Terian's voice twisted with contempt.

"...Clearly, they feel they've brainwashed you sufficiently by now, though, *na?*" he said, those sculpted lips frowning more. "They wouldn't have let you out of your cage at all, if they didn't. So, what did you promise them, Revi'? Did you promise to be a good little boy, to not go anywhere or do anything without their permission? Is this group here to protect you? Or to make sure I don't corrupt your mind with the *filth* of common sense?"

Revik didn't speak.

He found himself reorienting around Terian though, seeing him more clearly again.

He got enough distance from that initial shock of being so near to his light that he could feel the reactions there.

Terry wasn't as blasé about seeing him as he was pretending.

Revik could feel sparks of that reaction, even if he couldn't untangle them.

Not all of it was anger.

Whatever Revik felt, it was too complex to simply be labeled anger. He could also feel strongly how careful he needed to be with whatever was going on in Terry's light. It would be better not to agitate the Rook even more, not when he was like this.

Terian glanced briefly at his pet, the Revik look-alike.

When he looked back at Revik himself, he smiled, but Revik saw that harder look stand out more prominently in his amber-colored eyes.

Something about that expression caused Revik to tense.

He felt another probing dart of light from the other seer, stronger than before.

Balidor again blocked it.

Not just blocked it—Balidor shoved Terian away from Revik's light.

That time, Revik sent a flicker of gratitude to the seers standing behind him.

Terian frowned.

He stared up at Revik's face. He began tapping his long fingers on the body of the organic rifle he wore. The cadence was rhythmic but weirdly distracting, almost like one of those repetitive noises they would use in interrogation cells to cause stress reactions in their subjects.

Revik glanced at the rifle a second time.

The thing truly was state-of-the-art. About six generations ahead of the relics that Revik and the Adhipan infiltrators wore.

When he glanced up, those amber eyes hadn't left his face.

"Come now, Revi'... tell me," Terian cajoled, when the silence stretched. "Confess your sins to *me* this time, brother, since you never bothered to tell me anything before you left. Is it really true? Are you a believer again, Revi'? Like you were back when we found you in that shithole in Berlin? Are you truly 'in penance,' as the rumors tell me? Or is this just another act to save your worthless skin?"

Clicking softly, Terian shook his auburn-haired head.

"*Gaos.* I confess… it bothers me, brother. It troubles me greatly to see you like this. I never thought I would have to witness the day that you became such a hypocrite again. You always had an enormous capacity for self-deception, of course, but this…"

Terian trailed in his words, still staring at Revik's eyes. He rested both of his forearms on the barrel of his gun.

He focused more intently on Revik's face.

After a few more seconds of staring, the Rook's lips curled into another smile.

"Gods," he murmured. "But they haven't taken all of you, Revi', have they? Not yet. I can still see you there, brother, even under all of that kneeler crap. Tell me, did they really think they could take a poisonous snake and turn him into a fluffy bunny rabbit?"

Terian's smile grew wider.

Another probe of his light darted out.

Revik flinched at the intensity he felt behind it. Before his infiltrator mask could break, Balidor blocked Terian again, pushing him off Revik's *aleimi*.

Even so, that one was close enough, Revik found his nerves worsening.

Briefly, he had to fight not to take a step back.

"How long do you suppose this transformation of yours will last *this* time, Revi'? How long before those appetites rear their ugly heads? Before the hunger to have them sated grows too much for you? Your new friends may think they know you, brother, but I *do* know you. I know you far better than they ever will. Better than you perhaps know yourself."

Again, Revik didn't speak.

He fought to push away the images that rose in his light.

He felt Terian pushing more of those images at him, trying

to spark more memories, more feelings. When Balidor blocked them, Terian shifted focus. He aimed those same images at the Adhipan seers who stood behind him, meaning Mara, Yumi, Dalai, Vikram.

And Dalejem. He aimed those images at Dalejem, too.

Revik's jaw clenched. He didn't look back, but felt his shoulders clench.

He forced the infiltrator's mask down tighter. He stared at Terian alone.

The amber-eyed seer was smiling now.

Revik fought with words, some way to pull this back, when Terian abruptly straightened from his more languid pose.

When he spoke next, his voice had turned flat. Business-like.

"So what's the parlay, Revi'?" he asked. When Revik didn't speak, Terian's voice shifted to an open impatience. "What is it that your kneeler masters have to say to us, old friend? What would you like to *plead* for, on their behalf?"

Revik felt his jaw harden more.

"Galaith agreed to this," he growled.

Terian laughed. He held up his hands to the rest of the Org operatives. Revik watched his fingers. He frowned at the mocking peace sign Terian made in seer sign language.

"You are quite safe, Revi'. Quite safe. Do not worry, my brother." Terian grinned, motioning around the clearing at his seventeen visible agents. "None of my people will shoot you, I promise. Tell me your new friends' concerns and wishes. I won't bite."

Revik glanced behind him. He felt the movement in the Barrier as much as in the physical. The Adhipan leader had shifted position, and now stood closer to Revik, only a few feet away on his left, nearly even with him in the clearing.

The message there was clear.

Revik looked back at Terian, then deliberately rested his hands on his hips.

He'd gotten the message, too.

"Fine," he said. He motioned that he understood, as much to Balidor as to Terry. He repeated the message for the parlay that Balidor and Vash had given him before they arrived. "You need to back off, Terry. Now."

"Do I? Now?" Terian said, his voice openly amused.

Revik chose to ignore it.

Like Balidor, he wanted this over.

Terry was dragging this out on purpose, and Balidor wanted it to stop.

"...The prisoner we took," Revik cut in, his accent growing more prominent. "It is legal for us to have her, by the old laws. It was a mistake you made, bringing her here. It violated not only the ancient laws, but those of your own making—"

"Those of *our own* making, Revi'?"

"Yes," Revik said, biting back anger. "She's pregnant. Don't pretend you didn't know... or that to take a pregnant female captive in a human-run work camp doesn't go against about a dozen laws of our people, yours and mine. To imprison one who carries a child of our race is unpardonable, and you know it. She should never have been there."

Terian laughed, forcing Revik silent.

Revik stood there, silent.

He watched Terry laugh.

"She shouldn't have been in *Saigon,* either, Revi'," Terian said, his voice holding a colder edge. "...And yes, I know exactly who the cunt is, Revi'. And I know exactly why you're so hell-bent on protecting her, brother. Which is a bit rich, Revi', given she's about to birth another male's pup. Do you plan to take the child with you, too, Revi'? Bring her back to Asia with you, so the three of you can play house in the caves of the Pamir?"

"It's not like that," Revik growled, unable to stop himself.

"Ah, hit a nerve, have I?" Terian said.

"Stop making this about me!" he snapped.

"About you?" Terian raised an eyebrow, his voice shifting to a mock innocence. "Whatever do you mean, Revi'? This is about *the good of the race,* is it not? Isn't that what you would have me think?"

"Stop playing games. You know damned well what I mean."

"Do I?" Terian's gaze flattened to a cold veneer.

It held enough fury that Revik flinched, in spite of himself.

"What do I care that you're still trying to fuck the cunt, Revi'?" Terian asked. "What do I care that she's mated? Pregnant? That she blatantly infiltrated you, used your hard-on for her light to manipulate you into betraying all your friends? That she somehow then coerced you to come out here *yet again* to protect and defend her from all that's evil in the world? Why should I care that you're still sniffing around her ass like a drunk adolescent? How is that *my* problem, Revi'? Shouldn't that be her mate's concern?"

Revik clenched his jaw. His hands balled into fists at his sides.

*Don't rise, brother,* Balidor murmured. *It's what he wants.*

Terian's smile crept back across his dark lips.

"You really are *blushing* again." The Rook clicked his tongue, his smile widening as he shook his head. "I wouldn't have believed it if I couldn't see it with my own eyes. *Gaos.* It's almost giving me a hard on now, Revi'—"

"Damn it, Terry," Revik snapped, again speaking before he could pull it back. "You're breaking treaty. Moreover, you *know* you are, and so does Galaith. What the fuck do you want? Do you really plan to gun us down over a pregnant seer?"

"What makes you think Galaith would stop me, if I did?" Terian asked.

He paused deliberately. He stared at Revik's eyes.

His voice grew a few shades colder.

"...Or were you really under the impression, Revi', that I was the only one to hold a grudge over you leaving?"

Revik fought against the emotions he could see in Terian's eyes, the conflicted loyalties he could feel his old friend trying to raise in Revik's own light. The doubt. That implication that he'd betrayed them. The implication he'd betrayed Galaith.

That he was at fault.

*Tell him,* Balidor prodded him. *The words Vash gave you. It is time, brother. We cannot prolong this much longer. He is growing increasingly unstable, your Rook friend.*

Revik frowned at the "friend" comment, but didn't bother to refute it.

He did give Balidor a brief glance. He turned away when he saw him nod.

Revik realized he was right.

About the instability, anyway.

"It's part of the *other* treaty, Terry," Revik said. He turned back to face Terian. "The one he made personally with Vash. After the war. Tell Galaith that."

For a moment, Terian just stared.

Revik found himself lost in that stare briefly.

He fought not to care about what he saw, but felt himself drawn into the edges of feeling anyway. He saw reactions move and configure behind those amber eyes, saw tastes of emotion and personalities there and gone.

This was the body of Terian's with which Revik was most familiar.

It was the one Terry seemed the most fond of, too.

Generally speaking, the Terian Revik knew landed most of his light body inside this vessel when it wasn't needed elsewhere. He'd managed to kill it more than once, but got his scientist pals to clone it again and again. Terian himself was an experiment of sorts, Revik knew. He couldn't remember if he'd been Galaith's experiment exactly, or Terian's own experiment, but he wasn't like ordinary seers.

It was one thing Revik remembered clearly about his ex-partner, even if details around the specifics had faded from his mind.

Terian split his light body out into multiple physical bodies in the living world.

It made him more or less impossible to kill.

Revik remembered Terian calling it "riding corpses." He seemed to find the wording funny for some reason, although Revik had a memory of it disturbing him, even as a Rook.

Most of the Org soldiers here wouldn't know that, though.

Revik wondered if Terian's new boy-toy even knew... the lookalike.

Terian had other quirks with his bodies, in addition to favoring this one.

He dyed the hair on all of his male bodies to this same auburn color, unless there was an operational reason why he couldn't. Revik couldn't remember the reasons behind the preference, or even if he'd ever bothered to ask him while they'd been friends, but he remembered the detail with surprising clarity.

He tried to pull his feelings apart from everything he could see in that face.

The memories were fleeting, but Revik could feel tastes of emotion there, and not only in the seer standing before him.

The truth was, Balidor was right.

Terian *had* been his friend.

Maybe Revik even still felt that way about him in a strange sense.

Truly, though, their relationship had always been more of big brother to little brother, with Revik playing the role of mentor and protector. It had always been that way, part of some unspoken agreement between them, or possibly some directive from Galaith.

Even so, when Revik lived inside the Pyramid of the Org, Terry might have been the only thing standing between him and total disconnection with other beings.

Revik had been lonely in the Org, he remembered that much.

He had been intensely lonely, at times.

He'd been lonely even when he had lovers that lasted more than a few days or weeks, even when he *tried* to connect with others. Too often, friendships in the Org got mired in political complications, in power differentials, in agendas. The ones that didn't often fell flat, or turned competitive in some way, mired in superficial, petty bullshit of one kind or another.

Terian at least gave a damn.

As batshit crazy as Terry was, he'd been capable of warmth—affection, even—at least with Revik himself. He'd been intensely loyal with him, too, in a way that completely superseded his political ambitions... and Terry's ambitions had never been small.

Revik swallowed. He refocused on those amber eyes.

He didn't want to give a damn. Hell, he couldn't afford to give a damn.

Not now.

Even as he thought it, Terian broke the silence.

"And what 'other treaty' would that be, Revi'?" he asked, lifting one eyebrow.

Leaning forward, Terian again rested his arms on the modified gun. Revik couldn't help looking at it, even as a thought slid through his mind that he would miss some of the Org toys. Galaith, unlike the Adhipan and the Seven, worked with an almost unlimited budget, in no small part due to his strong ties to the human business world.

Terian's voice sharpened.

"Revi'? What bullshit is this, old friend?"

Revik sighed a little, at least internally.

"I don't know the specifics," he said. "I'm just an emissary too, brother."

As soon as Revik said it, he felt his mistake.

Hostility swam through the light of the Org seers in front of him, and not only from Terian. Revik felt it most strongly from the gray-eyed seer who looked like him. It felt as if the male wanted to hit him across the mouth with the butt of his rifle for his words.

It took Revik a second more to realize that the word that so infuriated them was "brother."

They hated that he'd called Terian brother.

"Ask Galaith," Revik said, if only to end that silence.

He felt their hostility sharpen and his muscles bunched up. He shifted his weight. He felt his light and body begin unconsciously gearing up for a fight.

"Just fucking *ask* him, Terry," Revik snapped, hearing adrenaline reach his voice. "Why are you prolonging this?"

"An emissary. Is that what you are, Revi'?"

Revik's jaw tightened. "Terry."

"...How incredibly formal and official it all sounds. 'Emissary.'" Terian's lip curled, but Revik felt the coil of anger there. "Do you really think—"

"Terry," Revik cut in, warning. "Ask him, or end this. We'll find another way to talk to your boss, if you're not capable of passing on a simple fucking message."

His ex-partner's amber eyes changed again.

The fury in his light turned cold as ice, stripped of pretense.

Revik felt others in the clearing react to the shift, especially on the Org side. Being hooked into the construct, they probably felt the real emotion there, without the shields that stood between Revik and Terian now.

Revik caught movement as the Org seers looked at one another, their faces visibly tense as they shifted their weight.

He glimpsed them rearranging hands on weapons and holsters.

Revik saw Terian give his new boyfriend a look then, as if warning him about something, or communicating something perhaps. It occurred to Revik they were probably all talking outside of his hearing, even more than he'd realized.

The Adhipan seers might be, as well.

Revik's eyes followed Terian's to the look-alike with the black hair.

The gray-eyed male looked nervous, but more angry than nervous.

Revik wondered if Terry's fuck-toy had any idea how dangerous his new playmate was.

Even as he thought it, Terian looked back at him.

"I have relayed your message," Terian said, surprising Revik, not only with the words but with his matter-of-fact tone. All traces of that previous fury appeared to have vanished, for the moment, at least. "It probably doesn't surprise you that he requires proof?"

Terian lifted an eyebrow, staring at him.

Revik nodded, albeit reluctantly.

He'd expected this, but it was the part he dreaded, too.

It was also the part Balidor and Vash warned him about.

"Yes," he said, hearing the reluctance in his voice. "Only him, though," he warned, giving Terian a harder look.

Revik saw a bare smile touch Terian's lips.

Then, the shield around him began to reconfigure.

Revik felt Balidor there.

He felt Vash, even Dalejem briefly, then—

Fuck. Holy fuck. He couldn't do this.

He really couldn't do this.

But it was already too late.

## CHAPTER 16
# EXTRACTING A TOLL

Galaith's light descended over Revik's.

It happened without preamble, without warning—with no way for him to prepare.

It felt like hot mercury being poured over his skin.

It clung there, melding into parts of Revik that hurt from the contact.

Even that confused him, though. The pulls and revulsions and resonances blended into one another until he couldn't decide if it was the contact itself that hurt, or the absence of it, prior to now. Had he actually missed this, somehow? Had he missed Galaith?

Could anyone sane really *miss* this?

Sickness washed over him as he struggled with the thought. It pulled at him, pulled at his separation pain, even as he felt grief from the other being's light, a wanting of him.

It had been so long since any being wanted his light like that.

Revik's nausea and separation pain worsened.

He fought not to cry out.

He knew they could probably all see it in his face, in his light, even as he felt Balidor and the others let this happen.

They opened him up deliberately when he tried to get away. They allowed Galaith to see the information they'd given him, what they'd imprinted on his light before they reached the clearing.

It was Kali, giving birth.

It was markers in her light... markers in her child's light.

Revik could see Vash and Galaith standing in a Barrier field of some kind. Galaith wore an avatar, like he always did, but Vash looked the same as he did in real life, in his physical body. His long face smiled sadly as he nodded to Galaith's words.

They shook on that thing, whatever it was.

*I was not the one to take her,* Galaith told Revik softly before he left. *Know that, brother Revik. And know that you are missed greatly here. Whatever you tell yourself, whatever your new friends tell you, you are missed painfully, my friend... and you are loved...*

Revik fought back another stab of pain.

He fought to extract himself.

That time, they let him go.

All the hands and arms around him in that space finally let him go.

The Adhipan shield wove back around his light. It blocked out those silver strands.

Revik felt worry there, apology, fear for him—

He felt Vash, Tarsi, Balidor, Yumi, Dalejem—

But he couldn't let them in either, not at first.

He couldn't stand to have any of them there, inside his light, or anywhere near him.

He slammed his own shield down hard over whatever he could protect. He knew it was futile, that his shield lived inside the shield of the Adhipan. He pushed all of them out almost without meaning to do it, or maybe just without being able to help himself from desperately needing the space.

It felt like he couldn't bear to have any light touching him but his own.

He even forced out Balidor, who stood right next to him. The gray-eyed Adhipan leader practically touched him with his body, even as he surrounded Revik with clear, fast-moving light. Revik didn't try to move away physically from the other's protective stance; he just stood there, breathing in and out, forcing emotion out with every breath, forcing out pain, thought, memory, his feeble attempts to understand.

All of it.

He closed his heart.

*Gaos.* Some childlike part of him didn't want to feel anything, ever again.

When Revik's eyes finally cleared, he found himself looking at Terian.

He couldn't tell by looking at the auburn-haired seer, just how much Terian had seen.

Right then, Revik didn't really care.

He wanted out of there. Now.

Before he could voice that desire aloud, Terian spoke, his voice cold.

"And how was it, Revi'?" he asked. "Did you show daddy your favorite bitch? Does he still love you, after all this time?"

Revik snapped back at him. Like before, he spoke without thought.

"Why don't you ask him yourself, Terry?" he growled.

His voice shook. His hands were shaking too.

Still, he'd meant his words to Terian sarcastically. Despite that fact, he saw his ex-partner's eyes shift the instant after he'd spoken them. Watching Terian's face, Revik realized the Rook was doing exactly as he'd suggested.

He was asking Galaith.

Revik just stood there. He looked around at the rest of the Org agents. He watched their faces as they stared back at him, as their hands and fingers rearranged themselves around different parts of the weapons they held.

Eventually, Terian clicked out.

Once he had, anger flared back into those amber-colored irises.

"So. You got what you wanted." Terian's jaw hardened. "How nice for you, Revi'. Galaith says we are to let you and your friends go."

His words had a strange distance to them.

Something about what he heard and felt there caused Revik to stare at his old friend warily.

"...Galaith *didn't* say, however, that we couldn't extract a toll before you go, Revi'."

Terian stepped closer to Revik.

No, he didn't step. He *glided* really, moving in that frictionless, deceptively casual way of his. Revik felt his whole body tense. Some less-conscious part of him picked up on the threat. He sensed the danger. That part sent up a flare to warn the rest of him—

It was the rest of Revik, the more conscious part, that got caught off guard. That part was still off-balance and shaking from having Galaith so intimately in his light.

That part let Terian get too close.

That part didn't see the knife.

That part only felt it when the sharp edge of the blade suddenly pressed to his throat.

Balidor's light flared in alarm...

...but Revik froze.

He stared into Terian's face.

He felt his breath stop and clench in his chest.

Instinct made him freeze.

He was too late, his mind told him. He couldn't push him off. He couldn't block him, or fight him. He wouldn't get out that way.

That way was closed.

Revik knew how good Terian was with that knife.

He'd watched him with it for years. He'd watched him use it and practice with it and play with it. He'd trained with him, sparred with him, honed techniques and new moves with him. Revik knew how fast he was. He knew how insanely liquid fucking fast he was.

Cutting instruments had always been Terry's favorite toys.

He liked blood. The more, the better.

He even liked it during sex.

Forcing the image from his mind, Revik kept his whole focus on the other seer. He fought with his own mind. He fought with his body, fought to remain utterly still, to keep from doing something stupid, something that would definitely get him killed.

He could feel the blade pushing in his breath. He knew he could cut himself, just by swallowing wrong, just by moving even a millimeter in the wrong direction.

Even so, the main emotion that writhed through Revik's light was anger.

Terian seemed to see it.

Or feel it, maybe.

Moreover, Revik's anger seemed to please him.

Terian smiled. He stepped nearer, angled the knife closer. "Maybe *I* want to extract a toll from you, Revi'," he said, his voice softer. "...before you go."

Revik glanced quickly around the clearing.

He reminded himself of the location of all the Org infiltrators.

He checked whether any had moved.

He felt Balidor beside him once more, closer than before.

Furious.

Adhipan leader Balidor was fucking *furious.*

Revik had no idea if it was at him, for letting Terian get that close, or at Balidor himself, for not seeing it coming, or at Terian for being a whack-job sociopath with a vendetta and a knife. Balidor may even have been angry with Galaith, for going back on their deal, or for having so little control over his people.

Revik could have told him not to waste his time.

Even Galaith didn't have much luck controlling Terian.

*Don't give him a reason to kill you,* Balidor whispered in Revik's mind.

Under different circumstances, Revik might have laughed.

Balidor's light remained calm on the surface, a reminder for Revik to stay the same. Even so, Revik could feel the fury seethe through the other's *aleimi*.

*…Give us a minute,* Balidor sent, his light still reassuring. *Vash is talking to Galaith.*

Revik fought back his own anger.

He forced stillness into his *aleimi*.

He understood what Balidor was asking him.

He wanted Revik to buy time.

Feeling his jaw clench, Revik returned his focus back to Terian.

"Don't do this, Terry," he said.

He didn't want to move his throat, so his voice came out soft.

"…You kill me, and the Org and the Seven break treaty," he said, still in that near-murmur. "The Seven might be peaceful at base, but they won't stand for that. You know it. So does Galaith…"

He remembered Kali's people, the ones her mate had called out to the jungle as reinforcements.

"…You know what's behind me in those hills. They'll hunt you down like a rabid dog, Terry, just to make the point. And just like that, you and me are dead, and this Cold War of ours… this relative truce… it all turns hot overnight. And then our people won't have a chance in hell, Terry. None of us will. We won't have to wait for the humans to kill us. We'll do it to ourselves."

Terian lips curved in a wry smile.

"Still the politician, aren't you, Revi'?"

"You know I'm right."

Revik didn't add that he knew Terian cared more about the fate of the seer race than he usually let on. Most in the Org did.

It was part of their ideology, twisted though it was.

"Do I?" Terian said coldly. "So why am I so confused by all of this, old friend?"

He pressed the blade tighter to Revik's throat and Revik flinched.

He closed his eyes longer than a blink.

"What are you confused about, Terry?" he asked, his voice still low.

"You, Revi'," Terian said. "I'm confused about *you*, old friend. Why are you doing this? Why would you *work* for them? What's in it for you, Revi'? Really?"

Revik felt his jaw clench.

"She's an intermediary, Terry," he said. "Don't tell me you didn't know—"

Terian let out an angry laugh.

He pressed down harder on the knife.

"You can't kill her." Revik raised his voice, even as he felt Balidor send a cautioning pulse his way. "You sure as fuck can't kill her child. You know what it might mean—"

Terian jabbed the blade deeper against his throat, cutting him that time.

Revik let out a strained gasp.

Anger swam through his light, along with more than one kind of pain.

"...Gods damn it, Terry!" he snapped. "Grow up! This isn't about me. Or us. And it isn't about her and me. There *is* no her and me. She's married, remember? Like you said, she's having another seer's child. She and I..."

His pain worsened.

"...I've never touched her, Terry."

When Terian let out another angry laugh, Revik felt his own anger worsen.

"...and if you think she's the real reason I left, you don't know me at all!" His voice lowered to a harder growl. "I didn't want to fucking *be* there anymore, Terry! I didn't want any of it. I hadn't been happy for years. I hated everything about what we were doing, how much worse we were making the world. Which you would have *known*, if you knew me even *half* as well as you like to pretend. Just let it go, for fuck's sake! It's over!"

But Terian only shook his head.

"No, brother," he said. "No, no, no... it's not over. It will never *be* over, because I can't just let you live a lie. I can't. You wouldn't let me, if our positions were reversed—"

"Live a lie?" Revik growled.

That time, he let Terian hear his contempt.

He remembered all those months in the caves, the memories they forced him to relive, all of those scenes, over and over again—how much he fucking hated himself, through all of it.

The more those images flashed behind his eyes, the more he didn't care if the other male did cut his throat.

Fuck it. Good riddance.

*No!* a voice snapped in his mind. *No, goddamn it! Don't go there! Don't you dare fucking go there!*

Realizing it was Dalejem, Revik felt his fury worsen.

But he didn't care what Dalejem or any of them heard about him anymore.

He didn't care what they saw about his past under the Rooks or at any other time.

They knew what he was.

Who the fuck was he kidding?

"Jesus, Terry." He aimed all his fury at the Rook. "What the fuck do you think I *did* under Galaith for all those years? You're so convinced that was the 'real' me, and this is some illusion... that I've been brainwashed or tricked or somehow got lost between Vietnam and India. You really think I've been snowed by the Seven? By the Adhipan? By fucking *Kali*, who only ever tried to help me? Who's never been anything but a friend to me?"

His jaw tightened when Terian pressed the blade harder against his skin.

Somehow, he didn't let it shut him up, even then.

"She's having a *child* right now, Terry," he growled. "Right now, as we speak. A child all of us should be trying to *protect*, not sell into slavery. Or use in some kind of juvenile pissing match with me."

He trailed when he saw the delight rise back to Terian's eyes.

*Gaos*. Why the fuck was he bothering with this?

Why was he even trying to reach him? Because he *was* trying to reach him, on some level, at least, even now. He might have started off trying to stall, to distract Terian for the Adhipan, but he'd practically forgotten that in the time since.

He was trying to talk to Terian.

He was actually trying to *talk* to him.

Terian couldn't even hear him.

And did he really need to confess his sins to the Adhipan?

Fuck them, too.

Fuck all of them.

He clicked under his breath, somehow ashamed of his anger, maybe because he knew most of it was bullshit. He found himself staring at Terian instead.

He looked into those amber irises.

He saw the crazy there, the instability, the cruelty, the confusion.

He felt real pity for him, maybe for the first time.

Revik might be a fucking mess, but at least he was starting to see the truth about who and what he really was. Unlike Terry, he no longer actively deluded himself into thinking he was the hero of this particular movie. He no longer believed he'd be proven right by history, by time, by faceless masses of seers and humans, by some higher power.

He no longer waited for the ticker-tape parades, for the statues erected of his likeness, for those who spat on him to apologize and tell him they'd been wrong.

He was just another cog in the machine.

He was just another stupid asshole who got deluded into fighting for the wrong side.

"Did it ever occur to you that maybe it was the reverse, Terry?" Revik asked. "That maybe *you're* the one living the lie? That I'm the one who finally woke up?"

"No," Terian said. He pressed deeper with the knife. "No, it didn't, Revi'."

Revik held up his hands. He moved more in instinct that time than conscious thought. He slid his throat and head back smoothly, carefully, slowly. He moved as much of both out of the way as he possibly could without taking more than a half-step back.

Terian made up the half-step with a full one.

Revik felt warmth pool at the neck of his armored shirt. His throat bled steadily now. Maybe he really was going to die out here.

He honestly didn't know if he cared anymore.

"Put the fucking knife down, Terry," he said, cold.

"I want my toll, first."

"Your toll?" Revik glared at him, barely masking the contempt in his voice. He was done with this. He was tempted to tell the other seer to shit or get off the pot, but he knew Terian would likely slit his throat the instant he said it.

"...What *toll*, Terry?" he asked instead.

Terian smiled. It was clearly the question he wanted asked.

He sidled closer to where Revik stood.

"I want you to let Quay here suck your cock before you

go." Those amber eyes glinted with a mad light Revik remembered. "I want to watch you come, brother."

His words managed to catch Revik off-guard.

Revik felt them like a punch.

That time, maybe to the solar plexus.

He barely had time to think before Terian was forcing him back, towards the side of the clearing. The auburn-haired seer angled his body and the knife to keep Balidor behind Revik. Revik matched his steps, again moving more in instinct than thought, gasping a little as the warmth increased at his throat.

Terry hadn't hit the artery yet, but Revik knew that was intentional, too.

Terian knew where all the arteries lived.

He studied anatomy obsessively when Revik knew him.

Genetics, too.

Revik pushed those flickers of memory out of his light.

As he did, Terian spoke again.

"I think hanging around the Seven hasn't done much for your sex life, Revi'," he said. He continued to match micro-movements with Revik, the knife pressed firmly to his throat. "...Really, I should probably make you give head to everyone out here, my friend. Including your kneeler brothers and sisters, since I'd hate for them to miss out on your talents... and clearly you haven't gotten nearly enough practice of late. That said, I'll be satisfied just to watch you come in brother Quay's mouth. Or you can blow me right here. Your choice."

Revik felt his light react.

Terian pressed the knife deeper, making him gasp.

More blood ran down his neck. It pooled thicker at the base of his throat.

"Just once, brother," Terian coaxed. "What could be the harm?"

"You've lost your fucking mind," Revik snapped. "Jesus, Terry. What the hell is the matter with you?"

"What is the matter with me?" Terian said.

Something in the other male's light shifted.

Then it abruptly opened. Terian's *aleimi* slammed into Revik with enough emotion that it overpowered the shield the Adhipan held over his light. The Rook's light swam into Revik's, blinding him with pain, not all of it his.

Terian's voice grew hoarse.

"I miss my *friend*, Revi'," he said. "I miss my goddamned friend. My friend who left without a word, who fucking *betrayed* me without ever giving me a chance to make things right between us. Is that really so hard to understand? Is it? All I'm asking is for a little token of his esteem before he leaves me again. Is it really so much to *ask*, Revi'?"

Revik felt his pain worsen.

He fought to extract himself from the other male's light.

He fought to distance himself from the pain that lived there.

In desperation, he looked for Balidor. He tried to find his face, his light, but Terian jerked the knife forward once more, cutting him again deeper.

Deep enough to noticeably increase the blood flow.

Deep enough to increase it a lot maybe, enough to scare Revik for real.

He let out a panicked sound. He jerked his head reflexively back from the knife, but again, Terian's fingers and feet followed him, until the front of Terian's body pressed up against his.

"Don't look at him!" Terian said angrily. "Don't look at your new master for *guidance*, Revi'. Look at *me*. Only at me."

Revik turned his head. He stared deliberately down at the other male.

Studying his eyes briefly, Terian smiled.

"That's better." Terian smiled wider. He exhaled with a kind of satisfaction. "We can be reasonable about this, after all. Come now, Revi'. Just do as I ask. I'm sure none of these fine new friends of yours would mind. Hell, I'm sure they'd appreciate seeing your talents showcased. Maybe they'll want a turn on you themselves when you're done."

Terian motioned to the Adhipan seers standing behind him with his free hand.

He never took his eyes off Revik's face.

"Are you really willing to risk bloodshed over such a small thing? Would you deny me even that, brother, after all our years of friendship?"

There was a silence while Revik fought to think past the other's light.

The Adhipan seemed to have their shield under control once more, but Revik could still feel Terian's *aleimi*. With him so close, pressed against his body and in his light, he couldn't keep him out, not entirely.

Nor could the Adhipan.

For a long moment, Revik fought with what to do.

He wondered at Balidor's silence, then wondered if Terian was keeping them away, if he'd found some means of cutting off Revik's link to the Adhipan altogether.

Before Revik found words, he felt Terian's hand on his belt.

Revik felt the other seer unhook the clasp. He did it easily, casually, without decreasing the pressure of the knife. Revik could only stand there, his whole body reacting, yet also going into a form of paralysis.

This wasn't happening.

This wasn't fucking happening.

The Adhipan weren't going to just stand there and let him—

Then Terian had his hand on Revik's cock, and Revik closed his eyes.

Enough pain rose in his light that it briefly blanked his mind. Disgust warred with that pain, revulsion even, a desire to wrap his hands around the throat of the other seer, but somehow, he still hadn't moved. Fear wound somewhere into all of it, the sudden certainty that even allowing this wouldn't keep him from getting his throat cut as he came.

The thought forced words to his lips, even as he remembered Dalejem was watching this.

All of them were.

They were just standing there, watching Terry do this.

They were just letting it happen.

"Terry, *jurekil'a mak rik'ali*. Stop—"

"Come on, Revi'. One blow job. What could it hurt?"

"You really are fucking crazy. You've finally cracked—"

"I want you on your knees, brother Revik. Now. Right now, in fact."

"Fuck you—"

"Revi'. Just do it. I can feel how hungry you are."

"Gods…" Anger warred with the pain, confusing him. He fought to think, to decide how he could get out of this, but his mind went utterly blank. He tried to slide back a step, but Terian gripped him tighter. He pressed the knife deeper, forced another gasp from him. The two types of pain mixed, confusing him more. But the separation pain had already begun to win.

It pulled at him, wanting him to let this happen.

Gods. He was desperate enough to nearly want this.

He closed his eyes as Terian continued to massage him. One of his hands gripped Terian's arm now, but he couldn't remember doing that, either.

"Stop it," he gasped. "Please, Terry. Please… don't do this."

He let out a low groan when the other male's hand tightened on him.

Terian clicked at him. He let out one of his batshit crazy laughs.

"Stop?" he said, mimicking Revik's pleading. "Who are you kidding, Revi'? You're so hungry right now, your light is practically fucking mine already. I'll have you begging me here in a minute. Hell, I could probably get you to do it now."

"No. I don't want this. Terry—"

He heard the lie in his own voice, and the truth in it, too.

He knew what Terry would hear.

"Come now, Revi'," Terian said, his voice cajoling. "Come, brother mine. I know what you like. Let go. Just let it happen."

"No, goddamn it—"

Revik's voice cut out when Terian used more of his light.

The Rook pulled on him sensually that time, and not only with the light in his hands. Revik let out another gasp, and then he nearly was begging him. The pain grew excruciating, impossible to think past. It took over so much of his light he didn't care about anything anymore. He closed his eyes, tried to shove it away, but he couldn't do that, either.

They were going to let Terian fuck him.

They were going to let it happen, right in front of all of them.

Memories slid out of the dark recesses of Revik's mind, a familiarity to this. It came with a self-loathing so intense it nearly blacked out his mind altogether.

"Come, Revi'," Terian coaxed, softer. "Come now. Come for me, brother. You know you want to. Just once, let me watch you. Then I'll leave you alone. Promise."

"Crazy bastard." Dehgoies gripped his arm harder, groaning. "Jesus... Terry. Fuck you..."

Terian laughed. "I'm trying to, brother. I'm trying. You need to imagine your precious cunt, while I jerk you off? Go ahead, Revi'. I don't mind. Pretend it's *her* stroking you. Pretend it's her mouth, not my fingers."

Revik let his mind go there, for the briefest instant.

He saw Kali there, saw those dark green eyes.

His pain grew so intense he nearly cried out.

"Ah, you like that," Terian said, his voice a murmur again.

"You like that a lot, don't you, Revi'? Tell me again how you're just friends, you and she. Tell me how *grateful* you are, about all the *help* she's given you since you ran away from me and everyone else who gave a damn about you. Then tell me how you aren't out here, hoping she might give you a pity fuck if you can just manage to separate her from her mate..."

Revik fought with the other's words. He tried to force them out of his mind.

He couldn't do that, either.

His words came out hollow.

Unconvincing, even to him.

"You've lost your mind, Terry. You really have—"

But another voice cut him off.

"Brother Terian. Let him go."

When Revik looked up, still more than half-blind with pain, he saw a gun pressed against Terian's neck. It wasn't Balidor who held it.

It was the violet-eyed seer.

The older one, the Rook with the iron gray hair.

"Let go of him," the seer said, louder. "Now, brother."

Hearing those words, Revik realized it was over.

Terian had stopped what he was doing.

He still held onto Revik. He gripped Revik almost possessively with the hand not holding the knife, but he had stopped what he was doing. The violet-eyed seer's words stopped him, which meant the seer with the Nazi scar likely spoke for Galaith.

It was over.

It was finally over.

Galaith was going to let him go.

Even as he thought it, the pain in Revik's light twisted.

It coiled around him, sparked out of his control.

It lost its purchase on Terian, on Terian's light—

—right before it turned inwards.

Emotion rose with the pain. That time it felt closer to fury, maybe even hatred.

Revik didn't even know who he felt that hatred towards until he realized he could feel Balidor's light once more, resting quietly next to his. Revik could feel the rest of the Adhipan seers there as well, and the thought again slid through his light that they just stood there, letting that happen. They hadn't done a damned thing to try and stop Terian.

They just let Terry molest him, right in front of them.

They hadn't spoken so much as a single word.

Logic tried to assert itself, to tell him they had little choice, that he, meaning Revik, didn't know what they'd been doing behind the scenes.

He didn't really care about logic, though.

Whatever they'd said to him before, whatever Balidor might pretend about Revik being under his protection, he was on his own.

He was really on his fucking own out here.

Feeling Balidor's light react to his thoughts, Revik slammed the shield back down over his *aleimi*. He stood there, panting. He closed his heart and light until he couldn't feel any of them anymore. He could barely feel himself.

He didn't want to share his anger with them.

He didn't want to share any of it with any of them.

He felt some of them react, Dalejem and Balidor especially, but he didn't care about that, either. He didn't fucking care anymore.

He was done.

He was really fucking done with this shit.

## CHAPTER 17
# DEAL WITH THIS

No one said much on the walk back.

Well… not that Revik could hear.

Then again, he didn't try very hard to listen.

All six of the other seers gave him a wide berth after they dragged him out from under Terian's knife. Balidor approached him not long after they'd left the Org's mobile construct, but Revik slammed out hard enough with his *aleimi* that the other seer promptly backed down.

After that, all of them left him alone.

Not long after they left the Rooks' clearing, Revik heard a shot echo through the trees from the place they'd left behind.

He didn't bother to try and figure out if that meant what he thought it meant.

He knew it wouldn't matter, even if he was right.

Terian couldn't be killed like that, not *really* killed, not anymore. It might shock Terian's men, including his new fuck-buddy, "Quay." It would likely be calculated to shock them, and to send a message, but that's all it would do, given who and what Terian was.

Shoving his ex-partner from his mind, Revik fought to erase his thoughts altogether.

He and the Adhipan seers walked the several miles back to the lower staging area.

Once they got there, Balidor informed the larger team, headed by Garensche, that they would be joining the rest of the Adhipan seers at a higher-level camp, one located a few miles south of where Kali and her husband now encamped.

Apparently, they'd been moved around the same time Balidor left to find Revik.

Kali and her husband Uye now camped in the center of that mysterious group of infiltrators who had come to protect her and her child from the Org.

The Adhipan would maintain the second camp as back up, from what Balidor said, in the event something happened and Galaith didn't honor their agreement.

They would not be joining the larger camp in those higher hills.

Revik barely listened as Balidor explained all of this.

He didn't look at any of them, or let any of them touch him, not even to dress the wound on his neck, although Yumi, and then Ontari, who didn't seem to know what was going on, at least not yet, both offered to do the latter.

Revik managed it himself.

Well, more or less.

He stopped the bleeding on the way back to Garensche and the others.

Then, once they'd reached the staging area, he opened his pack long enough to find the shirt he'd been sleeping in for the past few days, and tied that around his neck to keep the wound closed.

He knew he'd need help to stitch it up once they got to the upper base, but at least then he could ask one of Balidor's other seers to do it—meaning one he didn't know and didn't give a damn about. At the very least, he could find one who wouldn't ask him any questions.

He walked with the rest of them through the trees, silent.

On that leg of the journey, he could hear the other seers talking to one another in low voices. Most of that talking had to do with Vikram, Yumi, Dalai, Mara, and Balidor telling the others what had taken place while Revik "negotiated" with Terian.

Revik heard flickers of his own name in that, of course.

He ignored every part of it he could.

In the process, he shut down more of his light.

Dalejem remained notably silent. Dalejem was also one of the few seers who didn't try to get anywhere near Revik or his light.

Neither thing particularly surprised Revik.

He just wanted to get the fuck out of here now.

He wanted to go back to the Pamir, back to those caves, and not talk to anyone else for another five or so years… if not longer.

Hell, maybe he'd take a vow of silence and celibacy himself.

Maybe he'd end up a fucking monk, yet.

---

His anger didn't really crash until about two hours later.

By then, he sat in front of a real fire.

By himself, of course.

He'd asked one of the medical techs to stitch up his neck.

She informed him the wound wasn't bad, in terms of the cut itself.

She'd been more worried about the possibility of infection, and chewed him out for wrapping the shirt around it without putting any kind of disinfectant on the wound first, especially given they were out in the middle of the damned jungle.

She washed the cut carefully, put alcohol on it, then a

salve, then stitched it up and covered it with an organic bandage, which should have its own antibiotics in the gel that surrounded the wound.

Revik found himself touching the bandage periodically, anyway.

Tents were still being put up, but he probably could have found one by then.

Truthfully, he considered sleeping out there, in the open, even with the bugs and whatever else, if only because he didn't want to be that close to the light of any of them. He knew to sleep indoors he'd have to share a tent with at least two other seers.

The groups had remained more or less in their previous units, which didn't help.

It meant this fire provided the focal point for the same seers Revik had been traveling with for days now, along with a few others who came over to visit with friends.

Dalai had a boyfriend, as it turned out, a muscular, Chinese-looking seer by the name of Nurek. Revik recognized a few other faces from before they'd split into separate units, but he didn't have names to go with a lot of them.

He supposed it didn't matter.

They all gave him a wide berth, too.

He hadn't seen Dalejem since they'd gotten back to camp.

In the end, Revik just sat on a log by the blazing campfire, trying to pull his shit together before he made a final decision on where and how he could handle sleeping—assuming he could handle it at all.

Truthfully, he wished he could get drunk.

He considered asking someone if that was possible, but didn't.

He didn't ask about alcohol for the same reason he didn't ask anyone if they'd give him his own private tent for the night.

He could still feel flickers of light from the others in his group. They darted around him in rippling, if subtle waves. He felt concern in some of those touches, even worry, but he didn't want to deal with that, either.

He could feel them talking about him.

He didn't hear any of the specifics.

He didn't want to.

In any case, no one tried to sit by him.

They sat around the fire on different logs, most of those opposite where he sat, and talked quietly amongst themselves. Not content to simply avoid sharing Revik's specific log, they left a space of something like fifteen feet on either side of where he sat, clustering together on a few downed tree trunks across from him.

As per usual with the Adhipan leader, Revik didn't even see him until it was too late to avoid him. He didn't see his body, much less feel his light, until the older seer sat right beside him, on the same log.

Revik started to stand up. He moved without thought.

But that time, Balidor didn't let him leave.

His hand clamped down on Revik's arm, hard. He held Revik firmly in place.

"You need to listen to me, brother," he said.

His voice came out low, almost a murmur.

Even so, it held an open warning.

More than that, Balidor put light in his words, compelling Revik to obey them.

Reluctantly, Revik let his weight rest back on the log.

He didn't look over at the other male.

He kept his gaze trained on the fire, even as he fought not to react to the hand on his arm. He knew the other seer spoke aloud so they wouldn't be overheard, but he found it difficult to muster much gratitude for that, either.

Why the hell wouldn't they leave him alone?

"Revik." Balidor's voice grew harder, denser. It still carried that thread of *aleimi* and command. "You are losing control over your light."

Revik shook his head. He felt his mouth harden. "I'll be fine."

"You will not be fine," Balidor growled. "You are not fine now."

Revik fought with words.

In the end, he bit his tongue, saying nothing.

Balidor wouldn't let it go.

"You must do something about it," he said. "Tonight."

It wasn't a question, or even a request.

Balidor continued, "I cannot have a trained infiltrator out here in this state, brother. I cannot. You must understand my position in this."

Revik let out a humorless laugh.

Balidor cut him off.

"I mean it, Dehgoies." His words remained quiet, but pulsed with raw emotion now. "Why have you not asked anyone to help you with this? I expected you to. On the very first day we left those caves, I expected this. Why have you not done it?"

Revik fought not to turn his head.

He could feel the other seer pulling on him for that, trying to force him to make eye-contact, but out of sheer stubbornness, Revik wouldn't do it.

"What would be the fucking point?" he asked finally.

There was a silence.

Then Balidor let out a clicking sigh. He didn't loosen his hold on Revik's arm. "Brother, are you wondering why none of them has asked you?"

Revik shook his head. "No."

"Of course you are. Why would you not wonder?" Balidor's voice grew openly exasperated. "You must have felt their interest."

"What?" Revik couldn't help it. That time, he turned, staring at the older seer. "Are you trying to screw with my head, brother Balidor? Or do you simply think me an idiot?"

Staring back at him, Balidor exuded disbelief.

Then he frowned. He clicked in open irritation, even as he shook his head. The irritation didn't seem aimed at Revik that time, though. Not precisely, anyway.

"Brother, you are not thinking clearly," Balidor said flatly. "You are not. In fact, you are far deeper in this than I realized. Honestly, I would never have let you go near that Org bastard, had I fully understood the state you were in."

Revik flinched at the mention of Terian, but Balidor only hardened his voice.

"I ordered them to leave you alone. I *ordered* them, Dehgoies. You must understand this! I could not have them taking advantage of you in this state. I told them not to approach you unless you asked one of them for it directly. But you never asked. Not even when it was practically offered to you."

Revik felt his jaw harden more.

He found himself remembering his interaction with Dalejem that first day, out in the field with the guns, and the pain in his chest worsened.

"Why?" Balidor asked, exasperated. "*Why* did you not ask, brother?"

Revik looked back at the fire.

For a moment he actually tried to think about the other's question.

But he couldn't clear his mind enough to do that either, certainly not long enough to come up with any kind of real answer.

Anger coursed through his light, but it was more than that.

Or maybe it wasn't anger at all.

He felt his *aleimi* sparking around him in waves.

He realized they were being overheard. It felt like every fucking seer in this part of the construct was listening to them now, and the scrutiny sent Revik's light into another sparking flare, causing Balidor's hand to tighten on his arm.

"Revik. Do you need help to deal with this?" he said, lower.

"Are you offering, brother?" Revik asked humorlessly.

Balidor flinched. "That is not the kind of help that I—"

"Then no," Revik said, giving him a harder stare.

Returning that look, Balidor frowned.

"You know I cannot—" he began.

When Revik let out a harsh laugh, clicking as he shook his head, the Adhipan leader sent out a wave of denser light. He gripped Revik's arm harder.

"Dehgoies, you are not thinking clearly. You are not... or you would not question this!"

Revik only shook his head.

His vision blurred and he realized tears had come to his eyes.

Embarrassment touched him, but he was almost beyond the point of caring about that, either.

What the fuck did it matter out here? He didn't know these seers. He would never know them.

Even so, he didn't reach up to wipe the tears away. Pride, maybe. Or maybe he just couldn't make himself move enough to do it. Maybe he didn't trust himself not to punch the Adhipan seer in the face once he'd moved even that much.

But he knew the other seer was right.

He was losing control over his light.

Fuck, he'd already lost control over it.

He couldn't even force himself to try. Maybe he couldn't even force himself to want to try by then. But he couldn't bring himself to act either, at least not the way Balidor seemed to want him to. Who the fuck was he going to ask? Seriously?

With Dalejem gone, and clearly avoiding him, and the rest

of them sitting there, listening to this, who the *hell* could he possibly ask?

Next to him, Balidor clicked softly, although if it was in regret, sympathy, disbelief, or irritation, Revik didn't let himself think about too closely either.

"You know I cannot," Balidor said again, his voice gentle that time. "Even if that was a serious question... and I strongly suspect it was not... we do not permit sex between subordinates and their commanding officers in the Adhipan. Which is what I *am* to you right now, brother, whether you want to acknowledge that fact or not."

Revik nodded. He wiped his face in spite of himself.

When he didn't speak, Balidor shook his arm.

"Is there no one you would ask?" he said, his voice frustrated. "I am serious, Dehgoies. You have to deal with this. Tonight."

"Is that an order?" Revik didn't hide the bitterness in his words.

"Yes," Balidor said, his voice holding a thread of his own anger. "It *is* an order, by the gods. And if you won't adhere to it, then I'll have some of my people take you twenty miles down the mountain to a human brothel. You can deal with it *there,* if you're too much of a coward to ask anyone here. But you will *deal* with it, Dehgoies. Tonight."

Revik felt his jaw harden more.

Balidor wasn't finished.

"I am perfectly serious about the threat," he said, sharper. "You know the stakes out here. I cannot have you losing control... not any more than you have already. Not with Kali less than a mile away, and her husband with her. You are on the verge of losing control in a way that endangers things now, and I don't think any amount of masturbation is going to fix it at this point, brother," he added, his words brutally precise.

"You need another's light. I would prefer if you asked a

*seer* for that reason, versus the human brothel option... and not only for the logistical nightmare of losing three of my best assets for two days while they risk their lives, interacting with human locals simply to get one of their brothers laid."

Revik felt those words hit at him, too.

He didn't answer.

As if feeling some flicker of his thoughts, Balidor gripped him again, harder.

"They won't ask you, brother," he said, his voice still hard. "You need to hear me on this. I won't *let* them ask you. Not when you are in this state. You need to ask one of them yourself. I will not rescind that order, so don't even bother hoping for that occurrence."

There was a silence.

Then Revik nodded again.

When he still didn't speak, Balidor let out an irritated-sounding sigh.

He released Revik's arm abruptly and rose to his feet.

Revik felt the pulse of defeat in the other's removal of himself.

He expected the Adhipan seer to leave right away, but he didn't; Balidor only stood there instead, looking down at him. When Revik finally realized that Balidor would wait here, perhaps indefinitely, until Revik acknowledged him in some way, he looked up.

Balidor locked gazes with him once he had.

"I mean it, Revik."

His words bordered on cold.

They also sounded like a command.

Firelight reflected in those gray eyes, turning them orange, even as a faint frown touched the seer's mouth.

"I will give you one hour to ask someone. If you have not by then, you might as well gear up. I will have Gar and Vikram take you to the nearest human city this very night, with enough local currency to handle the problem. If you are thinking this threat is just me being theatrical, brother, you would be wrong."

With that, Balidor finally walked away.

## CHAPTER 18
# OFFER

Revik knew from the silence that the other seers around the campfire heard every word.

He felt flickers of curiosity again, as the seers sitting on the far side of the fire watched him. He could feel them wondering, almost on the surface of their lights and minds, what he would do. He even felt some wondering specifically if he would really walk twenty miles down a hill just to avoid humiliating himself in front of them again.

Feeling those pulses and flickers, Revik felt his jaw harden.

Before he knew he meant to, he spoke aloud.

He didn't even bother with the Barrier.

"You heard him," he said. "You know what I am asking of you."

The silence deepened.

When Revik continued to turn over words, Ontari smiled.

He blew warmth through the Barrier space.

*Was there a question in that, brother?* he sent softly.

Revik heard the teasing there. He felt the pain in his chest worsen.

He stared at the fire, knowing tears likely ran down his

face from the way the flickering flames blurred and clicked back into focus.

He didn't care anymore.

He couldn't think well enough to care.

"Do you need a formal question?" he asked finally.

He could feel all of their attention on him now.

He cleared his throat, wiped his face with the heel of his hand.

"I don't know how to do this," he said, clicking softly as he shook his head.

He said it quietly, but he could feel that most of them heard him.

"We need *a* question, brother," Poresh said carefully. His voice was less flippant than Ontari's had been, his eyes more serious. "It doesn't have to be formal. But Adhipan Balidor was pretty specific with us. Very specific, I would say."

Others murmured agreement as Revik listened.

He thought about that.

After another moment, he shoved it from his mind. He clicked to himself again, sharper that time, and in more irritation. He combed his fingers through his hair, and gave up somewhere in the same set of seconds.

He wouldn't handle this gracefully.

He had never handled this gracefully.

Usually he was drunk when he approached strangers.

When he looked up next, he sighed openly.

He let them all feel his frustration.

"How about an offer, instead of a question?" he said, meeting Poresh's gaze.

He glanced around at other faces. He heard the silence deepen, past the crackling of the fire, which overpowered the sounds of the jungle. He didn't know how to read that silence. He couldn't read any of them, really, although they could clearly read him.

"You know I need..." He hesitated on the word, turned it

over on his tongue, then walked past it with his mind. "...I don't have anything to offer in return," he added. "It would be a favor. I am asking for a favor, from one of you. I would accept that favor from any of you. With gratitude."

The silence continued.

Revik cleared his throat. He gestured vaguely with one hand.

"I have no money," he added, still staring into the fire.

He knew he was repeating himself, but couldn't seem to shut up, maybe so he wouldn't have to listen to their collective non-answer.

"...I have nothing to trade. I am asking... offering. To whoever is willing."

He fought with what else he could say, then fell silent. He shook his head.

*Gaos.* He had to stop.

He'd asked the question.

He'd done it, more or less coherently.

What the hell else did they want from him?

Wasn't that what Balidor wanted of him? To offer himself?

Or would the Adhipan leader still make him walk twenty miles through the jungle in the middle of the night, looking for some mountain shithole where he could buy sex from an impoverished human? Would he force Revik to do it even *after* he'd asked, simply for getting a resounding silence in response?

Revik honestly didn't know.

For all he knew, Balidor would order one of his people to take him up on it. Treat it as hardship duty, offer them some kind of perk for jerking off the ex-Rook for a few hours.

Revik wasn't even sure which thing he would prefer at that point.

Or which thing he wanted less.

He clicked again, softly, but didn't look up at any of them.

He considered leaving.

He considered just walking out, fuck what Balidor said, but Vikram spoke up before Revik could put that thought into action, either.

"Male?" Vikram said cautiously. "Female?"

Revik shook his head. "I do not care."

"What about one of each?" Dalai asked, her voice teasing.

Revik met her gaze. "I do not care about that either, sister."

The silence deepened again.

Then Ontari broke the silence with a near laugh.

"You do realize what you just did?" the seer asked him, smiling wider. "You just offered yourself to the entire *camp*, brother. All of us in hearing, anyway. What will you do if we *all* take you up on it?"

A few of the other seers sitting around him smiled.

Then someone stood up from a log on the other end of the fire.

Revik glanced over in time to see Dalejem's back as he left.

He hadn't known he was there, hadn't seen him sitting there in the dark, behind Poresh and Garensche and a few others, still wearing the armored vest from the walk through the jungle. Revik hadn't felt his light, presumably because Dalejem hadn't wanted him to feel it.

Now that he saw him, Revik felt his face flush.

It hit him, everything that he'd heard.

But he knew he needn't have bothered with that.

Dalejem heard and saw everything with Terian, in that clearing.

He'd obviously made up his mind about him then.

Even so, Revik found himself watching as the tall seer with the streaked black and brown hair walked away from the fire pit with measured steps, without so much as a backwards glance. They might have been talking about the weather and he'd simply gotten bored.

Or decided it was time for him to go to bed.

Revik watched his outline recede, at least until the darkness of the night and overhanging trees swallowed him. He felt nothing off the other male's light. He felt not a ripple of reaction, much less a thought aimed in Revik's direction.

From his light, he might not have heard Revik's offer at all.

Ontari glanced over his shoulder in the same silence. He followed Dalejem's retreat with his eyes before he looked back at Revik and quirked an eyebrow.

Revik felt the pain in his chest worsen.

By then, he had to fight to keep it off his face.

Eventually he could only stare at the fire again, not seeing it.

The pain pooled somewhere in his chest as the silence stretched.

It sharpened the longer he sat there, until it began to slide back into the forward areas of his light, to tug at different segments of his *aleimi,* to cloud his mind. He remembered what Terian had said, about Council-approved whores and his pain worsened, even as he considered leaving again... just walking the fuck out.

Maybe a human would be better.

Anything would be better than this.

He was contemplating getting up—

When someone appeared in front of him.

Their body blocked the firelight from his view.

Revik looked up at the shadowy outline, and saw Dalai standing there, with her boyfriend, the muscular seer named Nurek. They were holding hands.

When Revik glanced up, she smiled at him, holding out a hand to him, too.

"I think we got here first, brother," she said, her voice soft. "Is that all right?"

He stared at her hand.

Briefly, that heavier feeling of defeat swam over him,

something like surrender mixed with the knowledge that, even if this was pure charity, he wasn't in a position to refuse.

He barely hesitated before he nodded.

He slid his fingers into hers when she offered them again.

He was standing an instant later. He let her lead him towards the row of tents on the other side of the fire. He couldn't help but notice it was the opposite side of the jungle into which Dalejem had disappeared.

Maybe it should have told him something, that he noted that.

Maybe it should have told him something that he was thinking about Dalejem right then, even after the older seer left the campfire without giving him so much as a glance.

But Revik couldn't deal with that right then, either.

## CHAPTER 19
# OPENED AND HALF-WILLING

Revik barely entered the tent with them before they started undressing him.

He just stood there as they did it, unsure if he should try to help.

They seemed to know what they were doing, what they wanted.

Dalai stood in front of him. She unhooked the vest he wore carefully, only to have Nurek pull it off his shoulders from behind. Dalai grinned up at him then. She slid her fingers into his hair and tugged his mouth gently down to hers.

They kissed.

The kiss lasted for what felt like a long time, but through most of it, Revik found himself struggling, unable to relax.

He felt himself holding back too, trying to even get his bearings in this.

He supposed it was stupid, really, to try and think about it at all.

His mind told him that, but feeling the truth of it didn't really help.

It didn't really allow him to relax either, not enough to know what to do.

Dalai was unfastening the front of his shirt then, and the male seer tugged that off his back as well. Nurek yanked it and the armored shirt under it out from his belt as he removed it. Not waiting, Nurek yanked up the armored shirt next. He pulled it up over Revik's head and off his arms. It forced Dalai to break off their kiss long enough for her boyfriend to get the stretchy material off Revik's shoulders and head.

Then Nurek sucked in a breath.

"*Gaos,*" he murmured. He spoke louder then. He directed his words and light to his girlfriend. "Holy *d'lanlente a guete*... Dalai! Come here, *ilya*. Look at this poor brother's back."

He traced scars with his fingertips.

He cursed under his breath, in a different language that time, what sounded like a dialect of Mandarin.

"*Gaos,*" he murmured, softer. "Did you know about this, baby?"

Revik tensed. He felt the male's fingers run along more of the marks on his back, as if making sense of them by touch. When Dalai slid around behind him, her arm coiled around Revik's bare waist, she let out an even more shocked gasp than Nurek had.

"Holy fuck!" she said. "What the hell *happened* to you, brother?"

Revik gritted his teeth, not answering.

He just stood there while the two of them looked at him.

He didn't try to turn his head.

Both of them caressed the scars silently. They touched him from his shoulders to his belt, and Revik just stood there, enduring it. He didn't mind them touching him there. It was the staring he couldn't figure out how to manage, or how to stop.

When the other male slid an arm around him, clasping his

chest, Revik tensed. He closed his eyes as he tried to force himself to relax, to not care about this.

It was normal for seers to react to this.

It was normal; he didn't need to make a big deal about it.

He fought with what to say, but nothing came.

There was nothing he could say, really.

He didn't remember. He didn't remember how he got them, or what they meant. He didn't want to remember. He didn't even want to tell them he didn't remember, because he knew how that sounded, too.

He also knew that confessing that would only generate more questions.

Seers had photographic memories. To say he "didn't remember" was as strange as having the scars in the first place.

"It's all right brother," Nurek said from behind him. He massaged Revik's chest, then pressed against him and kissed his back. When Revik let out a half-gasp, the male held him tighter. "It's all right, brother," he said again. "We won't ask."

Revik nodded, grateful. He fought to relax, to lean into the other male, then felt hands on his belt and opened his eyes.

Dalai smiled at him from where she unhooked the clasp.

"We need to get him down," Nurek said to her. His voice still held that denser sympathy as he rubbed Revik's shoulder. He pressed deeper into Revik's back. "Get him naked and then get him to lie down, *ilya*. He needs fucking so badly I'm having trouble controlling my light."

Revik felt his tongue thicken, but he didn't speak.

Dalai smiled up at him, then at the other man.

She nodded to her boyfriend's words.

"I know," she said. "He's like a walking advertisement for sex right now, aren't you brother?" she teased softly. She deliberately caressed the front of his pants. "Even with the scars, he's young, though. How old are you, brother Dehgoies? Will you tell us?"

Revik fought to think. He felt his face warm.

"Seventy-nine," he said, after a pause.

Dalai flinched. She stared up at him.

Her hand remained on his crotch, but Revik felt shock emanate from her light. That same shock and surprise opened her purple and blue eyes wider, even as she glanced at Nurek, who laughed.

"Gods," he said. He kissed the back of Revik's neck. "We're fucking child molesters, *ilya*. Did you have any idea he was so young?"

Dalai shook her head, surprise still flickering through her light.

"*Gaos*, no," she said, her bewilderment audible in her voice. "I thought he had to be a century at least, given his time with the Rooks and his placement there." She looked at Revik, studied his face openly. "So, he's not even at his full weight yet. How is that possible?"

Revik started to tense.

He considered making a crack about them talking about him as if he wasn't there... but then they were both caressing him with their hands and light, and he found it difficult to hold onto his resistance, much less the thread of his thoughts.

His pain worsened the longer they touched him. He found his desire to fight them melting too, especially when they continued to warm him with their light as they explored him carefully with their hands. Dalai caressed him for a little longer, then returned her hands to his belt and finished unhooking the clasp.

Revik's body relaxed even more as she undressed him.

He leaned more of his weight against the larger male. He still fought half-heartedly with his light, but he knew he was losing that battle, too. Nurek was stroking him from behind and Revik let out another low groan—

When movement at the tent door jerked his eyes to the left.

By then, Dalai already had his clothes more or less off. She was pulling the last pant leg off his ankle. Half-struggling against the arm that now held him tighter, exuding reassurance, Revik found himself cringing, feeling overly exposed.

He didn't feel better when he saw who stood there.

Mara smiled at him. Those barely slanted, brilliant-colored hazel eyes slid down the length of him to linger on his now-uncovered erection.

Revik felt another conflicted stab of pain and unease at the intensity of her stare.

She wasn't alone. Ontari smiled at Revik from where he stood just behind her.

"Mind company?" Ontari asked Nurek politely.

He glanced at Dalai.

Dalai laughed, but slid her body protectively in front of Revik's.

Nurek held him more tightly against his chest, still exuding reassurance through his skin, and now an overt protectiveness, as well.

Revik felt a gratitude so intense it nearly brought tears to his eyes.

Dalai kept her voice light, but Revik heard that caution reach her words.

"Just how many are waiting out there to molest our poor brother?" She quirked an eyebrow at Ontari. "Do you have any idea how young he is? He's just told us, and now that I know, I think we'd better take it a little easy on him. At least until he's well enough to be more discriminating in his affections."

Ontari waved her concerns away with a smile.

"Oh, there were more," the other seer said cheerfully. "Believe me, there were more. Balidor capped it at the two of us, with admonitions that we play nice with his newest recruit. Besides, I think he'd prefer it if brother Revik could actually *walk* tomorrow."

Dalai laughed. She half-leaned against where Nurek held Revik.

Even so, she didn't move from her protective position in front of him. Revik felt the wariness of her light, and breathed another pulse of gratitude at her and Nurek.

Mara hadn't taken her eyes off him.

She raised her gaze from his lower body long enough to raise an eyebrow at his face directly. A smile touched the edges of her lips.

"You don't mind if we stay, do you brother Dehgoies?" she asked. "You did make an open offer. Were Ontari and I somehow not meant to be included?"

Revik fought with conflicted emotions as they flickered around his light.

Pain. Confusion. Distrust.

He didn't plan to speak, but did anyway.

His voice came out harsher than he intended.

"You don't want me," he said to Mara. "You made that more than clear. Why are you here?"

She smiled openly at that. She tilted her head at him, even as she made a dismissive gesture with her fingers. "We are a long way away from our introduction in those caves, brother. I had my role to play there, anyway. I would have thought brother Balidor told you that?"

Revik shook his head. A sharper panic tried to settle deeper in his chest.

"You don't like me," he said.

She smiled again. Her eyes grew more of a predatory glint.

"Do I need to like you?" she asked sweetly.

"If you're going to hurt me if you don't, then… yes," Revik said, his voice short.

His face flushed hotter after he said it, but he didn't lower his gaze.

He could feel Dalai hovering over him protectively again, even as she made a negative gesture to Mara.

"Maybe you should go, sister," she said, her voice worried.

Mara looked only at Revik, though.

"Brother," she sighed. She clicked softly. The coyness dropped from her voice, even as she rested her hands on her hips, frowning. "You are paranoid, indeed. Did you somehow miss that I've been flirting with you for days out here? That I offered to go along with Balidor and the others to protect you against that Rook? That your friend, Jem, has warned me away from trying to seduce you... repeatedly, I might add?"

At Revik's silence, she walked closer to him.

She glanced at Dalai as if for permission, then walked closer still.

After another few steps, she inserted herself between Dalai and him altogether.

She pressed her fully-clothed body up against his and wrapped her fingers around his cock. He let out a low groan, unable to pull it back.

"I want you, brother," she said.

Revik fell silent.

She looked at his face from where she leaned against his chest.

She watched him fight to control his breathing.

"Believe me in this," she murmured. "I want you... especially after your little display out there. You gave every male seer in this camp a hard-on, brother. You made every female wet, imagining you inside them."

When he closed his eyes, she smiled.

She pressed against him with more of her body.

"...The fact that you think none of us like you, or want you, or are affected by the insane amounts of pain you've been inflicting on us for the past weeks since we pulled you out of those caves, only makes us want you more."

Revik looked away, unable to hold her gaze.

He heard her smile, right before she started to massage him.

"Open your light, brother," she urged, her voice a purr. "Why won't you open your light to us? Isn't that the point of this little exercise?"

He groaned. His pain worsened when he realized she was using her light to try and open his. He felt her there, briefly, toying with him, and nearly lost it then and there.

"I won't let you come. Not that fast. Don't worry, brother."

"Fuck..."

"We will. Open your light. Please, brother."

He fought her, mindlessly that time.

Then he fought to do as she asked. He couldn't do either, but trying worsened the panic in his throat and chest. He heard her smile when he closed his eyes again, then she spoke softer once more, her voice a murmur.

"Gods, you are beautiful, brother. Even more beautiful than I imagined. How did someone as beautiful as you end up a Rook? We are all wondering this. Not only me."

He fought to hold onto his light, to keep her out, but only groaned.

When he let out another, heavier groan, she pressed into him with all of her weight. She slowed the movement of her hand as her fingers tightened.

Her light was growing hotter, more demanding.

"You like compliments," she said shrewdly, watching his face. "You like them a lot. Something tells me you also don't hear nearly enough of them."

Revik felt her slide deeper into his.

He let out another thick gasp.

As he did, the male behind him tightened his hold on him. He pressed an impressively-sized erection against Revik's ass and ground it against him.

Revik let out another sound and Nurek's pain worsened.

"Gods." Nurek kissed Revik's neck.

Hot, liquid light left the seer's tongue, making Revik light-headed.

Nurek bit him then, hard enough to make Revik gasp.

Fear washed through him, maybe even fear for his neck, some residual leftover after what happened in that clearing, but the muscular seer exuded nothing but reassurance, affection, warmth. He lightly stroked the bandage from where Terian cut his neck. He sent Revik another ripple of reassuring light, and that time he wove into it feelings of safety, of protectiveness, along with a wanting that made Revik lose control of his light.

He let out a heavier groan as he writhed in Nurek's hold.

Somewhere in that, he felt himself start to surrender.

He opened his light.

He opened it more, almost without him willing it that time.

He felt helpless.

He tried to relax into that, too.

"Gods." Nurek groaned, holding Revik tighter. "You aren't kidding about him, sister. Youngster or not... he's lucky we didn't all attack him out there."

"Is it rape when he asks us to do it?" Ontari mused from by the tent's opening.

Revik glanced at him, and Ontari smiled.

"I don't think he has any idea what he gave us permission to do," Mara said wryly.

She glanced at Ontari too, then looked looking back up at Revik's face. Her eyes held a denser scrutiny again, as if she studied his reaction to her words.

"He did not even seem to notice when every seer in that group started imagining taking him right there, by that fire," she mused. "Nor did he notice that the only reason we hesitated was because we couldn't believe he was serious. Dalai and Nurek just have better reflexes than the rest of us... and more power to them."

Mara smiled at Revik when Nurek laughed.

Then Mara's fingers tightened on him.

She massaged his cock harder.

"He's lucky Balidor intervened," she murmured, still watching Revik's face. "I think brother Balidor was in as much shock as the rest of us, or he likely would have stopped things sooner. I can only guess he thought for sure he was pushing brother Revik towards brother Jem with his ultimatum earlier... not into group sex with the rest of us."

Revik tensed at her words.

Mara sent a pulse of desire-filled heat.

She wrapped her light deeper and more possessively into his.

"Trust me, brother," she murmured. She pressed her body against his chest. "I am not making fun of you. Not in the slightest. We are all four grateful that was not the case... and for your generous offer out there. I would not be surprised if you find yourself the object of a lot of attempted seductions this week, however."

Nurek laughed again. He wrapped his arm around Revik tighter.

Revik felt possessiveness in the male, too.

His pain worsened, even as Dalai's hands slid over him, too.

"Can you feel his light?" the smaller seer murmured. She caressed his side. Her fingers traced his ribs up to his chest. "Gods. You are right, Mara. How did someone with light like this end up a Rook?"

Revik turned his head.

He saw Dalai smile at him.

He felt her pain wind deeper into Nurek's.

Revik's gaze slid higher then, looking over Dalai's head. He saw Ontari watching him now too, from a few feet away, his eyes faintly glazed. He was hard, Revik realized. He felt it on the handsome male seer before his eyes shifted down to confirm it.

It penetrated his mind that they were getting into his light.

They were opening him up, more than he'd intended... more than he probably should be letting them.

The thought panicked him, even as it made his erection worse.

He felt himself extending then, and Mara caressed the hard end of his cock as it revealed itself. Her fingers buckled Revik's knees.

Nurek held him up from behind, but Revik let out another groan, that one heavier than the previous ones, seeming to come from deeper inside his chest. He leaned harder into Nurek and the seer gripped him around the waist, pressing into him with his cock, even as he started pulling on Revik's light again, trying to get him to open more.

Mara tugged on his hair then. She forced him to look down at her.

He fought to focus on her face, panting. He felt his tongue thicken in his mouth.

Five years.

No one had touched him like this in over five years.

"Am I okay to stay then, brother?" Mara asked.

She pulled at him with her light, winding it deeper into his, coiling it hotly into his belly and groin. When he gasped, her voice grew openly cajoling.

"I'm asking you, brother Revik. I'll beg you, if you want me to... and I'll compliment you all night if you want that, too. I'll be very hurt if you say no, brother..."

He hesitated only a breath.

Then he nodded.

She gripped his hair tighter, and he closed his eyes.

"Tell me yes," she said. "Say it."

He let out another heavy groan, still not looking at her.

"Yes," he managed. "Stay. Please."

Smiling, she released him and stepped back.

When he opened his eyes, still fighting to control his breathing, she stood a few feet away. He pulled at her with his light, hard. He couldn't help it. He felt the void with her body and light away from his, so intensely it nearly brought tears to his eyes.

"Good," she said, sending him another flicker of heat.

He got the sense she was answering more than his words.

Before he could make sense of her expression, she glanced at the others.

Her voice and light shifted, until they held a near command.

"Get him down. Now," she said. "I think he's waited long enough."

"Do we flip a coin?" Nurek asked. He made his voice joking, even as he pressed against Revik from behind. "Or do we fight for it?"

"No," Mara said. She was still watching Revik's face. "I want to be the one to fuck him first. I will pay the three of you for that, if I need to."

Dalai laughed.

So did Ontari.

"I am serious," Mara said. "Name your price."

For a moment, Nurek didn't speak.

Revik felt him and Dalai exchange looks.

Revik himself just stared at the tall female, bewildered at the seriousness he felt in her light, and what he saw reflected in her hazel eyes. The others inside the tent seemed less surprised at Mara's words.

They also felt faintly hostile, which confused Revik, too.

He felt Nurek grudgingly concede with his light.

"Fine," he said. He released Revik's chest. "You can go first."

The big, Asian-looking seer kept hold of Revik's arm, even

after he released most of his body. Nurek gripped Revik tightly with his fingers, maybe to keep him upright, or maybe from the possessiveness Revik still felt rippling his and Dalai's light. The male seer stared at Mara as if assessing her in some way. As he did, he continued to support Revik with his light and hand. He wrapped a whisper of protective light around Revik's *aleimi*.

Whatever his precise reasoning for either thing, Revik found himself remaining by the other male's light. He did it almost unconsciously, without letting himself think too clearly about why, even after he noticed himself doing it.

Nurek gripped him tighter, maybe because he felt that, too.

Before Revik could clear his mind, or come close to controlling his light, the Chinese-looking seer aimed his voice back at Mara.

His tone grew openly warning.

"If you scare him, sister, or are unkind to him... or cause him to close on all of us again... I'll beat the crap out of you, Mara. I mean it. I don't give a fuck how much money you throw at us."

"He won't be the only one," Dalai muttered.

Mara smiled.

Her pale eyes shifted to Dalai, right before she quirked an eyebrow back at Nurek.

"You two really are quite taken with our Rook cub," she observed wryly.

"So are you," Dalai accused.

Mara shrugged. "I never denied that."

"I am serious, Mara," Nurek warned.

"Oh. I know you are, brother. I know both of you are quite serious. So am I."

She turned and studied Revik's gaze. "I won't hurt him. I have absolutely no intention of hurting him... in any way. Not unless he wants me to."

Revik felt Nurek's grip on him relax, but only marginally.

"You'd better not," the big seer rumbled.

Mara never took her eyes off Revik.

"You see, little brother?" she said softly to him.

She stepped closer to where he stood by Nurek and Dalai. She moved like a panther that time, that predatory glint back in her eyes as she looked over his body.

"...You have us fighting over you already."

## CHAPTER 20
# FRIENDS

Revik woke to a ping to his light.

He didn't know that at first.

He slid back into consciousness as if riding a heavier wave out of the depths of some darker ocean.

It wasn't tiredness he felt exactly.

Well, it wasn't tiredness that made it so difficult to open his eyes in those first few seconds. It was more like he'd lost track of himself somehow. He'd forgotten how to work any part of his body or light in the intervening hours since he finally forced himself to sleep.

He probably *was* tired, though.

He had a memory of Nurek urging him to sleep, to try at least, stroking his hair and face and pushing at his light, trying to get him to lose consciousness, to relax. The older seer had teased him gently, massaged his shoulders, murmured in his ear.

He'd said something about dawn approaching.

He'd said something about Revik needing to be something a little more coherent than one of the *upara d'kitre*... the walking dead... or Balidor would chew out the rest of them for abusing him, and making him worthless for the day.

Nurek reminded Revik they all would need to work that day.

He also teased Revik gently they'd all want him just as much tomorrow.

The last made Revik flush with embarrassment when he realized that was more than half the reason his body had been reluctant to go unconscious for any portion of the night.

Even just the last hour before dawn, his body fought him.

Some part of him believed it would be another five years before anyone agreed to have sex with him again.

So yeah, probably not a lot of sleep.

The second ping, Revik felt.

By then, he was awake enough to open his eyes.

He stared at the strangely liquid organic material of the tent. He shifted to his back then and adjusted his weight. He grimaced a little at the soreness of his body even as he felt limbs wrapped around him from more than one side.

Looking down, he saw Dalai's dark head resting on his chest.

She'd shifted with him from where she'd leaned on his side. Nurek wrapped around her from behind, his face smoothed in sleep. On Revik's other side, Mara pressed against him as well, her back and rear molded against his ribs and hip, her face tilted upwards as she slept.

Ontari lay on his stomach next to her, his head cushioned in his arms.

Revik felt eyes on him and looked towards the tent's door.

Dalejem stood in the opening at the front of the tent. He stood as far away from Revik as he possibly could while still having any part of himself inside the tent.

His face held no expression, but Revik could feel him waiting.

*Who is it you need?* he sent, his thoughts cautious, and quiet.

*You, brother,* Dalejem replied.

Dalejem's thoughts felt as empty as his expression.

Revik hesitated. He fought to take in the utter emptiness of the other's eyes.

Something about the look there made him wary.

*Is something wrong?* he sent, after a pause.

Dalejem just looked at him, then at the seers lying next to him.

*I'll wait outside,* he sent.

He receded from the opening, seemingly the instant he sent the thought.

Blinking to clear his vision, Revik carefully lifted Dalai off him. He repositioned her next to him on the softer mat. Then, moving slowly, he slid out from under Mara too, using his feet and legs to inch his body evenly down the mat.

He tried really hard not to jar it enough to bother their sleep.

He waited until he reached the end of the soft pad to try and climb off.

He still hoped to keep from waking any of them for real.

It occurred to him only then that they'd all been lying there uncovered, and that he was hard, just from waking up with so many hands on him, and so much skin pressed against his.

Remembering Dalejem standing there, he grimaced.

Moreover, he wondered just how long the other seer had been forced to stand there, between the tent flaps, waiting for Revik to feel the pings, to wake up.

Truthfully, he didn't want to know.

Still blinking and fighting to clear his vision, he looked around for his clothes.

All of those he saw belonged to other seers. He remembered how the evening had started, and looked to the other side of the tent.

They'd undressed him close to the tent's opening.

As he sat there, it occurred to him that others might have

seen more of his night's activities than he'd really wanted to think about at the time.

They all shared a construct, after all.

He shoved the thought from his mind.

He pulled himself stiffly to his feet and winced once he'd fully straightened.

He paused long enough to briefly stretch his arms and back, then made his way to the other side of the tent and dressed quickly. He threw the two shirts and armored vest around his shoulders without fastening the latter up.

He grabbed his boots and the two gun holsters he'd worn at the end. He checked the guns in rote before he shoved them back into organic holders.

He sat on the floor of the tent to shove his feet into socks and boots and to buckle them up before going outside. He did it more for the insects, parasites, and other things that might get on his skin than because he worried about the bottoms of his feet particularly.

It was already hot, even just a few hours after dawn.

He was sweating by the time he got the last boot done up and pulled himself back to his feet.

When he left the tent, he found Dalejem standing there, waiting for him.

The dark-haired seer turned when Revik walked out.

He didn't smile, or even really acknowledge Revik with his eyes or his light.

His expression remained as blank and emotionless as before.

When Revik just stood there, Dalejem motioned with his head for Revik to follow him.

They walked through the rows of tents without speaking, then out into the trees that started on the other side of the wide clearing.

Dalejem headed into the jungle, walking almost due west.

Revik followed him down the narrow, twisting path that

lived there. He didn't think overly about where they were going at first. He found himself noticing that Dalejem wore only sidearms, and that he had a machete stuck in the back of his belt, so they might be walking for a while.

Was this sentry duty? Or something else?

Frowning a little, Revik waited until they were a good distance from all of the tents, and out past the edges of the open construct before he ventured another try at speaking.

"What's going on?" he asked. "Are we on patrol?"

Dalejem didn't turn.

He continued to walk the narrow path, which began to curve upwards through the trees once they reached the next bend. Revik could feel it leading them higher up into the mountains. He touched his hip, realized he hadn't brought a canteen with him, and frowned.

"Brother?" he tried again. "Is something wrong?"

"Why would anything be wrong?" Dalejem asked.

His voice remained as expressionless as before.

Revik's frown deepened, but he didn't try to answer at first.

He started fastening up the front of his vest.

As he did, he sped the motion of his feet. He had to work a little to keep up with the other seer, despite his long legs. When he got close enough, Revik reached out. He laid a careful hand on Dalejem's shoulder, not really thinking about why as he did it.

As soon as he touched the other male, Dalejem came to an abrupt halt.

He turned on him, his green eyes cold.

"What?" he said. "What the fuck do you want?"

Revik took a half-step back. He stared at him.

There was no mistaking the hostility in the other seer's voice.

There was no mistaking the hostility in his eyes, either.

Revik had never seen the other seer angry, not like this.

Thrown by the expression on his face, he blinked.

He stepped back even more.

"Sorry. I just..." He hesitated. He watched the other male's face warily. Revik's hands hung at his sides now, instinctively in a position ready to fight. "What's wrong with you? Where are we going?"

"What the fuck difference does it make?" Dalejem snapped. "Why can't you just *follow orders* for a change, Dehgoies? Without all the goddamned questions?"

Revik just stared at him. He looked from one of his green eyes to the other.

"What's wrong?" he said. "Just tell me, goddamn it!"

Dalejem let out a humorless laugh.

Frowning, Revik was about to try again—

When the other seer turned on him.

He moved so fast, Revik didn't have time to even think about getting out of the way.

Dalejem swung, hard.

His fist connected shockingly with Revik's face, just under his right eye.

Revik's head snapped back and to the side.

Dalejem hit him hard enough that he nearly knocked him down.

Only years of fight training kept Revik on his feet, and even then, he gave ground.

He staggered back. He held up his hands instinctively, balled them into fists.

"*Gaos,*" he gasped. "What the fuck?"

Dalejem just stood there, panting. His light exuded so much anger Revik backed down, in spite of himself. He retreated another full step.

He held his hands up in more of a peace gesture.

"Brother," he said, fighting to get his equilibrium back. "Brother, talk to me. What is it? What did I do?"

"What did you *do?*" Dalejem let out a disbelieving laugh,

his eyes hard as glass. "Are you really fucking asking me that right now? Are you? You goddamned little *shit...*"

Revik flinched. He felt his skin flush, his face wince.

Fear rippled somewhere in his chest.

It wasn't fear of being hurt, not physically.

Dalejem had always been laid back. Calm. Warm.

Almost Zen in his approach to things.

That's how his light always felt to Revik, anyway.

Even as Revik thought it, he saw those sharp green eyes shift to look past him, back in the direction of camp. Maybe because his light was more open than it had been in weeks, months, maybe even years, Revik felt something from him in those few seconds.

A snapshot reached him, crystal clear.

In it, he got a good long look at exactly what Dalejem had seen when he'd walked through the flap doors of that tent.

That fear in Revik's light worsened, even as his mind fought to catch up.

"*Gaos,*" he said. "You're pissed about that?"

Dalejem's eyes shifted back to Revik's, holding a coldness that made Revik pause.

Pain coiled sickeningly through his light and gut, even as he shook his head.

"Gods. I didn't think..."

He paused, fighting to think, to make sense of this. He looked up, that fear flickering back through his light. He remembered Dalejem fighting with Mara that first night he was here, Mara making that crack about Dalejem telling her to keep her hands off him.

"You and Mara?" he asked. Panic reached his voice. "Gods, Jem... are you sleeping with her? Why the fuck didn't one of you tell me?"

"Holy fucking *gods*, Revik!" the male snapped. His words burst out of him like an explosion. "You can't possibly be as fucking stupid as you are pretending right now!"

Revik stared at him.

It felt like the seer had hit him again.

When Dalejem started to walk away, Revik lurched after him. He did it without thinking about whether that was particularly wise, either.

"Wait!" he snapped. "*Wait*, goddamn it...!"

He reached for him again, but Dalejem turned on him, his eyes holding an open threat.

"You touch me again, and I'll beat the living hell out of you. You little *fuck...*"

Meeting Revik's disbelieving stare, Dalejem returned it with one of his own.

His expression bled closer to incredulous as he studied Revik's face.

"What? Did you expect me to *like* it that you've whored yourself out to the entire camp, brother? And just how, exactly, did you expect me to react? Or did the thought cross your mind even once?"

At Revik's silence, Dalejem raised his voice.

His words twisted into a harder sarcasm.

"You know, I spent most of last night wondering if you were *angry* with me, brother," Dalejem said. "I wondered if you were trying to get my attention in some way, maybe get me to admit I wanted you, that I would be jealous if you slept with another. I wondered if you were angry that I didn't get you away from that psychopathic Rook. I wondered if you were angry at *me*, specifically, for that... since I told you I would protect you. I wondered if my goddamned *helplessness* in that situation is why you shunned me the whole walk back to camp, closing your light to me entirely... refusing to let me in at all."

He took a step closer to Revik.

He stared furiously into his face.

"I felt *guilty*, goddamn it," he growled. "I felt like I'd let you down... that we hadn't done enough to let you know how fucking *panicked* we all were when that piece of shit had that knife cutting into your throat. How afraid we were that he would kill you, right in front of us. And on the comm we have Vash telling us to stay back, Galaith telling us that red-haired fuck was capable of killing you in cold blood, that he was unstable, and overly-emotional about you. I wondered if this goddamned sex offer of yours…"

He waved a hand, clenching his jaw.

"…Was you *punishing* me for that. For not doing enough for you… during or after that mess. I thought you were *angry*, Revik."

The green and violet eyes hardened, right before Dalejem took a step closer.

He lowered his voice to a colder growl.

"Then, watching you with the rest of them, I realized… no. No, I'm an idiot. He's not angry. He's not thinking of me at all. He's just a messed up little shit who doesn't give a fuck. Which shouldn't have surprised me, goddamn it, but it *did.* It did surprise me. You're lucky I didn't walk into that tent and beat the hell out of you right there…"

Revik stared at him in disbelief.

Dalejem didn't seem to care how he reacted anymore, though.

He muttered what sounded like more curses, that time in a language Revik didn't know.

Dalejem still muttered as he turned his back on Revik, leaving him there.

He began walking even more rapidly into the jungle, that time without looking back.

Revik just stood there, watching him go.

It hit him, as Dalejem's form receded, that the seer had woken him.

He'd told him they were under orders.

*Had* Dalejem gotten orders to wake him? He clearly didn't want to be out here with him, not unless the whole point of this exercise was so that Dalejem could chew him out.

As he watched the older male walk away, Revik fought back and forth on whether he should try to follow him, even if Dalejem didn't want him there.

He might really be supposed to be out here with him for some reason.

Well. Unless it wasn't just about reaming him out.

Unless Dalejem brought him out here to kill him.

The seer let out another harsh laugh.

He came to an abrupt stop on the path in front of him.

"Don't fucking tempt me... *Rook.*"

Revik flinched, in spite of everything.

It was the first time Dalejem had ever called him that.

"What are we doing out here?" Revik asked. "Why won't you tell me?"

Dalejem shook his head in annoyance, clicking at him.

"Orders. What do you think? Orders. You think I wanted to spend my fucking morning looking at you? No. I got woken up, same as you. I got *told* to go get your sorry ass out of the remnants of your public orgy, and to go on patrol with you. I think this is brother Balidor's way of telling me to get over it... but he can go fuck himself, too."

When Revik didn't answer, Dalejem glanced over his shoulder.

He gave Revik an even colder look.

"Seriously. Are you brain damaged, brother? Did the Rooks do something to your mind while you were with them for so many years?"

Revik's muscles tensed, rendering him silent.

Maybe because the words hit a little too close to home that time.

Dalejem stared at his face, as if seeing the reaction.

The handsome seer's long jaw hardened more.

"Do you really think I would have *willingly* walked into

that tent?" he asked, his voice openly angry again. "You piece of shit *Rook*. Do you seriously think I would have just stood there, watching you sleep with a hard-on, waiting for your friends to wake so you could blow them again?"

Revik felt his own jaw harden.

He didn't speak when the other seer threw up his hands, exhaling in disgust.

When Dalejem turned, once more walking away from him, Revik didn't move.

Pain rose in his light as he watched the other male leave that time, enough that his throat abruptly closed. He found himself following the other mindlessly, barely seeing the trees around him as he placed his feet, not sure why he was still trying to keep up.

He fought to control his emotions, his light, wondering why it wasn't easier after the night before instead of harder. He found himself wiping his face angrily, fighting back tears.

"I thought we were friends," he said.

His voice was low, a mutter mixed with a growl.

Somehow, even walking a few yards in front of him, Dalejem heard it.

The seer stopped.

Revik tensed when he did, stopping, too.

He watched Dalejem's back warily in the pause, but he still flinched when the other male turned. Then he couldn't get out of the way fast enough when Dalejem suddenly came at him. Letting out a gasp of surprise, Revik actually considered running away, taking off into the trees, but the other seer closed the gap between them in what felt like a blink.

Then he had ahold of Revik's armored vest.

Before Revik could writhe free, Dalejem slammed Revik's back into the nearest trunk. It happened to be a large kapok, with wave-like roots jutting out of the sides, and Revik let out a stunned gasp when his spine made contact with one of those roots.

He gripped the other male's arms. He panted, tried to decide if he should call for help. He was still trying to decide when Dalejem released him just as quickly, stepping back.

Revik stared, stunned when he saw tears in the other male's eyes.

That panic returned to his chest. It forced words out of his mouth, almost before he knew what he was saying.

"You didn't want me!" he cried out. "You fucking *told* me you didn't want me... that first day we were here!"

"Bullshit!" Dalejem snapped. "Bullshit! You lying little *fuck!* I practically asked you for it!"

Revik stared at him. He felt the pain in his chest worsen.

He bit his tongue. He fought to think about Dalejem's words, to reason through them, if only to keep his emotions under control. He fought to think back over that day, to remember the exact words they'd spoken to one another out on the edge of that field.

Like all seers, he had a photographic memory.

He could remember the *facts* of things, even if his feelings twisted what they meant.

Once he had replayed Dalejem's words to him that day, the pain in his chest worsened. He played the words again, realized that his state of mind and the pain he'd been in, embarrassment about Kali and whatever else, had warped that conversation, too.

He hadn't heard him correctly.

Dalejem had been trying to tell him something, but not the thing Revik had heard.

Maybe he couldn't let himself go there at the time.

Maybe Balidor was right.

Maybe it was just cowardice.

He bit his lip, staring at the jungle floor without seeing it.

He'd been so sure they would all look at him the way the seers of the Seven had looked at him. More so, given the reputation of the Adhipan for being holy, for being above reproach in terms of ethics and rigid codes about light and dark. He remembered Seertown. He remembered those stares, the fearful flickers of light, the disgust. He'd felt those things the whole time he was there, up until the day he left Vash's enclave in the Himalayas for the Pamir.

He'd felt similar things from pretty much every seer there, apart from Vash himself.

It had been easier to try and prepare himself for being hated.

It had been easier to close that door before anyone could slam it in his face. For the same reasons, it had been easier to assume the worst in every word and interaction, rather than try to look at the situation objectively.

Realizing he hadn't learned a damned thing from those monks, in five years of staring at walls and trying to see himself clearly, Revik felt his nausea worsen.

As the pieces fell into place, he felt the pain in his chest worsen, too, even as he raised a hand to his head, clutching at his hair.

"I'm sorry," he said.

Dalejem let out a humorless laugh.

"I am," Revik growled. "And fuck you for not telling me. You must have known I didn't understand. What's your excuse for not making sure that I did?"

Dalejem gave him a disbelieving look.

"We were under orders! Balidor—"

"I don't want to hear any more about *Balidor!*" Revik snapped. "What? Are you a goddamned robot? You couldn't see that I wasn't thinking clearly? That I was afraid? Jesus, Dalejem. You, of all people. You knew what a mess I was... and I thought we were friends! I thought we were *friends!* Why didn't you tell me?"

"Tell you *what*, precisely?" Dalejem said. "That I wanted to be the one you came to?"

"Yes!" Revik said, frustrated. "Yes! And why not? You

must have known I wanted that. I might have been fucked up in the head, but you weren't. Hell, if I'd known you were open to it at all, I would have *begged* you, brother."

"Yet you never asked me!"

"I *couldn't* ask you!"

"But you can offer yourself up to *every single one* of them instead?"

Revik stared at him. He felt his jaw harden. "Yes."

Dalejem's jaw tightened, too.

He stared back at Revik, even as Revik felt a pulse of pain leave the other male's light. He winced against that pain, not wanting to feel that either, but he wouldn't let himself block it, or push it away, even when it hurt.

"Why?" Dalejem asked, his voice lower.

Revik clicked softly. He shook his head.

"Gods. I don't know. I don't *fucking know.*" Thinking about his words, he realized that wasn't entirely true, either. "I didn't want any of them," he said. "It was easier."

Dalejem gave him another disbelieving stare.

Then he laughed, a sound that managed to convey nothing but pure anger.

Staring at Revik in fury, he paced the ground in front of him. He glared openly at where Revik stood with his back against the kapok tree.

"Bullshit!" Dalejem burst out angrily at him. *"Bullshit,* Revik! You told us you wanted Mara when you first laid eyes on her. You weren't in that monk's cell *five minutes* before you told all of us about wanting to fuck her!"

Revik shook his head. He clicked at the other male angrily.

"No," he said. "That was different."

"What is different?" Dalejem said. "What is *different* about that?"

"It *is* different!" Revik growled, giving him a cold look. "That was my *dick* talking. Not my mind. Not even my light... which would have fucked anything that *breathed* at that point in time. I offered myself to all of them because I don't know any of them. Not apart from you, and you left. You walked out of there... before I even knew you were there. After that, I didn't *care* anymore. I didn't give a damn who it was. The who of it was incidental. I as much as told them that when I made the offer."

Dalejem folded his arms.

His expression had blanked once more, but not before Revik felt the open skepticism flicker across Dalejem's light. He saw it flash briefly in Dalejem's clear, green eyes. Revik saw the distrust there, even through the infiltrator's mask he wore.

He saw it, and just waited.

He didn't even know what he was waiting for at that point.

For the other to yell at him again?

To tell him he was liar, some kind of master manipulator... again?

Revik held the other's gaze until Dalejem looked away.

The green-eyed seer stared at the ground.

He gave Revik another hard look.

"Does it matter to you now, Rook?" he asked bitterly.

Revik felt his jaw harden to granite. "What difference does it make now? I can't do anything about it now!"

Dalejem's arms unfolded. He walked up to Revik again.

Revik couldn't help it, he flinched.

But the seer didn't hit him.

He reached for him instead. He placed his hands deliberately on Revik's belt.

Revik was hard in about two seconds.

Even so, he grabbed the other's wrists, stopping him.

"No." His voice came out low, almost forced. He shook his head. "No."

Dalejem looked up. Pain lanced through Revik's chest

when he saw tears in the other's eyes again. "You'll do it for them, but not me?"

Revik's pain worsened. He closed his eyes. He gripped the male's wrists tighter.

After he'd controlled his light, he shook his head.

"I... I care about you," he managed. His words came out close to angry. "I *care* about you. What part of that don't you understand?"

"How about none of it," Dalejem snapped.

"You do understand. I know you fucking do."

"No!" the other male said, staring at him in disbelief. "No, I don't! If we are only friends, as you feel the need to hammer into me again and again... then what difference does it make? Or do you only fuck people you feel nothing for at all, Revik? People you'd just as soon walk away from, so you don't have to care if they lived or died?"

Revik flinched.

It took him another second to realize at least part of that was because Dalejem used his given name.

Even most of the previous night, Revik hadn't heard his actual name all that often.

Dalejem walked closer to him.

He slid his hand roughly into Revik's hair.

He gripped it tightly with his fingers, holding him still. He started caressing Revik's neck and jaw with his other hand, like he had that first day, out by the field. He put light into his fingers, more of it when Revik opened, a lot more of it, enough to blank out Revik's mind. Light came from Dalejem's chest, from his belly and hands and Revik groaned.

He fought to pull himself free, gasping.

When the other male released him, standing back, Revik fought to control his breathing.

Once he had, he felt anger slide forward in his light.

"You won't even accept affection from me?" Dalejem asked, frustrated. "I won't try to *fuck* you, Revik. You've made your feelings on that topic crystal clear. If we really are friends, like you keep saying, then why can't I—"

"We're not friends," Revik cut in. "We're not."

He looked up. He gave the other male a harder look.

For what felt like a long moment, the two of them just stood there.

"Then what the fuck are we?" Dalejem snapped.

Revik only shook his head, not answering.

He felt the surrender in his own light, seemingly right after the seer spoke. Some part of him had already given in to this. He couldn't even be sure why he'd been fighting it.

Dalejem must have felt the change in his light.

That time, when the other seer moved towards him, Revik deliberately softened his body. He leaned against the tree, opening his light, opening his hands and arms to make it clear he wasn't going to stop him. When Dalejem got close enough, Revik tried to open the other seer's light, too. He slid himself deeper into him as soon as Dalejem reached for his belt.

That time, when Dalejem started undoing the clasp, Revik let out a heavy groan.

He began unhooking the front of the armored vest the other male wore.

He had it open and was yanking it down his arms and off his shoulders, when Dalejem stopped him, gripping both of his wrists.

"What are we doing here?" Dalejem asked.

His voice came out low, a near murmur.

He met Revik's gaze from only a few inches away, reminding him they weren't far off one another in height.

"What are *you* doing, brother?" Dalejem asked. "Now. With me. What is this? You haven't been clear with me about any of this."

Revik felt the pain on the other male and closed his eyes, longer than a blink.

He slid his hands into Dalejem's hair.

He pulled on him, hard, with his light and fingers. Hearing the other seer let out a pained breath, Revik lowered his head, unthinking, and kissed him. He used so much of his light in his tongue and lips that Dalejem groaned against his mouth.

He gripped the front of Revik's vest.

When the kiss deepened, Dalejem slid his hand deliberately down over the front of Revik's pants. He massaged him with strong fingers as they continued to kiss.

By the end of the second kiss, Dalejem was leaning on him, his arm wrapped around Revik's waist. Revik gripped his hair tighter, fisted it in his hands, and kissed him again. He opened his light more, and the other male let out another low groan.

Revik got lost there, somehow.

They kissed like that for a long time, for what felt like an endless amount of time.

He found himself pulling more, harder and yet more subtly on Dalejem's light. He pulled on it and wound himself into it. He experimented until he was panting against the other seer's neck and mouth. He lost himself in another kiss, still gripping the other's hair as he pressed his lower body against him, against his hand, against his body.

*"Gaos,"* he heard Dalejem murmur when they came up for air. "Of course you'd fucking kiss like this. Of course. A fucking toddler, and you kiss like this—"

"Brother, I—"

"Shut the fuck up, Revik."

Confusion swam over Revik's light.

Then the other seer had his hands on him again. He started massaging him for real, then taking off his clothes. Revik stopped thinking at all once Dalejem began opening his light more, pulling on him, asking Revik to do the same.

When Dalejem didn't stop, Revik's light continued to open.

He pressed his whole body against the older seer's. He let out a low groan.

Somewhere in that, he remembered where they were.

Staring around at the jungle, half-dazed, he fought to think.

"How long has it been?" Dalejem asked.

Revik turned, staring at him.

The question confused him.

The night before. Dalejem saw it. He knew about—

"I didn't mean since you had an orgasm, Revik," Dalejem said icily. "I meant since you kissed someone you actually liked."

Revik froze.

Thinking about the other's words, he fought to answer them. His mind went utterly blank, and not only from the memory wipe Vash and Galaith performed.

"I don't know," he said, gruff.

"You don't know?"

Revik shook his head, his voice still low. "I don't. I really don't."

Dalejem's sculpted lips twisted in a faint frown.

Revik didn't see anger in him that time as much as a wanting to know, an almost frustrated desire to understand something he clearly didn't understand. Revik still watched his face when Dalejem slid down the front of him, until he was on his knees.

He started unfastening Revik's pants with rough, deft fingers.

Revik let out a startled gasp.

Before he could recover, Dalejem yanked Revik's belt open entirely. He finished undoing the front of his pants, sliding his hands between Revik's thighs...

When the green-eyed seer stopped.

He looked up, that perfect mouth set in a hard line.

"No," he said.

"No?" Revik's voice came out nearly hoarse. "No? Now? Why?"

"No." Dalejem abruptly regained his feet. He looked Revik straight in the eye. "We're going back. You're taking a fucking *shower*, brother. You can at least do that for me. I'll try to let it go, what you made me listen to for most of last night, but don't expect me to bathe in it. Don't expect me to be very nice about it for most of today, either."

Revik stared at him for a moment.

Then he felt heat warm his cheeks, even as he fumbled with his belt to get it back on and done up. Pain rippled his light. It made him feel sick, but he remained silent.

Really, he couldn't find much to say in argument against the other's words.

Still, being cut off from Dalejem's light so suddenly left him lost-feeling, in enough pain that he found he couldn't meet the other seer's gaze.

Embarrassment pulsed off his *aleimi*, making that worse.

Flickers of memory rose around the night before, seen through a different lens now that he knew Dalejem had witnessed some, most, or possibly all of it. Revik shoved those memories aside a moment later, knowing the other seer would likely feel him thinking about that, too.

He would especially feel it given how close they stood, and how much they'd just wrapped into each other's light.

Revik didn't really know how Dalejem might react to seeing that again, after everything they'd just done and said.

He didn't really want another punch in the face, or a knee to the groin.

He also didn't want Dalejem to walk away.

When he looked up next, the green-eyed seer was only waiting for him.

He stood there, patiently holding out a hand.

Before Revik could take it, Dalejem retracted his fingers, frowning.

"Gods," Revik said. He fought an urge to shake him, maybe even to hit him. "What? What now? I'll take a fucking shower, okay? I just want you to take it with me—"

"It's not that."

"Then what?" he said, frustrated.

"Are you going to rescind your offer?" Dalejem asked.

Clenching his jaw, he faced Revik directly, hands on his hips, his lips curled in a frown.

His words sounded a hell of a lot more like a demand than a question.

"Am I just next on your list, Dehgoies?" he asked. "Or are you going to tell the rest of those fuckers to back off? To leave you the hell alone?"

Revik stared at him, blank.

Watching him, Dalejem frowned harder.

"You're not going to continue sleeping with them?" he demanded. He pushed at Revik harder with his light. "Because if you are, you can forget about sleeping with me, brother. In fact, if you are, you'd better stay the hell *away* from me, because I really might hurt you again. Next time, it might be more than a black eye."

Revik's jaw hardened in a frown.

He stared at the other male, half in disbelief now.

For a longer moment, he debated whether to speak.

Then he shoved caution aside, and just said it.

"What are you really asking me, brother?" Revik heard the edge creep back into his voice. He switched to formal Prexci, maybe to better make his point. "Are you asking me for an agreement? Or just toying with me by implying it? Would you rather just *take* the right to order me around, like some kind of control-freak *dulesri*? Or do you intend to *ask* me for it, as if you actually saw me as an equal?"

There was a silence.

In it, Dalejem blinked, staring at him.

Then the older seer burst out in a laugh.

For the first time that day, it sounded like a real laugh.

Revik felt a heated flicker of desire off the other male, too.

"Nicely said," Dalejem smiled.

After another pause, he smiled again.

He clicked at Revik softly.

"An agreement, brother," he said, giving him a slight bow. His voice grew formally polite, even as he switched to the same language Revik had used, despite the smile still teasing his lips. "I am asking you for an agreement, if you are amenable to the idea. One that preferably doesn't involve you offering yourself as a fuck-toy to every other seer in hearing distance. One that might just keep you *alive*, if you intend to share a bed with me."

Revik felt the pain in his chest worsen, but only nodded.

"You are not as... laid back... as you pretend, brother."

Dalejem gave him a denser look. "You think I am manipulating you?"

Revik shook his head. "No. That's not what I meant."

"Do you think you are too young for me, brother?"

Revik frowned, staring at him. "No. I wasn't saying that, either."

There was a silence.

Then, remembering something else, Revik looked up, his mouth firming.

"I have to go back," he reminded him. "After."

"Back?" Dalejem's eyes blanked. "What does that mean?"

"The Pamir," Revik said. "I have to go back to the Pamir. To the caves. To those monks. I'm in penance."

Looking at him for a longer moment, Dalejem nodded.

He offered his hand again.

"We'll talk about that when it happens," he said neutrally.

Feeling the reassurance in the other's light, Revik felt his shoulders start to relax. Even so, he glanced around at the trees, feeling suddenly nervous as he looked at the other male.

He hadn't been involved with many males.

None really, apart from sex.

Well, none other than Terian... who was such a freak show deviant coupled with a mass of complicated mental illnesses, Revik couldn't imagine how any aspect of that particular relationship would help him navigate this one.

When he continued to stand there, Dalejem cleared his throat.

"Are you coming?" he asked. His eyes grew patient once more. "I will take the shower with you, if you want. If that was your next question."

"Don't we need to be out here still?" Revik asked. He heard the stall in his voice. "Balidor. Didn't he want us to walk the perimeter or something? Patrol something?"

Dalejem smiled. That time, it barely touched his mouth.

"He's letting us off the hook, brother," he said gently.

After the barest pause, Revik nodded again.

That time, he took the hand offered to him.

He found himself clutching the fingers tightly in his own.

He knew his skin was hot, borderline sweaty, but he didn't let go, and he couldn't quite meet the other's gaze.

## CHAPTER 21
# RESCINDED

They didn't have sex in the shower.

Revik wanted to.

He let it go when he realized they were being watched, that Dalejem was right, that the showers were too public, especially given that it was broad daylight and they stood in a row not far from the mess tent... not to mention the fact that the wall only covered about half of his body with translucent organic sheeting.

In the end, Revik shoved the other seer out of the cubicle altogether, naked, and still wet, and finished showering alone.

Even so, he felt flickers of curiosity aimed at him by passing seers.

Some clearly felt what he'd been doing the night before.

Some just heard about it, or heard his offer around the fire.

Some stared at his scars, seeing their patterns on his shoulders and upper back as they walked behind him outside the shower cubicle.

When Revik finally left that cubicle, Dalejem was gone.

He snaked his light out cautiously to look for him.

He wrapped the towel more tightly around his waist as he did.

Revik grew aware of even more eyes on him and his back once he left the area of the showers. Ignoring those stares as best he could, he walked through the camp as casually as he could. It wasn't easy, given that he wore only a towel and borrowed shower sandals that Ontari had lent him days earlier.

It should have been easy though.

All of them used those showers.

Some of it was that he felt lost.

He didn't particularly want to ask anyone where Dalejem's tent was.

He didn't really want to be out here on his own much longer, either.

Feeling a whisper of irritation from Dalejem himself, who clearly felt the attention on Revik's body as he wandered around camp in a towel, Revik smiled faintly, but not with a lot of humor, right before the seer sent him an abrupt snapshot of where he was.

When Revik showed up outside Dalejem's tent a moment later, smacking at bugs landing on his legs, then frowning when he remembered what the monks would say about that, he hesitated again. He wondered if Dalejem would actually screw with him by sending him to the wrong tent. Somehow, after their confrontation in the jungle, Revik had an easier time imagining the other seer throwing him a random test, just to see what he'd do.

Even as he thought it, Dalejem appeared in the tent's opening, frowning at him.

The green-eyed seer no longer even wore a towel.

Revik stared down at his muscular body, right before he glanced over his shoulder. He moved to block Dalejem's nakedness from view of the wider camp before he'd thought about what he was doing.

He gripped his own towel tighter in his hands and scowled at the shockingly handsome seer. He found himself remembering again just how good-looking the other male was. Dalejem got stares everywhere he went, from males and females alike. Revik remembered how stunned he'd been by Dalejem's appearance the first time he saw him.

He'd been nearly star-struck by it.

Even for a seer, Dalejem was mind-numbingly beautiful.

Seeing him naked didn't exactly lessen that impression—and that was just his physicality.

It didn't even take into account his *aleimic* light.

"You really think I'd send you naked and wet to another's tent?" Dalejem asked him incredulously. His dark hair hung to his shoulders, straight and still dripping with water.

Revik felt his tongue thicken.

"Are you going to let me come inside?" he asked.

"That depends." Dalejem cocked an eyebrow at him. "Did you tell them?"

"What?" Revik stared at him. He saw other seers pass out of the corner of his eye, felt them notice and stare at Dalejem's nakedness. "Get back inside your fucking tent!" he growled. "Can we talk about this in there?"

"No," Dalejem said. "Did you tell them?"

"Tell them what?"

"What the fuck do you think?" Dalejem scowled at him for real.

Revik just looked at him, then tensed, hearing laughter behind him as a group of female seers passed by the two of them from a few yards away. He glanced over his shoulder in time to see one of them looking pointedly at Dalejem's cock, a smile at her lips.

Revik didn't hear exactly what she said to her friend, but he got the overall gist.

He glared back at the other male.

"Are you fucking with me right now?" he asked.

"Meaning what?"

"Are you trying to make me jealous?"

"I'm honestly not sure. Why? Is it working?"

Revik felt his anger worsen, even as he glanced behind him again. "Am I supposed to make an announcement in the construct? Right now? Seriously?"

"Why not?" Dalejem's eyes grew a touch colder. "You seemed to have absolutely no problem announcing your sexual needs to all of them last night, brother."

"Balidor gave me a fucking ultimatum—" Revik growled.

"To ask *someone*," Dalejem snapped. "Not *all* of them. Not every damned seer in the *gaos di'lalente* camp, brother Revik."

Realizing Dalejem was dead serious, Revik exhaled in open anger.

He opened his light. He sent up a flare in the construct, if only to get the seers in the immediate vicinity to notice him.

Silence fell over their whole area of the working Barrier space.

With it, Revik felt attention on him from at least a dozen presences, and suddenly, he felt a lot more naked than he had with just the towel.

*I'm rescinding my offer of last night,* he sent clearly into that quiet, waiting space. *If you're wondering why I'm interrupting your goddamned breakfast to tell you that... ask brother Dalejem,* he added, letting his irritation be felt in the construct as well. *I'm finding he's a bit of a control freak.*

Revik heard laughter.

Some of it was physical, from seers near enough for him to hear.

Some was in the Barrier.

In the pause that followed, Revik continued to feel open amusement in the Barrier construct, along with knowing smiles about him and Dalejem, a few flickers of surprise and even a few pulses of annoyance.

Some of those he even recognized by then.

Ontari was one of the loudest in terms of amusement.

Revik couldn't focus on any of that for long, though.

Dalejem was still standing there, arms folded, naked.

Moreover, he was now mouthing words at him.

Realizing what the seer wanted him to say, Revik clicked aloud, shaking his head.

*I am also no longer taking offers,* he added in that same space. He rolled his eyes openly at the older seer. "… Although I'm pretty sure that was implied with the first thing," he added aloud to Dalejem, his voice holding a touch of real annoyance. "Now will you go back inside your goddamned tent? Or are you making an offer of your own right now?"

Smiling, the seer bowed.

He receded backwards through the flaps of the tent and held one side open for Revik to enter after him.

After the barest hesitation—Revik did.

# CHAPTER 22
# OLDER, AND ADHIPAN

Once they were both inside, Dalejem didn't wait.

He caught hold of Revik by the arms. He forced him back, then down on his sleeping mat, pinning him to the surface with his legs, weight, and hands. His fingers moved to Revik's wrists where he held him to the soft cushion.

Then he hung over him.

He studied Revik's face in the dimmer light.

"Are you really okay with this? You should probably tell me now. I likely won't be able to hear you on this later, *ilyo.*" He watched Revik's face cautiously. "I think Balidor thinks I've snapped... that I bullied you into being my sex slave in a fit of jealousy."

Revik rolled his eyes, clicking a little.

"He's not entirely wrong," Dalejem added.

Revik laughed at that.

He couldn't help it.

He was having trouble focusing though, especially when the other seer began exploring him cautiously with his light. Revik felt threads of the older male's *aleimi* wind into his chest and abdomen. The subtlety there, the heat behind it... *gaos*.

He closed his eyes.

Fuck. Fuck...

His tongue thickened.

He could feel his light starting to open.

He broke out in a sweat.

"I thought I was just an ex-Rook?" Revik blurted. He bit his lip when his pain worsened. "Who cares what I think? It's all karma and bad spaces on my part anyway. Is it not, brother?"

Revik meant the words as a joke.

Also, maybe, it was a cowardly way of lightening things, of using humor to dodge the intensity he could feel in the other's light. Whatever Dalejem was doing to him right now, it already felt more intimate than anything that happened the night before.

When Revik glanced up, the other seer wasn't smiling.

A frown pulled at his handsome brow as he stared.

"Don't talk like that anymore, Revik," he said, his voice serious. "I mean it. I hate it when you say things like that to me, brother. I don't want to hear it any more. Not with me. Say it to one of the others, if you need to."

Revik flushed. He felt his mouth harden.

Defensiveness rose in his light.

"You don't want to hear about that?" he asked. "About me having been a Rook? I *was* a Rook, Jem. I don't think anyone's going to let you forget that, especially if we're fucking."

Dalejem winced.

"Don't call me Jem, either," Dalejem said. "I like that you call me by my full name. Hardly anyone ever does. Not even Balidor calls me that. And no, I didn't mean you having been a Rook. I know you were a Rook. I don't care. I meant about you being bad now. I meant that tired internal monologue of yours, about you being somehow wrong or irredeemably evil because of what you did in the past."

Revik stared at him.

"But it's true, isn't it?" His jaw hardened when the other seer didn't change expression. "My light *is* corrupt now. It will always be corrupt from what I did."

Dalejem's expression grew genuinely angry.

"Your light's not fucking *corrupt*, Dehgoies! Gods above! Are you an old man? That's old fashioned, to think that way. And dogmatic. And untrue."

"Don't call me Dehgoies," Revik said, his voice curt. "I don't like it."

"Fine... Revik," Dalejem said, clicking at him. "But if that was another attempt at distraction, I meant what I said. Stop thinking of yourself that way. It's pissing me off. That's not what those fucking monks are teaching you in those caves, is it?"

Briefly, Revik's anger retreated.

He thought about Dalejem's question.

He frowned, then slowly shook his head.

"No," he said. The truth of that hit him as he said it. "No. That's not what they teach. That's not where I heard that."

"Good." Dalejem exhaled. *"Gaos.* Then listen to them. *They* are your teachers. Not those ignorant assholes in Seertown." His eyes grew shrewd. "Is that why you don't like to be called Dehgoies? Because of your adoptive family?"

Revik felt his jaw harden again.

Annoyance mixed with his pain. He fought to untangle them, couldn't.

Dalejem exhaled. He clicked under his breath.

"I don't care, Revik." He shook him lightly. "I'm not one who gives a damn about the ridiculous pecking order of the old families. I couldn't give two shits that 'Clan Dehgoies' is one of the first. Or how much they think of themselves for that reason."

"They do not like me," Revik said.

"Is that all it is?"

"Isn't that enough?" Revik stared at him. "I never asked to be given their name. I did not want it, and they did not want me. I don't care if the others call me Dehgoies, but I don't want *you* to call me that. Do you have a fucking problem with that, brother?"

Dalejem soothed him with his light.

He sent a softer thread of that heat into his skin.

"It is fine, brother," Dalejem assured him. "I never disagreed with your request."

Realizing he was overreacting, Revik's embarrassment returned.

"I'm sorry," he said, gruff.

"No." Dalejem shook his head. "Don't be sorry. I have no problem with any of what you are doing, Revik. I won't call you Dehgoies."

Revik nodded, but now worry coiled around his light.

It began to turn into a denser paranoia.

He fought to let it go. *Gaos.* He had to let it go.

He didn't want to say anything.

He didn't want to make this weird. He knew he could be overly blunt.

He knew he had a tendency to make things weird.

"Are you having second thoughts about me, brother?" he blurted.

He fought to keep his voice subdued. He struggled not to push, not to make it weird. He struggled to keep every thread of hostility out of his light.

"This isn't the conversation I thought we'd be having in here," he said. He closed his eyes. "Do you not want to do this with me now? Just tell me. It's fine. Okay? It's fine. Just tell me. I can go. I'll go work… have them put me on the rotation. Just tell me what to say. What you want me to tell the others."

Dalejem gripped Revik's wrists more tightly.

When Revik opened his eyes, Dalejem stared at him.

Incredulity stood there.

Then pain. His light wound heavily into Revik's without warning. More pain lived there, liquid heat that broke Revik out in a sweat before he could get out of the way. His breath stopped. His heart stopped. Dalejem threw so much of himself into Revik's *aleimi,* Revik thought he was having a heart attack.

Jesus fuck. He thought he might die.

He let out a pained groan.

Dalejem wrapped a hand around Revik's throat.

His mouth fell to Revik's ear.

"You're not going anywhere, brother," he murmured.

Revik let out another pained sound. He was breathing too much, losing his ability to hold onto his light. He felt the other seer doing things to him, pulling on him—

Fuck. Fuck... he had no way to deal with this.

He didn't know how to deal with this.

Dalejem had still barely touched him.

Revik fought briefly to free his hands. It might have been a test in part, to see if he could get away with it. When the other smacked him warningly with his light, ordering him to lie still, Revik went soft under him. He closed his eyes.

He forced himself to try and relax.

He felt Dalejem's pain worsen as the older seer hung over him.

Revik fought him, but his pain only paralyzed him more.

The fucker wouldn't touch him. *Gaos.* He really wouldn't touch him.

When Dalejem continued to flood heat and pain into Revik's light, Revik lost touch with the room. It occurred to him, as he lay there, he might be in over his head.

Dalejem was older than him. He was older, more experienced.

He was better trained.

Fuck, he was Adhipan.

When he opened his eyes next, Dalejem was panting, his skin hot.

The breathtakingly handsome seer softened as he met Revik's gaze.

"*Gaos.* You really are fucking beautiful," he murmured. "I hate her for it, but Mara was right. That look on your face when you start to lose control... *gaos di'lalente rasul.* Your light turns so goddamned submissive it's feels like an attack, *ilyo.* Like an outright manipulation. Some part of me believes you are fucking with me, trying to make me lose control..."

Revik's jaw hardened.

He felt his skin grow hot.

He tried to stay still. He couldn't even meet the other's gaze.

"*Gaos*... and now you're blushing." Dalejem's jaw hardened. "You're fucking *blushing,* even as you pull on my light, even as your light begs me to fuck you." A colder look rose to those pale green eyes. "You have no idea how goddamned jealous I am right now, brother. For last night, but not even just for that. I know you prefer females... you must turn into a goddamned child with them. Like a begging, submissive, sex-starved child..."

Revik winced. He fought not to let his mind go there.

He felt Dalejem pull harder on his light.

"You fucker," Dalejem said. "You absolute fucker."

Revik looked away. Embarrassment made it difficult to think, to breathe.

Embarrassment, pain.

"You prefer females." Dalejem nudged his mind. "You prefer them, Revik."

Revik winced. "Fuck off... *gaos,* fuck off..."

"Just admit it. You prefer them. Don't lie to me."

Revik's pain worsened. He fought to breathe, to even

think. He felt his pain turning on him, turning him emotional. Jesus, Dalejem didn't want him. He didn't really want him. He was angry at him. This was just going to be revenge.

This was going to be Dalejem torturing him because he could.

The green-eyed seer studied his face. A frown touched his lips, his eyes, his brow.

Before Revik could decide what to say, how to ask—

Dalejem lowered his mouth.

He kissed him. His deepened the kiss once Revik started kissing him back.

They kissed until Revik's light began to open for real, until he started losing that clenching around his chest and heart, then losing himself, first in the pain, then in the sensation, then back in the pain when it grew unbearable again.

Pretty soon it slanted out his mind.

When Dalejem abruptly ended the kiss, Revik groaned.

He groaned, felt his light tilt out of his control. He felt sick again, desperate, lost in a way he hadn't the night before. Vulnerability lived there now, not only fear. He found himself acutely aware of the other's light, of his mind probing his.

"Are you going to let me in?" Dalejem asked, as if he'd heard him.

Revik hesitated, then nodded. "Yes."

"Really? You'll *really* let me in?"

"Yes."

The older seer's expression grew taut. He kissed him harder, using enough light in his tongue to black out Revik's vision. Dalejem yanked the towel off Revik's waist, and Revik felt himself handing over more of his light, even as that feeling of vulnerability worsened. It sparked a near panic in parts of his *aleimi* when Dalejem fought to open him more.

"Gods." Dalejem frowned, looking down at Revik's chest. "Those fuckers marked you all over." He met Revik's gaze, his green eyes hard. "I'm not going to be very nice about this, *ilyo.* I might need some fucking reassurances before I'm nice. I want to hear things from you... while you're in a mental state where I can actually believe them."

Revik closed his eyes.

He was too conscious of the other's hands to think clearly.

"I'm sorry," he managed.

Dalejem gripped his hair tighter. "You aren't yet, you little fuck, but you might be later. I'm not sure if I'm up for being gentle with this."

Revik couldn't answer that, either.

He fought to keep it off his face, but the other's words immediately made his pain spike. It grew bad enough to blind him a second time. When he could see again, Dalejem was watching him. His green eyes held a harder scrutiny.

Revik saw the understanding there and winced.

"That Rook was right?" Dalejem's voice came out neutral, despite the look in his eyes. "You want me to hurt you? I can do that, Revik. I can hurt you if that's what you want."

Revik felt the other male thinking about the scars on his back when he didn't answer. Revik didn't feel judgment there, although he'd been looking for it. Instead, he felt the other seer trying to decide what to do with that information exactly.

"It helps me... open," Revik admitted.

He watched that otherworldly, shockingly handsome face nervously.

He fought to read him, to gauge his reaction.

"Is it the only thing that helps?" Dalejem asked.

Revik fought with embarrassment.

He tried to think, to answer his question.

"No," he said, then amended, "...Sometimes. It was difficult for me. It still is. In the Rooks, I think it was more about sensation. Intensity. The constructs made it hard to feel much, so we all overcompensated, usually in all the wrong ways.

Terian was big on that kind of thing. He was big on pushing things—"

"He was your lover, then? That Rook in the clearing?"

Revik hesitated. "Yes."

"For how long?"

Revik thought about that. He felt his face warm.

"We were exclusive for a while." He fought to remember those years. He clenched his jaw when he only got impressions, pieces. "He was unstable. I wanted women, and…"

Realizing what he was saying, he flushed.

"It was different," he said. "With Terry, it was never much more than sex. We were friends." Flinching when he replayed his own words, Revik added, "I mean, we were *really* friends. I took care of Terry. Watched out for him. He was my brother. He had a tendency to get obsessive, though, including with me. So, I distanced myself. In the end, I broke it off. He didn't take it well. He didn't take it well at all… especially at first."

Dalejem's hand slid sensually around his cock.

Possessive. Demanding.

Revik felt the anger there, but he could also feel past it now.

He let out a startled groan.

He felt Dalejem's want, maybe for the first time. His groan turned into a drawn-out cry when the other male pulled on his light, then even more sensually on his cock. Revik stared up at the tent's ceiling, panting. He fought to relax, to calm down whatever it was in his chest that wanted to overreact to this.

*Gaos.* He barely knew this seer. He'd only known him a few weeks.

It didn't feel like that, though.

It didn't feel like that at all.

"No," Dalejem murmured. "No, it doesn't feel like that, Revik."

Dalejem's light coiled hotly back into his.

He began opening Revik deliberately. He unwound structures around Revik's heart, pulled on things in his belly before Revik knew what he was doing. It left him so open, so completely fucking vulnerable, he didn't know how to fight it, to bring any part of himself back. He grew conscious of the age difference between them again.

It hit him that he didn't even know what that age difference was.

Regardless of the exact number of years, Dalejem would likely be better with his light than any seer Revik had ever been with. There was a reason why seers coveted older, light-talented sexual partners from among their own kind.

Dalejem was Adhipan.

Of course he would be good with his light.

Dalejem grunted.

He let go of Revik's wrist. He hit into his light warningly as he did. He told him not to fucking move. He told him without saying a word, even in his head.

"You had a lot more Adhipan with you than just me last night, brother," he muttered.

"Shut up about that," Revik said.

He closed his eyes.

His heart stopped when the other's fingers stroked his cock and balls.

He felt like he was going to fucking die if he didn't do more than that soon.

"Tell me you like women, Revik."

"I like women." He let out a harder gasp. "So what? So fucking what? I'm a seer."

"Which means what? Exactly?"

"You know what it fucking means." Revik let out another pained groan. His eyes closed as he fought to control his light. "It means it doesn't fucking matter. It means light matters. Light is the only goddamned thing... light is everything, brother."

Some of that heat in Dalejem's *aleimi* grew less hard.

His hands explored Revik's body. He massaged him deliberately, light in his fingers, light in his tongue and lips, light in his legs and chest where he pressed into him. Revik closed his eyes, unable to control any of it. He fought the part of himself that panicked as his pain gradually worsened. He felt the other male's light in his, trying to get him to react, learning him.

When Dalejem continued at that careful, patient pace, Revik started to lose it for real. He pulled on the other seer violently. He begged him with his light.

Dalejem shifted focus, using his light to calm Revik down.

It did the exact fucking opposite.

He cried out. He started fighting him for real, struggling to get free. Dalejem sent another dense ribbon of pain and Revik groaned aloud.

It fucking paralyzed him.

"*Gaos*," Revik said. "Please. Let me give you head—"

"Not yet."

"Please." His voice came out gruffer, deeper. "Please. *Gaos*. Please—"

"No. I watched you last night. You like giving head, brother. A little too much."

Revik's skin heated more.

Embarrassment hit him, but that only wound into his pain, too.

He bit his lip, wanting to argue.

"How long are you going to punish me for this?" he asked. "For what I did last night? For what a fucking mess I was? For liking females?"

"As long as I fucking want, brother."

Revik let out a weak groan when Dalejem's hand went back to massaging his cock.

Within seconds, every nerve ending in his body felt like it was on fire. Whatever Dalejem had been doing to him with his light, it heightened everything Revik could feel, every breath and touch, every kiss and brush of the seer's tongue. Revik's breath stuttered in his chest. His muscles locked until he couldn't move.

For a long moment, he couldn't think at all.

When his vision finally cleared, he was clinging to the other male's arms. His light was so wrapped in Dalejem's he could barely see.

He whimpered. He whimpered and the other seer groaned.

Revik could tell without looking he was fully extended.

He felt the other male thinking about fucking him again, about intercourse, and Revik let out a heavier groan, clutching him tighter.

"I saw you." Dalejem switched topics without changing tone. "As a child. A real cub. When we shared light, I saw you like that." Pain reached his voice. "You were so goddamned adorable. You made my heart hurt. I wanted to protect you. *Gaos.* So fucking badly."

Revik felt his skin flush hotter. His muscles clenched painfully. He tried to see what the other male was talking about, but that time, Dalejem pushed him gently away.

"You don't need to see that right now, Revik."

"You won't tell me?"

Dalejem looked at him. He nodded slowly. "I will," he said. "But not right now."

Revik stared at him, fighting confusion. Another whisper of shame wanted to crawl over his light. He couldn't see anything about what Dalejem meant, what he'd seen, but the feeling of shame lingered as he lay there, until he had to fight not to let it show.

"No, brother." Dalejem clicked at him softly, reassuringly. He caressed his face. "No. I did not bring that up to embarrass you, or make you afraid. I'll never share anything about you with anyone, Revik. Not unless you ask me to."

Revik bit the inside of his cheek.

"I understand—" he began.

"Do you?" Dalejem mused. He watched his face. "I wonder if you do. I wonder if you've had many people you can trust with information about yourself."

He waited to see if Revik would answer.

He leaned down and kissed Revik's ear.

"You can trust me, Revik," Dalejem murmured. "You can trust me. I promise. I would never use such a thing as a weapon against you, or judge you for anything in your past."

He paused a second time. His voice grew a touch harder.

"Well... apart from maybe orgies with my friends."

Revik let out an involuntary laugh.

It turned into a groan when the other seer started massaging him again, then another when he wouldn't stop. Pain blinded him when Dalejem made it clear he wouldn't let him come.

"Please..." he said. *"Gaos.* Please..."

"I want you to trust me, Revik."

Revik shook his head, but not really in a no.

"I do," he said. "I do. It's just—"

"—You don't really trust anyone," Dalejem finished for him.

Revik hesitated. He fought to think past the other's hands and light.

"I don't know," he said truthfully.

The older seer started touching him more deliberately again.

Revik felt himself sinking into the mat, losing touch with what they were doing, with what they were even talking about. He cried out weakly when Dalejem started stroking the *hirik,* the hard end of his extended cock lightly with his fingers.

"Fuck," he gasped. "Fuck... please. Please..." His pain spiked. His light ripped out of his control. It made his voice deeper, harder. Words came out of him. They left his lips without any attempt to censor or filter.

"You're a fucking tease," he groaned. "A sadist. A power-hungry, jealous, control-freak sadist. You don't even like me. You don't want me. You're just so goddamned *mad* at me you're getting off on this…"

He felt the other react to his words.

At least some of that reaction was humor.

Revik realized Dalejem was muting those reactions too, at least from where Revik could feel them. The other seer was totally in control of his light, so pretty much the exact opposite of Revik right then. Which only made Revik's paranoia worse.

It also meant Dalejem could probably do this to him for hours, if he felt like it.

Maybe he would. He clearly wasn't hurting for sex.

Then again, given how Dalejem looked, not to mention how he used his light, he probably had sex pretty much whenever he wanted it.

"Last night I didn't," Dalejem muttered.

He met Revik's gaze when he looked up, his mouth hard.

"The rest is more or less true. Does that bother you, *ilyo?*" Dalejem's voice grew a touch colder. "Are you jealous of my success in fucking? Maybe you hope you will pick up some tips? Learn to replicate my success?" The green eyes hardened more. "Has it really been that interesting, listening to camp gossip about me, Revik?"

Revik couldn't answer that, either.

Truthfully, it only confused him.

No one told him camp gossip.

Dalejem let out a low laugh. He still stroked his *hirik* with his fingers, holding him down with that hand fisted in Revik's hair.

His light completely dominated Revik's.

Revik couldn't come. He couldn't do anything.

"You're going to have to relax, Revik," Dalejem said. "You're going to have to do what I ask for a little while... then maybe I'll forgive you."

Revik met that pale-eyed stare. He tried again.

He softened his body even more.

"I'm sorry," he murmured, looking into his face. "Please, *gaos*. I'm sorry. I'll do whatever you want. Anything." He kissed him lingeringly, using his light. He pulled on him slowly, sensually, even as his hand slid down his body.

"Please," he murmured. *"Gaos,* please... let me kiss your cock. Let me fucking touch you, at least. Even if you don't want me, I can—"

Dalejem laughed.

He sent a dense ribbon of liquid heat into Revik's belly.

It made him jump, then wince against a shock of harder pain.

Revik ended up lying there, panting.

He fought to pull back his light.

Fuck, he fought to breathe.

He was still fighting to move when Dalejem brushed Revik's hand easily off his chest. He gripped Revik's hair more firmly in his fingers. Once he had him more or less on his back again, he studied his eyes.

"You're a dangerous little fuck," Dalejem said affectionately.

Revik winced at the "little" comment.

Dalejem felt it.

"I meant age, brother." He rolled his eyes, clicking. He started massaging Revik's body again with his free hand, starting with his chest. "Very little else of you is 'little,' brother... certainly not this," he said, tiling his chin pointedly at Revik's cock.

Revik groaned involuntarily.

He fought the other's hold even as Dalejem's tongue

brought another low cry to his lips. When he could see again, Dalejem frowned.

"Why would you take my words that way?" he asked.

Revik let out another gasp when Dalejem stroked his *hirik*.

"Please," Revik said finally. "Please. Gods, please. I'll end up fighting you for real. I swear to the gods. I won't be able to help myself if you don't let me—"

"Stop begging me, brother," Dalejem said.

His words came out almost soft.

Revik's pain worsened.

When he looked up next, Dalejem's eyes had grown sharper, more predatory.

"You're going to get what you want," Dalejem assured him. "It's not been easy for me, holding you off even this much. Although I confess, some part of me would really like to see what you do if I deprive you long enough. You're still holding back... with your light, especially. You're holding back a lot. It's driving me fucking crazy..."

Dalejem shifted his body over him, until he was half lying on him.

Revik's pain violently spiked.

"Balidor gave us the day off," Dalejem added. "So technically, I guess you're right. I could deprive you all day if I wanted. I could jerk off a few times and fuck with your light for hours. I have food in here. Water. My bunk mates have already been relocated to other tents. You can scream at me all you want, brother. You can beg me all you want, too."

Revik felt the other seer's pain grow more prominent in his light.

"Either way, other than when you have to take a piss, brother, and barring any kind of emergency, I wouldn't expect to leave this tent anytime soon."

Revik felt another wave of that unbelievable pain.

The pain itself was starting to turn him on now.

It overwhelmed him, emptied his mind.

*Gaos.* He couldn't fight it at all.

The other male had his hands on him again. Like before, it shocked Revik. It yanked him out of his head when he realized how much more open his light was, even now. He gasped, fighting to pull himself back... then abruptly lost control over his light entirely.

He let out a cry that was openly pleading.

Then Dalejem started giving him head.

He watched Revik's face between bouts of sucking on his cock. When Revik fought him, mostly in instinct, without awareness or even real consciousness of why, Dalejem switched to using his hands. He talked in his ear, massaging his cock and the *hirik* until Revik didn't know where he was. He had no idea how long that went on, either.

It seemed to go on forever.

It seemed to go on until his body turned into liquid pain.

He just knew at some point, they were fucking.

Dalejem was inside him, and Revik lay there helplessly. Dalejem warned him not to move, not to do a fucking thing, not to struggle.

Revik opened his light and Dalejem groaned.

For the first time, Revik felt the other male lose control.

He struggled to remain silent as Dalejem started fucking him for real. He fucked him slowly, violently as he pulled out at the end, aiming with a precision that blanked out Revik's mind. Gods fucking in the stars... it felt good.

It felt so goddamned good. *Gaos.*

He really thought he might die.

Revik felt Dalejem fighting not to come and let out a heavier groan.

Then he was panting, crying out, whimpering.

He felt Dalejem's light react violently to that, too.

It hit Revik that others could probably hear them outside the tent. He felt Dalejem's awareness of that, too. A lingering jealousy still lived in the older male's light, along with an open anger about the night before.

Revik felt both things intensify—

—just before Dalejem arched into Revik harder. His light slammed into Revik's with so much force some part of Revik left his body entirely. Feeling the softness there, the wanting, Revik groaned aloud. He fought the green-eyed seer with his hands, gasping in pain.

He found himself pleading with him again, losing track of his own words.

It didn't matter. None of what he did or said mattered.

None of it got Dalejem to loosen his stranglehold on Revik's light.

He didn't tell Revik to be quiet. He didn't try to stop him from losing control. It took Revik a few minutes longer to realize Dalejem wouldn't answer him, not anymore.

For now, at least, he was done talking.

## CHAPTER 23
## ALWAYS

Revik let out a sigh. He leaned his head back on the dirt, closed his eyes.

He knew the other wouldn't let him get away with lying there for long.

He closed his eyes anyway, then shielded them with one hand. He gaze up through his fingers at the slanting green and gold light filtering through the leaves of the trees.

When Dalejem tugged on his hair, using his light to pull at his attention, Revik tilted his head back. He smiled at the seer's face. He adjusted his back on the rough ground as he did, moving a jutting tree root to a more comfortable place by his spine.

"We're supposed to be training, you know," the older seer chided.

Revik nodded. The smile still pulled at his lips.

Dalejem rolled his eyes in exaggerated seer-fashion, clicking at him.

Revik heard the other seer's amusement that time, and let his smile creep wider.

"Don't give me that look," Dalejem scolded. He prodded

Revik's shoulder with a booted foot. "You are a positively shameless flirt."

Revik chuckled.

Dalejem went on in the same tone. He gestured sharply with a hand.

"Adhipan Balidor isn't going to let us keep getting away with this, you know. He pulled me off regular rotations, brother. He allowed it as a favor to you, to let me help you with this, and we've spent two whole days out here now, mostly fucking and staring at clouds. With some light picnicking and a few naps in between."

Revik let out a low chuckle.

He turned over onto his stomach and exhaled. Then, gauging the other's light briefly, he crawled up leisurely to his hands and knees.

He kept moving forward in that way until he was more or less in the other's lap.

When Dalejem burst out in a laugh, Revik smiled. He met the older seer's gaze from only a few inches away, then lowered his head and pressed his cheek against his. He nuzzled him briefly before sliding his face down to kiss the seer's throat.

Feeling the other's breath stop, Revik lowered his mouth still more. He kissed him where his neck met his shoulder, where he already knew Dalejem's skin was sensitive.

Revik slid his hand inside his vest. He pulled on his light lingeringly as he let out a low groan. His fingers massaged the muscles along Dalejem's abdomen and chest.

"You are impossible," Dalejem grumbled. "A hopeless sex maniac."

"Tell me to stop," Revik said.

Dalejem didn't tell him to stop.

Revik kept going until the green-eyed seer made a low sound, from deep in his chest. He wrapped an arm around Revik's neck when Revik's hand slid further into his clothes.

When Revik started unfastening Dalejem's shirt, though, the older seer frowned.

"Are you really so determined to never relearn your infiltration skills, brother?" he complained. "You might need them, you know. Or do you plan to join those monks of yours on a more permanent basis?"

He blinked, then let out another low sound when Revik's hand traveled lower.

His voice grew the faintest hint of a gasp.

"Did it occur to you that maybe Adhipan Balidor has an ulterior motive in this? One that might allow us to spend a lot more time together than just these few weeks, brother?"

Revik raised his head. He studied his eyes, then frowned at him.

"What?" he said.

Dalejem laughed at his expression, clicking in amusement. He slid his fingers into Revik's black hair. He gripped him fiercely in his fingers.

"Damn you," he said.

Dalejem gazed over his face. Pain reached his expression as he studied Revik's eyes. It hardened the smile toying at his mouth.

"I'm hard as iron now," he murmured. "But I'm quite sure you knew that, already." He caressed Revik's face. His voice dropped to a murmur. "You are beautiful, brother. Gods, you're so fucking beautiful. Are you trying to drive me crazy on purpose?"

Revik closed his eyes, longer than a blink.

He leaned his face against the other seer's.

"Are you going to tell me what you're talking about?" Revik asked. He nudged him with his chin, sharpened his voice. "...With Balidor?"

Dalejem laughed. He pushed at his chest.

"You already know what I'm talking about." He clicked at him in a faint rebuke. "Balidor wants to recruit you to the

Adhipan. If we actually spent this time out here doing what we're *supposed* to be doing, it might convince him to do it sooner rather than later."

Revik frowned for real. He stared into the seer's light green eyes.

"Bullshit," he said, blunt.

Dalejem laughed again.

"Gods, you look young sometimes," he said, affectionate. "But you can't be serious with this disbelief of yours. What in the gods do you think we're doing out here? We could fuck in the tent and be more comfortable, you know. And for them, there would be the added bonus that they could watch... hardly an unwelcome pastime for most seers."

Revik's frown deepened. He sat back on his heels, rested his palms on his thighs.

He stared at the other seer in confusion.

"Why would Balidor want me in the Adhipan?" he asked.

Dalejem burst out in another laugh.

"You are joking, right?"

Revik shook his head. "No, brother. I am not."

Sitting up, Dalejem stared at him. His green eyes flickered with a thinly-veiled shock. He stared at Revik's face. As he did, his incredulity grew more visible.

"Gods. You're not joking, are you? You really are serious."

Revik felt his puzzlement turn to irritation.

"Are you going to just keep saying that?" he complained. "Or are you going to tell me what you're talking about? I'm not joking. I'm clearly not joking. And I have perfectly valid reasons for asking."

Revik let his irritation become more audible.

"...Is this something to do with Kali?" he asked. "Because my actual sight rank is shit since I left the Rooks. I don't even remember most of what I knew there. And what I did know I'll have to entirely relearn according to Vash, given how I did those things before. Not to mention how dependent I was on the Rooks' construct to do pretty much *anything* with my light. It truly would be like recruiting a monk."

Thinking about that, turning it over in his mind, his frown turned into a scowl.

"Why in the gods would Balidor want me anywhere *near* the Adhipan, given who I am?" he asked. "I'd be a walking target, in addition to the rest."

He stared at the dirt.

*"Gaos.* Does he think I could give him intel? On the Pyramid? Because I *would* do that, brother, of course. I would do it any way I could. He does not need to recruit me for that. I would tell him or show him anything he wanted."

Revik frowned, still thinking.

"Truthfully," he admitted. "I'd be shocked if that wasn't all gone, though. There is no way Galaith would allow me to leave the network with that information intact. He would guard that information first. Definitely before anything more transitory. The Pyramid mattered to him more than anything, brother. That, and the succession order."

When he glanced up, he flinched.

Dalejem was staring at him in open disbelief.

He was gaping at him, really.

"What?" Revik frowned. "What did I say now?"

Dalejem shut his mouth with a snap.

The incredulity never left his eyes, or his voice.

"Do you have any fucking idea what your potential sight rank is, brother? Any at all?"

Revik stared at him, half in puzzlement.

He thought about the question. Slowly, he shook his head.

"No," he said. "How could I? I haven't been tested since—"

"Fuck testing." Dalejem frowned at him openly. His eyes looked faintly disturbed now. "Who said anything about testing? Do *you* know what it is?"

"No." Revik frowned back at him. "How could I?"

Dalejem just stared.

Then he sat up, abruptly. A string of curse words in Mandarin burst from his lips.

He still sounded and felt mostly incredulous, borderline shocked.

"Gods, Revik! You *are* serious." Dalejem leaned closer. He gripped his black hair in a muscular hand. "Why in the seven realms do you think Galaith had you so high in the structure of the Pyramid at your age? You're a fucking *savant,* brother. You've got more above your head than most of us have ever *seen*, apart from maybe Balidor… or your blood-aunt, Tarsi."

Revik blinked.

Then he scowled. He wondered if Dalejem was pulling his leg.

Dalejem burst out in another incredulous laugh. At Revik's irritated look, the green-eyed seer held up his hands in a peace gesture.

"Okay, brother," he said. "Okay. Fine. Then tell me. Explain this to me. Why do *you* think Galaith had you down as his successor, out of all the hundreds of thousands of seers at his disposal in that Rook network?"

Revik clicked under his breath.

"It's different in the Pyramid, Dalejem." He met the other's gaze seriously. "I honestly thought everyone in the Adhipan knew all this. Abilities don't mean the same when you're a Rook. Sight rank doesn't mean the same. We *borrowed* the abilities of other seers… a *lot* of other seers. There's a whole library of skills inside the Org network. Any one of us could access these things. What we could do had very little relationship to anything we were born with—"

But Dalejem was shaking his head, clicking louder.

"It's not that simple, and you know it, brother," Dalejem warned.

"It *is* that simple."

"No," Dalejem said, sharper. "It is not."

At Revik's silence, Dalejem exhaled.

"*Gaos,*" he said. "How can you be so fucking intelligent and so completely dense at the same time? It is a puzzle, brother. Truly."

Revik felt his fingers clench on his thighs.

"Fuck you," he said coldly.

Dalejem let out a humorless laugh. "Gods. You're turning me on like you wouldn't believe right now, brother, so don't tempt me…"

Seeing Revik's jaw harden, Dalejem caught hold of his arms. He yanked him closer, so that Revik half-leaned on his chest.

"I am not making *fun* of you, damn it." That denser affection warmed Dalejem's voice. "I'm dead serious. How did you not know that Balidor wanted you to become one of us? Everyone in the camp knows. They have known since you first arrived here. Bringing you here has been one giant recruitment exercise, brother. One you have passed with flying colors, by the way… apart from the severe amount of slacking we've been doing these past weeks."

Revik shook his head. Pain sharpened in his chest.

The pain worsened as he thought through the other's words.

For a few seconds, he let himself get lost there.

He let Dalejem's words become real in his head.

He thought about living in the Pamir with Dalejem, rather than in the cold, empty caves of the monastery by himself. He thought about what it would be like to go on ops with him, to share a bunk with him, to be able to train with him and the others like he had been.

Pain slid hotly over his light.

Revik felt a slow, dense tug of the same coming off the seer holding him. It pooled like molten lava in his chest.

"You'd like that?" Dalejem asked, softer.

Revik rolled his eyes, clicking.

Still, he felt his face warm when he nodded.

Glancing up, he gave Dalejem a harder look.

"Would you?" he asked, sharp.

Dalejem rolled his eyes. A smile teased the edges of his perfect mouth.

"What do you think, brother?" he asked, grunting. "I'm about to forget all of my resolutions again today, and undress you once I'm done reassuring you... which should give you some indication of how much I like that idea."

He smiled at Revik's averted eyes, then shook him a little.

"And for that matter, why do you think Balidor assigned *me* to do this job, rather than another of his seers? Do you think that was purely generosity of spirit on his part?"

Pausing, the green-eyed seer answered his own rhetorical question, puffing out his cheeks before he spoke.

"He thought I had sufficient motivation to try and make you *work* at this, brother," he said, as though the answer were obvious. "He thought I might have my own reasons to want to see you pass the trials sooner rather than later."

Revik nodded. Still thinking, he felt a denser heat return to his chest.

He gave his boyfriend a harder look.

"You would not lie to me about this, Dalejem? Because that would be... unkind."

Dalejem's eyes and voice turned incredulous.

"No. *Gaos.* What possible motive would I have to toy with you like this? You think I don't want you to come with me? I'm in *love* with you, brother. I've all but told you that."

Revik's anger deflated, all at once.

He stared into those green eyes. He felt the pain in his chest worsen.

"You love me?" Revik asked.

Dalejem laughed. "You look surprised."

"I am surprised," Revik admitted.

He hesitated, thinking about the other's words, about

what he felt himself. He tried to decide if he should say something in return.

Before Revik could make up his mind, Dalejem shook him lightly by the arms.

"No," the other said, clicking softly. "Think about it later, Revik. Tell me what you feel later. Don't tell me anything now."

Revik hesitated, then nodded to that, too.

He studied the seer's eyes. He focused on the violet rings around the lighter green of his irises. Pain shivered through him, stronger that time, enough that his vision blurred.

"Can I give you head?" he asked.

He paused on the pain that slid off Dalejem's light.

He waited a beat longer, then stroked the other's bare arm.

"We can work on infiltration after that. Or shielding. Or whatever you want. I'll work harder at it this time. I vow it."

Dalejem burst out in a laugh.

"Is this a bribe?"

Revik smiled. His hand dropped to the other's thigh. He massaged it slowly with his palm. "You have given me an incentive," he said, inclining his head.

Dalejem slid his fingers into his hair. He gripped Revik tighter that time.

"Fine," he said. "Promise me you will really *try*, though, brother. You should be able to do these things in your sleep, Revik… I mean it. So promise me you will really *try* to work at this today, at least for some part of today."

Revik nodded. He acknowledged the other's words with a gesture.

Then, quirking an eyebrow, he said, "You mean on the infiltration, right?"

Dalejem laughed aloud at that.

He let out a low gasp a moment later though, as Revik began unfastening his pants.

"I do love you, brother," Dalejem said, his voice a murmur. "Those aren't just words."

Revik hesitated. Embarrassed somehow, he let his voice turn teasing. "Is this a sex-love, brother?" he asked, returning his eyes to Dalejem's belt.

"You mean a crush?" Dalejem's eyes turned faintly predatory. "A fixation?"

Looking up, Revik shrugged, answering only with his eyes.

Dalejem laughed again.

Revik could feel the other seer liking the expressiveness of his face and eyes, even his silences when they contained more than one meaning, and the way Revik had a tendency to talk with his hands. Dalejem liked those things about him enough that another ribbon of pain coursed through the green-eyed seer's light as he thought about them.

The intensity of Dalejem's pain tightened Revik's chest.

He found himself caressing Dalejem's jaw. *Gaos.* He wanted him again. He let the other seer feel his want.

"I may have those things, too," Dalejem admitted. "The sex-crush. The fixation. But no. It's not only that, brother."

"How can you be sure?" Revik asked.

Hearing his own voice, he realized the question was real.

Dalejem caressed Revik's face with light fingers. He fingered the last remnants of the bruise he'd given him when he'd punched him in the face, weeks ago now. He frowned as he touched the faint discoloration gingerly, and Revik clicked at him, shaking his head.

"Don't apologize again. I mean it."

"It is inexcusable. A child's answer to jealousy, to possessive rage—"

"Not again," Revik warned. "I mean it. Let it go." He muttered darkly under his breath. "I would have done the same to you. Probably worse. I would definitely do worse things now. Assuming I could handle it at all and didn't completely freak out."

When Dalejem clicked at him, Revik nudged him with a hand.

"Answer the question. Stop distracting me."

Dalejem smiled.

He began massaging Revik's chest with strong fingers.

"I can tell the difference, brother," he said, his voice a murmur. "If you are going to tease me for my age, at least give me credit for it now and then. Fixations and crushes are for now, for today, for tomorrow... for whenever my cock gets hard around you, which, admittedly, is most of the time right now. The other, is, well..."

He made a vague gesture with one hand.

"The other is always," Revik finished, pulling it off the seer's light.

He knew the quote.

He remembered it from the caves.

There was a silence after he said it.

In it, Revik felt his face warm.

He looked away from Dalejem's face when that silence stretched. He gazed out over the valley from their small corner of the jungle. Refocusing his eyes on that distant curve of sky, he saw a black, red, and yellow bird flying between canopies across the field, what might be a toucan from the brightness of the plumage.

Revik was still looking out over that expanse, at the muggy, yellow-tinted sky, when he jumped a little, feeling the other's hands on him.

Dalejem didn't smile that time when Revik turned.

He only looked at him, his green eyes serious.

"Exactly that, brother," he said, caressing his face. "Exactly what you said."

Revik felt the pain in his light worsen, right before he lowered his mouth.

## CHAPTER 24
# CHANGE IS COMING

They got back to the camp late.

Well... later than they had planned.

The sun had just sunk below the highest of the distant mountains, coloring the muggy air a pale pink and blue, streaked with swaths of orange and red.

Before Revik wandered off to find them food, he watched Dalejem head for their tent to drop off the pack he'd brought with them up the hill.

They'd spent the rest of the afternoon working on sight skills.

Well... mostly.

Dalejem started him on blocking at first.

He moved Revik into identifying resonances shortly after, then began testing his actual working skills. Dalejem started the second half of their work by instructing Revik to demonstrate his ability to locate a number of different people and places. He threw him a lot of secondary and tertiary links, then greater as he progressed, to see if he could follow the trails.

Revik lost himself inside the complexities of different Barrier frequencies and lights. It was strange as hell remembering spaces and structures he'd forgotten in his five years in those caves. It was stranger still to operate them like this, with light that felt closer to the light of the monks, definitely a lot closer than anything he'd used as a Rook.

Towards the end of the session, Dalejem even tested him on a time jump.

He used one of his own past ops as Revik's target.

By then, Revik found he was actually enjoying himself.

Well, he *was* enjoying himself... until he saw too much of the evening after the operation itself, and a fleeting imprint of Dalejem spending the night with Yumi, which caused another argument between them.

Revik finally shut up about it when Dalejem pushed back, pointedly asking Revik questions about Mara, then about his time under the Rooks, and finally about his fixation on Kali, and how Revik reacted to her in Saigon.

Somehow that argument ended in them fucking, too, although Revik couldn't remember who started things that time. He only knew that halfway through it, he'd almost forgotten why he'd been angry in the first place, and by the end he didn't care at all.

Then, when they were on their way back down the hill, they ran into Yumi, Dalai, and Ontari on their way back to camp, and Revik found himself remembering why he'd been angry and got jealous and annoyed all over again.

They'd more or less sorted that out by the time they re-entered the main construct.

Anyway, as Dalejem reminded him, more than once on the walk back, it was normal for seers to get angry with one another while setting boundaries around a new agreement.

They would both be touchy for a while, he said.

Revik didn't bother to tell him he hadn't been in any kind of "agreement" like this with another seer before, so he wouldn't really know.

At base, he knew Dalejem was right, of course.

Just anecdotally, he knew that, given that seers had been telling him such things more or less his entire life. He'd also observed it from the outside, just from watching new couples among his own kind where the light-connection was strong.

None of that really helped, of course, in terms of how he actually felt.

He still had to bite his tongue when Yumi winked openly at Dalejem on that trail, right before she smirked down at where the two of them held hands.

"Have a good afternoon together, brothers?" she had asked with a smile. "You both look... disheveled," she added, her smirk growing more apparent.

"Please just let it go, brother," Dalejem said, when Revik saw him next. "I did not *keep* anything from you. I told you I had not been with anyone in an exclusive way in years, and that is true. Anyway, it was nothing. A bad night with too much pain."

Standing there, Revik only nodded, biting his tongue.

He'd brought two mugs of *chikre* over from the mess tent, a kind of meal-like soup in lieu of dinner. He carried them over to where Dalejem sat on a log around the fire, where he'd saved the two of them a spot to sit. Revik stretched out his hand to offer the larger of the two mugs to the other seer.

Smiling up at him, Dalejem caressed Revik's thigh through his pants. He accepted the offering with a pulse of warmth.

"Is that really all you want?" Revik asked him, gruff.

When Revik sat down next to him, Dalejem wrapped a muscular arm around his back.

*You don't have to worry about me, brother,* he told him softly. *Truly.*

Revik nodded. He forced his shoulders to relax.

Balancing his arms on his thighs, he exhaled again, then forced himself to let it go.

He hated how fucking young he felt in his reactions to this.

He hated wondering if Dalejem had slept with every seer in the camp, male and female, given that he'd worked ops with all of them over the years.

When he glanced across the fire, he saw Mara watching them, a hard look in her hazel eyes.

Revik didn't let his gaze rest there for long.

Even so, he felt Dalejem stiffen.

"Don't play these games with me, brother," Dalejem murmured.

Revik shook his head, clicking softly. "I'm not."

"I mean it—"

"I'm not," Revik cut in. He looked at him seriously. "I promise you. You don't need to worry about me, either. I swear it. No games."

Dalejem studied his eyes. Then he nodded, visibly relaxing.

"Okay."

Revik watched the seer drink the *chikre,* and a sliver of pain touched him again.

He forced himself to look away. He could feel they were being watched by others in the construct. He didn't want them looking at Dalejem that way, too. He didn't glance away in time, though... at least not before Garensche burst out in a low chuckle from a few yards away.

"They are disgustingly cute," he boomed in his deep voice, ostensibly talking to Vikram, but grinning directly at Dalejem and Revik. "I wholeheartedly agree, brother. It is quite vomit-inducing. We should seriously consider banning them from sitting with the rest of us."

From the other side of the fire, Ontari laughed.

"That is not too extreme, brothers?" Ontari called out.

He winked at Revik when he caught his eye.

"I do not think so," Garensche said, his voice still loud. "If they won't share, then I think they should take their toys into the other room."

"Don't call the ex-Rook a toy in front of Jem," Mara said. Unlike the others, her voice held a darker bite. "He tends to get touchy about that kind of thing."

Revik saw Ontari put a hand on her thigh when she said it. He shook his head perceptibly, and she gave him an annoyed look, pursing her lips.

Dalai smiled at Revik from the other side of the fire.

"Now that the Bridge is born, maybe the fact that Dalejem has given himself to another is another sign of the impending Displacement?" she teased. She leaned against the chest of Nurek, who sat on the log with her. "I never thought I'd see the day, myself."

Revik frowned. He glanced between her and Dalejem.

He fought with whether to ask, when Dalai looked at him, laughing.

"He is quite the rogue, your Jem," she joked. "I think I can say, entirely without hyperbole, that Jem here had the absolute worst reputation of just about any seer in—"

"Shut the fuck up, sister." Dalejem leaned forward, his light an open threat. He rested his arms on his thighs, met her gaze with a predatory stare. "Now."

Revik glanced at him, frowning.

"Worst reputation," he muttered.

Dalejem flinched, but didn't take his eyes off Dalai.

"We might need to have some words later, sister Dalai," he said, his tone the same as before. He glared around at the others. "I might have to have words with more than one of you... since you all seem to have forgotten your goddamned manners."

His eyes rested for a beat too long on Mara's at the end.

Dalai only laughed, clicking at him.

Revik could feel that Dalejem wasn't amused.

He no longer wanted to ask. Maybe in part to distract

himself, he turned his mind to the other thing Dalai had said. Glancing at Dalejem, he contemplated asking, and found the green-eyed seer watching his face, his expression cautious.

"The Bridge?" Revik cleared his throat. "That is confirmed then? The elders have finished their assessments of her light?"

Ontari nodded, making a "more or less" sign with his hands.

Dalajem's fingers dug into Revik's back. He massaged the muscles there deliberately, putting light into his hands, working it into Revik's skin.

It didn't help Revik's concentration much.

It also didn't help him with his light, which again seemed to be twisting out of his control. He felt Dalejem pulling on him, even grounding him in a way, but while it reassured him on one level, it also made the pain worse, and made him more aware of his own instability.

A part of him didn't care about any of it.

That same part was so wound into Dalejem's light, he knew the others could see it, and could likely see the possessive pulling of it, the way that vulnerability practically shone in the space. He knew he wasn't over what Dalai had said.

He wasn't over what he'd seen while Dalejem fucked Yumi, either.

Dalejem's fingers grew stronger, more filled with light.

*Do not worry about me, brother,* he murmured in Revik's mind. *Do not worry... please. They are giving us shit because it is the seer way to give shit to new couples, at least when those couples are serious enough to warrant it. You know that.*

When Revik only nodded, Dalejem gripped him tighter with his free hand.

*They also know we are both easy marks right now, which is an additional source of amusement.*

Revik felt his jaw tighten more. He didn't answer.

He was an easy mark. A little too easy right now.

Dalejem answered his other question aloud, after the too-long pause.

"Yes," he said neutrally. "They are saying it is her now. The Bridge."

Revik nodded, silent.

That information twisted his mind in other directions though, making him wonder just how fucked up his light truly was right then. He stared into the fire and fought to ground himself. He tried to think through his reactions logically.

There was no logic to this, though, not now.

Remembering what Kali said to him by that swimming pool in Saigon, Revik fought with a sharper pull in his light, what felt almost like claustrophobia, mixed with a darker feeling he didn't want to probe too closely.

Whatever it was, he couldn't quite shake it off.

Nor could he eradicate the memory of Kali's serious eyes, how sure she'd sounded when she told Revik he'd have some kind of relationship with her daughter.

Those words felt more like prophecy now than they ever had... and they'd upset Revik at the time, too, for multiple reasons.

That feeling of prophecy didn't make him feel special.

More, it felt like a train bearing down on him in the night, one he couldn't see, couldn't outrun, couldn't avoid by changing direction.

Revik felt Dalejem's hands grow stronger on him. The green-eyed seer massaged his back skillfully, patiently, trying to get him to relax. Revik tried to do as he wanted. He tried even as he avoided the other's gaze, unable to help himself.

He stared into the fire. He followed the sparks and flames with his eyes.

He didn't look up until Yumi spoke.

She was watching him shrewdly when he raised his eyes.

The tattoo on her face appeared to move strangely under the liquid orange of firelight.

"It won't be long now, brothers and sisters," she intoned softly. "It won't be long, so we should enjoy this time, this quiet before the storm. It won't be long now. I feel it very strongly tonight. Since we got here, really."

There was a silence after she spoke.

Ontari broke it. He smiled at her, a cup of *chikre* clutched in his muscular hand.

"It won't be long for what, sister Yumi?" he asked.

"Before our lives change again." Yumi turned her eyes to his. That seriousness grew more prominent on her face, in her voice. "With the Bridge here, nothing is certain any more, my brothers and sisters. Nothing."

She made an elegant gesture with one hand.

She looked back at Dalejem and Revik.

That time, a smile reached her eyes.

"Only love is certain," she said, her voice warm, along with her light. "Only love can take us through these times. Remember that."

Revik tensed at her words.

He tensed before he even fully understood them, feeling them lodge somewhere in his chest, along with Kali's words from five years before.

Yumi continued to smile at him as he sat there, that deeper meaning shining out from her dark eyes.

"Only love is always," she said, quoting the same passage as Dalejem had, earlier that day.

Revik sucked in a breath, staring at her.

Next to him, he felt Dalejem's light react, too.

Yumi only smiled, her eyes flickering away, roaming over the rest of them.

"Treasure it, brothers and sisters," she said, speaking to all of them. "Treasure all of it. For this world is not long for us now."

She raised her mug in a toast.

Revik watched, unmoving, as the others around the fire followed suit. They raised their mugs as she did, their faces as serious as hers.

"Treasure the always moments," Yumi said. "For they are rare. And while forever, they are fleeting, too. Especially in these uncertain times."

A more serious mood fell over the small group around the fire.

Revik watched as the Adhipan infiltrators raised their cups in a silent salute, drinking to seal Yumi's words within their hearts.

Even Dalejem joined them, his mouth and eyes as serious as the rest as he took a long drink of the *chikre* Revik brought him.

Only Revik sat there, unmoving, his fingers clamped around his own metal cup.

He watched them all drink, feeling that dread settle deeper into his light.

## CHAPTER 25

# SUMMONED

"**B**ecause she wishes you there, brother," the Adhipan leader said. "Why else?"

He frowned down at Revik where he sat at a wooden table.

Balidor glanced at Dalejem, who sat next to Revik and somewhat behind him on the long bench, then back at Revik himself.

"She wishes you there," he repeated. "So you will go."

Revik shook his head.

He did it without raising his eyes. He stared at the plate in front of him on the table. He rested his arms on the wooden planks.

He shook his head a second time.

Or possibly the third time.

"I don't think it's a good idea," Revik said. "I don't want to go."

"She asked for you," Balidor said, exasperated. He looked at Dalejem again. "She wishes to speak with both of you, actually."

Revik looked up at that, his face taut. "What?"

He'd moved his body in the pause, almost without

knowing he'd done so. He inserted himself between the Adhipan leader and the man sitting next to him. He'd done it with his light even more than his body, and from behind him, Revik felt Dalejem smile, even as his fingers gently squeezed Revik's shoulder, rubbing the muscles in his back.

*It's all right, brother,* he murmured. *Relax.*

Revik glanced at him, feeling his face warm. Then he looked away from both of them. He gazed off into the jungle without really seeing it.

"What does she want?" he asked finally.

"She wants to see you," Balidor repeated, his voice holding more of an edge. "It is a great honor, Dehgoies, to be asked for by name like this. She has given birth to an intermediary being. Moreover, she is an intermediary being herself—"

"I understand that—"

"Do you?" Balidor retorted. "Because this window is closing, brother. It has been for over a month, and she is finally safe to be moved. She wishes to see certain people before she goes. She asked for you *specifically*, brother. You were the very first name on her list."

When Revik didn't look up, or change expression, Balidor's voice grew openly exasperated.

"Brother!" he said. "She will go into *hiding* after this. You must know that. Do you have any idea how many seers would jump any obstacle to be granted the honor you have been given? It poses a risk for her to stay here now. Extending her time here by hours, much less days, only increases that risk. Do you really not understand the gravity of that, given what this birth means... not just to her, but to all of us?"

Revik felt his jaw tighten more.

He didn't look over.

"They really think it is her?" he asked. "The Bridge?"

"Yes," Balidor said, impatient. "Yes, they think it is her.

Kali has said so all along. Now the Council is saying it, too. And Tarsi."

"What about Vash?" Revik asked.

"Vash *is* the Council," Balidor said, exasperated. "Of course he agrees with this. If you ware waiting for an official pronouncement of some kind, you will be waiting forever… he cannot risk such a thing, given the target this will place on all their backs. For you to even *know* these things is a huge honor."

Revik nodded. His jaw hardened more. "Vash is absolutely certain then? Or is he merely deferring to Kali, given who she is?"

Balidor rolled his eyes. "When have you known Vash to defer to anyone, solely because of who they are?" He placed his hands on his hips. "And if you are looking for more precision than that, I am not at liberty to share his impressions, brother."

"Do you believe it?" Revik looked up at him almost accusingly.

Balidor clicked at him, but some of the charge dissipated from his light.

"Yes," he said, his voice more subdued, more sincere-sounding. "Yes, I do believe it, brother. Apart from Vash and Tarsi believing it, I have also seen things that convince me, yes." Pausing, he added, "And I am learning to trust her… your Kali."

Revik winced at his phrasing, but Balidor ignored that, too.

"She is definitely a seer of far-reaching sight," Balidor said. "I feel no duplicitousness in her at all. Moreover, her daughter's light is…" He trailed, his eyes growing distant. "…It is unique, brother. It is beyond unique. I believe Kali is telling the truth."

"Assuming she knows the truth," Revik muttered.

Dalejem squeezed his shoulder.

Clicking to himself, Revik fought with his own light.

He was still sitting there, silent, when the green-eyed seer pulled him even closer, wrapping his arms around Revik's waist. Revik felt Dalejem look up at Balidor, but he still jumped when his boyfriend spoke.

"We will go," he said, ignoring Revik's flinch.

His words were decisive, uncompromising.

"We will?" Revik retorted, looking at him.

"Yes," Dalejem said, smiling back. He winked, then his eyes flickered back up to Balidor. "When does she want us?"

"Two hours," Balidor said at once.

Balidor hesitated. He looked between the two of them, as if about to say more.

Then he seemed to think better of it, and simply walked away.

Revik watched him go.

Once he could no longer see the Adhipan leader, Revik turned his head, frowning at the green-eyed seer who sat beside him. His anger lost some of its charge when he saw the other's face. He found himself studying the seer's eyes instead, tracing the violet rings around the cooler green of that sharp, intelligent gaze.

"You are speaking for me now, brother?" he said finally.

Dalejem chuckled.

Leaning past him, he tugged Revik's fork out of his hand. He scooped up a mouthful of the pile of refried beans, cheese, and salsa Revik had on the plate in front of him. Revik couldn't help reacting a little, watching the seer eat his food.

In the end, he just watched him, silent. He tried to decide if he was angry or not.

Dalejem chewed and swallowed, then paused to kiss Revik's neck.

"Don't be afraid," he said. "You will be fine, brother."

Feeling what the other meant, Revik tensed.

He gave Dalejem a harder stare.

"You think I don't trust myself with her?" he asked angrily.

There was a pause.

In it, Dalejem studied his expression cautiously.

Then he shrugged. He placed the fork back on Revik's plate.

"I think you are worried about offending me, yes," he said, matter-of-fact. "I think you are a little worried about her husband, too."

Feeling Revik's anger sharpen, Dalejem wound his arm further around him. He pulled him tighter against his body. He silenced him with his light, even as he sent warmth into his limbs. His fingers and palm massaged Revik's chest.

"I think you are happy," Dalejem said, his voice a murmur against his neck. "I think you have not been happy for a long time, brother, but you are now. As am I. I think you do not want to do anything to fuck that up. And I don't, either."

Revik stopped struggling at that.

He stared into the jungle, thinking about Dalejem's words.

He couldn't help but hear the truth in them.

He lost his train of thought when the other male started massaging him more deliberately again, his hands moving lower on his body.

"You won't," Dalejem murmured, kissing him. "You won't fuck it up, Revik."

Revik frowned, thinking about that, too.

"How do you know that?" he asked finally.

He heard the bitterness in his own voice.

He didn't look back to see if Dalejem heard it, too. Even so, he felt the other's smile, right before Dalejem pressed his face against Revik's neck.

"I won't let you, brother," he said, kissing him again.

Thinking about that, Revik found himself relaxing into the other male's chest. After another pause where they simply wound into one another's light, he sighed again, nodding as he closed his eyes.

"All right," he said, reluctant.

"All right?"

"Yes," he said.

Dalejem laughed quietly. He kissed Revik's shoulder as he slid his hands under his shirt. Revik felt the other seer wanting sex. He knew they were supposed to help Yumi and some of the others scout a Barrier anomaly Balidor had observed, what looked like a larger force coming out of a hidden base somewhere deep in Argentina.

He knew that anomaly had a number of them concerned.

The main theory now was Black Arrow, but apparently the signatures didn't fully match what they had mapped of Black Arrow infiltrators or their training methods.

Revik also knew his part of that probably wouldn't take two hours.

Well, not for the preliminary work. He could probably start in an hour, then finish the rest after his meeting with Kali.

Thinking about that now, with Dalejem's hands on him, he didn't move.

He just sat there, feeling the other seer breathe, listening to his heart beat against his back. His mind flickered to the handful of seers talking by the fire not far away, and then to the fainter sounds of birds and monkeys coming from the jungle.

He *was* happy, he realized.

More than anything, the realization surprised him.

It also made him inexplicably sad.

## CHAPTER 26
# INTERMEDIARIES

Revik stood outside a long, hut-like structure. He grew overly conscious of stares as a group of indigenous humans watched them warily from a nearby fire pit.

Dalejem stayed close to him.

He also wrapped Revik in his light, but it didn't really help all that much, the longer they waited out there. Revik found himself looking between the humans and the hut's door, conscious that he knew both not enough and way too much about what waited for him inside the thatch-roofed structure.

The not particularly friendly stares of the locals weren't helping.

He'd already been warned against pushing these humans.

He couldn't even push them to look away.

While this particular tribe had no contact with outside humans at all, Kali was an honored guest here, having some tie that went back to her own childhood years, which Balidor explained had been spent in this part of South America.

Revik didn't ask how long ago that was, but he definitely got the sense it was the ancestors of these particular humans, rather than the humans themselves, who had been the ones to forge that particular bond with Kali herself.

He also strongly suspected all of that took place long before official First Contact between humans and seers, and long before Europeans made their way to this part of the world, at least in large numbers.

He didn't know how old Kali was.

He'd never thought to ask her that question during their brief time together in Vietnam, but he'd known she was significantly older than him.

Now he wondered if perhaps she was older than Dalejem.

She might even be older than Balidor.

Revik had always struggled to discern the ages of female seers, even more than he had with males. He'd also learned, from trial and error, not to guess.

Dalejem chuckled, clearly hearing him.

When Revik glanced at the other male, Dalejem grinned. He leaned down to kiss him on the mouth before he went back to sitting on the rock outside the hut, his arms folded.

Revik watched him sit. Then he looked back warily towards the local humans.

They definitely seemed protective of her, of Kali.

Being an intermediary, she likely had the ability to create and cultivate alliances that differed from those more accessible to run-of-the-mill seers. Even so, this overt protectiveness of theirs raised questions in his mind.

Did they know anything about the myths?

Did they have some awareness that this baby was important, in addition to Kali herself? Did they see Kali as one of their own somehow?

With the Barrier shield strongly surrounding their human lights, it was impossible to tell. He picked up on their protectiveness, but that was about it. And hell, he could have seen that with his eyes, even without his light.

They stared at Revik and Dalejem warily.

The fear Revik picked up was definitely more for Kali and her child than it was for themselves, or for their village more broadly.

They stared at Revik even more than they did Dalejem.

Revik wondered about that, too. It might simply be that they thought he looked human. Many seers—and humans—were thrown by how his appearance straddled the two races. Also, they weren't close enough to see that his eye color was clear, not gray or blue.

To them, he probably looked like a light-eyed human, if a tall one.

Realizing he was staring again, and that it wasn't endearing him to any of them, Revik shifted his gaze back to the long hut with its palm-covered roof.

Most of the structure was open, to catch the breeze as it wafted through.

They had created a private, separate structure in the middle of the building, however, so even with his military-trained seer eyes, Revik couldn't see very far inside.

His view was cut off by what looked like organic and cloth curtains that hung from the rafters maybe ten feet from the main door. He saw gourds hanging from the ceiling, what looked like indigenous mats on the floor. The mats were made of woven grass and more palms, unlike the organic and semi-organic cloths the Adhipan used in their tents.

Revik's light still darted around them in quick scans when Dalejem wrapped an arm around him again, calming him with his light.

*They will come for us now, brother,* he sent, soft. *She is asking for you. She wants us each to come alone, though.*

*Alone?* Revik sent, tensing.

*One at a time,* Dalejem clarified. His hands continued to massage Revik's back, almost without Revik noticing he was doing it. *Calm down, brother. Her husband is there. The child, too. You won't be alone with her.*

Revik felt his irritation returning.

Dalejem blew more warmth over him.

*That wasn't an accusation. Calm down. You're not reacting to what you think you're reacting to, anyway. At least not from what I can tell.*

*Meaning what?* Revik sent, looking at him.

*Meaning, I think Kali was probably right,* Dalejem sent cryptically. His light continued to probe Revik's gently. *She was right. She has never been the true source of your distress.*

Feeling Revik about to ask, Dalejem went on before he could.

*In Vietnam,* he clarified. *You told me what she said. About you reacting to her daughter more than her. I don't think Kali is the issue this time, either.*

Revik felt his jaw clench.

He didn't answer him, though.

Anyway, he didn't have time.

One of the local humans appeared in the opening leading into the hut.

He pointed directly at Revik's face. Revik found himself looking at the bright orange paint on the man's skin, the piercings and tattoos covering his face and in his ears.

The man pointed to him again. He said something sharp in his own language.

Revik didn't try to read him for specifics.

Anyway, the message was pretty clear.

He nodded, then held up his hands in a peace gesture.

Revik started to move towards the opening of the hut... but Dalejem caught hold of him, stopping him before he got very far. Revik stiffened and turned. He'd only just faced his lover when Dalejem began kissing him.

He put light into his tongue and hands. He kissed him harder.

His fingers clasped Revik's arms.

Then Dalejem coiled his light into Revik's intensely

enough and possessively enough that Revik let out a surprised sound, then got instantly hard.

He kissed the other seer back, losing himself in light. He only pulled away when the male human started shouting at him again from the doorway.

When Revik broke off the kiss, looking over, the male human shouted louder, gesturing sharply from the dark opening between the two wooden poles. When Revik still didn't move, the human stomped his bare foot.

Feeling more eyes on him, Revik glanced over at the fire pit as he took a step away from Dalejem. He saw the female humans there staring at the two of them, their eyes wide in dark faces. From their expressions, Revik could have just turned into a ghost.

He didn't probe that any deeper, either.

*Come back to me, brother,* Dalejem sent to him softly.

Glancing at him, Revik nodded.

He swallowed a little as he released the other's hand.

Then, hardening his light against any more outside impressions, he followed the painted human into the darkness of the palm-roofed hut.

---

THE HUMAN PULLED BACK THE CURTAIN. HE PUSHED REVIK through the opening before Revik had really wrapped his mind around entering.

He found himself standing just inside the door, in a warmly-lit space taken up mostly by what looked like a Western-style bed.

A dark-haired woman sat on the thick mattress. She leaned against a wooden backboard, surrounded by pillows. The mattress itself looked to be resting on a frame made of the same type of wood as what formed the outside frame of the hut.

The mattress might have been palm fronds stuffed inside cloth, or maybe something the seers brought with them from the United States, but it looked comfortable.

A man lay sprawled on the mattress next to the woman with the dark hair.

He wasn't looking at her, or at Revik. He smiled down at a small bundle wrapped in a blanket who rested between them.

Revik realized that must be the baby.

He avoided looking at all three of them directly, especially Kali.

He shifted his eyes up instead. He studied the netting that surrounded their little enclave, seeing human fabrics wound in and around the organic cloths that kept out insects and at least some of the heat and humidity. He followed the construction with his eyes, noting where the morphing organic cloth hung from wooden poles, creating a makeshift roof, like they'd built a full-sized tent inside the hut.

It was definitely cooler in here.

The fabric must have properties with which he wasn't familiar.

Someone had hung what looked like indigenous religious totems over the bed, along with a Christian cross, something wooden, that looked old.

Above all those things, and dwarfing them in size, hung a traditional seer image of the sword and sun in blue and gold.

The more local-looking totems evoked protection to him, so were probably meant to keep out bad spirits. Revik studied them briefly with his eyes and light, then felt a ripple of amusement from the bed, from a presence that had to be Kali.

"Do you plan on acknowledging me at all, brother?" she asked bemusedly.

Feeling at least two sets of eyes on him now, Revik tensed.

His face warmed despite the cooler air inside the tent.

He lowered his gaze reluctantly, and found Kali smiling at him.

She looked genuinely happy to see him, which threw him a little.

It also rendered him briefly mute.

Clearing his throat, he bowed, formally.

"I hope you are well," he said.

She laughed, and he flinched a little.

He remembered that laugh.

It sent a shiver of memory through him, of standing on the banks of the Saigon river with her, flagging down a boatman so he could get her the hell out of there. He pushed the memory from his mind, even as he glanced at the male lying next to her.

The male seer had looked up from the bundle on the bed. His fingers continued to stroke a small arm Revik could see. Feeling a strange pain in his chest at the sight of that pale, soft skin, Revik flinched, then looked up.

When he did he found the male watching him warily.

Revik shifted his weight. He looked at Kali.

"You wanted to see me?" he said.

She laughed again, clicking at him in mock annoyance. "*Gaos,* brother! Do I warrant so little warmth from you? Won't you come here at least? Give me a kiss?"

Revik's jaw hardened. He glanced at her husband.

"I would rather not, sister," he said. "No offense."

At that, the male grunted.

It was almost a laugh.

"I won't hurt you, pup," he said, his voice darkly amused. "Not that I want to discourage that concern in you…"

He trailed, glancing at his wife, sharply enough that Revik got the sense she'd poked him with her light. Rolling his eyes at her, the big-shouldered male clicked under his breath, then gave Revik a more measured, if only marginally more friendly look.

"I am Uye," he said.

Staring down at the tiny fingers wrapped around his thumb, Revik swallowed.

He still didn't make any move towards the bed.

"You are with someone now," Kali said.

Revik turned. He found her green eyes studying him shrewdly.

"You are," she said, watching his face. "Are you not?"

He nodded. "Yes."

"Will we meet this mystery person?" She quirked an eyebrow at him. "Why did you not bring him with you?"

Revik felt his confusion worsen.

Hesitating, he glanced behind him, at the curtain that covered his exit.

At a loss, he looked back at her, his voice uncertain.

"He is here," he said. "Outside."

She smiled. "Why did you not bring him in?"

Revik stared at her, even more thrown. "I was told you wished to see each of us alone."

He saw confusion rise in her light and expression.

She exchanged puzzled looks with Uye.

Revik added, "You asked to see him. He is here because you summoned him, sister. I thought you knew."

Kali's lips pursed.

She glanced at her husband a second time, but Revik saw more understanding there that time. Revik saw the big male shrug, no expression in his blue eyes. He gave Revik a fleeting look before his eyes returned to the bundle lying near him. Once he focused there, his eyes grew instantly warmer and softer.

They held a love Revik could almost feel.

The feeling of protectiveness emanating off the other male grew so tangible, Revik couldn't help but feel that too, even with his light mostly closed. He found himself noticing that

Uye had a healing burn on his neck, cuts on his hands and arms.

He remembered Uye had been in *Guoreum* with Kali.

The Rooks and Black Arrow agents put him in solitary to try and recruit him. They would have beaten him, if only to disorient his light, and probably starved him, too. Not to mention the games they would have played with his mind and *aleimi*, looking for pressure points.

It must have been bad if Uye was still healing from the ordeal.

Revik glanced back at Kali when he felt her light. He found her watching him again, that denser scrutiny back in her light-filled eyes.

"Why did you request Dalejem?" Revik asked. "What do you want with him?"

There was a silence.

Revik saw a deeper understanding flicker in her eyes, even as she and her husband exchanged another set of looks. Then Kali looked at him, smiling.

Revik felt himself react to the warmth in her light, in spite of himself.

Uye gave him a sharp look, and Revik took a step back, so that his back came nearly to the door of the small enclosure.

In the same instant, he shielded more of his light.

"Do you not want to hold the baby, brother?" Kali asked, her voice holding affection.

"No," Revik said, unthinking.

Uye grunted another laugh, glancing at his wife.

"You do not?" Kali asked, puzzled.

Revik shook his head, once. "No."

That pain returned to his chest, sharper.

Revik saw Uye staring at him once it had, a harder look in his blue eyes.

That time, when he looked at his wife, Uye frowned. Revik saw the male look at the baby on the bed, then back at

Revik, right before Uye's light thickened perceptibly. His complex-feeling *aleimi* enveloped the baby lying on the bed in an even denser shield.

Kali clicked at her husband, a gentle rebuke.

Revik could tell by the expressions on their faces that they were probably talking.

"Did you want something from me, sister?" he asked finally.

Both of them looked over, as if he'd interrupted them.

Realizing he had, Revik made an apologetic gesture with one hand.

"I am sorry," he said. "I don't know what I'm doing here."

Kali sighed at that. She sat up more on the bed and combed her dark hair out of her face with her fingers. Then she shoved the covers aside. She swung her long legs over the side, and Revik saw that she was wearing a pale green skirt, lighter than her eyes, along with the tunic-like shirt he'd noticed already. The style of the clothes looked Indian almost.

She got to her feet, and walked right up to him.

Revik just stood there as she embraced him. He closed his light even as his eyes flickered nervously to the male on the bed.

When Kali smacked him lightly on the chest, Revik looked down, startled.

"I thought you would want to see her," she said reproachfully. "I thought you would want to see *me*," she added, even more reproachfully. "Instead you stand there, refusing to say hello, acting like I am torturing you, brother, by even inviting you here. Is Uye really so frightening? Or is it the baby you are so afraid of?"

The male on the bed chuckled softly, glancing up.

Smiling at Revik for the first time, he rolled his eyes a little, looking fondly at his wife.

Revik found himself relaxing slightly.

"I'm sorry," he said.

She smacked him again, and he jumped.

"Don't be sorry!" she scolded. "Say hello."

Revik rolled his eyes a little, clicking under his breath. "Hello, Kali."

"Are you glad to see me?"

"I am glad to see you are well," Revik said. He felt his jaw harden. He glanced at Uye before adding, "I was worried about you. I am glad you will be leaving soon. All three of you," he added, seeing Uye's quirked eyebrow.

"And you are afraid of my daughter, too?" she asked.

He shook his head. "No." He fought to think, then sighed, clicking at her more normally. "Kali, I feel strange. What you told me in Vietnam... how am I supposed to react to that?"

Uye grunted from the bed.

He glanced pointedly at his wife.

Revik distinctly got the impression it was an "I told you so" type of look.

Kali only laughed. She slid her arm around Revik's waist. "You don't want to hold your future love interest in your arms then, brother?"

"As a baby?" Revik retorted. "Not particularly. No."

Thinking about her words, he felt his frown deepen.

He met her gaze directly. He let her see the frown, even as he shook his head.

"I'm not comfortable with this, sister. I think I should go."

Kali released him with a sigh. He saw the knowing look in her eyes. "Because you are in love now?" she asked him gently.

Revik felt his face warm.

He glanced behind him, at the blank wall of curtain at his back. Revik clicked under his breath. Even he heard the faint irritation in the sound he made.

"Stop picking on him, wife," Uye said from the bed. "I'd just as soon he *not* have an interest in our daughter yet, if it's all the same to you."

Kali rolled her eyes at her husband. Her mouth firmed as she looked up at Revik, studying him more carefully with her leaf-colored eyes.

"Brother," she said gently. "I am happy for you. Truly."

Revik shook his head, but more because he didn't know what to say.

He glanced at the bundle on the bed, in spite of himself.

For the first time, he opened his light, just a little.

Just enough to feel... something.

Maybe to convince himself he wouldn't feel anything at all.

Instead, that pain in his heart worsened, grew unbearable.

He felt the familiarity there.

He felt it, and found himself fleeing from it.

"I have to go," he said.

Hesitating, he leaned down. He kissed Kali on the cheek.

"I wish you all health and happiness, sister," he said. He meant it, even as he closed all three of them out of his light. "I'm sorry I didn't try to thank you sooner, for what you did for me in Saigon. And to apologize for my behavior there. I really am sorry. It was inexcusable, the way I behaved, Rook or no."

Hesitating, he looked up. He met Uye's gaze.

"I am sorry to you as well, for my behavior with your wife, brother. Truly. I was sorry even then, even in that state."

Uye grunted, but his blue eyes softened somewhat.

"I appreciate that, brother," he said, once again caressing the arm poking out of the bundle on the bed.

Revik hesitated. He nodded then, looking down at Kali. "I should go."

She nodded, wordless.

A faint sadness rose in her eyes as she looked at him.

"Brother... before you go." She laid a hand on his arm before he could move away. "I must remind you of something, now that your mind is clearer than when we last met."

She paused. "Remember your promise to me, brother. Please. You must keep that promise to me. You cannot tell her. You cannot tell her anything about us."

Revik frowned. He stared down at her.

"Tell her?" His frown deepened. "Tell who?"

Kali clicked at him, even as Uye made an amused sound from the bed. She gave her husband an annoyed look.

Then she sighed and pushed her long, dark hair out of her face.

"I apologize," she said to Revik. She glanced again at her husband. "My husband says I always forget to speak ten words out of the twelve I must convey…"

When Revik's confusion only worsened, Kali clicked again, seemingly at herself.

"Our daughter, brother. You will meet her one day, when she is grown. When you do, you cannot tell her about us. You cannot tell her how you met us here, or that we met in Vietnam. You cannot tell her anything about me or Uye."

"Why not?" Revik asked, bewildered.

She shook her head.

"You just cannot," she said. "She would go looking for us. It would be very dangerous for her. I don't mean to sound melodramatic, but if that were to happen too soon, it would be dangerous for everyone on the planet, human and seer. So you cannot tell her. You cannot. You promised me, before you left me on that pier, that you would not tell her."

Revik felt his confusion worsen. He looked between the male on the bed, and the dark-haired woman standing in front of him.

"*Look* for you?" he said. "Why wouldn't she know where you are?"

"None of your business, pup," Uye growled from the bed.

Kali clutched Revik's arm.

She gave her husband a fleeting warning look.

"Be polite, husband," she scolded.

Her green eyes returned to Revik.

"I cannot explain it all to you, brother," she said gently. "I wish I could, but I really cannot. Just remember that I said this, and vow to me you will do as I ask. If you *truly* want to repay me for what I did for you in Vietnam, then promise me you will do this for us."

Revik stared at her leaf-green eyes.

It was no use, though; he knew he would not understand.

He exhaled in a sigh.

"Of course," he said. He made a seer's gesture of a promise. "I vow it."

He probably could have walked away. He didn't, though.

Something made him hesitate as he continued to watch her eyes.

"Is there anything else you want of me, sister?" He glanced at Uye. "...Either of you?"

From the bed, Uye let out another half-laugh.

Kali only shook her head. She smiled at him.

When Revik turned to go, however, she stopped him again.

That time, she clasped his hand.

Revik turned.

He was shocked to see tears in her eyes.

"You are loved, brother," she told him softly. She clasped him tighter. Her words turned almost fierce. "I hope you know that. You are very deeply loved."

Revik felt his confusion worsen, along with a denser pain.

He didn't understand what she meant.

He didn't want to understand.

Feeling another pulse of light off the bundle on the bed, he found himself struggling to breathe, feeling suddenly claustrophobic again.

He wanted to get the hell out of there.

At the same time, he didn't want to jerk his hand away from the female seer. He glanced at Uye, and saw the male watching the two of them, no expression on his face. Giving the Bridge's father a last nod, Revik turned to go.

He disentangled his fingers gently from Kali's as he did.

"I should go," he said, softer.

Kali only nodded. Her fingers reluctantly released his.

Revik turned to leave.

He'd just reached for the cloth door, when Uye raised his voice.

"Revik!" the seer said.

Revik froze. He turned his head, his fingers already grasping the organic curtain. He met the gaze of the male seer on the bed.

The blue-eyed seer stared at him.

Zero compromise lived in those ocean-colored eyes.

"You may be loved," he said, his voice holding a soft lilt of humor. "But you hurt my daughter, brother, and I will *hunt* you. I will hunt you to the ends of the fucking Earth. You'd better hope you're dead before I catch you, too."

A pulse of that protective light shimmered off his prone form, even as a smile touched his sculpted seer's lips. "...No offense."

Revik swallowed.

Then, tightening his grasp on the curtain, he nodded.

His face warmed as he gestured to the seer that he understood.

Then, pulling back the organic cloth with a sharp jerk...

He fled.

## CHAPTER 27
# FEAR

Revik waited outside, on that same rough boulder, as Dalejem disappeared inside the hut.

He waited for a long time.

It was getting dark then, and still he waited.

He found himself wishing he had a packet of *hiri* with him, even though he hadn't smoked the seer cigarettes in years, not since he'd first gone to stay with those monks in the Pamir.

*Hiri* tended to mellow him out, and calm his stomach when he felt like this.

His gaze tilted up.

He watched the stars begin to appear between the branches. He watched as they multiplied in the sky, watched them move slowly on their curved tracks. He fought not to mark time with his light or his eyes, but some part of him did it in rote.

Even when he didn't attach numbers to that time, he felt the length of it.

It felt like Dalejem had been in there for a long time.

Far longer than Revik himself had been.

Then again, Revik hadn't really tracked how long he'd

stood inside that curtained space, not until he got outside and saw that the position of the sun had changed.

He watched the humans whose village it was cooking over their fire pit.

They were boiling something in a large, cast-iron pot. He watched them talk, listened to them laugh with one another as they gathered around the light.

Revik had been sitting there long enough now that he didn't garner more than the occasional curious stare. He saw an older male on the far side of the clearing, apparently doing his own thing. Whatever it was, it didn't look cooking-related.

He burned some kind of plant as Revik watched.

As he did, he chanted over the red stone basin.

Revik reached out his light tentatively to feel what the man was doing. He asked permission from the Barrier if he could see what it meant.

Immediately, the space opened.

Revik saw beings there, connected to the Earth.

Again, he got a strong feeling of protection.

He felt love there. Real love.

Love for Kali and the Bridge.

With that love, Revik felt something that evoked a kind of pact.

His eyes clicked back into focus.

He saw the medicine man looking at him, once he could see again.

Revik raised a cautious hand in greeting, signaling his thanks, and the old man laughed. He shook his head in amusement as he turned his attention back to his offering smoke.

Revik sighed. He wrapped his arms around his ribs as he averted his gaze. He wished again he had the *hiri*, or maybe just something to eat.

He kept his light away from the hut.

He hadn't let his light go anywhere near it, not since Dalejem first disappeared inside.

Even so, he felt pain in his heart a few times.

In his mind's eye, he felt flickers of that bundle on the bed. He could feel other things now, too. Protection. Love. A kind of silent guardianship that felt deeper than both of those things. A dense, golden light stood over this place. Wherever it originated, it shrouded the whole clearing in a living Barrier mist.

Something about that light opened his heart more than he really wanted it open.

Revik could feel the parts of him that it pulled.

All those things made him want to stay farther away, not get nearer.

He was starting to get restless again when a figure appeared at the door.

Revik blinked.

Then he made out the form of Dalejem, and stood up.

The other male saw him when he did and walked directly up to him.

"Come." He avoided Revik's eyes. "Let's go."

"What?" Revik stared at him. "What did she say to you?"

Dalejem paused that time.

He looked at Revik directly.

In the faint light from the distant fire, Revik saw a glimmer of emotion there. It was too dark for him to get more than a fleeting glimpse, but he couldn't unsee it. He also couldn't catalogue it in a real way, nor could he use his light to comprehend what it meant.

Then he realized why.

Dalejem had his light shielded.

For the first time in weeks, he was keeping Revik out.

Dalejem continued to look at him, that faint sadness in his eyes. He studied Revik's face from behind what looked and felt like an infiltrator's working mask, even as he pretended it wasn't there. His light exuded warmth from his heart, but he was gone.

Revik could feel that absence.

Then Dalejem inclined his head.

He aimed it towards the path back down the hill.

"Let's walk and talk," he suggested. "I'm hungry."

Revik just stood there.

He felt a dense pain building in his chest.

He turned his head. He stared into the darkness of the opening into the hut, feeling an anger coil in his heart. It shimmered hotter and angrier before he could pull it back. He felt himself losing control over his light.

He couldn't make himself care about that, either.

"She told you." His voice grew into an open accusation. "She told you. Didn't she? Even after I made it clear what I chose—"

"Brother, calm down."

"Fuck you with your 'calm down'! I don't want to *calm down.* Just fucking *tell me* what she said to you, Dalejem." His voice grew openly bitter. "Whatever it was, your choice clearly differed from mine."

"Not here," Dalejem said.

"Yes, here!" Revik growled. "I want to talk about it here! Right now!"

"Brother." Dalejem's voice grew warning. "This is not a good place for this."

He pinged Revik's light, nudged his eyes towards the fire pit.

Revik turned at the impulse, unable to help himself.

Once he had, he saw that all the humans sitting there had fallen silent, even the medicine man by the stone basin. Those nearest stared at Revik and Dalejem from the flickering light of the flames, their expressions still, yet somehow almost forbidding in that orange light.

"We cannot fight here," Dalejem said, soft. "They won't permit it. Not this close to her."

Revik felt his jaw harden.

He could feel what Dalejem meant.

He just didn't care.

When Dalejem tried to take hold of his arm, Revik jerked it away. He took a full stride backwards, once again struggling to breathe, fighting not to yell at the other male. His jaw hardened as he stared at Dalejem through the dark.

Then, realizing he was on the verge of striking him, he turned, abruptly.

He began walking down the path into the jungle.

He closed his light, but he knew the other seer followed him.

He knew it without turning his head.

CHAPTER 28
# LOVE

Revik considered picking a tent at random to sleep in.

He considered avoiding the other seer altogether.

He didn't eat with him, although eating alone was almost worse.

He felt eyes on the two of them, whispers of speculation about what had happened.

A few of them frowned at Dalejem, probably because they could feel Revik's anger at the other male from where he sat on the opposite side of the fire. Revik didn't look at them. He dug into a plate of chicken and rice without tasting it, without looking at any of them.

He had no idea how Dalejem himself reacted.

Even so, Revik fought with what to do as he ate.

Then, halfway through the meal, he realized he didn't have any appetite left.

He walked his plate over to a bucket they'd been using for scraps. He dumped the remainder of his chicken inside and washed the plate in the plastic bin.

He put it on a rack to dry.

He stood there a few seconds more.

He considered just walking, disappearing into the jungle,

but when he turned around, Dalejem stood directly behind him.

Without speaking a word, he took Revik's arm roughly in his hand. He started pulling him towards the tent they'd been sharing, walking fast.

Revik considered fighting him.

Then he considered screaming at him.

In the end, he didn't do either.

Dalejem tugged him inside the tent flaps and Revik braced himself, sure the seer would try to force him to talk. Instead, Dalejem closed the flaps to the tent, then turned around and promptly started to undress him.

Revik felt his pain spike when the other seer yanked the shirt off his arms.

Dalejem tugged roughly at his belt. He unhooked it without preamble, then swiftly unfastened his pants. Revik only stood there. He fought back anger, nausea, what felt like a black hole that lived somewhere in his chest.

Something about the abyss that lived there felt more familiar than even her light.

The familiarity of both things crippled him.

They also made him want to erase himself, to cease to exist.

That darkness wanted to annihilate him from the inside out, to stamp out the last part of him that felt anything, that gave a damn about anything.

He didn't know he was crying until Dalejem caressed his face.

"Brother," he murmured, kissing his tears. "I love you, brother. Don't do this. Please."

"You're leaving me," Revik said. It wasn't a question. It was barely coherent. "You're fucking leaving me... because of that bitch."

He didn't know what he was saying.

He barely knew which of them he was talking about.

The other seer pulled him deeper into the tent, then down onto the mat.

Revik barely knew where he was, what was happening, and then the seer was inside of him, pinning him to the floor.

He felt something in his heart give out.

He closed his eyes, right as Dalejem let out a heavier groan.

"*Gaos,*" he panted. "*Gaos.* You're so fucking open right now... your light. It's so beautiful, brother." He arched into him harder. "I love you," he murmured against his neck. "I love you... please. Gods. Please hear me."

He cried out as his light swam over Revik's.

He fought to open him more, to pull him apart from the inside.

"Gods, don't do this, brother," Dalejem pleaded. "... Please. Please. Let me in. I can feel so much of you right now. Let me all the way in, please."

Revik closed his eyes, blinded him with pain, even as he fought to block it.

"I love you, brother," Dalejem murmured, softer. "Let me in, brother... please."

Revik stared up at the roof of the tent.

He felt like his chest had been hollowed out with something like a broken bottle.

But Dalejem was right, too.

He could feel how open he was.

He gasped out tears, even while he came. He groaned when the other male managed to open his light enough to get him there. Then Revik just lay there, unable to move as he spasmed against the other seer. He felt desire building again in Dalejem's light by the time he'd finished, and Revik wrapped his hands around the other seer's neck.

His chest started to hurt all over again.

"I hate you," he told him. He clung to him tighter. He

gripped Dalejem's hair, his hands in fists. He knew how young he sounded, but he didn't care. "I fucking hate you."

Dalejem stroked his face. He kissed him, slid his light deeper into his.

"I know, brother," he said, soft. "I know."

"I hate you."

Dalejem pooled even more of his light into him.

He cradled him in his arms, tears in his eyes.

Revik gripped him harder.

He fought to breathe.

He pressed his face against Dalejem's shoulder as the other seer wrapped him in his light. He felt Dalejem grow even softer. He coaxed Revik open gently as he stroked his hair.

Revik didn't remember them talking after that.

Truthfully, though, he didn't remember much of anything after that.

## CHAPTER 29
## ALONE

Kali and her people left the next day.
Revik barely listened as Balidor addressed the entire group.

The Adhipan leader spoke through the Barrier, using the construct so he didn't have to shout to be heard over the sounds of the jungle and the rustle of clothes and murmurings of the over one hundred infiltrators gathered in the main area of camp between the several dozen tents.

They all stood together anyway, roughly centered in the area of the main campfire and mess tents.

The current group was now bigger than any Revik had seen outside the Org.

He didn't know who all of these seers were, but they all felt like Adhipan or Seven to him now. He no longer felt that distinct flavor of the seers who came specifically to guard Kali, Uye, and their child, the ones who finally got the Org seers to back off.

He did see more he thought he recognized from the Seven's Guard.

They were Vash's people, infiltrators and military-trained seers who operated directly out of Seertown. Those same seers primarily defended the Council, Revik knew, along with the monks and government officials who lived in the Himalayas.

Revik fought not to look for Dalejem's face in that crowd.

He hadn't seen him since that morning, when he'd crawled out of the tent while the other seer was still asleep.

Revik had barely slept himself.

He found himself lying there for hours.

He stared up at the dark ceiling of the tent, his light and mind hollowed out.

When he couldn't stand lying there any longer, he'd gone for a walk in the jungle in the hours before dawn. The walk culminated in him watching the sun come up from a hill not far from where Kali's people had camped.

He felt pings to his light a few times while he sat there.

Some of those pings were questions.

Some were pleas.

Dalejem wondering where he was. Dalejem wanting him.

Dalejem asking him to come back.

Revik shut him out.

He didn't answer him, and eventually, the questions stopped.

When he came back to the camp for breakfast, an hour or so later, he didn't see the green-eyed seer anywhere. He also didn't find him in the tent they'd been sharing, which looked more or less how Revik remembered it looking.

Now, however, standing in the crowd of other seers, he wondered about that, too.

He scanned through his memories, recreating his brief stare through the contents of the tent. He tried to decide if things had been missing from that tent.

He wondered if he'd deliberately not looked very closely.

For the same reason, his focus remained elsewhere for most of Balidor's speech.

He still heard snippets.

He heard most of it truthfully, but also filed the majority of those words away in the back of his mind. He listened without fully comprehending Balidor's words as he started to look for Dalejem in earnest, if still discreetly.

Balidor's speech formed a kind of backdrop as he scanned the crowd for Dalejem's face, as he catalogued the features around him.

*...have been asked to split our forces, following our break of the camp here,* Balidor sent, his tone businesslike inside the construct dome.

*...We have been asked by the Council, in particular by Father Vash, to expend at least some of our resources to try and learn more about this force from the south, since they do not appear to be affiliated with SCARB or the regular Org hierarchy. The rest of us will be joining our brothers and sisters back in Asia, so as not to alert the Org to the movements of sister Kali and her husband and child. She and her mate say they are well-fortified now, and by those who know well how to keep her safe, and out of view...*

Revik watched a colorful bird where it alighted on a nearby palm tree.

The bird called out a musical string of notes, and another bird, from deeper inside the jungle, answered it, repeating those same notes back.

The pain in Revik's chest returned as he listened.

It grew into a low, dull throb under his ribs.

*I am sorry I could not tell any of you this earlier,* Balidor sent somberly into the construct. *But we are losing one of our brothers on this day. For reasons of security, we could not announce his departure until now. But know that it is his wish that it be so, and that it is a higher calling to which he has been sent. I know many of you will still be grieved to see him go.*

Revik flinched, expecting to hear his name.

He had already been told what his fate would be.

Ironically, it would be the exact one he had asked for, so Balidor was right in a way.

It had been his wish.

It just wasn't his wish anymore.

He'd understood Balidor's reasoning when the Adhipan leader explained it. The order had come down from Vash himself, in any case, so Balidor hadn't much say in how it unfolded. In this decision, it seemed, Balidor had only been a messenger.

Ironic, really, given who he was.

But maybe not all that surprising.

Revik felt some hint of Kali behind those orders, as well.

It crossed his mind, in a bare flash of paranoia, that she might have done it to separate him from Dalejem. The thought pained him, so he didn't entertain it for long.

Would they really do that?

Would they really break up a love-bond, just to suit some fucking prophetic figment of Kali's imagination? Even Kali made it sound like the whole thing wasn't written in stone. Were the Council, Vash, Kali, and whoever else really so calculating and cynical?

*...Brother Dalejem,* Balidor sent, his thoughts holding a thread of sadness. *He will no longer be wearing the Adhipan colors, my brothers and sisters...*

Revik's head and eyes jerked around.

He stared at where Balidor stood in the open area by the fire pit.

As he did, Revik felt his breath stop in his chest.

But he had known. Of course he'd fucking known.

He'd know what Dalejem decided.

*...Brother Dalejem has been given another assignment, my brothers and sisters.*

Balidor's thoughts felt solemn but quietly happy, too.

They echoed through the Adhipan construct.

*It is an assignment for which he was chosen by the gods themselves. We are to wish our brother swift wings, and send him all our love as he embarks on this new calling. It is one that speaks to his higher light, to a great need in his soul. None of you will be surprised by this, I suspect, for there was always something special in brother Dalejem, something that would make such a calling seem natural now. It reminds us, as if any of us needed reminding, what an honor it was to serve with him, and to be privy to his light and wisdom all these years...*

At every word, Revik felt his breath squeeze tighter in his chest.

It felt as if he'd fallen under the weight of a stone.

His heart crushed inside bones and earth like the tightened fingers of a fist. He went back to scanning faces in the crowd. He looked for Dalejem openly now, with no thought to being discreet, but he already knew what he would find.

He didn't see the green-eyed seer anywhere.

*Of course, brother Revik will also be returning to his enclave in the mountains,* Balidor added, his words inside the Barrier space still weighted with feeling. *I know you will join me in feeling immense gratitude for what our young brother has risked for us, both body and light, by joining us in our mission out here. Not to mention what he endured personally in order to keep the Bridge and her family safe at this critical time...*

Revik continued to look for Dalejem, ignoring the smiles aimed in his direction, the pings of warmth from nearby seers as they acknowledged Balidor's words.

Revik didn't feel Dalejem in any of it.

He didn't see his face.

Hesitating only another second, he opened his light.

He looked for him openly, searching for the familiar resonance. A few seconds later, he pinged him, and when that didn't work, he called out to him in the space.

Finally, in desperation, he opened his light completely.

He offered it up, begged the other seer to answer him.

Dalejem didn't answer, though.

He didn't answer because he was no longer there.

When Revik sent out a harder blast, using more of his

light, he saw a few seers around him flinch. They turned their heads in surprise, but none of them were Dalejem either.

He really wasn't there.

He was really gone.

Pain hit Revik's heart as he found he understood, as the reality sank into his awareness.

Dalejem was gone. He'd left with Kali.

He was just... gone.

He cried out, unthinking, even as eyes turned towards him again in surprise, their expressions twisting in sympathy when they saw who it was. Revik stared back at all of them but saw none of them. He fought to shut himself down, breathing too much, until he couldn't see, couldn't hear the words being spoken by the gray-eyed seer, even from inside the Barrier.

He felt hands on him, voices in his mind and his ears.

He felt their concern flicker around him, but he didn't want to listen.

He didn't want to hear any of it now.

*Gaos.* How had he gotten so good at lying to himself?

He knew what Jem had chosen.

He knew before he left that hut.

Somewhere in that, someone must have knocked him out.

They must have, because all at once, the world eclipsed around a single dot.

---

...AND REVIK WAS SOMEWHERE ELSE.

Wind played gently with his hair. It whispered softly by his cheek.

He stood at the edge of the world, gazed out over a landscape of endless light.

A golden ocean lived there.

As the ocean appeared gradually out of the light-filled mist, sand spilled out under his feet, which were now bare. High cliffs rose on either side of him. A small island appeared in the surf, covered in trees and birds, so vibrant with life it caught his breath.

Red and black clouds massed at the horizon.

They were distant still, only a warning, not anything he could yet touch or feel.

Something about just being here both calmed his heart and made it so full he couldn't breathe. He stood there, alone. He soaked up the life around him, the scents on the air, the dome of blue sky above, the perfect, crystal-clear waves.

He could just be here.

For now, he could just be.

There was nothing else, not yet. Whatever would come, he wouldn't have to face it yet. He wouldn't have to face it by himself. He *knew* that, somehow. He knew it with all of his light, all his heart. He knew it to be true.

For now, it was silent.

The world held him, still as a stopped breath, full with flower-scented wind and the curling white foam of aquamarine waves and the flash of wings from calling gulls.

Those same rolling waves lapped shores of pure, white sand. They wetted his bare feet. The shockingly clear, pale blue sky swam overhead, still as glass but filled with light, so much light. The light shimmered around him, tiny fragments of living presence and meaning where birds flapped silent between beats of his heart, fish swam leisurely in deep waters.

He was alone here.

He was alone.

But somehow, maybe for the first time, being alone was okay.

## CHAPTER 30
# RETURN

Revik opened his eyes.

He realized only then that someone had entered his room.

It occurred to him a few beats after, he'd opened his eyes because that same person had touched him gently with their light.

He didn't feel any alarm.

He let himself come back.

He let himself return to the room slowly, to his body, until he felt the room reveal itself around him. He felt the stone and air and his flesh and bones grow substantial around the spot where he sat cross-legged on the floor. The floor grew solid under his legs.

He smelled the particular scent of the rock walls, the smell of incense probably from the open door that led out of his cave-like room.

Sitting had gotten easier for him.

It had gotten a lot easier.

Revik craved these sessions now, hungered for them. It wasn't for the escapist reasons he might have expected when they first brought him here.

The opposite felt true, really.

He could feel the difference the sessions were making in how he approached the world. He could feel the difference in his state of mind, in how he viewed himself, how he assessed other beings.

More and more, Revik felt the layers of who he was being slowly peeled back, exposed to the light so that he could finally just accept what lived beneath all of the countless masks and veneers. He could finally just allow himself to be, without trying to change any of it.

He could allow the world to be, without trying to change any of that, either.

On the other side of all that fighting and resistance, things felt simpler.

They felt a fuck of a lot simpler.

He was starting to crave that simplicity.

Moreover, it started to feel more and more like his true self.

At the very least, Revik could now see some fraction of the truth behind the things and people he had been. He could see the common thread running between them, some deeper core to his light—that thing which seemed to remain there, no matter what he did or who he was in the outside world.

Truth lived in that core.

There was nothing in that core to hate.

There was nothing in it to judge, to fix, to manipulate.

It just was.

It existed.

It also felt completely and totally like him.

For now, that was enough. For now, connecting to that part of himself *was* the goal. Revik found the more he did it, the more he lost any interest in his own past, or even what he told himself about who he was now. All those stories just ceased to be interesting to him. They also ceased to really tell him much about who he was, either in the good sense or the bad.

The world felt larger here.

Too large to waste on meaningless regrets.

Sometimes he found that funny, that it took this—sitting alone in a semi-claustrophobic cave—for the world to open up for him. In here, he felt weirdly freed from all the constraints he put on himself, on his life, on who he was able to be, on the future of the world.

Here, it really felt like anything could happen still.

It felt like losing hope was just one more illusion, one more lie in the dark.

When Revik finally opened his eyes and looked up, he found Tulani standing in his doorway, smiling at him. The old monk wore sandals and sand-covered robes, like he always did. His long, dark hair wrapped into a clip at the base of his skull.

Revik blinked to clear his eyes then rubbed the back of his neck.

He shifted his weight on his thighs before stretching out his legs and feet.

"I apologize, brother," he said, smiling at Tulani. "Have you been waiting there long?"

"Not long, no," the other said. "No need for apologies, my friend."

"You needed something?" Revik asked politely.

Tulani nodded, his smile growing warmer. "You have a visitor, brother."

For the first time, Revik's smile faltered, but more in surprise.

"A visitor?"

"Yes. He just arrived. He is most anxious to see you."

Revik just stared at him for a moment, his mind blank.

He still didn't feel any alarm, but confusion swam over his

*aleimi* as he tried to think through possibilities, then to pull answers from the monk's own light.

The male laughed as he blocked his attempt.

"No, no," he chided affectionately. "You must come see for yourself."

"Is it Vash?" Revik asked, his voice curious.

The seer clicked at him teasingly. "You are so suspicious, brother! It is quite funny, you know, given where you are. Do you really imagine enemies coming out of the rock walls to get at you here? Carrying guns, perhaps? Or just very large sticks?"

Revik clicked in a wan humor, too.

It was difficult to remain tense around Tulani.

It seemed, sometimes, like all the old monk did was smile.

He pulled himself stiffly to his feet. As he did, Revik smiled back at him. He made a polite gesture with one hand. "Well?" he prodded. "Are you going to take me to this mysterious guest? Or must I find them on my own in this maze, too, brother?"

Tulani laughed. He waved for Revik to follow him.

"I will take you," he assured him. Tulani glanced over his shoulder as he walked down the narrow passage. "We would not want to lose you in these caves, brother. Although I am quite certain you would not be the first acolyte to get lost in here."

Revik snorted. He nodded a polite greeting to two other monastics as they passed, who smiled at him and Tulani in return.

Revik glanced down at his feet, noting he was barefoot.

That wouldn't matter, though.

Even if they were leaving the caves, it shouldn't matter now.

It was nearly summer in the Pamir.

It was easy to forget about clothing here, and even seasons, inside these walls.

While the caves remained cool in the hottest of the summer months, and in the snow-covered winters, they never got truly hot or truly cold in either.

Revik marked the passage of time mostly when he decided to go out for fresh air, and for real exercise, which he never seemed to get inside the caves.

With the monks' blessing, he spent more than a few days out in the wilderness, at least once a month. He spent that time meditating too, and out hiking on the peaks, even in the dead of winter, even through the shifts in climate that made those winters more brutal of late, despite the wildfires and droughts happening in other parts of the world.

Thinking about that now, Revik sighed a little wistfully.

Maybe he was due for another of his treks.

It would be nice to be out there now, with the rivers and waterfalls full, the plants bursting with new life under the late-spring sun.

He followed the much shorter male through the tunnel's twists and turns, until it hit him they were heading for one of the common areas. Those larger caves often acted as impromptu reception spaces when they weren't filled with socializing monks.

Tulani made the last turn then, and the cavern walls opened up. A much, much larger space expanded around them both. Revik realized the monk had brought him to the least-often used of these massive halls.

It was an enormous, ancient-feeling cave, one that used to serve as a meditation hall before they'd moved those functions to a smaller part of the underground city.

Revik's eyes slid up the rock walls in a kind of wonder.

He remembered this as one of his favorite spaces in all of the Pamir. Something about the remnants of light that clung to these walls pulled at him. They opened his light. They enveloped him in feeling. They even made him feel safe.

Everything about this place had a familiar feel to it, one that wasn't solely comforting, but immersed him in a sense of—

Well, family.

He felt family here.

He felt an intense feeling that he belonged.

It was not something he ever expected to feel inside these walls.

His eyes paused on the faded mural someone long-ago painted on the fire-blackened stone, probably more than a thousand years before he'd been born.

He found himself staring at the figure at the top of all the rest.

She wore all white. In one hand she gripped a lightning staff.

One of her bare feet rested on the Earth, the other in the heavens.

The staff spun gold and white upward, formed an arc of cabled brilliance that reached from Earth to a shimmering, deep gold sea surrounded in dark blue clouds.

She stood alone in the night sky.

*She holds the Light between worlds...* Revik's mind murmured.

When he looked down, he saw a man standing there.

The man gazed up at the same mural.

Even as Revik took in the infiltrator's uniform, the black armored pants and organic vest, the male seer turned.

His green eyes widened when he saw Revik.

Then he burst into a grin.

Revik just stood there.

He felt nothing but shock as he stared at the other seer.

It had been more than two years since he'd last seen him.

Before he could recover, Dalejem walked right up to him. He embraced him tightly, wrapping his muscular arms around Revik's waist and back. He clasped him more tightly still and Revik felt Dalejem's breath hitch.

His fingers gripped Revik's shoulder, then his neck.

"*Gaos.*" Dalejem's voice came out hoarse. The older seer released him long enough to look at him. "*Gaos.* You look so different, brother. So fucking different. Your light... it is even more beautiful than I remember. You are positively glowing, my friend. Truly, I almost did not recognize you..."

His words trailed.

Dalejem studied him openly with his eyes and light, even as he continued to run an infiltrator's scan over Revik's entire *aleimic* body.

Revik wondered if the other male knew he was doing it.

The green-eyed seer still held his arms.

He still gripped him tightly, smiling, as tears ran down his face.

"What are you doing here?" Revik asked.

The words were clumsy.

Revik winced at how clumsy they were, but he couldn't figure out how to soften them.

He stared at those green and violet-ringed eyes, feeling a strange combination of pain and happiness at seeing him there. The pain part of that shocked him. It clenched in his chest, even as he stood there, staring at Dalejem's face, watching the infiltrator look at him.

"*Gaos.*" Dalejem wiped his eyes. "I am so happy to see you, brother."

Revik felt that pain in his chest worsen.

He watched the other male cry.

He struggled with the parts of himself that wanted to cry, too.

Remembering where he was suddenly, he looked around.

But Tulani had already left them.

"And what am I doing here?" Dalejem asked. Humor touched his voice as he shook Revik lightly in his hands. "I *missed* you, goddamn it. What the fuck do you think I'm doing here? I missed you like crazy. I wanted to see you, brother, now that I finished my training under my new order. I was given some time before I started my first assignment."

Revik fought to get his equilibrium back.

His chest hurt badly now. He shook his head. He fought to disentangle himself from the other male's light. "No. I can't do this, Dalejem... no."

"Brother." The other seer caught his arms. He pulled him gently back. "Brother... please. Let me see you. I can't stay long. Just let me *see* you. Let me say goodbye to you this time at least. Let us leave one another as *friends*, goddamn it!"

Revik shook his head.

He fought the closing in his heart.

He hadn't felt anything like this since he left Brazil.

He hadn't closed like this with anyone, not in months.

He'd been trying so hard.

He'd told himself he'd made so much progress.

Yet here he was, right back where he had been all those months earlier, when he'd first gotten here, a goddamned mess of self-hate and broken light.

He couldn't look at Dalejem at all now.

At the same time, he didn't fight him all that hard, either.

He ended up following, stiff-legged, as Dalejem brought him to a faded couch that squatted directly under the mural. Dalejem sat him down, then curled up on the cushions beside him. He pulled Revik closer as he warmed Revik's light with his.

Revik felt the other male's hands on him then, touching him, caressing his skin, and winced in spite of himself, pulling away.

"Jem... no," Revik said. "I said no," he growled, glaring at him.

"Don't call me that."

"Fuck you."

"Gods, brother... I don't want to fight." His green eyes filled with tears, even as he caressed Revik's face with his hands. "You left that morning. *You* left, brother. Before I could explain. Before I could tell you anything. I looked for you everywhere before I left. I called for you. I wanted so badly to talk to you about this, about why I did what I did—"

"I know why you did it," Revik said. "You did it because she is the Bridge... and I am not."

Dalejem stared at him.

Pain filled his green eyes.

"No, brother," he said. He shook his head. "I did it because Kali asked me to do what *felt right* to me. She asked me to look, high up in my light. She told me to ask that higher, clearer part of myself, the part that loves unconditionally... and she urged me to do whatever that part said. She had me ask what felt right for you. She had me ask it what felt right for me. She had me ask it what felt right for the world. All three answers were the same."

He caressed Revik's jaw. The handsome seer shrugged his shoulders, shoulders that were even more muscular than Revik remembered from the jungle.

"Once I'd done that," Dalejem said. "Once I could see that she was right, that the higher parts of me agreed, I could not choose differently."

"You could not?" Revik asked bitterly.

"No." Dalejem frowned. "Could you? If you loved me?"

Revik's jaw hardened more.

Before he could think of what to say, Dalejem kissed him. He kissed him harder, his hands wrapped in Revik's hair. He leaned into his chest, coaxed his mouth open with his tongue and lips, and kissed him again.

Revik found himself kissing him back. He fell into it before he knew he meant to, until he gripped the male's long hair in his hands. He lost himself in his light. He pulled on Dalejem to open that light more.

When Dalejem did, Revik let out an involuntary groan.

He kissed the other seer again.

He held him tightly enough that time, he might have been hurting him.

When they next parted, both of them were panting.

Dalejem's hand fell on Revik's groin. He looked up at Revik's face, those green eyes glazed, and he gasped when Revik pressed his erection against his palm.

Revik's fingers tightened. He gripped Dalejem's face in his hands.

"Explain," Revik growled. "You said you wanted to explain things to me that morning. So fucking explain them now. Fucking talk, Dalejem. Is that all it was? This seeing of 'rightness' to leave me?"

The seer closed his eyes.

Pain came off him in a dense cloud.

Revik's jaw hardened more.

"You broke my fucking heart," he said.

Dalejem groaned. That pain coming off him worsened until Revik looked away. Dalejem leaned closer. He pressed his face against Revik's, caressed his hands, kissed his neck. He made a low sound when Revik's light opened, almost against his will.

Gods. He couldn't do this. He couldn't fucking do this again—

"Brother, you understand," Dalejem murmured. "I know you do. It's why you got so angry at me that night. It's how you knew... before I'd told you a damned thing. It's why I didn't *have* to tell you anything. You understood from the moment I did. Before, maybe."

"I understood?" Revik growled. "What did I understand exactly, Dalejem?"

"That I serve the Bridge."

Revik's jaw hardened until it hurt.

He released Dalejem's face. He leaned back abruptly on the couch.

"So?" he said coldly. "You want a fucking medal, brother? Your own set of angel's wings?"

"You understand," Dalejem said, clicking softly. "I know you do."

Revik found his eyes shifting up.

He stared at the white figure at the top of the mural, and his jaw hardened more.

"So Kali managed to split us apart." He glared at the other seer. "It occurred to you, didn't it? That getting you away from me might have been their goal?"

Dalejem shook his head. "I do not think so, brother. She cried when I told her. She cried when I said how I felt about you. They both seemed surprised. Her and her husband both."

"That you gave a shit about me? I'm sure that *was* a surprise," Revik growled.

Dalejem stared at him. "No. Not for that. That my heart told me I should go with them."

Revik swallowed. Pain still wanted to fill his chest.

"Maybe it wasn't her, then," Revik growled. "I noticed Balidor and Vash didn't want me in the Adhipan, either. Not once you were spoken for."

"Revik... *gaos*. No." Dalejem gripped his thigh. He shook his head as the pain coming off him worsened. "No. You know that is not true. That's not what you think, either. It's really not."

"Then what is true?" Revik growled. "What do I think, brother?"

Pain rose to his heart, even as he tried to answer his own question.

"What is *my* purpose, Dalejem? What is *my* truth? What would that higher part of me have said, if our positions were reversed?"

Dalejem looked at him, his green eyes sad. "You know I

can't tell you that, brother. But if you stay here, it will become clearer to you. I am sure that is why Vash—"

"You don't know that," Revik cut in. "You don't know fuck about me."

Seeing the hurt in the other's eyes, his jaw hardened.

He fought to swallow, staring at the other male's face. "What am I doing here, Dalejem? Because it feels a hell of a lot like I'm being pushed aside, hidden out of the way... and not only by Kali. Or Vash. Or Galaith. Or you."

He watched as a distressed look rose to the other's face.

Guilt hit at him as he realized what he was doing.

He was wrong. *Gaos.* He was wrong in this.

He was acting wrongly.

"I am sorry, brother," Dalejem said, his voice softer. "I wish I could tell you what you want to know. I wish I could so much... but I can't. All I can say is, you are not forgotten here. They have a job for you, and it is an important one. They need you here for that. For now, at least."

Revik fought not to think about his words.

He could feel the truth there.

He didn't want to feel it.

The vagueness didn't help. The vagueness made him want to believe it was all bullshit, that they were all lying to him. In the end, the inability of Revik's mind to make sense of that vagueness brought another swell of frustration and grief.

He looked at Dalejem.

He fought not to react to the sadness in his green eyes.

"Who asked for you?" Revik asked. "Who exactly? Do you know?"

Dalejem exhaled shortly. He tilted a hand over his knee.

"I do not know, brother," he said. "Who knows anything with these things? Kali said only that she knew it should be me. She saw me with her daughter... protecting her... presumably through one of her prophetic visions. She could not risk her daughter's life by sending me away. Not even for you, brother."

Revik didn't speak.

He felt the part of him that wanted to be angry about it still, to have someone to blame. But it hurt to be angry, even now. Maybe especially now, since he could already feel that Dalejem wouldn't be staying.

When he looked up next, the seer was wiping tears from his face.

"Only for the night, brother," he said. "They gave me leave to see you, but I cannot interfere with your work here." He hesitated, then added, "It is unlikely I will be able to come back. They warned me about this. I can't tell you particulars, brother. I wish I could… I only know we are going into hiding, and the tie between you and the Bridge is strong. It cannot be visible. It would be dangerous for both of you."

Revik nodded. He stared at the stone floor.

He'd known that, too.

He didn't know how he'd known, but he'd finally stopped asking himself that question.

It was pointless.

He lifted his gaze to the mural. He felt some part of his chest unclench as he stared at the black rock. He drank in the elaborate paintings of the seer pantheon there.

Tulani may have picked this room on purpose.

In fact, as Revik thought about it, he grew more and more certain the monk brought him here with intention. Knowing Tulani, he would see it as a favor, a means of reminding Revik of the broader perspective surrounding his own, considerably smaller problems. Tulani would see it as one small nudge past the pain and into the truth of things.

The truth of life. The truth of Dalejem.

The truth of Revik's own role in this, whatever that ended up being.

Tears came to his eyes as he thought it, but he took Dalejem's hand.

He raised it to his lips. He kissed his palm, then pulled the seer closer so he could wrap his arms around him. He felt Dalejem's immediate relief, an almost mind-numbing feeling of gratitude as Revik wound his light and body around his.

For a long moment, they just kissed, half-lying together on the old couch. They held one another, immersed in each other's light. They caressed one another through their clothes, then kissed for a while longer.

"I missed you," Revik murmured.

He kissed his cheek, then rested his face against the other male's. He tugged him closer until he'd pulled him, armor and all, halfway into his lap.

Pain bled out of the other seer.

Pain, and so much love, Revik closed his eyes. He bit his tongue as he opened to let it in. Then he was stroking Dalejem's hair and back, opening his light more as he felt the seer sigh against him, gripping him by the arm and shoulder.

For a long time after that, neither of them spoke.

As they lay there, Revik found his eyes scaling that rock wall.

That time they stopped on a second, softer image of the woman in white, one nearer to the bottom of the Earth. The Dragon God swam by her through stars, his tail curled around Tortoise. The softer woman rested near their light, but she didn't look at either of them. The smile she wore aimed at a different being, and him alone.

She still held that charged light between her hands, but it looked softer than the lightning above. Inside that glowing circle, Revik saw a faint image of a golden ocean.

Next to her, a boy sat smiling, his eyes filled with joy as he played in the star-filled sky.

Between his hands glowed a blue-white sun.

It was him the woman in white smiled at.

It was him who entirely held her gaze.

Revik felt tears return to his eyes as he traced the course of those lines. He watched the boy laugh where he held the sun between his hands. Between those curling flames, bisecting light and dark, a perfect white sword glowed softly in the night sky.

The golden ocean pulls at him, even faded and dark, a bare scratch in the stone, but Revik remembers that, too, and not only from the lines he's read in the old books.

He remembers what it was like there.

It is real to him now.

He wonders sometimes if parts of him live there still. If he waits for her there.

If he waits on that shore.

He feels himself sometimes, watching from the golden sand.

Waiting for the rise of that blue-white sun.

## WHAT TO READ NEXT...

Check out the first book in the main BRIDGE AND SWORD series, which takes place not long after this one!

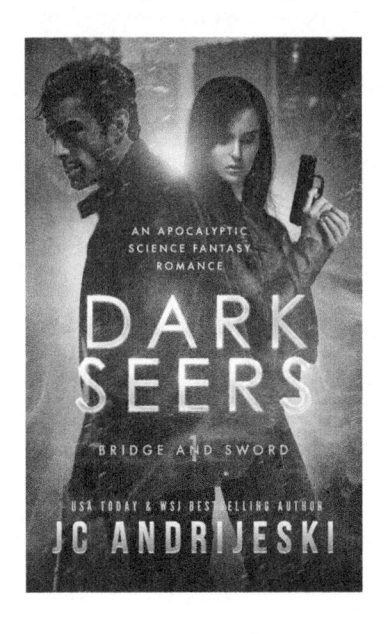

**DARK SEERS**
**(Bridge and Sword: Book One)**

*BOOK ONE only 99 CENTS!*

Link: https://geni.us/BS01

**The way he stood there. His angular features. Precise, interesting, sensual. Freakishly tall, with pale, unnerving eyes. He moved unlike anyone I'd ever seen. He also wasn't human.**

Like most humans, Allie only glimpses Seers at a distance,

usually in sex clubs, or on the leash of the wealthy and powerful of San Francisco. Fascinating, beautiful, deadly, Seers exist totally outside the sphere of ordinary people.

You have to be rich to own a Seer. You have to be rich to get anywhere near one.

Allie's more focused on getting her mom to a therapist, on keeping her friend, Cass, out of crap relationships, and making enough money so they don't lose the house. When Revik shows up at her work, she assumes he's just some eccentric, another weirdo with an odd fixation on her. But in Revik's world, dark, terrorist Seers run everything, and now they're targeting Allie.

Revik tells her Seers believe she will free their people from enslavement.

They believe she will kill all the humans.

They believe she will destroy the world.

Now she's on the run, the police have her family and friends, and the only person left is a hot but surly Seer with seriously terrible communication skills and a frightening ability with a gun.

She has to find a way out. She has to keep her family safe. Revik is all she's got.

***Psychic suspense. Apocalyptic. The first chapter in an epic,***

*soul-crushing, world-spanning science fantasy that can get dark, dark, dark... but also contains a lot of light.*

**THE BRIDGE AND SWORD SERIES** is a dark, gritty psychic warfare epic from a USA TODAY and WALL STREET JOURNAL bestselling author. Set in an alternate version of Earth where a second race of beings called "Seers" live alongside humans, this is for fans of romantic, character-driven science fiction and fantasy worlds, filled with twists and turns and backstabbing betrayals, with heroes and villains who are often the same people.

*GET THE EBOOK FOR ONLY 99 CENTS!*

*See below for Sample Pages!*

**WANT TO READ MORE?**
Check out the next BRIDGE and SWORD companion book,
featuring Balidor and Cass:

**A GLINT OF LIGHT**
**(A Bridge and Sword Novel)**

Link: https://geni.us/Glint-BS

*Everyone said to let her go.*
*To let the devil and her dark masters have her.*
*But he can't do that.*
*He just can't.*

Everyone told him Cass couldn't be saved.

All of them, even Allie and Jon, Cass's childhood friends, believe she's too far gone.

She chose the darkest of dark paths, betraying everyone who loved her, nearly killing her best friend, Allie, and destroying Allie's mind in the process. After Cass became a minion of the dark being, Shadow, she nearly killed them all. After everything she put them through, the rest of their team mostly wants her dead.

But Balidor can't bring himself to let her go.

Using his vast abilities and psychic training, he leads Cass through the darkness of her own mind, trying desperately to bring back the woman he loved before Shadow broke her.

*SERIES NOTE:* This is a companion novel to the *Bridge and Sword* world and takes place between books #8 and #9 in the main series.

# FREE DOWNLOAD!

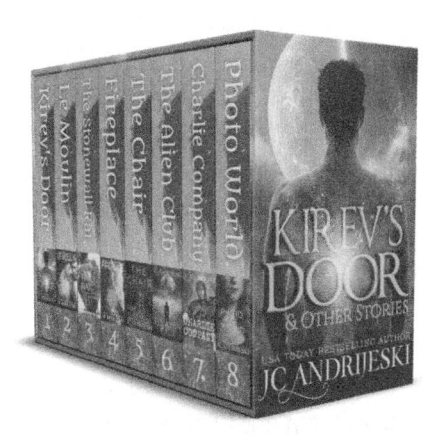

Grab a copy of KIREV'S DOOR, the exciting backstory of the main character from my "Quentin Black" series, when he's still a young slave on "his" version of Earth. Plus seven other stories, many of which you can't get anywhere else!!

## This box set is TOTALLY EXCLUSIVE to those who sign up for my VIP mailing list, "The Light Brigade!"

**GET MY FREE BOOK!**

Or go to: https://www.jcandrijeski.com/mailing-list

# REVIEWS ARE AWESOME

A Note from the Author:
Now that you've finished reading my book,
PLEASE CONSIDER LEAVING A REVIEW!
A short review is fine and so very appreciated.
Word of mouth is truly essential for any author to succeed!

Leave a Review Here:
https://geni.us/ExRook-BS

~ SAMPLE PAGES ~

*DARK SEERS*
*(BRIDGE AND SWORD: BOOK ONE)*

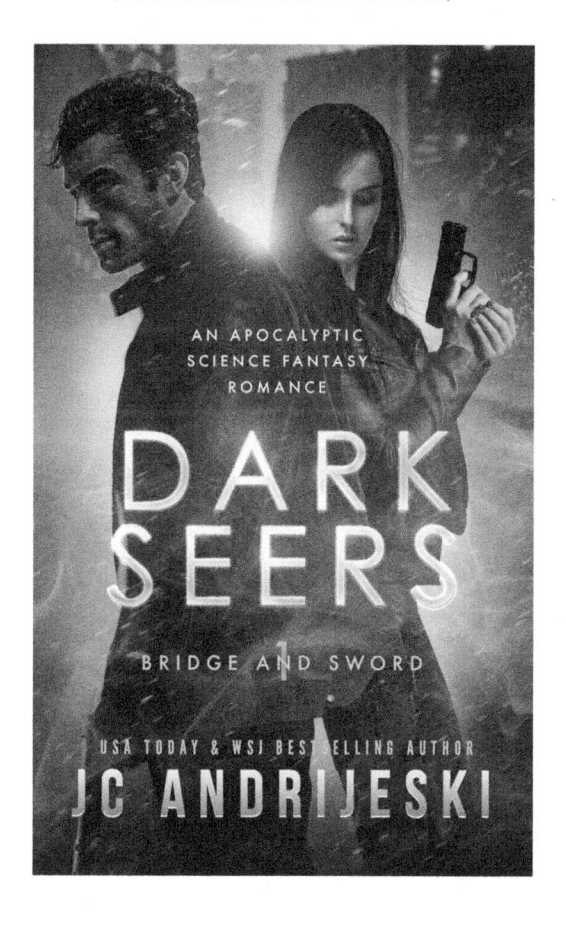

# 1 / ALLIE

"HE'S BAAAACK..." MY BEST friend, Cass, grinned at me from where she leaned over the fifties-style lunch counter, her butt aimed at the dining area of the Lucky Cat Diner where we both worked.

Given that our uniforms consisted of short skirts and form-fitting, low-cut blouses, Cass was giving an eyeful to at least a few of our regular customers.

Oblivious to that, and to the men sitting at the counter, pretending not to stare at her ass as she stuck it up in the air, she grinned at me, her full lips more dramatic than usual with their blood-red lipstick.

"Did you see, Allie? Your buddy? He found your section again."

I muttered something.

I might have rolled my eyes.

Mostly, I continued my personal, ongoing battle with the diner's decrepit espresso machine.

"What's the pool up to now?" Cass asked. "Seventy? Eighty?"

"It's over a hundred now." I used the metal stopper to compress finely-ground espresso beans into a metal filter. I tried to be careful, but still managed to spill a small pile on the linoleum counter.

"Sasquatch threw in twenty yesterday," I reminded her.

Thinking about that, I grunted.

"He must really want the cash. He walked right up to the guy. Asked him his name, point-blank. Said he wouldn't leave until he told him."

Cass's eyes, with their thick black eyeliner, widened. "What happened?"

"Same thing that always happens, Cassandra. *Nada.* That guy could stare down a professional killer. He probably *is* a professional killer."

My best friend laughed, kicking up her high heels, which were red-vinyl platforms, more seventies than fifties, not like it mattered. Again, the nearby men pretended to sip their coffees as they surreptitiously checked her out.

Cass had a red thing going lately.

Her long, straight black hair had dark red flames coming up from the tips, the color matching her lipstick, eyeshadow, fingernail polish, and the five-inch heels.

Two months ago, everything was teal.

She could get away with just about any color or style she wanted, though. She just had that kind of face, not to mention a gorgeous body. Cassandra Aria Jainkul was, and probably always would be, one of the most physically beautiful women I'd ever seen in my life, even compared to feed avatars and movie stars.

I hated her a little for that, sometimes.

Looking up from where I was still doing battle with the diner's antiquated espresso maker, a machine I was convinced had it in for me, personally, I blew strands of my much less dramatic dark brown out of my face.

I glanced at the man in the corner booth.

I didn't tell Cass, but I'd seen him walk in.

Hell, I *felt* him walk in.

It was weird being so attuned to the guy.

He'd never said a damned thing to me either, apart from relaying whatever single-item purchase he wanted off the diner's menu. He never came in with anyone else. He flat-out ignored my few attempts at small talk. He never made eye-contact.

He generally stared out the window, or down at his own hands.

Mr. Monochrome took the practice of ignoring other human beings to the level of art.

The extremes he went to avoid conversation didn't just verge on rude.

They *were* rude.

Yet he didn't exactly come off as a dick, either.

My mind superimposed various stories—undercover cop, international fugitive from justice, spy, private detective, terrorist for the seer underground.

Serial killer.

Of course, this was real life, so the reality was likely a lot less interesting.

Jon, my brother, simply referred to him as "Allie's current stalker."

Which wasn't totally fair, to be honest.

This guy didn't give a shit about me. Apart from eating at one of my tables every day, Mr. Monochrome ignored me along with the rest of humanity.

He likely worked at one of the tech companies nearby and came to the Lucky Cat because we still accepted cash. Most places in San Francisco didn't.

So yeah, a tinfoil hat weirdo, maybe.

But likely a harmless one.

I glanced at the monitor on the wall.

The news feeds still played up there, showing the reaction to the latest terrorist attack in Europe. I watched the President of the United States give a speech from behind a podium, but the volume was too low for me to hear his actual words. His blond wife stood beside him, hands clasped, a solemn look etched on her face.

I knew neither one of them really looked like that, of course.

According to the Human Protection Act, both were required to wear avatars to avoid being targeted by seers working for enemy governments.

The rules against real-time images kept getting stricter, too.

Even the landscape around them had to be digitally altered now.

I told myself I didn't need to hear the President's actual words.

I'd listened to dozens of Caine's speeches already, just like everyone else. President Daniel Caine was the most popular president we'd ever had. There was already talk of adjusting the presidential term limits a second time, to allow him to run for a fifth term.

Opposite Caine's wife stood his Vice President, Ethan Wellington.

Wellington's avatar showed him to be a handsome black man in his late forties, roughly the same age as Caine. I remembered reading somewhere that they'd gone to school together. Both were young, energetic, articulate.

Both of them bothered me.

I honestly couldn't have said why, exactly.

Hell, even *Jon* liked Caine, and he hated most politicians. Objectively, I got it. I even agreed with Jon's reasons whenever we talked about it.

Caine had done a lot of good.

My distrust of him felt practically physical, though.

I glanced at Mr. Monochrome again, wiping the counter off with a wet rag where I'd spilled the espresso grounds. If I was right about my tinfoil hat theory, he likely believed a lot of the same wild theories my brother did. Jon had a whole paranoia thing about seers, in particular. He was convinced our government used seers to spy on our own domestic population.

To be fair to my brother—and possibly Mr. Monochrome—I *had* noticed a lot more seers on the streets lately.

Of course, rich people had been importing privately-owned seers to San Francisco for decades. The difference was, they used to hide it. Owning a seer had become a status symbol in recent years—a way to mark yourself as part of the uber-wealthy, or an executive in a forward-thinking corporation.

I'd read in the feeds somewhere that a highly-trained seer could go for more than the cost of *buying* an apartment in San Francisco.

So yeah, being a peon myself, I couldn't get very close.

A few times, I got within a dozen yards of one, though.

Like most people, the closest I'd likely *ever* get to a real-live seer was a glimpse of one on the street. All my knowledge of the seer race would come via online feeds, movies, stories from my friends. The seer sex-fetish bars were way out of my price range too, even if I'd been into that kind of thing. No amount of tips, tattoos, digital renderings, or coffee-shop gallery paintings would ever buy me access to that world.

So yeah, unless I had a rich relative somewhere I didn't know about, I would have to appreciate the beauty of seers from afar.

I was curious, though.

Most people were curious, I suppose.

Cass poked my arm, pulling me out of my reverie. When I looked over, she raised her eyebrows suggestively.

"What'll you give me if I go over there right now?" she grinned. "...and offer to blow him if he'll give up his name?"

The man at the counter next to her coughed, spitting out some of his coffee.

## 1 / ALLIE

Glancing at him, I grunted.

I looked at Cass, only to realize I'd completely forgotten the cappuccino I'd been making. I turned my back on her briefly, and hooked the metal filter into the corresponding threads on the machine. After a bit of a struggle, I got it locked in place and stuck a wide-mouthed coffee cup under it, hitting the red button.

When I heard the tell-tale hiss, I turned towards her.

"What'll I give you to blow my stalker? Hmmm." I folded my arms, pretended to think. "How about a grilled cheese sandwich? You like those, right?"

She smacked my arm. "Cheapskate."

"What were you hoping for? I'm basically offering you my dinner."

"Right. I'm thinking you just don't want me to blow your new friend." Grinning faintly, she gave me an exaggerated wink. "I guess I'd better let you blow him instead. If you do a good enough job, maybe he'll tell *you* his name."

When I smacked her with the counter rag, she laughed.

"Hey, starving artist." She nudged my arm. "We're going out tonight, right? You're still in your *I'm getting even with my lousy, cheating, fuckwad, loser ex-boyfriend by going out to clubs, getting rip-roaring drunk with my best pal Cass* phase, right?"

I grunted. "I think that phase has run its course."

"Aww." She pouted. "One more night. It's Saturday."

I shook my head. "I'm supposed to work at Spider's new shop tomorrow. He and Angie wanted to see a few more designs... so that's what I'll be doing tonight. I can't draw drunk, so partying's out, sorry."

She frowned, and that time it looked real. "Boring. At least call that Nick guy. Get him to come over and screw your brains out when he gets off work."

I grimaced. "Ugh. No. I had to end that."

"What?" Her mouth puckered disapprovingly. "Why? He was cute!"

"He started getting weird."

"Define 'weird,' Allie."

"I don't know." I shrugged. "Just weird. Clingy, I guess."

Staring at me in disbelief, she snorted.

I heard real irritation in her voice.

"Jesus. The magic pussy strikes again." Leaning her ass on the counter, she frowned. "You'll have to give me your secret one of these days, Al. I think I have the opposite... the anti-magic, dick-repellent pussy. They all want to bang me, then... *poof!* They're gone. You get marriage proposals. I get vomit-stained notes on my bedstand."

I let out an involuntary laugh. "You have bad taste in guys, Cassandra. That's not the same thing as being dick-repellent or whatever. If I slept with those guys, they'd leave me crappy notes, too."

"Sure, they would."

"They would," I insisted. "And you know it."

Mollified slightly, she propped her jaw on her hand, looking down the bar.

"Maybe," she admitted, glum. Perking up slightly, she glanced over. "Hey, is Jon coming in today? After his morning kung fu class?"

"Far as I know." I jerked my jaw towards the cat clock with the eyes that flicked back and forth. "He should be here any minute."

"Now, *he's* someone I'd blow for free," she said wistfully.

I grimaced. "Seriously? Can you just... not? Talk about him like that? He's my brother."

"Your brother is seriously fine. And he's your *adoptive* brother. No reason to get all skeeved hearing me lust over your *non*-blood relative."

I flung the rag over my shoulder. Bending down, I looked under the bar for almond milk. "You know he's gay, right? I mean, it's not like we haven't known that since kindergarten."

She sighed wistfully. "A girl can dream."

Internally, I sighed.

Cass had always oscillated between *bad for her* and *completely unattainable.*

Her entire sex-partner-picking meter was broken.

"You're sure he's not bi?" Cass asked hopefully. "Even a little? Like a secret bi?"

"You're welcome to ask him."

"Maybe I'll just show up at his place in a trench coat and a teddy. See how he responds to real-life stimuli."

The men sitting there all looked away as her eyes turned in their direction, trying to hide the fact that they were staring at her.

"Yeah," I grunted. "Good luck with that."

Walking the cappuccino over to the guy at the counter who'd ordered it, I walked back to her, shrugging. "Personally, though, if you're going to start going after guys who aren't card-carrying members of the bag-of-dicks crowd, I'd suggest trying with males of the species who actually like sleeping with, you know, *women.*"

"Where's the fun in that?"

Still thinking, I added, "Jon has good taste in guys. Instead of playing 'scare the hot gay guy,' maybe just ask him for tips on how to pick up, you know, men. With an emphasis on guys who aren't anything like your father or your bag-of-dicks brothers."

She laughed, but I saw my words reach her, even as she shook her head ruefully.

"Yeah," she conceded. She dumped part of a saltshaker on a napkin and spread the granules around with a finger. "How's your mom doing?"

"She's okay."

"Really?"

I looked up from where I'd been rearranging a stack of paper napkins.

Seeing the probing look in her eyes, I exhaled.

"Let's see. Her last bender was two weeks ago, so she's probably due for another one. Last time I went over there, she was watching old tapes of us with my dad, when me and Jon were kids. She yelled at me when I tried to turn it off, then started crying."

"Jesus Christ." Cass winced. "You need to get her help, Al."

"And pay for it how? My stellar blow jobs? I already had to drop out of school." I grunted, dumping the old almond milk carton in recycling and straightening. "Even if I added blow jobs to my repertoire of gigs, I doubt I'd pull in enough to pay for a week of rehab, and she needs more like a year, plus counseling."

Frowning, I found myself thinking through it for the thousandth time, despite my own words.

"Jon would help, but he doesn't have any money, either. He'd have to hit up one of his tech partners, and I don't want to ask him to do that, not until he's more established. Then there's the little problem of her flat-out refusing to go. We tried to get her to a grief therapist and she wouldn't even do that. She won't even *talk* about Dad. She watches those videos of him, you know, before he got sick… I swear she wants to pretend it never happened. Like he's on a business trip or something."

Cass frowned, watching my eyes. "I really like your mom."

I nodded, my chest tightening. "Me, too."

A throat cleared.

A male throat.

I turned, startled at how close they were.

Pale, glass-like eyes met mine.

A narrow mouth hardened under high, sharp cheekbones and an angular but handsome face. He was tall as hell. I'd known he was tall of course, but somehow I hadn't fully realized *how* tall, not until now, with him standing right in front of me.

His coal-black hair hung longish, cut in a way that struck me as expensive.

His watch looked expensive.

An expensive-looking coat hung from his broad shoulders. His headset looked expensive. The rest of his clothes were black and nondescript, but they looked expensive, too.

It was Mr. Monochrome.

And he was staring straight at me.

# 2 / MR. MONOCHROME

HE CLEARED HIS THROAT again. I heard impatience that time. Annoyance.

"May I speak with you?" he asked. "It's important."

I blinked.

Nope. He was still there.

He was also definitely talking to me.

I glanced at Cass, who was staring up at him, too, her red-lipsticked mouth ajar where she leaned over the lunch counter, her short-skirted butt in the air. When I glanced back at Mr. Monochrome, he hadn't followed the direction of my gaze.

Those pale eyes remained on me.

"Now, Alyson," he said.

I wasn't someone who generally had to listen to people who spoke to me like that. One benefit of working jobs I didn't care about.

Even our boss at the diner, Tom, didn't go there with me.

Then again, Tom didn't exactly carry this guy's presence.

Also, my head only came up to about the middle of this guy's chest. He had one of those frames that made him appear more lean than bulky, more of a runner type than a weightlifter. Now that he stood in front of me, though, I decided that might be deceptive, too. Up close, he looked more like one of Jon's martial arts buddies.

The muscles this guy wore definitely looked functional, not purely decorative.

The weirdest part was definitely that stare, though.

His piercing gaze stunned me in some way I couldn't articulate to myself, maybe in part because his eyes weren't at all what I expected. I'd known his irises were on the light side, but I hadn't realized *how* light. Looking at them now, they appeared to have almost no color at all. I supposed technically they must be blue or gray, but they reminded me more of crystals I'd seen in New Age rock shops. Their lightness was made stranger by his pitch-black hair, but I didn't see how they could be contact lenses.

Maybe they had a virtual component?

Maybe he'd gotten some kind of augmentation surgery?

Mr. Monochrome stared at me while I drank him in.

Then, without warning, he moved.

Before I could get out a single word, he caught hold of my upper arm. His fingers felt like flesh-wrapped steel; they closed around my bicep and I immediately panicked.

He gripped me tightly enough that I let out a surprised yelp.

I fought him, jerking back...

...when something slammed into my chest.

Liquid heat, reassurance, presence, light... I don't know what the fuck it was, but it confused me, calmed me, and completely wiped out my ability to think.

I didn't tell myself to stop fighting him.

I just... stopped.

When my vision cleared, he was watching me, wary.

"All right?" he asked.

Thinking about his question, I nodded.

He gestured with a hand.

I followed the motion with my eyes.

He moved oddly. I liked it. Every movement contained grace, an effortless fluidity. An animal quality, I thought... like a big cat. Everything about it precise. The small, vague but expressive gestures, those little adjustments of his body and face.

The way he stood there. His angular features.

Precise. Interesting. Sensual.

It pulled at my eyes, at some other part of me.

The fascination felt visceral.

I tried to think what it reminded me of.

I realized it didn't remind me of anything.

It was new.

"Come," he said, gruff.

Before I'd made sense of the word, he was leading me through the opening in the linoleum-topped counter.

I followed the tug of his fingers.

I couldn't think of a single reason not to.

---

CASS FOLLOWED BEHIND US. I was aware of her, but I didn't look back.

Her voice grew increasingly frantic.

"Allie! Wait!" She reached for me, catching hold of my arm. "Wait!"

The man holding my hand didn't wait. He scarcely glanced at her, scarcely paused his steps. Focusing on the diner's front door, he continued to walk us in that direction. He dragged Cass along with us until she was forced to let me go.

"Hey!" Cass burst out. "Wait! What are you doing with her? STOP! STOP!"

I heard the fear in her voice.

It didn't alarm me.

It just felt... irrelevant.

The man holding my hand remained silent.

Despite his silence, I felt tension vibrate his presence, all the way down to his fingers. Aggression wrapped in stillness, a hard line of thought moved precisely in the background, calculating things. Time. How much time was left. Distance. Documents needed. Law enforcement. Weapons. Car.

He needed a car.

A different voice took my focus off him.

It was hard, loud, and it came from right in front of us.

It was also extremely familiar.

"What the fuck do you think you're doing, man?"

My mind wavered...

...then it clicked back, sharpening.

My brother, Jon, stood in front of us. His long, dirty-blond hair was up in a half-ponytail, probably because he'd just walked here from the martial arts studio where he worked.

He stared from my face to the man holding my hand.

Jon's hazel eyes focused on that hand, the one gripping mine, right before they slid up, measuring the man attached to it.

He seemed to make up his mind.

"Let go of her, man," Jon said. "Now. Or I'm calling the cops."

My brother's voice was blunt, with no hint of empty threat.

He spoke without emotion, his eyes matching the steel underlying his words. It was his martial arts voice, the one he used with his students. I knew that voice. I'd seen it in action when I'd gone to his fights and other events.

I'd never seen it used like this.

Something about it brought my mind back, marginally, at least.

I tugged on my hand in the tall man's grip, trying to retrieve my fingers.

The man glanced at me, his grip tightening.

*Calm down,* I heard distinctly in my mind. *Now, Alyson.*

That time, it didn't calm me.

I still couldn't quite force myself to speak. I frowned at him instead, gritting my teeth as I fought to clear my mind, to understand what was happening, what I was doing.

The man in front of me faced Jon. "I won't hurt her."

Jon frowned. He looked at me. "Are you all right, Al?"

*Answer him. Tell him you're fine.*

I frowned, looking at the man holding my hand. For the first time, it crossed my mind to wonder what was wrong with me.

Why did I want to do as he said?

*Tell him,* the man's mind prodded, insistent. *Tell him you're fine, Alyson.*

"I'm fine," I blurted.

My voice sounded doubtful.

Jon's eyes never left my face.

He didn't direct his next words at me, however.

"What's going on here, Cassandra?"

"I don't know!" Worry sharpened her voice. "He just fucking *grabbed* her and started walking for the door. They didn't even talk. It was like he drugged her or something... she just *went* with him..."

Jon's mouth hardened.

He glared at the man holding me, then held out his hand.

"Come here, Al." Jon motioned towards me, a brief flick of his fingers. "Right now. Get behind me."

*No.*

I bit my lip. "No."

"Alyson!" Jon's voice hit into me. "COME HERE. NOW."

I started to move forward, but the man holding me tightened his grip.

"No." He looked at Jon, then at Cass. "There isn't time for this."

His voice was deep enough to shock me.

He also spoke with an accent. I don't know if he'd been hiding it before, or if I just hadn't heard him speak enough words to catch it, but I heard it clearly now.

It sounded European to me.

Really, it sounded German.

Jon stared up at him. "Excuse me? You need to let go of her. Now."

"Don't make me force the issue, Jon." The black-haired man glanced at Cass. "Cass. I'm trying to help her."

Jon's light eyes widened. For the first time, his voice grew openly hostile. "Do we *know* you, man? How do you know our names?"

There was a silence.

Then Mr. Monochrome turned his head, fixing that cold gaze on me.

*Tell them you're coming with me willingly,* his mind sent. *Tell them we're going outside to talk. Tell them it's all right... that they can watch us from inside.*

"What?" I stared at him, bewildered. "That's my brother."

"I know who it is," the man growled out loud. "Either you deal with this, or I will."

Abruptly, he tensed.

Holding up a hand to silence me, he turned towards the diner's front door. Every muscle in his long body clenched. His arms, chest and shoulders grew taut.

His grip on my hand tightened.

Before I could turn to see what he was looking at, he moved, sliding his free hand into the jacket he wore. When he removed it, his fingers held a gun.

He wrenched me closer to him and aimed the barrel of that gun at my head. I let out a gasp when he flicked a metal bar on the end, and pressed the barrel firmly to my skin. Everything about the gesture was smooth, practiced, expert.

My heart jackhammered in my chest. Adrenaline flooded my limbs.

He pressed the gun tighter to my temple.

*Don't fucking move, Alyson. Do what I tell you.*

Cass screamed.

I heard other people, diners probably, reacting around us.

I heard Jon yell at Cass to get back, to go behind the counter.

I felt strangers panicking, their minds crashing into mine. I heard chair legs screech as they moved back, as everyone got out of the way.

But none of them were why Mr. Monochrome pulled the gun.

None of them even registered on his immediate radar anymore.

He didn't plan to shoot Jon, or Cass.

He barely noticed they were there.

He stared only at the new man who'd just walked into the diner.

**WANT TO READ THE REST?**
**Click the link below!**
**DARK SEERS**
**(Bridge and Sword: Book One)**

*BOOK ONE only 99 CENTS!*

Link: https://geni.us/BS01

**BOOKS IN THE SEER WORLDS...**

BRIDGE AND SWORD SERIES
(RECOMMENDED READING ORDER)

DARK SEERS (Book One)
DEATH SEER (Book Two)
*ALLIE*
ROGUE SEERS (Book Three)
SHADOW SEER (Book Four)
*REVIK*
SEER KNIGHT (Book Five)
SEER OF WAR (Book Six)
BRIDGE OF LIGHT (Book Seven)
*TERIAN*
*THE EX-ROOK*
SEER PROPHET (Book Eight)
*A GLINT OF LIGHT*
DRAGON GOD (Book Nine)
*GUARDIAN SEER*
SWORD & SUN: Part 1 (Book Ten)
SWORD & SUN: Part 2 (Book Ten)

ALSO: *"Fireplace" and "Le Moulin (short stories) are both FREE in exclusive box set when you sign up for my mailing list!*

QUENTIN BLACK MYSTERY SERIES
(RECOMMENDED READING ORDER)

BLACK IN WHITE (Book #1)
*Kirev's Door (Book #0.5)*

BLACK AS NIGHT (Book #2)
*Black Christmas (Book #2.5)*
BLACK ON BLACK (Book #3)
*Black Supper (Book #3.5)*
BLACK IS BACK (Book #4)
BLACK AND BLUE (Book #5)
*Black Blood (Book #5.5)*
BLACK OF MOOD (Book #6)
BLACK TO DUST (Book #7)
IN BLACK WE TRUST (Book #8)
BLACK THE SUN (Book #9)
TO BLACK WITH LOVE (Book #10)
BLACK DREAMS (Book #11)
BLACK OF HEARTS (Book #12)
BLACK HAWAII (Book #13)
BLACK OF WING (Book #14)
BLACK IS MAGIC (Book #15)
BLACK CURTAIN (Book #16)
BLACK TO LIGHT (Book #17)

Vampire Detective Midnight Series
(Recommended Reading Order)

EYES OF ICE (Book #1)
MIDNIGHT FIGHT (Book #2)
THE PRESCIENT (Book #3)
FANG & METAL (Book #4)
THE WHITE DEATH (Book #5)
MIDNIGHT CURSE (Book #6)
MIDNIGHT COVEN (Book #7)
ALMOST MIDNIGHT (Book #8) ~ coming soon!

## Seer Wars
(Will be released in Serial + Novel Format)

A NEW WORLD (Seer Wars Season 01) - *complete, with novel version coming soon!*
A NEW ENEMY (Seer Wars Season 02) - *serial in progress*
A NEW APOCALYPSE (Seer Wars Season 03) - *serial version coming soon!*

# THANK YOU NOTE

I just wanted to take a moment here to thank some of my amazing readers and supporters. Huge appreciation, long distance hugs and light-filled thanks to the following people:

Sarah Hall
Elizabeth Meadows
Rebekkah Brainerd
Joy Killi
Amelia Johnson

I can't tell you how much I appreciate you!

JC Andrijeski is a *USA Today* and *Wall Street Journal* bestselling author of science fiction romance, paranormal mysteries and romance, and apocalyptic science fiction, often with a sexy and metaphysical bent.

JC's background comes from journalism, history and politics. She also has a tendency to traipse around the globe, eat odd foods, and read whatever she can get her hands on. She grew up in the Bay Area of California, but has lived abroad in Europe, Australia and Asia, and from coast to coast in the continental United States.

She currently lives and writes full time in Los Angeles.

For more information, go to: https://jcandrijeski.com

- patreon.com/jcandrijeski
- amazon.com/JC-Andrijeski/e/B004MFTAP0
- bookbub.com/authors/jc-andrijeski
- tiktok.com/@jcandrijeski
- facebook.com/JCAndrijeski
- instagram.com/jcandrijeski

Made in the USA
Las Vegas, NV
04 February 2025